MURDER
OVER
BROKEN
BONDS

MURDER OVER BROKEN BONDS

A WALL STREET MYSTERY

REBECCA SALTZER

LEVEL
BEST BOOKS

First published by Level Best Books 2023

Copyright © 2023 by Rebecca Saltzer

This novel is entirely a work of fiction. The names, characters and incidents portrayed in it are the work of the author's imagination. Any resemblance to actual persons, living or dead, events or localities is entirely coincidental.

Rebecca Saltzer asserts the moral right to be identified as the author of this work.

First edition

ISBN: 978-1-68512-291-1

Cover art by Level Best Designs

This book was professionally typeset on Reedsy.
Find out more at reedsy.com

To my mother, Marlys Anne Hughes Saltzer

Contents

Praise for Murder Over Broken Bonds

"A bond analyst at the firm of Spencer Brothers, sharp-witted and innocent Anne Scott is about to step into the back alleys of Wall Street, where corruption, murder, philandering, and fraud lurk in the corners. With a plot that builds to a tense climax and a helpful glossary for readers not familiar with Wall Street jargon, author Saltzer leads us into the heart of investment brokers, bonds, traders, and the men and women who inhabit the world of money. *Murder Over Broken Bonds* will shock you, scare you, disgust you by the chicanery, and delight you by the young protagonist's determined insistence on justice. Just be sure to check your investments before you read this book."—Libi Siporin, author of the Leah Contarini Mystery Series

"*Murder Over Broken Bonds* is an engrossing page-turner that sets money, greed, lust, and murder against a backdrop of financial wrongdoing within a 1980's NYC trading firm. In her debut novel, Rebecca Saltzer weaves the lives of bond analysts, lawyers, and other questionable characters together as they try to discover the truth without becoming the next victim. *Murder Over Broken Bonds* is a clever, fast-paced novel that will leave the reader wondering right up until the final pages."—Desmond P. Ryan, Toronto Police Detective (Ret'd), author of The Mike O'Shea Crime Fiction Series and The Mary-Margaret Cozy Series

"Put on your pinstripes and slog the day away in a cubicle on Saltzer's Wall Street to make your six figures plus annual bonus. Join the in-house lawyers, bond analysts, and traders teetering on that high wire between regulation and temptation as they scheme their way to the corner office. Now throw in the mysterious death of a sleazy investment banker. Will you be cunning enough to penetrate the darkest secrets and see through the desperate lies when one of your co-workers is the culprit?"—June Trop, author of the Miriam bat Isaac Mystery Series

"*Murder Over Broken Bonds* is set in the fast-paced world of stocks and bonds, where big money means big opportunity for corruption. When bond analyst Anne Scott discovers irregularities in her company's municipal bond portfolio, she's thrust into an investigation no one wants her to pursue. Least of all, the handsome Michael Kingston, the top executive who orchestrated the shaky transactions. As Anne pursues the truth, the search turns deadly. First one, then another, of the bond developers dies a suspicious death. And Anne receives threatening phone calls. Could she be the next victim? Debut author Rebecca Saltzer delivers a powerful behind-the-scenes look at dealmakers who succumb to the biggest murder motive of all: greed. You won't want to miss it."—Anna St. John, author of *Doomed by Blooms*

Prologue

January 17, 1989

The city was just beginning to wake when the pills were stirred carefully into his favorite coffee blend, its nutty aroma rising to greet him as he walked through the door. Still shivering from his walk in the crisp pre-dawn air, he set his briefcase down and gladly accepted the warm cup.

An hour later, he swaggered into the conference room, greeting his three other business partners like long-lost friends. Had anything worked out with that lovely waitress? Wink. Wink. And what about that promised game of Squash? To a casual observer, there would be no hint they had met beforehand and developed a plan. As they continued their lively banter, he began to feel warm and clammy and a rumbling of irritation. It looked like they would be getting a late start because the woman who had insisted on the meeting had not yet bothered to arrive.

She appeared as if by magic moments later, looking vibrant and sensuous, her cheeks flushed from the cold. Ignoring the sudden urge to pull her toward him, he closed the door and pointed to the one remaining chair.

And then the meeting he had been dreading finally began.

Everyone was civil at first, unsure of what would happen. It soon became clear that the woman's comrade-in-arms, a dry, dull lawyer, planned to walk through every excruciating detail of the financial enterprise. As his allies shifted in their seats, rolling eyes at one another and sighing deeply, he began to feel vaguely nauseous. "Is this really necessary?" he asked at one point, aware that if the stuffed shirt insisted on continuing in this manner, the meeting would never end.

There was a short, still silence while Mr. Boring considered his reply.

Of course, the lawyer insisted on continuing in the same plodding and tedious manner, egged on by his fawning accomplice, who sat in rapt attention, a small smile playing on her silky lips. He found himself growing increasingly annoyed by the pair, but particularly with the uppity young Brit, his nondescript suit, and clipped manner of speaking. It was obvious the pinhead was going to be a problem.

Ignoring the headache that was clamoring for attention, he turned his thoughts to the vacation house he had recently purchased in the Caribbean, imagining his girlfriend lounging comfortably on the veranda. She would look perfect in a banana-yellow bikini with a margarita in her hand as she basked in the sun's warm rays and slowly turned a golden shade of bronze. Just envisioning the scene caused a wave of heat to pulse rhythmically within his chest. He twitched as the warmth rose up his neck, fanned over his cheeks, and then slowly drained out through his fingers and legs. Hoping that no one had noticed, he pulled a handkerchief out of his pocket to mop his wet brow.

"Do you have anything to add?" The lawyer fixed his reptilian eyes on him, waiting for a reply.

"Not right now," he said, his headache throbbing painfully as his vision began to narrow. Was he coming down with the flu? It was the height of the season, after all. He tried to focus on the conversation at hand. It was important to get through this meeting and convince these two twerps to focus their attention elsewhere and forget about the bonds.

And then his most reliable partner began to erupt, spewing brainless comments, his face a deep shade of red. The rest of the coalition looked at him warily, obviously wondering the same thing. *Why couldn't the idiot just sit still and shut up?* Normally malleable and easy-going, Red-face was becoming a huge liability and had to be stopped.

Immediately.

Summoning his remaining energy, he called a recess, and the partners privately reconvened in his office to review their strategy. It wasn't rocket science. All they had to do was pretend to cooperate. Were they in agreement? They nodded. No more outbursts. Everyone would stick to the script.

He lingered behind for a minute with the excuse that he needed to make a quick call. But the truth was that he needed a moment to catch his breath and briefly rest. He was feeling light-headed and wobbly, as if he might fall, and there was an odd tingling in his feet, almost a trembling, that seemed to be moving upward toward his knees.

He moved his finger toward the intercom button, intending to summon his secretary. She could bring a glass of water and two aspirin to quell his banging head. At the same time, he would instruct her to destroy the checks. The tiny slips of paper had long ago served their purpose and were now the last piece of evidence linking him to the transactions in question.

But before he could complete the operation, his world turned dark.

Instead, she would open the door a few minutes later with a relaxed, cheery smile, no idea anything was amiss. She would assume he had fallen asleep after arriving at work so early that morning and gently tap his shoulder in an effort to avoid startling him. But that light touch would be enough to upset the delicate balance, causing his chair to roll sideways and his lifeless body to slide. The shiny mahogany desk, carefully polished to glimmer and gleam, would provide no opposing resistance to the motion, and she would watch in horror as he landed on the floor with a loud, echoing thump.

1

The Money Trail

Two Weeks Earlier

I t began as a routine check on some housing bonds that one of the
traders had acquired earlier in the day. Vito had purchased them
blindly, at a bargain basement price, and now it was up to Anne to fill
in the details so he could turn around and sell them at a profit. She began
by calling the bank overseeing the terms.

"We've had no problems with them." The trustee sounded bored. "The
interest payments have always been on time. It's a solid performer."

She knew Vito would be relieved. He had taken a risk in buying them
without having that information securely in hand. She tapped her pen
lightly on the desk and asked idly how much money the bank was holding
in reserve, in the event of a cash shortfall, thinking it would complete her
records.

"I don't have the exact numbers in front of me," he replied. It was almost
imperceptible but nonetheless caught her attention. She was certain he had
hesitated before answering, "It's whatever's spelled out in the prospectus."

Anne abruptly stopped tapping her pen.

"How much cash *do* you have on hand?" she asked carefully and then
waited, feeling a bit like a fox hunting a rabbit, closing in on its den.

The ensuing silence spoke volumes. In her mind, she began to take aim. "Are you telling me there's *no* money set aside?" and in response to his stuttered replies, "At all?!" As the answers slowly trickled out, she continued digging deeper, recording little nuggets of information on the notepad in front of her.

After hanging up the phone, she left her tiny, brown cubicle on the edge of the trading floor and walked briskly past five equally drab cubicles that housed the rest of the municipal bond research staff, coming to a stop as she scanned the trading operation. She spotted Vito sitting in his regular spot, tucked in a long row of desks that was one of many rows of desks filled with traders who bought and sold municipal bonds for Spencer Brothers in New York City. The floor around them hummed with the sounds of people talking, phones ringing, photocopiers grinding, fax machines beeping, and an occasional harried trader barking orders across the room to one of the support staff. The arrangement reminded her of a busy parking lot in which all the available spaces had been taken, and the cars that didn't already have one were left to mill around, waiting for one to open.

"What d'ya mean the bank doesn't have the money?" Vito asked, drawing his head back and squinting his eyes. "They always have the money. That's their job," he insisted, "to handle the money." He looked as if he didn't quite believe her.

She, too, had been flabbergasted to discover that the trustee did not actually hold any of the bond proceeds or manage the interest payments. She had never heard of a municipal bond issue where the real estate developer was handed the construction funds to spend as he wished, when he wished, without any sort of direct supervision. "It's odd," Anne agreed. "I'm not quite sure what to make of it. The good news is that all of the interest payments have been on time so far."

"Vito!" A junior trader sitting diagonally across interrupted. "A hundred of those Detroit bonds just came up." His face had a look of eager anticipation, like a dog expecting to be taken for a walk.

"Sit tight!" Vito ordered, glancing quickly at his screen. He swiveled around to face her, his eyes darting back and forth as he spoke. "What about the project? Does it look profitable?"

That was just one of many questions she had. "He doesn't know," she replied, making sure to stand tall, with both of her feet firmly planted on the floor, knowing that if he sensed any hint of insecurity, he would rip her apart without a moment's hesitation. "He suggested I ask the builder, but I haven't been able to reach him."

The trader shifted uncomfortably in his seat, his large frame straining against the stark white shirt he wore, causing a button near the center to look perilously taut. After a string of expletives, he said, "I own a bunch of these bonds. You need to get ahold of that guy."

Anne nodded. It was crucial she reach the builder. Not only to confirm what the trustee had told her, but to make sure there was sufficient cash flow to pay the upcoming interest that would be due in a month. For all they knew, the bonds were on the verge of default. "It's my highest priority."

His shoulders relaxed, and Vito resumed studying the numbers dancing lazily across his computer display, alternately offering bonds for sale and then listing ones that had already been taken. "Let me know when you have something more," he said, his eyes still glued to the screen.

She started to turn toward her cubicle, but stopped when she heard her name being called out from somewhere to the left. She pinpointed the source standing halfway down the row with a phone in each hand.

"Hang on," the stalwart trader said into the receivers and then pressed them both to his chest. "Got a sec?"

She nodded and took a step in his direction, bracing herself for whatever might come next.

The trader returned the left phone to his ear for a moment and mumbled something before slamming it down. "Eat that!" Chuckling, he put the remaining phone back on his right ear. "I'll take six hundred." He high-fived his trading assistant, mouthing *sucker*, and then picked up where he had left off with Anne. "Any progress on those Nebraska Airport bonds?"

After updating him on the financial state of the bonds (surprisingly stable, probably a good buy), taking down the name of another that a junior trader was interested in purchasing (probably a pass, but she'd confirm and get back to him), and clarifying a complicated bond provision for one of the salesmen (his client would be second-to-last in the bankruptcy line), she finally made her way off of the trading floor, grabbed a Coke and Hershey's chocolate bar with almonds from the snack machine, and returned to her cubicle. She kicked off her shoes, pulled the tab off the can, and called the real estate developer's office in Atlanta, again without success.

"Anne!" One of the secretaries yelled out, just as she took her last bite of chocolate. "There's a broker on line two who's having a cow about some hospital in Philly."

She twisted her dark blond hair into a bun, securing it with a pencil, before picking up the phone and beginning the post-mortem: the hospital was in receivership, there was no chance of making the bond investors whole, the financial picture was grim.

Anne looked up from jotting some notes to see Donna, one of her co-workers, standing at the entrance to her cubicle. A chain smoker, she rolled an unlit cigarette back and forth between her fingers, which sported neon pink, glittery polish on long, pointy nails.

"Vito's sweating bullets out there," Donna said, followed by a raspy cough. "A million more of those same bonds just came up for sale."

Anne drew a sharp breath. It was possible somebody was dumping them, that they knew something was terribly wrong.

"Is the housing project okay?"

Anne bit her lip. It was the million-dollar question. "I don't know," she said, feeling like a failure as Donna's bloodshot eyes scrutinized her. "I'm having trouble reaching the developer. Every time I call, his secretary says he's in a meeting."

"Keep pushing."

Anne looked at her, surprised. The two of them were peers who normally worked independently. It wasn't The Puff Queen's place to tell her how to do her job. And she had been pushing. Quite hard. She began to wonder, *why the sudden interest?*

Donna leaned toward her, reeking of stale cigarettes. "I just overheard some discussion about layoffs," she whispered.

4

Layoffs? Anne blinked. It was the last thing she needed to hear. It had been less than six months since she had bitten the bullet and purchased a condo, discarding the random assortment of banged-up second-hand tables and chairs from her apartment-renting days, instead filling it with sleek, modern Crate and Barrel furniture and trendy rugs that coordinated in style and color. Between the mortgage and other general expenses, she would be in a tough spot if she lost her job right now. And her smug sister would have a field day.

"Equities lost a wad last month," Donna hissed, revealing her nicotine-stained teeth. "Word is that Spencer Brothers is scrounging for cash."

No wonder the atmosphere on the floor had seemed more fierce than usual the last few days. Anne took a deep breath and looked at the folders and financial statements scattered over her desk. "Just like Pinkerton Investments," she said slowly. The previous week Pinkerton had closed up shop without warning, giving their employees one week of severance pay.

Donna twisted the point of her long black heel back and forth on the carpet. "Exactly. Now's not the time to get on Vito's hit list. The last time there were layoffs—" She was interrupted by the sound of Anne's phone ringing. "Hopefully, that's the builder," Donna said, tottering away.

Anne felt a rush of anticipation as she turned to answer it. Maybe she would finally get some answers. And Vito off her back.

"Miss Scott?" A deep, gravelly voice said cheerfully. "I'm glad I finally reached you."

She tapped one foot against the other, willing the conversation to be short, while the broker on the other end of the line began to explain his customer's financial predicament.

* * *

As trading neared its close, Anne dialed the number for the developer in Georgia once more.

"I'm sorry," his secretary spoke pleasantly, with a slight southern accent, "but he's on the other line. Would you care to leave a message?"

Anne frowned. She had already left several that day to no avail. There was no question in her mind that he was trying to avoid her. "I'll hold."

"I'm not sure how long he'll be."

Anne said nothing in reply, letting the awkward silence hang heavily between them.

"Wouldn't you rather leave a message?"

"No," Anne said firmly.

The woman sighed. "Let me see what I can do."

Anne swiveled back and forth in her chair as she waited, oblivious to the various conversations and political maneuverings taking place in the adjoining cubicles. Her attention was riveted on the problem before her and the growing impatience she felt at this man's deliberate game-playing.

After several minutes, his secretary returned to the line. "Miss Scott?"

Anne could tell from the woman's tentative tone that she was in the unenviable position of delivering bad news. Again. Her eyes narrowed as she waited to hear the excuse this time.

"He asked me to tell you that he's gotta' scoot and suggested you call back in the mornin'."

Scoot? Anne snapped forward in her chair. That was it. She had had enough of his runaround. She took a deep breath and ramped up the pressure. "You tell him if he doesn't pick up the phone this instant, I will contact the *New York Times*, the *Wall Street Journal,* and whoever else I can think of! Does he really want that kind of adverse publicity?"

She had begun by speaking slowly, in measured terms, but by the end, had accelerated her pitch and speed so much that the words came out quickly and forcefully. Perhaps too forcefully.

"Oh! My goodness! I'm not sure that's necessary."

The secretary sounded stunned, and Anne felt a pang of guilt. Her issue was with the builder, who refused to take her call, not this poor woman on the other end of the line. As Anne waited to see what would happen next, she hoped none of the bond analysts in the adjoining cubicles had overheard her. She could already envision the potential jokes it would engender about her being overwrought, on the verge of a nervous breakdown, and in immediate need of a chill pill. But it was imperative to reach him. He was the next link in the chain, and threatening to contact the newspapers was the only concrete idea that had flashed into her mind as a way to get his attention. It was times like these when she wished she had more privacy.

"Let me just check—" the secretary sounded flustered. "Perhaps he—" There was a rustling that sounded like her hand was covering the phone. "Well, what do you know!"

Miraculously, he was now available to take the call.

"I'm fixin' to leave in just a few minutes," he began with a gracious southern drawl, "but I can chat with you briefly."

Anne explained that she was a bond analyst at Spencer Brothers, an investment bank in New York City, and then inquired about the housing project the bonds were supposed to finance.

"It ain't been built yet."

She felt her eyes widen. "Why not?"

"The ground's frozen. We're waitin' for it to thaw."

"But it's been four years…."

"We've got lots of projects on our plate."

He paused, and she heard what sounded like spitting in the background. *Chewing tobacco?*

"Honey, how old are you?"

"What?" she sputtered.

"Your age," he drawled. "I'm wondering—"

"Why do you ask?" she replied warily, reminded that she would be turning thirty in three months' time and was still single, not that it was any of his business.

"You don't sound like you have much experience with financing construction projects."

Seriously? He was going down this path? She took a deep breath. "Actually, I've been a bond analyst at Spencer Brothers for the last eight years. In my experience, a four-year construction delay is…unusual."

"Don't know what to tell ya."

There was a brief pause, and she debated whether to push him harder on the issue.

"Is that everythin'?" he said, with a tinge of annoyance, followed by another spitting sound.

"Not quite." She shifted to the subject of the construction money. "The trustee tells me they turned the entire $45 million over to you when the deal closed. Where has that money been sitting while you wait to break ground?"

"Listen, honey," he replied slowly and deliberately, "whoever gave you that piece of manure is dumber than a sack of rocks. I ain't got the money."

She felt her pulse quicken, but tried to maintain a level tone. "Are you saying the bank never gave it to you?"

"That's right, honey. I never touched it."

"Then who *did* they give it to?"

"Dunno."

She blinked, trying to make sense of what she was hearing. "If you don't have the money and the project hasn't been built, then how are you paying the interest due every six months on the loan?"

"Lady," he answered in a tone of slight alarm. "I ain't got nothin' to do with that loan. It gets paid in some other way."

"What way?"

"Cain't say for sure."

"You have a $45 million construction loan, and you don't know how it gets paid off, and you don't know where the money actually is?" She knew her tone sounded incredulous, accusatory even, but she didn't care. She was fed up with his nonsense and determined to get to the bottom of the missing funds.

"Y'all are barkin' up the wrong tree." His voice had risen an octave. "You should be talking to Marvin Goldberg. Not me."

"Who?"

"Hang on."

He put her on hold and then returned after a few moments with a telephone number.

"Marvin runs a small boutique up in your neck of the woods, *Onyx River Investments*." He paused, and she heard him spit again, louder this time. "He's the one you should've called in the first place, honey. Knows all about the bonds and the money."

And how would she have possibly known to call this Marvin person? He was not mentioned in the prospectus. In fact, it seemed like a number of pertinent details were missing from the official documents she had pulled that afternoon while waiting for this potato head to take her call.

"Now, I was just gettin' ready to head out for my golf game when you called," he continued. "I don't want to keep the boys waitin' so you'll have to 'scuse me. Y'all have a nice day." The words tumbled out quickly, without pause, and then he hung up before she could say another word. She felt like a fleck of dust that had been roughly brushed off of his jacket.

A shadow darkened the edge of her cubicle. It was Vito again, wondering whether she had learned anything more about the bonds.

Anne drew herself up in her bulletproof, grey Brooks Brothers suit, hoping the nail polish she had applied to the small hole near her big toe was keeping her stockings intact. She stole a glance down at her feet. *Damn.* A run extended across the top of her foot and halfway up her leg. "I'm still working on it," she said, crossing one leg in front of the other, hoping to hide the telltale streak, and then relayed the conversation she had just had with the real estate developer.

As she was finishing up, two junior traders wandered over and stood a few feet behind.

"It's Miller time," the short, squat one said, his eyes roving over Anne as if she were a lobster he might choose for dinner.

"Gimme a sec," Vito barked in return without so much as a backwards glance, and then softened his tone as he addressed Anne again. "Who did he say you should talk to?"

"A Marvin Goldberg from something called *Onyx River Investments*. I've never heard of him or that firm before."

"Hmmm." The trader appeared to take the news in stride.

"We're heading out," the tall, built one said, starting to move away.

"Give it a rest, boys!" Vito yelled back, his gaze fixed on Anne, unwavering. Behind him, she could see Mutt and Jeff conferring.

"I was just about to give this Marvin guy a call," Anne said, checking her watch. It was getting late. She hoped he would still be in the office.

"Meet us there," the two guys called out in unison and disappeared from view.

Vito winked. "When you reach him, he's gonna' tell you how great these bonds are. Mark my words."

It was typical trader swashbuckling. Now that he owned the bonds, they were the greatest thing since sliced bread. No doubt, he had claimed they were the worst piece of garbage known to man when he had been haggling with the seller over whether to buy them in the first place. Anne smiled thinly. "Let's hope you're right."

He turned to join his friends, calling over his shoulder, "I'll check back with you in the morning."

As she dialed Marvin Goldberg's number, she tapped her foot nervously on the floor. Was he the next step in the money trail? Or would he turn out to be another dead end? She leaned back in her chair and began counting.

When he answered his phone after the very first ring, she sat straight up, surprised, and then explained the purpose of her call.

"You got nothing to worry about," he responded coolly, his strong New York accent flattening every word. "The money is safely invested."

"Where?"

There was a pregnant pause as she waited for the hurricane to roll in.

"The Oko Sychaito Bank in New York. It's in a guaranteed investment contract with them."

She breathed a sigh of relief. The Oko Sychaito Bank was a huge Japanese bank with branches all over the world. It certainly wasn't going to collapse tomorrow. If he was telling the truth, then the money was safe for the time being.

"How come none of this is mentioned in the prospectus?"

"Oh," he said offhandedly, "the lawyers advised us to keep the description simple. It facilitated marketing. And," he added, "we wanted to close the deals before year-end. We weren't about to start questioning our legal counsel and miss the boat on these babies."

Of course not. Heaven forbid there be any delay in the receipt of their fat fees just because the financial disclosures were a little fuzzy.

"Can money be withdrawn from the investment contract in the next few years in order to underwrite the construction costs?"

"No." His laugh sounded harsh, and his tone slightly condescending. "The investment is like a certificate of deposit that you or I might buy at our local bank. The money is invested for the duration of the contract."

"How long is that?"

"Thirty years."

Anne closed her eyes and shook her head. "I've never heard of a municipal bond structured like this before."

"Oh, there are many," he responded quickly. "You'd be surprised how common it is. In fact, your firm, in particular, was very active in marketing them for several years."

"Really," she replied as evenly as possible. "Do you recall *who*, in particular, specialized in these bonds?"

The telephone crackled during the silence that ensued, and she began drumming her fingers nervously on the desk.

"Michael Kingston," he said brightly. "Know him?"

She groaned inwardly. Everyone at Spencer Brothers knew Michael Kingston. He was an investment banker with a reputation for being aggressive and hard-driving, a hustler who clinched big deals. With his winner-take-all mindset, he generally left a trail of twisted wreckage behind in his turbulent wake. And he carried a lot of clout.

She ventured one more question. "There's something I don't understand. If the money is tied up in this investment contract you mentioned, how were you planning to build the project?"

"Yeah," she could almost hear him shrugging as his voice traveled down the telephone line, "that's not my area of expertise," and then insisted that he had to take a call on his other line.

2

The Shark

Wednesday, January 4, 1989

The next day, Anne headed out to the trading floor with Jennifer, one of the other analysts in her group, just as the lunch bags were being wheeled in. Similar in age, the two had become friends during their years of working together in the Municipal Bond Research Group. They occasionally went out for drinks after work and enjoyed commiserating about the sluggish secretaries.

"Standing lunch?" Jennifer asked.

"Definitely." Anne was ready to take a break and chat for a few minutes.

After wading through the sea of bags, they each found their respective names scribbled across the top and headed toward a long row of waist-high, gray file cabinets just outside their cubicles. The primary function of the thirty or so drawers was to hold financial statements, analyst notes, and other information that the research group maintained about various bond issues. However, the cabinets also functioned as a makeshift dining table when the analysts chose to step away from their desks and eat together.

"I'm so sick of these sandwiches," Jennifer said with a sigh, tossing her long brown hair over her shoulders where it cascaded in perfectly formed, flowing waves.

"Me too," Anne said, self-consciously touching her own wavy tresses, which never seemed to hang where they were supposed to.

"You get what you pay for," one of the salesmen muttered as he passed them on his way out to the trading floor.

"I'm just saying it would be nice if we had more options," Jennifer replied, rolling her eyes at his retreating back and flinging her arms in a show of exasperation, but he did not appear to hear her.

He had a point, Anne conceded silently. The lunches were free, but that was because they were expected to continue working through the hour without pause, just like the bond market, which did not stop when the clock struck noon. Technically, the small break they were taking at that moment was a violation of the protocol.

They set their bags down and began inspecting the contents.

"I've been looking at some pretty weird housing bonds for one of the traders," Anne said as she pulled out her chocolate bar.

"I was wondering what you've been up to." Jennifer held up an orange package and sighed. "They gave me the wrong chips again. Want to trade?"

Anne glanced at the label, made a face, and shook her head.

"What's weird about the bonds?" Jennifer asked as she threw the chip bag over the cabinets, just missing the trash barrel on the other side. "Damn." She walked over to the other side to properly dispose of it.

"Well, for one thing, the bank trustee doesn't hold the proceeds from the bond sale. And he didn't seem to know who does."

"That makes no sense."

"You're telling me. And not only that—"

"Hang on—your bow's coming undone."

Anne's fingers flew to her neck.

"I always had the same problem when I wore them," Jennifer said with a kind smile.

As Anne firmly re-tied the ribbon, she studied Jennifer's sophisticated designer skirt and top. The ensemble flattered her natural curves, broadcasting to the world that she was an attractive woman. Despite the harsh, fluorescent office lights, her blouse almost shimmered, like the Manhattan skyline on a foggy night. In contrast, Anne felt frumpy in her conservative gray suit with its big padded shoulders and masculine-looking button-down shirt. The accompanying bow tie was uncomfortable and restricting, almost strangling. "I have half a mind to rip this thing off."

Jennifer laughed. "Don't do that. It's a flattering color for you, and it contrasts nicely with your suit."

A couple of years earlier, Jennifer had given up the corporate uniform, announcing one day that she was done with dressing like a man just so she could be taken seriously. Anne wished she had the nerve to do the same, but androgynous power suits signaled to the world that she was a professional. And they were an effective way to deflect unwanted attention, or at least keep it to a minimum.

"Do you know who *is* holding the money?"

"The Oko Sychaito Bank," Anne replied, holding her Coke safely to the side as she popped the lid in case it exploded violently. "But it's locked up in an investment contract, so the funds can't actually be used to build the project."

"That's a new one."

"I know. I don't think we're talking *Michael-Milken-junk-bond* kind of stuff," Anne made air quotes, "but something is definitely off. The good news is there doesn't appear to be much risk of the bonds defaulting."

"Well, that's a positive. Who brought them to market? Wait!" Jennifer thrust her hand out in a blocking gesture. "Let me guess. *Fly-By-Night* in Wichita, Kansas?"

"We did," Anne said more disparagingly than she had intended.

Jennifer's arms dropped limply to her side. "Seriously? How did something like that ever get past our internal review committee?"

Anne raised her eyebrows and gave an exaggerated shrug. Obviously, someone with clout had profited. Enormously. She then asked whether Jennifer had ever interacted with Michael Kingston.

"No." Jennifer paused and bit her lip. "Although…do you know Kelsey O'Brien?"

Anne shook her head.

"I didn't think so. She's one of the grunts in Michael Kingston's group. We met a few years ago at an alumni gathering. I was pretty impressed when she told me she had been hired directly out of college in the summer of 1982."

"Wow." That was in the midst of the worst recession since the Great Depression, when hiring had been virtually nonexistent. Kelsey must have been outstanding to have snagged a Wall Street job offer that particular year.

"We immediately clicked when we realized we both work for Spencer Brothers." Jennifer paused, suddenly immersed in thought. "She's made a few comments about him, but…"

"But what?" Anne waited for the punchline.

"Well—she's pretty intense. A total workaholic, from what I can tell. I'm not sure how great a judge of character she is." Jennifer took a bite out of her sandwich.

Every investment banker Anne knew worked eighty hours a week, slaving away to put the finishing touches on a deal, computing expected returns and other key financial parameters on multiple spreadsheets, until finally, it could be shipped down to the trading floor and brought to market.

"Just because she works hard—" Anne started to say.

"That's true. I was thinking more about her overall resilience."

"Why? Is it particularly low or something?"

"No. I was thinking it might be unusually high."

Anne searched Jennifer's face.

"It's just that—" Jennifer hesitated, looking uneasy. "Well—she's tough as nails and might not be put off by things the way other people would. I mean, someone in Michael Kingston's position must be something of a snake, but to hear her tell it, he's a teddy bear."

Anne took a sip. "So, she likes him?"

"Totally. She said he's a great person to work with. Smart. Funny. When I last talked to her, she loved her job and was making a ton of money."

Anne was pleasantly surprised. She had expected to hear he could be difficult, over-bearing even, given his reputation as a no-holds-barred deal-maker.

"Honestly?" Jennifer confided, "It was a little depressing talking to her. I was rather envious."

Anne understood how she felt. While she and Jennifer were well paid, their jobs necessitated sparring with the traders on a daily basis, which required a great deal of stamina. The buyers and sellers of bonds often resorted to bullying if they didn't hear what they wanted and had no qualms about publicly chewing someone up and spitting them out with a string of obscenities hurled throughout the process. When compared with the rough and tumble of the trading floor, the more refined and upscale nature of investment banking certainly held some appeal.

"The guys on the floor can be so difficult..." Jennifer's voice trailed off.

That was putting it mildly. They were a breed unto themselves. Extremely intense individuals, they thrived on risk, peppered their speech with profanity, and generally burned out by the time they were in their mid-thirties.

"I'm sure investment banking has its dark side as well," Anne said. "Killer hours. Pretentious know-it-alls prancing around in brightly colored suspenders with a few women tossed in for variety."

"That reminds me," Jennifer added with a surreptitious glance around, "Kelsey said Michael Kingston's *really* good-looking. But, he's married, so no potential there...."

"I have zero interest in dating co-workers," Anne said firmly. "Remember the last time you—"

"Don't remind me."

"I'm just saying—"

"Well, don't. And since we're on the subject of men." Jennifer gave her a sideways look. "Have you heard from Paul?"

Anne shook her head, a pang of regret stabbing her in the chest. She missed him, but was unwilling to continue a relationship with someone who had announced, after two years of being her steady boyfriend, that he didn't think he could marry her as long as she made more money than he did. It was mind-boggling.

And untenable.

Jennifer leaned against the cabinet, a frown creasing her face. "I figured with some time apart, he'd change his mind."

Not Paul. He was way too stubborn.

"I mean, seriously, someone needs to tell Beaver Cleaver that this is the eighties, for god's sake."

Despite her hurt and anger, Anne gave a small laugh. "Believe me. I tried." And had failed.

Miserably.

They were now at an impasse. An academic at Columbia University, he would never earn as much as she, and Anne was not about to give up her job, stepping down her ambitions, just to soothe his male ego. He'd had a good six months to revise his position and hadn't budged. In retrospect, she should have pressed harder to understand his feelings on the matter before investing so much time in the relationship.

"His loss," Jennifer said, obviously trying to make her feel better.

Anne shrugged, wanting to sweep it from her mind, and quickly shifted gears. "I'm glad to hear Michael Kingston sounds decent, because I'm going to need to ask him some rather touchy questions."

Jennifer shot her a warning glance. "It's probably no accident that he became a managing director. He may be nice to work with, but you're likely to find it's an *entirely* different ballgame once you start grilling him about some flaky deals he put together...."

* * *

The meeting with Michael Kingston was scheduled for the following morning. Anne felt a flurry of butterflies as she stepped off the elevator and walked over to the receptionist, her heels echoing on the shiny marble. After giving her name, she was permitted to proceed through the tall glass doors into the investment banking sanctuary and found herself in a well-appointed seating area, complete with coffee, tea, and an assortment of fresh fruit, chips, and candy bars neatly arranged on a side table. A fountain gurgled gently in the corner. She stood for a moment and absorbed the dignified, almost serene, ambiance of the place and then grabbed a chocolate bar before continuing to his large (even by investment banking standards) plush corner office.

She was greeted by a man with short-cropped brown hair wearing suspenders and an elegant silk tie, who she guessed to be in his mid-forties. Tall and lanky, with brilliant blue eyes and a dimpled chin, he was, as Jennifer had relayed, jaw-droppingly handsome.

"You must be Anne." He shook her hand firmly and flashed a big smile. "Michael Kingston. It's a pleasure to meet you."

"You too." She smiled in return, but could not help feeling a bit like a guppy in a shark tank. Like most successful investment bankers, he projected confidence and trustworthiness, a person eminently capable of leading a business or municipality in need of capital through the labyrinth of Wall Street's complex corridors. His solid stance and deep, clear voice gave a sense of infallibility. And yet she knew he was nothing more than a salesman, good at reading people and using that information to manipulate them.

They all were.

As they chatted about the spectacular view of the Hudson his window afforded, she got her first full look at the surroundings. She saw a man of impeccable tidiness and meticulous organization. Books neatly lined the shelves of his bookcase, and small mementos of various investment banking deals were carefully arranged on the top of his credenza. His polished mahogany desk glistened under the light cast by an antique-style bronze lamp, displaying an open and inviting workspace without the customary clutter of most busy executives. Not even a paper clip was out of order.

"We should probably get down to business," he said, waving at one of the chairs opposite his desk and flashing a big wide smile that showed two rows of perfect, white teeth. "Although I always enjoy chatting with a beautiful woman."

Yikes! Was he flirting with her? She gave a small smile and quickly sat down, landing with a hard thump on the edge of the chair.

"I realize the bond structure is a little unusual," he began jovially, as if they were the best of friends.

You think? Anne said silently. She had never seen anything like it.

His eyes crinkled, and a smile played at the corners of his mouth. "But I'm sure someone like you appreciates how clever it is. We managed to achieve a fairly high-risk financing at triple-A rates."

As he sat there, smugly congratulating himself, she was reminded of a puffed-up bird. "The bonds certainly appear to deserve their triple-A rating," she replied. "I see little risk of them defaulting. What I don't understand is why they should be exempt from federal income taxes."

"All municipal bonds are exempt from federal income taxes." His voice was syrupy smooth. Too smooth.

"Yes, but they're also supposed to serve a public purpose. I'm not seeing how these bonds do that since the money is tied up in an investment contract with the Oko Sychaito Bank. The funds aren't available to build the low-income housing project."

He tilted his head slightly downwards and peered at her ever so condescendingly. "I think you've missed a key point, but it's not surprising as these bonds are very complicated."

"Okay," she said, careful to betray no hint of her annoyance at being treated like a bumbling idiot. "Help me understand." Meanwhile, the words *arrogant, pompous,* and *jerk* paraded through her mind.

His face took on a look of deep concentration while he formulated a reply. "We are *actively* working to find a savings and loan institution that can provide a construction loan for the housing project. Once we pass that hurdle, the homes will be built." He gave her that big, wide smile again.

She tried to choose her words carefully. "But if you're going to get a separate loan to finance the project, then someone *could* argue there was never any need to issue the bonds in the first place and that they were solely a mechanism for generating large fees...."

"Well." He sniffed. "The deals were all approved by the firm's investments committee. They *carefully* review all bond issues before committing the firm's *hard-earned* capital toward underwriting endeavors. In addition, we have a legal opinion stating that the bonds *deserve* their tax-exempt status."

"I saw that," she said. "But what was the basis for that legal opinion? That's what I don't understand."

He smiled piously. "That's a question you should probably be asking the bond attorney. Me?" He waved his hand dismissively, "I'm just the deal maker," and then clucked magnanimously, "—the one who made the investors a ton of money."

He clasped his hands on his desk and leaned toward her.

"Sweetheart, let me give you some advice. Our firm has made a *lot* of money on these deals. You would do best to leave well enough alone." He paused, his eyes boring through her, but Anne refused to look away from his unrelenting stare, unwilling to be cowed by him. "Especially given the current financial environment."

A reference to the rumor of impending layoffs? An icy chill crawled up her spine.

The corners of his mouth curled downward. "I, for one, see no reason to stir the pot at this juncture."

Anne assured him that she had no interest in stirring up any pots unnecessarily and thanked him for his time.

* * *

She was stopped on the way back to her desk by a junior trader, who told her he had acquired a large position in some hospital bonds and wanted to designate them as the firm's *High-Yield Bond of the Week.* "We need you to write a short article that will help us get the word out to our brokers." He gave a little chuckle and then came out with the words that put her on high alert. "They're a great deal. Really cheap."

She had not calmed down from meeting with Michael Kingston yet, and now Mr. High Roller was asking her to help him peddle some more crappy bonds. She eyed him warily. "Great deal for who?"

"For everyone!" He crossed his arms, acting personally affronted.

When she heard the name of the hospital in question, she shook her head. This particular bond did not belong on anybody's *Buy* list, especially the mom-and-pop investors he was proposing they target. "It's a total dog," she replied. "We can't make it the *High-Yield Bond of the Week*. It's way too risky for people saving for their retirement."

His eyes hardened.

"Seriously. Only institutional or especially savvy investors should be buying those bonds."

The trader shrugged his shoulders. "Your boss already okayed it. He said you'd write it up."

Anne felt a surge of anger as she watched the trader saunter away. The head of the research group was forever making pronouncements off the top of his head without thinking through the consequences. Just last week, he had pontificated about some hospital being a great investment when, in fact, it was in dire financial straits. (It turned out that he had confused it with another similarly-named hospital in a completely different city). The week before that, he had recommended a trader purchase some electric utility bonds, but failed to review their latest financial statements. That particular screwup had cost the firm close to a million dollars, and she knew the trader was still annoyed about it.

She charged full speed into his office, ready for battle.

"What were you thinking telling the traders that such a crappy bond could be *High-Yield Bond of the Week*? It's *totally* inappropriate for mom-and-pop investors." She threw her arms toward the ceiling in frustration. "I refuse to write it up."

"Yeah? Well, I don't give a damn," came the sharp reply. "I've just been fired."

She stopped dead in her tracks and looked at the tall, portly man standing behind his desk. He was partially obscured by a large, cardboard box and appeared to be in the process of filling it with personal items scattered about his office. She stood there for a moment, unsure of what to say.

"You're on your own." He dropped the book he was holding into the box, where it landed with a loud thud.

As far as Anne was concerned, she had always been on her own at Spencer Brothers. It was a sink-or-swim environment filled with an ocean of high-rollers, all frantic for the next financial home run. Nothing would change with his dismissal other than no longer having to waste time and energy fighting his ill-conceived recommendations. "Good luck with—" she started to say.

"Whatever," he cut her off with a wave of his hand.

She opened her mouth and then shut it again, realizing there was nothing more to be said. He would pack up in the next hour and then be escorted out of the building.

"I'm ready to move on anyway," the beleaguered man said with a forced smile that was more of a grimace, eerily reminding her of Michael Kingston's shark-like grin.

The thought of Michael gave her a momentary twinge of panic. He had obviously been annoyed by her pointed questions. What if he complained about her to the head of trading? It would be her word against his. She looked at the shocked man standing in front of her and swallowed hard. There was no probationary period at Spencer Brothers. No opportunity to fix any perceived performance issues. When someone got the axe, it happened immediately, without warning. Would she be next?

"The smartest thing you could do is to start looking outside of this place pronto. If I were you, I'd check out that all-woman firm that's starting up." He motioned toward the trading floor. "You're never going to get anywhere with these dinosaurs in charge."

She felt herself mentally withdraw, as if she were closing the castle doors and pulling up the drawbridges. In previous conversations, he had shown little interest in her career, dismissing her request to transfer elsewhere in the firm so that she could broaden her experience, claiming that the trading floor could not afford to lose her. She studied him coolly. Was he genuinely trying to offer her advice or simply advancing his own personal agenda?

"It won't matter how hard you work or how good you are." He gave a dry laugh. "Look at what they've just done to me."

Seeing the humiliation on his face, Anne found herself feeling sorry for him, but at the same time, reminded herself that the man had been an ineffective manager, sorely lacking in leadership skills. She had never understood his promotion to the manager position in the first place. In point of fact, it was going to be a big improvement with him out of the picture.

"Thanks," she said. "I'll keep that in mind."

She slowly retreated from his office, her mind bouncing back and forth between images of her ex-manager angrily salvaging the remnants of his time at Spencer Brothers and Michael Kingston leaning back in his big executive chair, glowering at her for suggesting there were any problems with his bonds.

* * *

"He's an idiot," Jennifer said, "who couldn't care less about your career." They were sitting at the Sea Tavern down the street from their office, having a drink with Jennifer's boyfriend before heading home for the evening. "I'm glad they finally showed that loser the door."

Anne nodded in agreement. The truth was she felt the same. But the conversation had made her uneasy, reminding her of how quickly one's fortunes could change.

"And you shouldn't worry about Michael Kingston, no matter *how* ticked off he seemed." Jennifer fixed her gentle brown eyes firmly on Anne. "You were looking out for the trading interests of the firm, which is what you are *paid* to do."

"I agree," said Jennifer's boyfriend, Mel, who had already promised to keep anything they said confidential.

"After meeting with him today, I'm even more convinced these bonds don't deserve their tax-exempt designation."

"But is that really such a big deal?" Mel asked, raising an eyebrow. He was a lawyer who specialized in wills and estates rather than corporate matters.

"Well—" Anne replied, twisting her wine glass between her fingers, "Imagine some broker called your grandmother and told her about some great bonds she could buy."

"My grandmother knows better than to trust brokers," he said smugly. "She hides her money under the mattress."

"Okay. Let's say he calls Jennifer's grandmother instead. And she *doesn't* manage to hang up before he tells her they're rated AAA."

Jennifer rolled her eyes. "She'd probably listen to his whole spiel just to be polite."

"Exactly." Anne nodded. "—and, since her lovely granddaughter has already told her that AAA is the *highest* rating a bond can get, she's convinced they're a really safe investment."

"Her granddaughter *is* quite lovely," Mel said with an appraising look, causing Jennifer to blush slightly.

"Not only that," Anne continued after taking a quick sip of wine, "her grandmother doesn't have to pay taxes on the interest she earns because they're municipals."

"I could actually imagine this happening," Jennifer said, looking vaguely concerned.

"The bonds sound like such a great idea that she decides to invest her entire savings, thinking that she'll just live off the interest for the rest of her life."

"I need to make sure my grandmother checks with me before buying anything from anybody," Jennifer muttered, putting her head into her hands.

"I still don't see why it's such a big problem," Mel said, sounding peevish.

"The *problem* is how it all ends." Anne paused to take another sip. "Everything probably goes along fine for a couple of years until suddenly the IRS decides these bonds don't deserve their tax-exempt status. Bummer! Now her accountant tells her she has to pay taxes on the interest."

"Sure." Mel shrugged his shoulders dismissively. "No one wants to get a bill from the IRS. But still, it wouldn't be the end of the world." He flagged down the bartender and ordered another beer.

"Ah, but we're not done yet," Anne said in a tone suggesting that the world was indeed about to stop spinning on its axis. "It turns out the IRS is really ticked off about these bonds and decides to tax the bondholders *retroactively*. Now Jennifer's grandmother has to amend all of her tax returns for the last five years."

"That would be the pits," Jennifer said, eyeing Mel.

"—and she has to pay back taxes and interest that has accrued, and probably fines as well."

"That would be the *serious* pits." Jennifer's face took on an even sterner expression.

"Bottom line," Anne finished gravely, "Jennifer's grandmother doesn't have enough money in her bank account to pay everything off."

Mel squirmed in his seat. "Time to sell the bonds and get her money back. After she has settled everything with the IRS, she can look for a better investment." He looked nervous as he glanced over at Jennifer, probably wondering whether his response had passed muster.

Anne shook her head and then continued solemnly. "Her grandmother can't sell the bonds to anyone because no one in their right mind will buy them now that they have all of these *known* legal issues...But, the taxes are due. So now she's in danger of losing her house and having to sell her wedding ring."

"No way!" Jennifer sat straight up and crossed her arms. "I'm supposed to inherit that ring." Her eyes took on a fiery look.

"Sounds like she should sue the hell out of Spencer Brothers," Mel said quickly and then took a large gulp of his beer.

"Exactly. Now you can see why I'm so concerned."

3

Ascending the Throne

"Who do you think they'll put in his place?" Anne asked the next day while several of her co-workers stood around the file cabinets eating lunch. Even though the previous guy had been universally disliked as a manager, his sudden termination had created a sense of panic in the group.

"If they choose William, I'm quitting," said Donna, tapping a cigarette on her lighter.

The weary-looking analyst standing beside her gave an obvious look of disdain. "There's no way they'd put *him* in charge." As Carter spoke, a small piece of unchewed food tumbled out of his mouth. "William's got less experience than I do, and nobody likes him."

"I don't know," Donna countered. "He seems to—"

"William is nothing more than a termite who's taken up residence on our floor," he pronounced with a wave of his hand. "They won't give him a second look."

"You may be underestimating—" Anne began.

"What?" Carter snorted. "His winning personality?"

"He's good at what he does." William also seemed to get along well with

26

the traders and had an uncanny ability to schmooze with management, despite being something of a loner.

"Oh please," Carter scoffed. "He's just a brown-noser. And he's so secretive about everything."

Anne thought *reserved* a more accurate description. And *cunning*. Potentially dangerous, if crossed. Whether Carter liked it or not, William was probably in the running. Fortunately, Anne had never had any issues with him.

"Donna has the most seniority."

Anne cringed silently at the sound of Elise's whiny voice emanating from somewhere behind. Often absent from the office, Elise was invariably difficult to deal with when she deigned to make an appearance. Jennifer had nicknamed her the Ice Princess because she was imperious and demanding, often acting as if she was above the rest of them. Whenever possible, Anne did her best to avoid interacting with the woman. Evidently, she was in today and had decided to join them.

"She's the most qualified person in our group," Elise's thin lips announced and then clamped together in a tight smile as she sidled over toward Donna.

Anne paused to consider the words rather than the person delivering them. Elise had a point. Donna had been with the firm for years, having worked her way up from the bottom. She knew the operation inside out.

Carter looked at Donna with an odd expression on his face. He appeared to be gauging her reaction, and it suddenly occurred to Anne that he might be interested in the position himself. She quietly studied the small, meek-looking man standing beside her. He squeaked a bit when he talked and was often made fun of by the traders. It was hard to believe he would be selected.

"Too many politics," Donna said quickly. "I don't want it."

Donna had worked her way up over the years, starting as a secretary. Never without a cigarette in hand, she wore bright, garish eyeshadow and heavy mascara. Her long fingernails were always painted in bright shades, sometimes sporting glittery sparkles and artful designs and her clothes appeared to have been purchased from the ultra-final clearance sale rack, the ones that absolutely no one else was willing to buy. She would never have been promoted on the investment banking floor, where customers occasionally visited, and hence polished appearances were important. But down on the trading floor, anyone could start anywhere and end up at the top, regardless of how gaudily they dressed.

"Wondering who they'll put in charge?"

They all turned in surprise to see William, who never joined them in standing lunches or casual conversations.

"Aren't you?" Carter chirped.

William gave a casual shrug. As usual, he never offered his thoughts about anything.

Just then, Jennifer appeared, breathless, with lunch in hand. The entire research group was now assembled. "I've been hanging out with a couple of guys on the trading floor," she explained. "I was hoping to catch some scuttlebutt about who our next manager might be."

They all looked at her expectantly and waited to see if she had anything more to offer.

"Someone stuck a mouse in Vito's sandwich, and they were all waiting to see how long it would take him to discover it." She shook her head. "I didn't hear anything else besides that."

They each looked down at their sandwiches. Carter started separating the bread from the filling.

"It took forever for him to find it," she continued. "I was afraid he might actually bite into the creature by mistake. I'm not sure the guys would have stopped him, either."

Anne found it hard to continue eating. The image seemed permanently imprinted in her mind. Lunch had arrived later than usual, and she had been starving before Jennifer showed up. "What did Vito do when he found it?"

"He just dumped the entire thing into the trash, cool as a cucumber, and told one of the trading assistants to order him something else."

They were interrupted by a secretary who said the phones were ringing off the hook. Grabbing the remains of their lunches, they quickly headed back to their cubicles.

* * *

As she nibbled on her sandwich, Anne sat quietly, thinking about next steps. Was there anything more she needed to verify? Any obvious loose ends? When none came to mind, she concluded that it was time to do something about what she had discovered. It was time to talk to Alex Hunter, Spencer Brother's in-house legal counsel, so that he could be apprised of the firm's unwise involvement in these troublesome deals and gauge the likelihood of lawsuits and other legal actions against the corporation.

She shifted from her cross-legged position (one of the less professional mannerisms she employed at the office), swung her legs down to meet the floor, and slipped her feet back into the awaiting pumps. Almost immediately, her shoulder-length blond hair fell haphazardly across her face. She pushed it away and then ran her finger down the list of phone numbers she kept pinned on the wall near her telephone, stopping when she found his name.

"Another trader gone astray?" Alex said when she explained why she was calling. "Already?"

It had been less than a month since the two had finished up work on another "problem trade," as they were euphemistically called. That case had involved a cocky, lone wolf who had gambled the firm's money on some bonds. And lost. Big time. If he had asked Anne her opinion prior to bidding, he would have been advised to avoid the bonds at all cost because they were an obvious disaster just waiting to happen. But like all traders, he was a risk-taker with a strong personality who did not like to be told what to do. Or what he should not buy. It was not the first time he had become the proud owner of "something worth close to nothing," but it would be his last. Shortly after Anne and Alex had pulled the facts together and determined there was no way to legally undo the trade, he was handed his walking papers and escorted to the door.

Alex gave an exaggerated sigh, as if to drive home the point, and then said,

"I'm free for the next thirty minutes. Can you drop by now?"

Anne headed straight for the elevators. When she arrived at his office, however, she found him engaged in a telephone conversation.

"We're not—" he said, motioning for her to take a seat in the chair opposite his desk. "No. Definitely not. We never—" He covered the receiver and mouthed, *I'm almost done.*

She looked at him, skeptical. He was unable to get a word in edgewise, and whoever was on the other end of the line appeared to be quite angry. Or at least not listening. Probably an irate investor.

"Even if that were so, the financial—" he said, shaking his head.

No more than thirty-five years old, Alex dressed like he was closer to fifty. Today he wore a tailored, navy pinstripe suit with a bland tie she never would have even noticed, except for a small dark stain, probably his morning coffee, which practically leaped out and begged for her attention. His white, pinpoint oxford cotton shirt was so heavily starched it looked as if it would stand up any moment and begin marching out of the room.

"Right. In that case—" He pulled the receiver from his ear with a look of surprise. "The wanker hung up!"

She loved his British accent and the various expressions that came tumbling out of his mouth.

"I've lived in the States since I was fifteen years old, and I'm still surprised at how rude some New Yorkers can be." Alex carefully set the phone down in its cradle and then looked up at her with a warm smile. "How's *your* day been so far?"

"In the course of researching a housing bond issue," Anne immediately started rattling, "I've come across a group of deals that are all structured in the same manner, have many of the same participants, were all underwritten by a handful of firms—"

"Hang on," he broke in quickly.

She waited while he rooted around the various piles of paper on his desk, produced a pen and pad, and then nodded at her, ready to take notes.

As soon as she mentioned Michael Kingston's name, Alex gave a tight smile. "He's like a magnet when it comes to problems, but he's also a rainmaker.

I think that's why the firm tolerates his antics." He squinted at her. "What has he managed to get us into this time?"

"Let me start by telling you about the prospectuses that were used to sell the bonds in the first place. Bluntly speaking, they're pathetic."

"And pathetic in this case is?" He sounded like a policeman reciting the details of a speeding ticket. *You were going forty in a twenty-five. That will be a $200 fine.*

"They're riddled with inaccuracies and contain several outright lies. They fail to mention key participants in the transactions, their personal interests, or conflicts of interest in the projects. Most importantly, they obscure the true purpose of these financings."

"Smashing." Alex set his elbows on the desk, interlacing his fingers to form a ledge, and then lightly rested his chin.

"Given the SEC's recent crackdown on flaky sales pitches, we could be in for some fairly rough riding on this issue alone. Not to mention the timing with all the leveraged buyouts...."

She left the rest unsaid. The newspapers were littered with stories about Michael Milken, Ivan Boesky, and other high-flying junk bond traders who had pled guilty to insider trading. They were the biggest scandals to hit The Street since 1938, when Richard Whitney, a former president of the New York Stock Exchange, was found guilty of embezzlement and taken to Sing Sing prison wearing a three-piece suit.

Alex frowned. "Bloody hell."

"The far more serious problem, however, is the structure of the bonds themselves."

"You mean it gets worse?"

She dropped her bombshell.

"In my view, these bonds *don't* qualify for their tax-exempt status." He took a deep breath and leaned back heavily in his leather, executive-style chair.

"As you know, investors purchase municipal bonds specifically to *avoid paying federal taxes on the interest they receive.*" She did not need to spell it out for him. Their clients purchased these types of bonds because they were special—the federal government was not allowed to tax them—but if there was something wrong with this particular set of bonds, if they violated the rules somehow, then that special exemption would be gone. "It could spell disaster for the firm."

"Like Drexel," Alex said, fixing his steel blue eyes on her.

She nodded, her face grim. In the last few months, Drexel Burnham Lambert had agreed to pay $650 million in fines, a consequence of failing to adequately police their employees. It was possible that some of the biggest investment banks on the street would be bankrupted by the illegal information swapping that had become all too common in the aftermath of Reagan-era deregulation. The question was where the bonds she had tripped over might fit into the equation.

"You've got my attention."

Anne began to describe a low-income housing project in Colorado as an example of how the bonds worked.

"In Aspen?" He raised an eyebrow. "As in the powdery ski-haven loved by the jet-setting crowd?"

"It's meant to provide affordable housing for the help. To give them the option of living somewhere besides a garage, camper, or tent."

"Not there. It's already been tried."

"Seriously?" Anne wondered if he was joking.

"There was a proposal to build subsidized housing on the east side of town that caused a big kerfuffle a few years ago." His eyes narrowed. "People with homes in the area were afraid it would bring an increase in crime. Eventually, the whole project was scrapped."

Yet another reason these strange bonds were problematic. "Well, even if the rich and famous were to allow the riffraff to enter their hallowed domain, this particular $53 million dollar project would not, and in fact, *cannot* ever happen."

"Because?"

"Because the money that was raised when the bonds first came to market has been locked up in an investment contract with the Oko Sychaito Bank." She pretended to hold a key and twist her wrist in a door-locking motion.

"It's tied up for the next thirty years."

"But if that's the case, there was never a plan to build the project in the first place."

"Exactly. Which means the bonds were not issued for a true public purpose. I don't see how they qualify as a *legally acceptable* way to issue tax-exempt bonds, despite the legal opinion from some schlocky law firm I never heard of stating that every one of these bonds supposedly deserves their tax-exempt status."

He rotated back and forth in his chair, looking puzzled. "And you said there are multiple bond issues like this one?"

She nodded. "At least eight that I know of. There could easily be more."

"How did they manage to escape detection until now?"

"Probably because the prospectuses don't even remotely correspond with reality. They don't bother to mention the Oko Sychaito Bank or the investment agreement or any of the other nitty gritty. An investor wouldn't have a clue as to the true nature of these things."

"Yet you noticed them."

"I did," she replied, but she might not have if it hadn't been for the trustee briefly hesitating that day. The bonds had appeared so dull and completely routine at first glance that the task of looking them over had been unceremoniously dumped in her lap by the Puff Queen, who had used words like *crap* and *waste of time* to describe them. When Anne subsequently relayed what she had unearthed about their unusual structure, it became painfully obvious that her co-worker was mortified to discover she had discarded what now appeared to be an interesting project.

"In time," she added, "others will notice them too."

Neither one said anything for a moment while Alex scribbled some notes. By the time they had finished, he had agreed that they needed to alert the Senior VP of Municipals. Anne gathered her things and stood up to leave.

"I almost forgot." She set a thick stack of papers containing information about the eight problem deals on his desk. "Some nighttime reading." She smiled and then swiftly disappeared out the door.

* * *

Anne returned to a department abuzz. The Senior VP had told one of the secretaries to round up all of the analysts. Everyone knew it could mean only one thing. He was about to announce who would be put in charge of the research department now that their manager had been fired.

Anne heard a couple of traders making bets as she passed by and saw the analysts gathered around the file cabinets at the far end, with the three secretaries flitting nervously around the periphery. She quickened her pace and headed over to join the group. When she reached them, Jennifer smiled and gave a small wave while Donna bit one of her multi-colored fingernails and studied the floor. The Ice Princess stood next to Donna, her arms crossed tightly over her chest, her face frozen in an anxious scowl. Steering clear of her, Anne went to the far side of the group and stood by Carter who was tapping his foot on the floor. William gave her a slight nod and then stared straight ahead.

When the big guy finally appeared, everyone stopped moving and stood rigidly in place. He got straight to the point. "William will be the interim manager," he said with no obvious emotion.

Out of the corner of her eye, Anne saw Carter blanch at the news that the termite would be ascending the throne.

The VP remained for a moment scanning their faces, perhaps waiting to see if anyone had any questions and then headed wordlessly back to his inner sanctum.

4

Minimizing Losses

Thursday, January 12, 1989

After the announcement, Donna locked herself away in her office for three days. No one dared to enter, not even the Ice Princess, who normally was joined at the hip with her. All of them were shocked that William had been designated interim manager. He was, in many respects, an unknown quantity. Reserved and more reclusive than the other analysts, he rarely ventured from his cubicle and never joined them when they ate. It was as if he lived silently amongst them, watching over their antics with a somber expression permanently etched on his face. William, for his part, said very little. He waited a few days before quietly moving the contents of his cubicle into the office that had been occupied by the previous research manager and then promptly disappeared for a week of supervisor training. It was during this time that Anne arranged a meeting with the Senior VP, Peter Eckert, to discuss the bonds.

At the appointed hour, Anne stood outside Peter's office and waited to be motioned to join him and his head trader, Nick Angelini, inside. They were visible through the long, thick glass that separated his office from the rest of the people on the floor.

In his mid-forties, Peter was one of the oldest people on the trading floor. Short, slightly overweight, and clearly balding, he had never married. Rumor held that he dated pretty women in their twenties, often secretaries employed by the firm. A relatively quiet man, he never projected the strong, take-charge attitude that might be expected from the manager of a three-hundred-plus-person department in the heart of Wall Street. Instead, he ruled quietly from his office and generally relied on his henchmen to be the public show of strength.

In diametric opposition to him was his head trader, Nick. Everything about the man suggested he was a force to be reckoned with. He jogged before work and lifted weights daily, making him lithe and muscular. And he was unusual in that he was one of the few traders to have graduated from college (from an ivy league college to boot). But the thing that set him apart most was his explosive temper. He could lose it at any time for virtually any reason. Anne always felt like she was walking on eggshells whenever she met with him.

She tried not to stare, but through occasional glances, saw Peter sitting silently, a look of consternation on his face while Nick made large, agitated gestures as he spoke. Gradually, her positive assuredness turned to dread.

Anne took a deep breath and again reviewed in her mind potential questions they could have and what she would say in reply.

"Nervous?" She heard Alex ask.

She whirled in surprise to see the lawyer standing just a few feet from her.

"A bit," she admitted, feeling sheepish.

"It'll be fine." He smiled and then looked down at the papers in his hand.

"I know," she murmured, trying to sound nonchalant, and then resumed trying to anticipate what she might be asked. Gradually she became aware of her co-worker Carter and one of the junior traders engrossed in a conversation in her periphery, about ten feet to the right. They both had their backs to her, probably unaware of her presence.

"I'd give her an eight today," the junior trader said while visibly eyeing the unsuspecting woman's chest area. They both snickered.

"Yeah," she saw Carter nod enthusiastically. "Maybe even a nine. I wouldn't mind a piece of that action."

Anne watched them with a mixture of curiosity and disgust and then stole a glance in Alex's direction, but he didn't seem to have noticed the conversation. Or perhaps he was just ignoring it.

"Yesterday, she was barely a five," the trader said with a derisive sneer, "but today's outfit is really hot."

Anne regarded him from where she stood. Short and stocky, he had small beady eyes above a prominent chin that jutted out at an odd angle, as if it had been broken at some point and never properly set. He'd probably only rate a 2 on a scale of 1 to 10 himself. Even more questionable was whether Carter, who had hair billowing in all directions, a pockmarked face, and pasty white skin, would fit within the parameters of the scale at all. In fact, his spindle-shaped body (making him look like a fish) and tendency to complain had earned him the nickname Carter-the Carper, or The Carp, for short. Of course, he had no idea that anyone called him that or that the traders occasionally made jokes about him belonging at the bottom of a stagnant, scummy pond.

"Now there's a babe." Carter motioned with his head toward a different woman on his left, causing him to turn and face more in Anne's general direction. "Too bad more of the girls don't dress like that," he said suggestively and chuckled in a way that Anne found particularly grating.

She saw Alex look over toward the woman in question and then quickly look away, giving a slight shake of his head. Anne looked back at Carter and the junior trader, wondering what would come out of their mouths next.

"A little scenery always livens the place up." The junior trader gave a wink.

"I'm with you. Yesterday—" Carter suddenly noticed Anne staring at them intently. He brought a finger to his lips to motion the trader to be quiet, cocked his head in her direction, and quickly took a few steps further away.

It had been obvious to Anne for some time that something other than natural selection had been at work in the hiring practices of the municipal bond department. The bevy of female employees did not even remotely resemble the corporate female population anywhere else. In fact, most of the women hired to work in this division were not only attractive, but exceptionally so. Only a few strays, like the Ice Princess, managed to slip through the cracks.

A light touch on Anne's arm startled her out of her thoughts. She turned to see Alex nod toward Peter's office and vaguely wondered how long he had been waiting for her to notice the open door. She quickly shook off her feelings of dismay as they headed in together. The rational, intellectual side of her brain knew that this meeting required her full attention, complete composure, and unwavering confidence.

Peter began grilling her like a drill sergeant before she had even finished describing the intricate structure of the bonds.

"Does our trading desk own any of these things?"

Naturally, he was more concerned about trading losses than customer losses or the potential that a fraud had been perpetrated upon the market as a whole.

"Roughly $7 million."

"Has the price dropped at all?" he asked gruffly.

"No."

He appeared visibly relieved. Earlier that day, several traders had whispered to her that it had been a bad month for the department in terms of trading losses. Anne figured Peter didn't want these bonds compounding his problems. She added a caveat to her previous statement.

"My guess is that in time, as the projects remain unbuilt, the market will begin to examine the bonds more closely, as I did, and start to find minor, unsettling discrepancies."

She paused as she heard Nick mumble something under his breath from the corner of the room and begin pacing in front of the long window that overlooked the trading floor. Peter motioned for her to continue.

"When that happens, the price will undoubtedly be affected negatively."

Out of the corner of her eye, she saw Nick tighten his fists into balls.

"The question is how long it will take others to discover the bonds."

"Exactly!" Nick said, pausing his pacing. "We're sitting on a time bomb!"

Peter motioned with his hand for Nick to tamp things down.

"This isn't the time to waffle around," Nick said, looking directly at Peter and ignoring the signal. "We need to dump these bonds now!"

Anne caught her breath and froze, trying to avoid showing any sign of surprise. She had never seen Nick challenge Peter so directly. Normally, they were aligned before bringing subordinates into a conversation.

Peter shot a warning glance, his gunmetal eyes studying Nick mercilessly, like a cat watching a goldfish swim around its bowl.

Nick threw his hands up in a gesture of frustration. "I'm telling you. These bonds are going to eat our lunch!"

Ignoring Nick pacing a small path on the carpet, Peter turned back toward Anne calmly, as if nothing had happened, as if she was the only person in the room. "So, the upshot of what you're telling me is that these bonds appear to violate IRS rules and should never have been issued."

"Precisely."

"It also sounds like the idiots who concocted this scheme went to great lengths to obscure the true nature of the deals in order to keep the IRS from catching wind of their little enterprise."

She nodded.

"And one of them works for us," he said with a wry smile.

She nodded again, more slowly this time, unsure of where he stood.

He clucked his tongue against his teeth. "I'll bet Michael made a pretty penny on these deals."

Of course he had, but so had all of the other participants in this transaction, including the developer (who wasn't actually building the project), the bond lawyer (who had opined that the bonds could be issued), Marvin Goldberg (the architect behind the scam), and the Oko Sychaito bank (where the money was currently invested). And of course, their own firm, Spencer Brothers, had profited handsomely as well when the bonds were initially brought to market.

"What is the total dollar amount we're talking about here?" Peter asked quietly, like a hunter moving in for the kill.

Nick stopped pacing and stood rigidly still.

"So far I've found seven deals underwritten by our firm that total approximately $280 million. There's at least one deal for $32 million underwritten by Pinkerton Investments, but I wouldn't be surprised if there are more," Anne said matter-of-factly.

Nick began clasping and unclasping his hands restlessly, as if they were cold and needed to be warmed.

"How exactly do these things work?" Peter tapped one of his fingers ever so gently on his desk, seemingly oblivious to the discomfort of his right-hand man.

"The funds locked up in the investment contract earn 9% interest while paying off the bondholders at the lower, tax-exempt interest rate of just 6%. When the bonds actually mature, the money initially invested in the contract plus the 3% surplus generated each year will be sufficient to pay off the bondholders as well as all the underwriting and other fees. It's really very neat and tidy."

"Not quite neat and tidy enough, though."

She shrugged almost imperceptibly.

"And Michael Kingston's response is to sweep the whole thing under the carpet?"

Nick had kept quiet for as long as he found physically possible. "Doesn't that moron understand the trading implications of letting us buy and sell this crap? If the press manages to get a hold of this story, these bonds are going to drop *instantly* in value."

He was absolutely right. Anne saw Alex nodding in agreement while Peter remained stone-faced, looking at no one in particular.

Nick set his jaw in a hard line and banged his fist hard on Peter's desk. "I refuse to be left holding the bag. My people have to be told immediately to halt trading in these things."

"Absolutely not!" Peter shot back, his voice rising to match Nick's in intensity. "I need to take this up the line before we go saying *anything* to *anybody* and inadvertently tip off the rest of the Street." He grimaced, a small twitch visible on the left side of his mouth. "Don't forget who brought them to market—we did."

The air in the room became heavy. He was obviously weighing the risk of a federal investigation against potential trading losses, unsure how to proceed. It was possible the firm would be liable for Michael Kingston's actions, for standing by quietly while their prize bull had steadily racked up fees that profited both him and Spencer Brothers.

"And we certainly don't want to give the *Sheriff of Wall Street* an excuse to waltz across our floor."

Ever since Black Monday some 15 months before, when the market had fallen 508 points, the greed-is-good mentality of Wall Street had been under siege. The US district attorney had made a name for himself, handcuffing high-profile traders and parading them across the trading floor. Dubbed the "perp walk," it was obviously meant to crush the arrogance of the suspendered yuppies who would do almost anything to make a buck. Peter's comment suggested the tactic was having an impact.

After what seemed an interminable amount of time, he turned to Alex and asked, "Are you absolutely sure these securities violate IRS rules?"

"As sure as I can be without having seen all of the legal documents."

"So there's a chance–"

"No." Alex cut him off, his voice firm, his eyes unwavering. "The only question is whether the IRS would actually choose to penalize investors. They're the innocent ones in this mess. And it's anyone's guess as to what the SEC might do to Spencer Brothers. We should *never* have allowed these bonds to get into the marketplace."

"Okay. I want this kept confidential. Does everyone understand me?" Peter's eyes rested briefly on each of them as he slowly scanned the room. He looked down and adjusted his cuff links and then looked back up at Alex. "Arrange a meeting with the rest of the bozos that were involved in this harebrained scheme so that you can resolve any of your unanswered questions. I want you to know these deals inside and out."

Alex nodded.

"After I've had a chance to think about this some more, we can make a final decision about how to alert our larger customers and, most importantly, how to avoid owning any of the bonds when the shit hits the fan."

He turned to address Nick. "Start reviewing all housing bond trades over $500,000 so that you can quietly ensure we don't own too many of these things at any one time." He swung his hand back and forth dismissively.

"Say there are some weird redemption provisions that are affecting the bond prices."

Nick made a face. Clearly, he was not in favor of feeding the traders some story about the bonds being subject to strange pre-payment rules.

Peter gave a loud sigh and looked down at his desk. "Or make up something else that sounds plausible."

They all stood still, awaiting further instructions.

When Peter finally raised his head again, he appeared surprised to see them still there. "Everyone's dismissed," he said quickly.

Anne felt her face go hot as they hustled out of the room.

"I can't believe we didn't realize he wanted us out of there."

Alex shrugged. "It wasn't clear."

Wasn't clear? Or had they missed a cue?

"I wouldn't worry about it."

Easy for him to say. Unlike him, she actually reported to the man. One word from him and she could be out the door. And he determined her year-end bonus. The last thing she needed was for Peter to question whether she was on top of her game.

* * *

"Who did you say you work for?" a disembodied voice emanated from the speaker phone in Alex's office. It belonged to David Singer, one of the so-called bozos. This was the first of several calls they were making that morning, inviting the key players in these deals to a meeting.

"Spencer Brothers in-house legal counsel," Alex replied, with a hint of a smile, evidently finding the man's apparent discomfort amusing.

"I see." There was a pause. "And why do you want to meet?"

"To discuss the bond structure. It's a little unusual. Since you served as bond counsel—"

"Have you spoken with Michael Kingston?"

"Actually, he's the one who gave us your name."

In point of fact, the handsome banker had been so slow in providing contact information they had given up waiting and sleuthed it out by themselves.

"I see." David coughed loudly into the phone, causing both Alex and Anne to jump back. "And he'll be there as well?"

"He wouldn't miss it."

Under no circumstances, Michael Kingston had said through gritted teeth, were they to hold a meeting without him.

There was a long pause in which nobody said a word. Anne kicked her foot nervously and stared at the silent speaker box. Presumably, the man was considering his options.

"What time?"

Alex gave her a thumbs-up signal and provided the logistical details. Anne began getting her thoughts organized for the next call they would be making.

"It's always interesting to see the reactions of these guys when their schemes start unraveling," Alex chuckled after they hung up.

The sun streamed through the window, illuminating his broad shoulders and thick sandy hair. Anne caught herself wondering if he had a girlfriend and then immediately stopped herself from continuing that train of thought. She never dated co-workers. It was her cardinal rule. "I wasn't sure he was going to agree to meet with us," she managed to stammer out.

"Me neither," he replied. "Let's see what the next one of these jokers has to say," and began dialing the number for *Onyx River Investments*.

"Hello?" She heard Marvin Goldberg's nasal voice boom out. And then, "Will Michael Kingston be there?" once she explained the purpose of their call.

"Absolutely," Anne replied. She tried not to laugh as Alex made a face. Michael's presence appeared to be supremely important to these guys.

"Okay. I can schlep over to your office easily enough," Marvin said, his New York accent permeating every word. "When is it again?"

The tight knot in Anne's stomach began to slacken as she provided the organizational information and wrapped up the call.

"Two down, one to go," Alex said, removing his jacket and loosening his tie. "This office always seems to warm up too much in the afternoon sun."

"At least you have windows." Anne smiled. Her drab cubicle was located within the interior of the building with a view of offices, adjoining cubicles, and the trading floor. It looked nothing like what they showed in the movies, which always had the iconic shot of a couple hundred traders jam-packed in the trading pit of the New York Stock Exchange, shouting out orders to buy and sell shares of stock, and the closing bell ringing loudly in the background. In the bond world, there was no bell. Deals were made via telephone, with traders scattered all over the country. They sat at desks in the building of the firm that employed them, and all of the support staff, including the research analysts, were crammed into the space that remained.

"Walter?" she initiated the next conversation with the Oko Sychaito banker. "We spoke last week about the bonds that your—"

"Oh yes. I recall. What can I do for you?"

"I'm here with Alex Hunter. He's one of our in-house lawyers, and we—"

"I'm sorry. Did you just say lawyer?"

"Yes." Anne locked eyes with Alex and raised her brow.

"Why is the legal department involved?"

Alex leaned in toward the speakerphone. "I advise the trading operation from time to time. These bonds are a little unusual and—"

"In that case, I should probably have an Oko Sychaito lawyer on this call as well," he replied, his words clipped and voice taut. "In fact, you should probably speak with him directly." Walter promptly provided the contact information and hung up the phone.

Anne leaned back in her chair. "That didn't go so well."

"Interesting how quickly he scurried for cover," Alex said with a wry smile. She nodded. That was one way of putting it.

"Keep your fingers crossed," Alex instructed as he dialed. "Fortunately, I know the guy he pawned us off on. We've worked together a few times, and I've found him to be a decent enough chap."

"Alex?" The lawyer's voice sounded friendly. "It's been a while. How are you doing?"

After they spent a few minutes catching up, Alex gave the reason for his call. Anne braced and waited for the reaction on the other end of the line.

"I'm not familiar with the bonds you're asking about. Which banker?"

"Walter Hughes."

There was a long pause.

"Are you still there?" Alex cocked his head at the speakerphone.

"Yes. Sorry. I recognized the name and was just trying to place him. I'll take a look at the documents and get a better understanding of our role in this investment. When did you want to get together?"

And so the meeting was set.

5

The Meeting

Tuesday, January 17, 1989

"Good morning!" said Michael Kingston as Anne walked into the conference room three days later at exactly 8:30 am. "I was beginning to wonder what had happened to you."

"Believe me." She laughed and glanced quickly around the table, keenly aware that she was the last to arrive. "You don't want to know."

It had been a hectic day so far. The ferry had been on the fritz, delaying her more than twenty minutes during her morning commute. Then to compound matters, the elevator had stalled between floors, costing her more valuable time. Anne had made it to her desk just a few minutes before the meeting was scheduled to begin. After ripping off her coat and sneakers, throwing on a pair of heels, and stowing her purse, she had headed up to the twenty-fifth floor, convinced she would never make it on time.

She sat in the remaining open chair and found herself next to Marvin Goldberg, the self-professed architect behind the scam.

"You're younger than I expected," he said as he shook her hand, his dark brown hair falling into his eyes (only it sounded more like *yawh younga* with his strong New York accent).

"You too," Anne replied.

"And prettier." He looked her up and down, his eyes lingering over her midsection in a way that made her want to throw on a big puffy down jacket and zip it up to her chin. "My card," he said, holding it out in front of her, his mouth widening into a lopsided grin.

She gave a polite smile and surveyed the man before her. He wore no tie, and his shirt was a disaster, covered with wrinkles and creases that must have come from days of being thrown in a heap, god only knows where. His business card said he was President of *Onyx River Investments*, but his scuffed black shoes, sagging grey socks, and ill-fitting suit told another story. He looked more like a homeless person who had wandered in off the street, or perhaps someone who had had a bit too much to drink and spent the night in his car.

In sharp contrast to Marvin Goldberg's rumpled appearance were the two Oko Sychaito Bank attendees. "Hello," the silver-haired one said, giving her a firm handshake, "Walter Hughes." He wore what was obviously a custom-tailored suit, accented with an ocean blue Hermès tie, and toyed with a Cross gold pen in his left hand.

"And I'm Paul Sherman, in-house counsel for Oko Sychaito—" the one with jet black hair said, reaching his hand across the table "—here to keep Walter in line." Also immaculately dressed, he wore an irritated expression on his face. Presumably, he was less than thrilled about having to help mop up the mess Walter had gotten the bank into.

"David," the man to her right mumbled as he gave her a limp handshake with cold, clammy hands. "Nice to meet you." Balding and graying slightly in a nondescript gray suit, he looked nervous and uncomfortable. Anne wasn't entirely surprised. He was the one who had said, unequivocally, that the bonds deserved their tax-exempt status—*and put it in writing*—when he provided the legal opinion that accompanied the bonds. If she were in his shoes, she would be feeling nervous too.

"Did you have any trouble finding our office?" she asked, trying to remember his last name.

He shook his head. "I've been here before."

Of course he had. The four of them were business partners. She kicked herself for asking such an inane question.

Alex began by carefully reviewing the details of the bond structure for the next twenty minutes. Almost immediately, everyone looked bored. Marvin Goldberg yawned and blew smoke rings. Walter Hughes tapped his gold pen against the open palm of his hand, all the while moving restlessly in his seat. David Something-or-Other began doodling on the pad of paper in front of him, and Michael Kingston repeatedly stirred his coffee between frequent glances at his shiny Movado watch. There was a palpable feeling of relief in the room when Alex finally finished.

"Given everything I've just outlined," Alex looked squarely at David Something-or-Other with a solemn expression on his face, "What is the legal basis for bond counsel's determination that these are tax-exempt securities?"

The lawyer's lips twitched during the ensuing pause. After a moment, he averted his gaze downward and resumed drawing. "The deals were properly structured to conform with the provisions of the tax code," he replied in a monotone. "However, my files are warehoused out of state, so I can't provide you with any details at this time."

"But the bond proceeds are locked up in investment contracts with the Oko Sychaito Bank—" Anne said, watching his pen shift from connecting a series of circles to outlining a single, sharp square, "—so they can't be used to build any of the low-income housing projects."

"I believe that is the case," was the terse reply. "Nonetheless, my firm stands by its legal opinion."

"Except that you're unable to enlighten us as to what specifically allows that designation," the Oko Sychaito lawyer said with obvious derision, "—because you don't have your files handy." He shook his head and frowned.

"That's correct," David Something-or-Other replied in the same monotone. "However, I reiterate that my firm stands by its original opinion."

"How long will it take to get your hands on those files?" Alex asked evenly, as if there were a chance the man would ever produce them.

"It's hard to say," he said, with all the energy and enthusiasm of a dead turtle. "We're rather short-staffed right now, but I'll have someone get right on it."

Alex briefly studied him before turning toward Marvin Goldberg. "I understand you're trying to find a savings and loan institution that might be interested in providing a loan to the developer."

"That's right," Marvin said, feeling around his coat pockets until finally settling upon the slightly bent cigarette he had, evidently, been hunting for.

"How are your efforts panning out?" Alex looked at him expectantly.

"Haven't had much luck so far," came the casual reply.

"Am I right in thinking you created this unusual bond structure? That you brought the idea to Spencer Brothers?"

"Yeah," Marvin shot a look of defiance at Michael Kingston. "I'm whatcha' call the brains behind the deal." He deliberately flicked the lighter and slowly lit his cigarette.

"Do *you* recall the legal basis for the tax-exempt status of the bonds?"

"Can't say I do." He puffed a smoke ring toward the doodling lawyer, who was repeatedly drawing over the same single square. "What I can say is I know I ran everything—" he paused for a brief moment to let his lips curl up in a defiant smile, and then repeated the word, slowly, drawing it out for maximum emphasis, "e-v-e-r-y-t-h-i-n-g past our bond counsel, who approved it as a legitimate structure."

David Something-or-Other's hand froze, and he visibly squirmed in his seat.

Marvin rubbed the stubble on his face and leaned back in his chair. "I'm no lawyer, just a hard-working businessman from the Bronx. Until legal counsel says otherwise, I assume the bonds deserve their tax-exempt status."

Alex directed his attention to the one remaining source of information. "What is the Oko Sychaito Bank's position on this?"

"We merely provided an investment vehicle for a pool of money," Walter Hughes responded icily, running a hand through his silver hair. "It's no concern of ours whether the bonds are tax-exempt or not."

The dark-haired lawyer accompanying Walter visibly bristled at his co-worker's reply.

"You're not concerned about the bank's reputation if the cat were to, somehow, get out of the bag?" Alex stared incredulously at him.

"The Oko Sychaito Bank didn't actually underwrite—" Walter began.

"We would be very unhappy if our involvement in this affair were made public," the accompanying attorney interrupted, all the while glaring at him.

Walter snorted. "But Spencer Brothers is actually responsible for—"

"We have no interest in being party to questionable transactions." The lawyer practically spat the words into Walter's shiny, silver hair. "Our bank prides itself on being regarded as discreet, trustworthy, and always above board." He turned his palms upward in a gesture of appeal. "Surely your firm is equally concerned about the potential effect on its reputation as well?"

"Of course," Alex said. "And before this mushrooms into a giant public relations nightmare, I want to be absolutely certain that I know exactly what we're dealing with."

"You're spazzing out over nothing," Marvin announced with a smirk, repeatedly flicking his lighter on and off. "Nobody's concerned about these bonds except for you." He jerked a thumb in Anne's direction, "And Nancy Drew over here."

She blinked, and her jaw went slack. *Seriously?*

"Let's keep this professional, mate," Alex said, warningly.

She gave Marvin a long look. By comparing her to a sixteen-year-old amateur sleuth, he had been trying to insult her, but he seemed to have forgotten that the fictional character was smart, resourceful, and always succeeded in solving the case.

His thumb froze above the sparker, which stopped the incessant flicking, but the smug smile remained. "Our investors are getting a good return, and their money is safe." He shrugged. "Sounds like a good deal to me. What more d'ya want?"

Michael nodded in agreement. "Well said."

"Unless the IRS catches wind of things," Alex retorted.

"And who's gonna tell them?" Marvin scoffed. "You?"

Alex shrugged.

David and Walter both looked around uneasily.

"Give me a break," Michael said, sounding a bit like an injured bird. "You can't be serious." He was hunched slightly forward, with tiny beads of sweat forming a constellation on his forehead.

"He's bluffing." Marvin clicked his lighter shut and carefully stowed it in his shirt pocket. "He doesn't have the balls. Besides, it wouldn't be acting in the firm's best interest to mouth off to the IRS."

Michael's hand shook slightly as he wagged his index finger back and forth. "A move like that could cause irreparable damage with some of our clients and perhaps even subject us to SEC fines."

"So, you guys admit that the IRS and the SEC wouldn't look favorably upon these deals—that the structure is, in fact, a little dodgy?" Alex watched them, unblinking.

All four were silent for a moment, and then Michael replied. "I can see that they might raise an eyebrow or two at the agencies, but it's *unnecessary–*" he paused, and Anne saw that his face had taken on a peculiarly gray pallor, as if he were about to be sick.

"—there's no good reason to subject the bonds to that sort of scrutiny." Marvin finished the thought for him with a cough and a small puff of smoke.

"Exactly," Michael said, carefully dabbing at his forehead with a handkerchief.

Again, the room fell silent.

"Is it true that the four of you each receive monthly *oversight fees* from the interest generated by the bonds?" Anne asked, shattering the uneasy quiet. She had seen mention of them buried in the prospectus, but there had been no explanation as to who was actually receiving the payments or why.

"What?! Where did you—" Walter sputtered, angrily scanning his partners' faces. "Who told you that?"

Her guess had paid off. They were personally profiting from the bonds by skimming money off the top.

"It doesn't matter where she got it," the dark-haired lawyer retorted without so much as a glance. "The only thing that matters is whether it's correct." His lips pressed together so tightly, they were in danger of vanishing.

"This is outrageous!" Walter threw his gold pen down on the table and gave Anne a withering look.

"Walter—calm down," Michael said with an exasperated sigh.

"Don't tell me to calm down!" He pushed his silver hair back, exposing his now beet-red face. "I don't know what the hell is going on here."

"You and me both," Marvin said, looking slightly perturbed for the first time since arriving. "Where exactly is this headed?"

Michael eyed Anne warily as he spoke. "I agree. How is this relevant?"

She pressed, full bore ahead, curious to see what else Walter might spill. "Well, the oversight fees are *unusual*, to say the least."

"Unusual?" Walter huffed. "So what?"

"It's not clear to me that they're even legal."

"Who the hell died and made you the grand arbiter of securities law?"

Damn. She had overreached, not only allowing him to avoid the question, but paving the way for him to attack her instead.

"I agree with her entirely," Alex said sternly, "and I'm a licensed, practicing member of the bar."

"Listen here, Perry Mason," Walter said through gritted teeth. "Any fees I've received are *totally* legal. *Totally!* How dare you suggest there is anything questionable about—"

"Walter—" Michael tried to break in.

"I'll have you know that I've been in this business for years, and my integrity is absolutely *impeccable*. If you're looking to find malfeasance," he gestured toward Michael, "just pick up a few of his rocks and see what crawls out—"

"Walter!" Michael interrupted angrily. "Put a lid on it." His handsome features now looked pinched and twisted, giving his face a pickled appearance. He stood abruptly. "I think we need a short break."

"Bloody Hell!" Alex threw his arms up in a gesture of frustration. "We're right in the thick of—"

"Walter. My office. Now!"

Grimacing, Alex pushed his chair back and unfolded his legs, so that he now matched Michael's height and intensity. "But—"

"Now!" Michael repeated, his eyes locked on Walter.

"What a bunch of tossers," Alex muttered under his breath as Michael and Walter headed toward the door with Marvin and David Something-or-Other in tow.

Anne looked over at the dark-haired lawyer from the Oko Sychaito Bank, who still remained in the room. He looked grim.

"I'm not quite sure what to make of all of this," he said, stroking his chin.

"Really?" Alex snorted. "I think it's pretty obvious."

Anne nodded in silent agreement. The question in her mind was where to go from here. "I've got an idea I want to bounce off the two of you."

Alex shot her a curious look and slowly sank back down into his seat.

"I know you were trying to get Marvin's goat with that IRS comment, but it got me thinking. What if Spencer Brothers and Oko Sychaito Bank were to approach the SEC together and lay out all the issues we see with these bonds?"

"You're suggesting we intentionally draw their attention to them?" Alex raised his eyebrows.

"Exactly. Anyone can see that the offering statements are misleading, which explains how the bonds made it past our oversight committee. Since then, they've been trading all over the Street, with no one else noticing a problem either. So, the powers that be should be able to imagine our shock—" she put her hand theatrically on her chest as if she were fainting in surprise, "when we came to realize a fraud had been perpetrated on the market."

"But they'll just—"

Anne put up a finger to stop him. With all of the insider stock trading scandals dominating the financial news in the last few years, he was obviously concerned that the SEC would hammer everyone involved in an effort to set an example for the rest of Wall Street. "Let me finish, and then you can trash it."

He put his hands up in surrender.

She ticked off the arguments one by one. "We'd make it clear that we began an internal investigation the *moment* we became aware there was something flaky going on." Tick. "We'd emphasize that those responsible will be held *fully* accountable." Tick. "We'd say we have new policies in place to avoid this problem ever happening again." Tick. "And then plead for forgiveness and *light, light fines*."

The bank lawyer's eyes brightened, and he gave a throaty laugh. "So you'd serve Michael, Walter, Marvin, and that idiot who acted as bond counsel to the SEC for dinner. Hah! What an entertaining notion!"

Alex nodded. "It's an interesting strategy for trying to mitigate the fallout. The last thing any of us needs is for the SEC to go ballistic after discovering the deals on their own."

"But," the dark-haired lawyer said slowly, deflating the growing enthusiasm in the room. "Even though I like the idea of being proactive, I'm fairly certain that the C-Suite at Oko Sychaito Bank will be adamantly opposed." He took off his glasses, blew lightly on the lenses, and rubbed them against his shirt. "My guess is that they'd prefer to wait until the issue came to light of its own accord. It's just possible it never will."

Alex's eyes narrowed. "And Walter's involvement could be brushed quietly under the carpet."

"Not a chance," the Oko Sychaito lawyer said darkly, slipping his glasses back on.

"But if we take the lead on approaching the SEC—" Anne began.

"I'm not sure we can trust them to keep a thing of this magnitude quiet. A public investigation would run completely counter to the bank's preferred manner of conducting business. They would see it as humiliating. For that reason alone, I expect they will respectfully ask you to refrain from pursuing that strategy."

Humiliating? It was an odd choice of word in the milieu of Wall Street. So was *respectfully*. And then it hit her. The bank was based in Japan. They were concerned about having their name tied in any way to a scandal. It was all about saving face.

"Rest assured," he sniffed. "Walter's well-being in this matter is completely irrelevant. In fact, by the time I'm done briefing the Senior VP, I wouldn't be surprised if—"

The door opened, and they turned to see David Something-or-Other return to the room with his hands balled into fists so tightly that his knuckles had turned white. Looking like a cobra, coiled and ready to strike, he walked wordlessly over to his seat and sat down stiffly in his chair.

After a moment, the Oko Sychaito lawyer pointed left and then right, asking, "Which way is the men's room?"

"I'll show you," Alex said, leaving Anne alone with David Something-or-Other, who had begun scratching tiny check marks on the same tired piece of paper he had been drawing on throughout the meeting.

As she watched him take quick, shallow breaths, she decided to break the awkward silence. "I think they're predicting a big snowstorm later this week."

"I wouldn't know," he said curtly, without so much as a glance in her direction.

Clearly, he had no interest in chatting. Since he wasn't a Spencer Brothers employee, she didn't think she should leave him alone, unattended. Wasn't there some corporate policy to that effect? She looked around at the four walls that confined her to the dull space, trying to remember. As the minutes ticked by, she started to feel annoyed. Why should she be stuck babysitting this guy? Alex was every bit as capable. She stood up, stretched, and prepared to poke her head into the hallway to see if he was anywhere within sight.

Just then, a tall, athletic-looking woman wearing pearls and an elegant, belted suit strode into the room and announced that Michael would be just a few more minutes.

"Thanks," David grunted. "Hey, Kelsey—" he began, but then stopped, looking away.

Kelsey? No doubt this was Jennifer's friend, who had spoken so glowingly about Michael Kingston. Anne decided to take the opportunity to quickly introduce herself.

"Yes," Kelsey said hospitably. "That's right. How's she doing? It's been ages since we've spoken. I keep meaning to give her a call."

As Anne admired the woman's perfect hair and makeup, she felt plain and unsophisticated in comparison. It had to have taken forever to achieve that look. Time she never felt she had.

"You should join us for coffee next time," Kelsey said after they had exchanged cards and additional pleasantries, promising that there would be absolutely no discussion about the Pandora bonds. "The ones you're meeting about right now," Kelsey answered Anne's momentary look of confusion. "We nick-named them that because they're just like the mythical Pandora's Box—it's hard to know exactly what's inside and even harder to predict what will come flying out."

She appeared amused by the description, although Anne found it rather disconcerting. These bonds had the potential to cost the firm considerably.

"So you helped Michael with them?"

"Yes," Kelsey said with a laugh. "*I* did all the heavy lifting, and *he* got all the glory."

Such was the life of any investment banking associate. Until she was promoted to Vice President, she would continue carrying the bags of the more senior people in the group with barely a mention. Anne briefly commiserated and then asked how many Pandora deals, in total, had been brought to market.

"At least fifteen—" Kelsey said, interrupted as the conference door opened and Walter Hughes marched in angrily, his silver hair bouncing with every step. Marvin Goldberg followed closely behind and blew a kiss in Kelsey's direction.

"Morning dahling," he said, accentuating his New York Accent.

Kelsey glanced down at her wrist, revealing an elegant, diamond-studded watch, and gave a small gasp. "Oh my God! I've got to get back." She lowered her voice to a whisper and gave Anne a small wink. "Good luck! This is a pretty tough crowd—make sure to stand your ground."

Anne looked over at David Some-thing-or-Other sitting morosely at the conference table, Walter Hughes twirling his gold pen nearby, and Marvin Goldberg puffing away in the corner. Now that Alex was back, she could make a quick escape and decided to wander down the hall under the guise of searching for a soda.

As she perused the corridors, she saw the associates and analysts who supported the investment bankers, quietly crunching numbers on their computers, hard at work to find ways to bring the next deal to market. She took a deep breath and thought about the meeting so far. Everybody seemed nervous except for Marvin Goldberg. Was it just a fluke of his personality, or were the others more deeply entrenched in this sketchy operation than he? And what about Walter's outsized reaction? It suggested there was more to these bonds than just the unethical fees.

As she rounded the corner, her heart jumped into her throat as she spotted the Ice Princess leaning against the doorframe of someone's office. *No way. Not now.* The last thing Anne needed was any more distractions. She did a one-eighty and headed in the opposite direction.

When she returned to the conference room, everyone except for Michael was in their seats. She joined in the idle chatter about the weather and the Yankees until, eventually, the room again fell silent, leaving her to wonder how much longer they would have to wait. As if reading her mind, Alex asked if anyone had any idea where Michael was.

"You might try his office," Marvin suggested with a shrug.

"Well, I haven't got all day," Walter said with a snap of his gold pen. "Perhaps this meeting should simply be adjourned."

"Let's give Michael a call," she said, already picking up the phone. Anne heard the familiar click as she was placed on hold, and his secretary went in search of him. After waiting a few minutes, she sighed and looked at Alex. "I don't know what her problem is."

"Do you think she forgot about you?"

Anne flipped her palms toward the ceiling and shrugged. "Who knows. At this rate, we'll be lucky if we get an answer to his whereabouts by tomorrow morning."

What the hell? Walter mouthed to Marvin.

Marvin shrugged and looked over at David Something-or-Other, whose attention was singularly focused on drawing little triangles around the edge of his paper.

Walter slowly scanned the room and then asked aloud, "What are we still doing here?"

When he got no reply, he crossed his arms and glowered at Alex. "This is beyond rude."

Alex shot Anne a look of annoyance, as if it was her fault that Walter was ticked off, but Michael was the one who was missing. All she had done was to report the facts, perhaps, she allowed, a bit more negatively than necessary.

"Let's give his secretary another minute," Alex said evenly.

"I don't have another minute." Walter's lips twisted disdainfully, as if the mere suggestion was a huge imposition. "I've already wasted enough time on this matter." He stood up as if to go.

"Walter—keep your hair on!"

Anne jerked in surprise at the sharpness of Alex's tone.

"Another one of your annoying British expressions?" Walter said, waving his hand in Alex's face. "We're in America, pal."

"Just give us a moment to figure out what's going on," Alex replied, sounding more conciliatory.

Anne watched the unfolding scene in exasperation. If Michael didn't return quickly, the entire meeting would disintegrate like a sand castle washed away on the beach. "I'll just walk down," she said, brushing past Walter, who remained locked in a staring contest with Alex.

"About time," he quipped.

Ignoring the barb, she reached for the door and narrowly missed being hit as it swung open, and Kelsey burst into the room. Anne stopped short when she saw the look of stunned bewilderment on Kelsey's face.

"I thought I—" Kelsey stammered, her eyes bright and her skin flushed. "I've got some—" she stopped again, looking wildly around the room.

Anne waited impatiently for her to spit out whatever she had to say.

"It's Michael—" she gulped.

"What? He's got to take some very important call?" Marvin rolled his eyes and patted his pockets, undoubtedly looking for another cigarette.

"I'm done waiting for him." Walter slid his gold pen into the side of his leather case and slammed it shut. "This meeting is over."

Anne felt her stomach sink.

"Hang on—" Alex barked. "She hasn't even—"

"He's dead!" Kelsey finally exclaimed.

Anne felt the world stand still as her mind disconnected from her body and observed the room from afar.

A chorus of voices erupted simultaneously.

"What?"

"How?"

"Bloody hell!"

"Are you sure?"

"I don't believe it."

Anne had a hard time believing it as well.

"An ambulance is on its way." Kelsey blinked several times. "But he has no pulse."

Someone, Anne did not register who, asked, "A heart attack?"

Kelsey shook her head slowly, looking visibly pained. "He left a note."

Suicide. Anne looked over at Alex, dumbfounded.

"And there was an empty bottle of pills on his desk."

An overdose? Anne thought of his wan, bleary-eyed appearance that morning. Had he already taken the drugs before the meeting had even started, feeling the effects percolate through his body while they blithely discussed the bonds? Or had he been nervously contemplating the idea? She gave an involuntary shiver.

"What did the note say?" David Something-or-Other asked sharply.

Kelsey waved her arm vaguely. "Something about the Pandora bonds. That he couldn't see any other way out. I don't know. I only saw it briefly."

Anne felt a heavy weight settle on her chest.

"I never would have expected..." Walter started to say.

"Me neither." Marvin looked like the air had been sucked out of him. "He was always such a fighter...."

"It doesn't make sense...." David looked back and forth at Walter and Marvin, like a terrified squirrel trying to decide which way to run.

"Does a note written in the depths of despair ever make sense?" Marvin asked, eyes wide, while Walter shook his head ever-so-slightly, almost, Anne thought, in warning.

"I guess not," David mumbled, averting his gaze to the table.

Kelsey shifted her weight back and forth as if she wasn't quite sure what to do with herself. "I should probably get back. Betty is hysterical." Her hands began to shake. "She found the body and all."

Anne's mind shot to his young secretary, innocently looking for Michael because he had failed to return to their meeting and then discovering him slumped over his desk, unresponsive. She felt a pang of guilt for complaining about Betty leaving her on perma-hold.

"That's awful," Alex said quietly.

"Especially since the two were so close—" Kelsey gasped and instantly clapped a hand over her mouth.

Anne saw a look of horror cross her face.

"Oh dear, I probably shouldn't have said that." With a look of chagrin, Kelsey ran out of the conference room.

Everyone stared at each other in dead silence.

6

Flagrante Delicto

"**M**s. Scott?" The detective motioned her in. "I just wanted to ask you a few routine questions." He appeared to be in his early fifties and almost bored with the formality of talking to her.

Anne gave a quick glance around the small room and nervously settled herself in the chair. It was obviously an empty office, with some castaway pieces of furniture and half-drawn blinds. She wondered what had happened to the prior occupant. Had he gotten fed up with Spencer Brothers and moved on to greener pastures? Or perhaps, failed to make the cut and been let go? She assumed it was a *he*, given the small bag of golf balls in the corner.

The detective picked up a pen, and her muscles went taut. "I understand you were one of the participants at the 8:30 meeting."

"Yes."

"How well did you know the deceased?"

Her mind jumped to the first time she had met Michael to discuss the bonds, his handsome physique and confident nature. She would never have expected to be discussing his death just a few weeks later. "Hardly at all," she replied. "I work on the trading floor and rarely spend time up here in investment banking."

"Did you notice anything odd about his demeanor this morning?"

Odd? All of the Pandora partners were somewhat out of the ordinary, each in their own individual way, but of course, Anne knew that wasn't what he was asking. "No."

"At any time during the meeting did he threaten to commit suicide?"

"No."

"Did he appear depressed or unhappy?"

"No."

"Do you have any idea why he might have chosen to take his life?"

The million-dollar question. *Why did he do it?* Presumably, he was afraid that his world was about to cave in. She looked directly at the detective. "It's possible he was concerned about his involvement in the bond deals we were meeting about."

He looked up from his note writing with a curious expression on his face. "Because?"

Anne briefly wondered if any of the others had mentioned the peculiar nature of the deals. "They didn't appear to have been structured appropriately to conform to the IRS tax code. There were ethical issues as well."

"In plain English, what does that mean?"

"It's possible that he, and several of the others in the room, were involved in defrauding the general public."

"Which others?"

She ticked the names off on her fingers. "Marvin Goldberg, Walter Hughes, and David, the bond lawyer. I forget his last name."

"Singer."

"That's right." She shifted in her seat. "The whole purpose of the meeting was to discuss whether that was, in fact, the case or not." The detective looked at her as if uncomprehending, so she tried to clarify. "Whether what they had done was fraudulent."

"And was it?"

She thought, *Of course! They were all acting guilty as hell.* But she knew that telling him would be a mistake. It might trigger an SEC investigation before her firm had had a chance to dump the bonds. Before they were ready. Her career would be destroyed in an instant. Instead, she said, "We never reached any conclusions."

"Can you prove they committed a crime?"

She hesitated. "No."

"Did Mr. Kingston know that?"

She thought for a moment. "I don't know," she said slowly.

"What would have happened to him if your allegations could have been proven?"

"If there were sufficient evidence of illegal activity, he could have been fined by the SEC, maybe even lost his securities license. Without his license, he would have lost his job. Most importantly, he might have been forced to hand over a portion of any illegally gained profits."

"What kind of money are we talking about here?"

"Somewhere around two million dollars derived from fees when the bond issues were first sold to the public, and then an annual income stream of half a million a year, from the investments they set up at the Oko Sychaito Bank."

"So, you think he was concerned that the scheme would be blown sky high," he said in summary.

"Maybe," she shrugged, "but I didn't really know him all that well. It could be that he had marital problems or something else that was disturbing him."

* * *

When Anne finally returned to her floor, she intended to walk straight into William's office, shut his door, and tell him what had happened. She thought he ought to be the first to know as the newly appointed head of Research. Instead, she found herself being pulled toward the file cabinets by Jennifer, who flew out of her cubicle faster than a hawk the instant she spied Anne.

"You're never going to believe what happened in my meeting," Anne heard herself practically hyperventilate, her heart beating furiously inside her chest as she frantically tried to maintain a façade of calm control.

"Michael Kingston decided to trade his fancy-pantsy life for a permanent dirt nap," Donna squawked from somewhere behind.

Anne gave a start and reached out for the cabinet to regain her balance as she turned to ask, "How did you hear?" To her surprise, she found William standing stone-faced beside her.

"Elise was meeting with someone in a nearby office," Donna replied while chomping her gum, a mixture of stale smoke and spearmint wafting between her words. "Now everybody in Municipals knows."

"Word is that he took an overdose of something that caused cardiac arrest," William said, his face impassive but his voice sounding slightly disconcerted.

Anne nodded. "One of the emergency people said it was digoxin, which is a fairly potent heart medication. There was an open bottle of it on his desk."

Jennifer looked quizzical. "I wonder if that's a painful way to go."

"I doubt it," Donna said with a dismissive bubble pop. "It sounds like it happened pretty fast."

"I just can't believe he did it." Anne began to tremble and took a deep breath to suppress her nervous energy. "After the coroner arrived, a detective interviewed each of us. He wanted to know if there was anything odd about Michael's behavior during the meeting."

"They brought in a detective?" Carter asked, approaching from the side.

"It's protocol," William explained. "For insurance and paperwork purposes."

"What'd you tell him?" Donna paused her loud gum smacking and looked at Anne intently. "Did you notice anything unusual?"

The image of Michael's pale face with beads of sweat popped into Anne's mind, and then she thought of the detective. Had she told him how ashen and strained Michael looked? Or was it Alex she had mentioned that to? She couldn't recall.

"Was he acting strangely?" Donna pressed again, followed by a loud bubble pop.

"There's no question he was stressed out..." Anne finally managed. "Definitely on edge...but nothing in his manner indicated that he was about to take his own life."

"Hmmm." William crossed his arms and began to study the file cabinet drawers.

"Well, one thing's for sure. It sucks for his wife. She won't get the insurance." Donna gave an exaggerated frown that looked more like a smirk, and her tone didn't sound the least bit sympathetic.

"What about his bonus?" Carter surveyed the group, his Adam's apple jumping up and down like a springer spaniel about to be taken outside for a walk.

"Bonuses don't happen for another month." William's response was curt and flat, clearly aimed at discouraging additional discussion on the topic.

"But his must be huge. Won't the—"

"Carter—" William looked exasperated. "It's not our problem."

"I was just—"

"Will there be any more follow-up?" William cut Carter off abruptly, his gray, wolf-like eyes focused on Anne. "From the detective?"

"I don't think so. He said he was going to fill out some paperwork and that would be the end of it." He had uttered the words with a casual shrug as he opened the office door to let her out, as if Michael's death was simply one of many mundane tasks on his to-do list, easily dismissed from further thought with the click of a pen. And yet it had shattered Anne's sense of normalcy, leaving her feeling anxious and unsettled.

"Everyone up in investment banking was totally caught off-guard by this," Jennifer said. "I just got off of the phone with Kelsey O'Brien. She was practically hysterical."

"Who?" William asked, looking far more interested than Anne would have expected, given his normal tendency to avoid these sorts of conversations.

"Michael's number two," Donna said, spitting her gum into the trash. "Did she have any idea he was thinking about offing himself?"

Jennifer shook her head solemnly. "Nobody saw this coming. Least of all Kelsey. She's been up to her ears working on some deal with another banker. Now she's kicking herself for missing the signs...you know...that he was depressed." Jennifer sighed. "But she was so wrapped up in her work that she didn't see it. And on top of that, she feels terrible about mentioning Michael's affair with Betty."

"What?!" Carter appeared taken aback. "Michael and his secretary were having a fling?"

"It can't have been much of a secret," William said drily. "Even I knew about it, and I don't go up there very often."

"Why did Kelsey blab about that?" Donna's bright orange lips formed a smug-looking smile, accentuating the yellowness of her uneven teeth.

"She blurted it out by accident when she came to tell us that Michael was dead." Anne closed her eyes, recalling the mortified look on Kelsey's face the moment the words were out of her mouth. "She was in total shock."

"Still is," Jennifer added.

"I guess that means Betty's available." Carter seemed to be thinking out loud. "I've always thought she was pretty cute."

Was he trying to be funny? Anne exchanged glances with Jennifer, who furrowed her brows in obvious revulsion.

"After the dust settles, maybe she'd like to date me," he finished with a self-satisfied grin suggesting he thought this was a serious possibility.

"Why not Kelsey?" William said, his voice flat and wooden.

"Is she single as well?" bleated Carter.

Even William rolled his eyes.

"On top of everything else," Jennifer redirected the conversation, looking everywhere but at Carter, "Kelsey has a ton of work she needs to finish up this afternoon. I don't know how she's going to do it."

"She's planning to stay in the office?" William sounded surprised. "I thought they told everyone who worked with Michael to take some time off."

"The woman's a total workaholic," Donna croaked. "She probably doesn't know how to spend five minutes away from the office."

Jennifer drew herself up tall so that her full six-foot frame towered over the rest of them. "I think that's a bit harsh. She's worked really hard to get to where she is. Now she isn't sure what's going to happen, who she'll be reporting to...it's all up in the air. And with these Pandora bonds on top of everything else, she's totally distraught."

"What are the Pandora bonds?" Carter asked, scanning everyone's faces.

"Not our problem," William replied brusquely.

Donna arched one of her heavily penciled eyebrows.

"This would probably be a good time—" William began.

"Is that what your meeting was about?" Carter interrupted, staring at Anne.

She gave a quick nod.

William cleared his throat and addressed the group. "While I'm sure Michael Kingston's death is a shock to everybody, I want to remind all of you to be mindful about what you say outside of here."

Anne felt herself drift away, uninterested in being lectured on the importance of keeping her mouth shut. *Seriously?*

"—friends, acquaintances…there are bound to be lots of inquisitive people asking why he might have taken his life and at this point—"

Blah. Blah. Blah. She thought. *Come on, William, let's wrap this up.*

"—leave the speculation to others and get back to work."

Finally.

"Oh. One more thing."

What now? Anne studied Donna's fire-engine red fingernails in an effort to hide her growing irritation.

"Elise had a migraine and left early. It's possible that the traders will need one of you to finish whatever she was doing for them."

She tore her eyes away from the talons and exchanged glances with Jennifer. The Ice Princess always had an excuse for ducking out.

As the group started to break up, Anne felt a sudden need to get out of the office and breathe some fresh air. She mumbled that she was going to step out for a while and walked briskly away before William could argue.

The chilly city streets did the trick, providing a respite from the morning, allowing her mind to clear. But when she returned to the building, she came face to face with a woman moving in the opposite direction through the revolving doors. She was slender and dark-haired with luxurious pale skin and light green eyes—like Kelsey, except shorter, and judging by the carefree manner in which she threw the plaid scarf over her shoulder, much happier. Anne immediately flashed to an image of Kelsey, struggling to deliver the grim news, frantically surveying the room as if she was looking for some sort of lifeline she could grab hold of that would allow her to escape the nightmare of Michael's death.

Anne moved to the side of the lobby, out of the way of the harried people rushing by, and took several slow, deep breaths. *Get a grip*, she told herself. It wasn't their fault that Michael had cracked under the pressure. He had chosen to get involved with these illicit bonds, potentially jeopardizing the firm's reputation and risking huge fines. She and Alex had just been doing their job, trying to tie up loose ends and find the best path forward. Her breathing normalized, and the tension in her limbs dissipated.

When she felt sufficiently composed to face the onslaught of questions from curiosity seekers in the office (she knew they would descend upon her in droves with one morbid question after another), she slipped quietly through the crowd like an eel in water and made her way onto the elevator, avoiding eye contact with the others already inside.

"You too?"

She turned to see Alex holding a hot pretzel from one of the street vendors and an unopened can of Coke.

"I needed to get away after everything that happened this morning," he said, smiling weakly.

She nodded as the elevator gave a small bump and began its ascent. "I had no idea he was feeling so depressed...."

"None of us did."

One of the suspendered yuppies in the elevator looked back and forth at the two of them. "Are you talking about the banker who killed himself this morning?"

"Here?" another one chimed in. "Which floor?"

Anne and Alex exchanged glances.

"How did he do it?" A third one piped up.

"Sorry," Alex said evenly. "We can't talk about it."

For the remainder of the time, the passengers rode in strained silence until a loud ding signaled arrival at Anne's floor. She stepped out, relieved to be freed from the cramped, airless space, and then took a deep breath and braced herself to face the next barrage of questions that would undoubtedly be coming her way.

Her expectations were right on target. In addition to the traders and salesmen (How long did it take them to move the body? Did anyone have to give him mouth-to-mouth resuscitation?), even Peter Eckert's secretary got into the act, accompanied by a full body shudder (I heard she touched the body not realizing he was already dead. Can you imagine?) More shuddering. (When he fell to the ground, do you think rigor mortis had already set in?)

As if Anne knew.

Or even wanted to speculate on the matter. *Ewwww!*

In addition to the general inquisition, Anne was greeted by twelve barely legible messages all demanding her immediate attention. She groaned inwardly and thumbed through the pile. After spotting the name Katie, buried near the bottom, she smiled with relief and reached for her telephone.

"Hi!" Katie's voice sang out.

Katie was probably her best friend from college. Unlike Anne, who had majored in the sciences and ignored business and accounting classes, Katie had set her sights on Wall Street as a freshman and carefully chosen to graduate with a double major in economics and math.

"Hang on. One of the managing directors is freaking."

After putting in a couple of grueling years as a low-life grunt for a big-time investment banker (as Kelsey was still doing), she had finally gotten herself moved into the vice-presidential ranks at a very small firm. Pleased with her career success, Katie was now starting to focus on her social life, or lack thereof. Panic about her marriage prospects had definitely set in, so she frequently called Anne to chat about these weighty problems. Today, however, was different. Like everyone else, Katie was curious to hear juicy details about the suicide.

She gasped audibly when Anne announced she had been in a meeting with the man minutes before his death.

"I've got to go to a meeting right now for a deal that's coming to market tomorrow," Katie interrupted while Anne was starting to describe the detective. "Can you meet me for dinner at the Sea Tavern? I want to hear everything."

* * *

Anne was seated comfortably at the bar sipping a glass of chardonnay when Katie breathlessly arrived. They moved over to a table and quickly perused the menu.

"You know," Katie said almost immediately, "I've interacted with Michael Kingston on several different bond deals, and I have to say that he *never* struck me as the suicidal type. Arrogant? Totally. Self-centered? Absolutely. But suicidal? I never would have imagined."

Anne's thoughts exactly.

"So tell me what happened!" Katie leaned back, sipping her wine, her nose, and cheeks still pink from the cold.

"Partway through the meeting, he said he wanted to take a break. I didn't think anything of it." Anne paused and pondered for a second. "Actually, that's not true. I thought it was incredibly obnoxious. I mean, he invited a few of the people back to his office and left the rest of us sitting there, just waiting. Like we had all the time in the world."

"Typical," Katie sniffed disdainfully. "The man thought he was God's gift to the human race."

"And then, when he didn't return with everyone else, I called his secretary."
"She's the one—"
"—who found him." Anne grimaced. "Yes."
Katie shivered. "Must've been a total shock."
Anne nodded. "She was a complete basket case afterwards and had to be physically helped off the floor."
"Wow." Katie took another sip of wine.
"But get ready for this—" Anne quickly looked around to make sure they weren't sitting near anyone she knew, "They were having an affair!"
Katie rolled her eyes. "That's what I heard."
Anne looked at her friend, dumbfounded. How had this man's sex life been such common knowledge? Her expression must have given her thoughts away.

"From one of the guys at my firm who happens to be dating an investment banker at yours," Katie explained. She lowered her voice and leaned in, "So how did you learn that he topped himself? Did you hear screaming or running feet or what?"

"His assistant, Kelsey O'Brien—"

"I know her," Katie jumped in. "Tall, athletic woman. I never found her very likable. She always kind of reminded me of the wicked witch from the *Wizard of Oz*. At any moment, I expected her to shriek with laughter and begin flying around on a broom."

"What? Her intensity, you mean?"

"No. Her personality. I hated having to deal with her. She was ruthless. And cold as stone. Like a mafia hit man."

Anne tried to reconcile Katie's description of Kelsey with the shattered woman she had met that morning, reeling from the shock and pain of Michael's death.

"She always did everything she could to be front and center," Katie continued. "If there was credit to be had, she made sure to grab it. All of it."

"If you'd seen how raw and exposed she looked," Anne began, "I mean...she was shaken to the core."

"Really?" Katie said quietly.

"She was a mess."

"That's too bad." Katie paused, a pained expression on her face. "I guess it's not surprising...They did work closely together for many years. If my boss were to kill himself...." She bit her lip. "You know what? I feel terrible about calling her a witch."

"Well—from what I hear, she's highly competitive, so I can see where you might have gotten a negative impression."

"Even so," she shook her head, looking like an unhappy puppy who had just been scolded for chewing the favorite oriental rug. "I retract the comment. It was a really catty thing to say."

"Don't worry about it." Anne smiled reassuringly. "Just don't tell Jennifer what you think. You remember her, don't you? She's one of the analysts in my group."

"Of course. How could I forget? She's the one who dated that trader who used to work on the floor below me. He wore those weird blue glasses."

"—and turned out to be a real slime bag."

"I know," Katie said, shaking her head. "Remember when he wore those grody jam shorts to that birthday bash?"

Anne rolled her eyes. "He waltzed up to me and said something like, 'Hey baby. Admit it. You're dying to have me.' I was like, 'gag me with a spoon!'"

Katie cocked her head. "I doubt I'll see Jennifer any time soon, but why should I be careful what I say to her about Kelsey? Are the two of them friends?"

Anne nodded. "She says that Kelsey thought Michael was just the cat's meow. It's almost like he took her under his wing. Of course, now her world has been turned completely upside down."

Katie squinted at her. "How well does she know Kelsey?"

"I'm not sure. They both went to the same university, but didn't meet until a few years later. It sounds like they get together for coffee once in a while."

"So, they're not that close?" It was more of a statement than a question.

"No," Anne said slowly, wondering where Katie was heading. "But why—"

"Does she realize that Kelsey was also sleeping with Michael?" Katie raised her eyebrows in a knowing fashion.

"What?!"

"Yep."

"Wait a minute. You're sure it's Kelsey and not his secretary you're talking about?"

"Positive," she tilted her chair back and crossed her arms. "I caught the two of them in *flagrante delicto*."

Anne was too stunned to reply.

"He was the senior banker on a deal our two firms were co-managing. The guy in charge of the deal. Imagine everyone's surprise when I returned unexpectedly to the conference room where we'd all been meeting… His lips were all over her, and his shirt was half undone…All I can say is it wasn't pretty."

"When did this happen?" Anne asked incredulously.

"A couple of years ago." Katie sniffed. "That Michael Kingston was something else."

"What do you mean?"

"The guy was a total pig." Disgust dripped from Katie's every word. "He'd sleep with anything that had two arms and two legs. He even had the nerve to come on to me."

"What?!?!"

Katie nodded. "During one of our business meetings. Even though he was married and obviously involved with Kelsey. Made me want to barf. Honestly, I wouldn't be surprised to hear that he'd come onto every woman that worked on his floor at one time or another."

"Funny," Anne said slowly, her eyebrows knitting together and her throat feeling constricted. "Both Elise and Donna in my department had fairly extensive dealings with the man over the years, and yet I never heard one word about this side of his personality."

"Are you talking about that crackpot in your department who's friendly as a glacier and her boss, Sergeant Dumpy?"

Anne just nodded mutely.

"Give me a break. They're probably the only two people in the city who would fail to make the grade of even Michael's pitiful standards," Katie said contemptuously. "Trust me. The man had a problem." She held up a finger. "Hold that thought. I'm starving," and flagged down a passing waitress.

"I wonder if Kelsey knew anything about his...proclivities...when she got involved with him—" Anne said as soon as they had finished ordering.

"She worked closely enough with him that she had to know," Katie replied confidently.

"But what if she thought he really cared about her? That their relationship was different?"

"I don't buy it," Katie replied. "My guess? She thought sleeping with him would take her straight up the corporate ladder. As for Michael?" Katie tapped her fingers on the base of her glass. "Well, I think sex was really important to his ego and sense of power. When the jerk made his move on me, I gave him a piece of my mind."

"I think I remember you telling me about this. I just didn't connect the event with the person."

A distant memory began to take shape in Anne's mind. Katie and Anne, having brunch on her patio, talking about a big-time banker who had made a pass at her and how she hoped that rejecting him would not damage her career. Anne had been proud of her friend. Still was. She knew other women who had quit their jobs after being propositioned by someone with power over them. Simply walked away. It took a great deal of courage to stand up to men like Michael Kingston and hold them accountable.

"After I told my supervisor what happened, my firm withdrew from the deal."

Anne desperately wanted to believe that Katie's boss had recognized the gross injustice of the situation, but the pragmatist in her had a hunch there was more to the story than that. "I'll lay odds ten to one they withdrew for reasons *other* than Michael's Neanderthal behavior," Anne said drily. "Or have I become overly jaded after eight years in this business?"

"Good bet." Katie sighed deeply. "In point of fact, the deal itself was pretty bizarre. I think at the last minute, the higher-ups at my company decided they would be better off bowing out."

Anne felt her antennae go up. "What was so unusual about it?"

"Well—it involved all sorts of unnecessary players, some of whom were rather unsavory characters. And, it just didn't appear to be on the up and up." Katie lifted her glass of wine and gave it a tentative swirl before taking a sip.

"What do you mean?" Anne felt a tingle of adrenaline surge through her chest as she waited for the reply.

"Suffice to say that it didn't appear to deserve its tax-exempt designation, despite the legal opinion of some random law firm from the middle of nowhere," Katie said cautiously.

Anne stared at Katie without seeing her. *Another Pandora deal. It had to be.*

"And it struck us as generally unethical."

"The structure?"

"The fees." Katie hesitated. "The whole thing."

Anne nodded, her mind racing.

"It was a senior banker at my firm who brought the deal in." Katie frowned. "I didn't want to have my bonus jeopardized or, worse, lose my job over one sleazy deal, so I didn't say anything and just quietly helped put it together." She shook her head. "The whole thing felt off to me. It was a relief when the firm decided to back out at the last minute. I'm certain it would have caused nothing but headaches for us to go forward with it."

Anne looked quizzically at her. "Do you remember who your banker was working with?"

"A guy by the name of Marvin Goldberg, from a small firm named after the same type of rock my mother used for the guest bathroom vanity. Onyx."

"*Onyx River Investments,*" Anne said slowly.

"That's right. Why?" Katie demanded, suddenly suspicious.

Anne regarded her friend for a moment. They had been very close since college. Katie had always been completely trustworthy and solidly reliable. She gambled. "Because our meeting this morning included that very person, in addition to some of his other cohorts who were involved in deals very similar to what you are describing. But that's between just you and me. I'm not supposed to talk to anybody about this."

Katie's eyes widened. "So, Michael's death is related to those deals?"

Anne nodded. "He mentioned them in his suicide note."

"That's a little unnerving."

"I'll say," Anne agreed. "It makes me really curious what happened during that private meeting he held."

"I'll bet."

Anne was suddenly tired of talking about Michael Kingston's death. The conversation moved on to other topics, and after another hour, they got up to go.

"Make sure you call me if there are any other exciting developments," Katie insisted.

"And you, please keep the stuff about the fishy deals under your hat," Anne replied and then headed toward the PATH tubes that would take her across the river to her condo in New Jersey.

7

On or Off the Record

The Following Day

The Wall Street Chronicle
January 18, 1989

Suicide at Spencer Brothers

Members of the bond community were shocked and deeply saddened to learn that investment banker Michael Kingston III, age 46, had been found dead in his office yesterday morning after taking an overdose of heart medication. A graduate of Harvard College and Stanford Business School, he devoted his career to structuring and financing public bond issues.

A spokesperson for the family said he had been an influential member of the Short Hills, New Jersey community where he resided with his wife and three children. In addition, he was a member of the Kingston Family from Newport, Rhode Island, which is known for its generous gifts to charitable organizations around the world.

Anne wasn't surprised to find a story about Michael's suicide in the business section of the paper on Wednesday morning. She was surprised, however, to learn of his blue-blood family in Newport. For some reason, he had struck her as more of a scrapper, someone who had fought his way to the top, rather than someone who had been born to a life of privilege.

She scanned the paper for any other articles of interest and, finding none, folded it up and went about her business. Before she had made it through the morning, however, she found herself caught, once again, in the middle of the trading floor, discussing the wisdom of purchasing a block of risky hospital bonds. A young trader was raring to grab them because they were so cheap.

Anne stood her ground and gave her view that the bonds were a poor investment. When he began to argue, calling her analytical abilities into question, she stopped him and said firmly, "I've given you my opinion. It's a mistake to buy them. I've got to go. I'm supposed to be at a meeting with the rest of our illustrious research team in the conference room." A couple of his trading buddies chuckled when she added, "Don't add these bonds to my list of problems."

She knew the he was annoyed, maybe even angry, but wasn't about to be bullied into making a bad call on a bond just to curry temporary favor. Experience had taught her that the trading floor was both fluid and merciless. Today's agreement to submit to trader pressure would be rewarded with that same trader hanging her out to dry the next if things turned sour. She strode confidently into the conference room, where the other analysts in her department were gathered.

"Did you see the article about Michael Kingston in the *Chronicle*?" Carter asked, pushing the open paper on the table toward her.

Anne nodded. "I didn't realize he was such a philanthropist."

"He got a whole column," Donna cackled. "I guess that's what living in Short Hills will get you."

"Can we get started with our meeting?" William asked tersely.

Donna flashed a look of annoyance before leaning down to rummage through her purse.

"You should all be aware that a reporter has been fishing around," he began. "One of the traders got a call early this morning."

"For the latest bond tips?" Carter chuckled.

William gave him an icy stare. "He was asking about Michael Kingston."

Anne felt everyone's eyes turn immediately toward her. *Could it mean word had gotten out about the purpose of the meeting?* "I haven't heard from him," she volunteered, her voice sounding thin and reedy.

"Shouldn't he be talking to people up in investment banking?" Donna popped a piece of gum into her mouth, dropping the crumpled wrapper onto the floor.

Jennifer shrugged. "He may be contacting people he knows personally."

"Probably trying to find out why Michael killed himself," Carter said with a loud sneeze, causing Jennifer and William, who were sitting on either side of him, to shift slightly farther away.

"I don't know what he wants," William replied with a quick wave of his hand, "but the Big Boss isn't happy about it. I caught an earful this morning."

"Why does Peter Eckert—" Carter began.

"The last thing the firm needs is for any of you being quoted, or worse, misquoted, on the front page of the *Chronicle*," William interrupted.

Carter looked confused. "So, does that mean—"

"Nobody is to talk to any reporters. On or off the record." William eyed them sternly. "Is that clear?"

Carter's head bobbed like a small boat cast adrift in the ocean.

William turned to face Elise. "Are you working on anything interesting?"

As she launched into a tedious explanation about some arcane bond provisions, Anne leaned back in her chair and quickly found her mind wandering to the meeting the day before, wondering when Michael had made the decision to pop the pills. Did he know he was going to do it prior to bringing Walter and the others back to his office? Presumably, the purpose of that discussion was to make sure no one gave the game away. But why bother strategizing if he was planning to kill himself anyway. Laughter intruded on her thoughts.

"Where?" William asked.

"Bermuda," Carter said with a straight face.

"No." William summarily dismissed his request to attend the conference.

Watching the color drain from Carter's face, Anne was reminded of Michael, who had looked pale and shaky during the meeting, as if he had already ingested the drugs. That would have given them time to work. But, then, why attend the meeting with the Pandora Partners at all? It didn't make sense, not that suicide, in general, made sense.

"Six?" She heard William say.

"Yes," Carter warbled. "I wrote the last one up yesterday and gave it to the secretaries to distribute. You're all welcome to read them if you'd like."

Anne groaned inwardly. He had to be talking about the number of reports he had written up, as if quantity was the only thing that mattered. When the previous guy had been in charge, the purpose of these weekly meetings had been to promote discussion on topics of general interest. Unfortunately, they had tended, in reality, to be dull and materially unenlightening. This meeting was proving to be no different than the others.

"How about you, Donna? Anything to report?"

She shrugged. "Nothing special."

"Okay. I think we're done here."

At last! Anne stood up immediately and breathed a sigh of relief.

William nodded in her direction. "Would you please stay behind for a minute?"

She looked at him in surprise and then watched everyone else slowly file out of the room, probably wondering the same thing she was. *What did he want to talk to her about? Privately?*

"Peter got a call this morning from some big wig up in investment banking."

She stood absolutely still, waiting for the other shoe to drop.

"Tread lightly with the folks in that group."

And what exactly did that mean? Her mouth suddenly felt dry. "Are you telling me to stop looking into the bonds altogether?"

"No." William's face was grim. "The trading floor has way too much money on the line. The fact that someone up there took the time to call probably means you're on to something, and they're worried. You still need to get to the bottom of this mess. Just do it carefully."

Her eyes narrowed. She was being given the impossible task of poking her nose into Michael's shady enterprise without actually making the investment banking titans angry. And if she failed?

William continued, "Those guys up there think they have more power than they do. It's ultimately Peter's call as to who gets fired in his own division. Not theirs."

"Fired?"

She couldn't hide her look of shock.

"Don't worry. We have your back. I'm just giving you a heads up so you understand the landscape you're playing in."

Minefield is what he should have said. Why hadn't she gone to medical school, like her sister? Doctors never got fired unless they truly screwed up. And everyone respected them.

"I have full confidence in you," William said, the ghost of a smile flickering across his perfectly shaved face.

She took a step back, feeling vulnerable and exposed, as if she had just stepped into the freezing cold without a jacket.

"Let me know what you find as you continue digging," he finished, his penetrating eyes never leaving her.

She gave a small nod and walked numbly toward the door. If push came to shove, would they actually protect her? William was brand new in this position, completely inexperienced in management. He might be promising more than he could actually deliver. Or worse, he might simply be saying what he thought she wanted to hear.

"What was that all about?" Donna accosted her as she was heading back to her cubicle.

"To warn me that the investment banking people aren't happy about having their bonds scrutinized," Anne said flatly.

"Tough." Donna spat the words out. "It's not their call."

In theory, she was right. The trading floor cared about one thing only—making money. But when one manager started calling another, it was less clear how the chips might fall. Her face must have betrayed her concern.

"No one down here gives a rat's ass what the investment bankers think." Donna sucked in her cheeks and blew a loud bubble. "As long as you give the trading desk information they can trust, you'll be fine."

Anne heard a shuffle behind her.

"Hey, I've got a bond I need some help with," a junior trader greeted them and then pointed at Anne. "By the way, is there any more news about the guy who killed himself yesterday?"

* * *

The moment she walked through the door that evening, Muffin greeted her enthusiastically. At work, she was dispensable, someone who could be fired at the drop of a hat, but to this cocker spaniel, she was the most important person in the world. She buried her hands in the dog's warm fur and felt an immediate sense of calm. Without Muffin, she would feel so much more alone. And stressed out.

She scanned the day's mail and noted an envelope from her mother. Opening that piece first, she discovered yet another article describing the perils of being female and waiting beyond the age of thirty to get married. Anne smiled. Mother was obviously concerned about her personal safety. According to the article, if she waited just a few more years, she had a greater chance of being gunned down by a terrorist than finding a spouse!

"Come on," she said as Muffin brushed lightly against her leg, "let's get you fed."

The two of them padded into the kitchen and then settled themselves on the couch. A glass of red wine within reach and Muffin curled up beside her, Anne picked up the spy thriller that her book group was reading and pulled out the bookmark. She was quickly immersed in the novel, oblivious to what lay in store in the next day's paper.

8

Half-eaten Scone

Two Days After the Meeting

The Wall Street Chronicle
Thursday, January 19, 1989

Mysterious Wall Street Death

Prominent Wall Street Banker Michael Kingston III, 46 years old, was found dead in his office Tuesday morning in what the police are now terming a suspicious death. Authorities have no comment at this time because the investigation is still pending. Sources at the firm of Spencer Brothers, where he had been employed, say that he abruptly left a meeting and was found a while later, slumped over his desk, having died from an apparent drug overdose.

S uspicious death?! Anne looked at the paper with a mixture of shock and disbelief. *The police said he committed suicide.* Suddenly the phone rang loudly and insistently. After three rings, she gave up waiting for one of the secretaries to screen her calls and picked it up herself.

"Have you seen the *Chronicle*?" Katie didn't even bother saying hello, already running a mile a minute. "What happened between yesterday and today to cause them to suspect foul play?" She continued without waiting for a reply. "I thought he left a note."

"He did!" Anne responded, her voice rising and panic welling up inside of her. "It was on the desk next to his body. It talked about his fear of being found out—" She paused, a realization sweeping over her, "—unless he didn't actually write it."

"Did the detective say anything that suggested he had doubts about it being a suicide?"

"No—this is just—"

"Weird," Katie said.

"Totally unnerving! For all I know, I was sitting face to face with a cold-blooded murderer just minutes before he actually murdered!" As Anne spoke, she envisioned the meeting and the various people in attendance sitting around the table. Walter, tapping that annoying gold pen. David Singer, doodling nervously, and Marvin Goldberg, puffing away on one of his slightly bent cigarettes. It was hard to believe that one of them had actually killed him.

"Maybe it was one of the investment bankers he worked with instead," Katie said, as if reading her mind. "Spencer Brothers is known for being dog-eat-dog...."

"Oh great. A fellow employee. I'm not sure that's much better! Hang on—I'm getting buzzed." Seconds later, she returned to the line. "I'm wanted down in the corner office—immediately! Talk to you later." Anne threw down the phone.

As she approached Peter Eckert's office, she could see him sitting at his desk, expressionless, while Nick Angelini gestured wildly and paced around the room. She took a deep breath and tried to appear confident as she stepped through the door to join them. Alex walked in moments later, appearing as uncomfortable as she felt.

"I *knew* something like this would happen," Nick greeted them with a morose glare. "Soon, these bonds will be worth nothing." He drew his hand across his neck, making a cutthroat gesture. "Zilch. Zippo. Nada."

Peter Eckert ignored the barrage of comments coming from his head trader's direction and asked if they had seen the morning paper. "Well then, I'm sure you realize that it's only a matter of time before the deals themselves are discovered and splashed across the front page of every major financial publication."

"I'm telling you!" Nick resumed circling the room, his hands clenched together. "We've got to reduce our exposure now!"

"We also have another more potentially serious problem," Peter said, adjusting his glasses.

"You mean that his death may have been murder rather than suicide?" Anne assumed they had been similarly alarmed by the news story.

"No," he responded dismissively. "Not that."

"Give me a break," Nick gave her a disparaging look, his tone suggesting she was a vacuous moron. "That's the least of our worries."

"Nick," Peter said firmly, "I'll handle this if you don't mind."

Anne waited uneasily, her hands gripping the arms of the chair, while Peter casually flicked a piece of lint off of his sleeve.

"There's nothing suspicious about Michael's death," he finally said, keeping his gaze averted.

Out of the corner of her eye, she saw Alex cock his head slightly to the side.

"For reasons that are not entirely clear," Peter continued, "Michael's widow has gotten it into her head that he was murdered."

"It's gotta' be the life insurance," Nick said disdainfully, as if she was no more than a petty swindler. "She can't collect if he killed himself." He flung his hands up in the air in an obvious show of frustration.

"I don't think so." Peter Eckert said slowly. "She comes from a *lot* of money herself. In fact, some people say that's the reason he married her."

"Then why does—"

"I don't know where she got the idea that Michael might have been killed. What I do know is that her family connections helped him get into investment banking in the first place. And now she's managed to pull some strings down at city hall. The police are going through the motions of investigating her claims, but don't actually take her seriously."

"You're sure?" Anne asked and then wondered whether she should have kept her mouth shut.

"I've spoken personally with one of the men in charge down at the precinct." Peter gave a wry smile. "He's adamant there's no real murder investigation going on. In fact, he's quite annoyed about the whole thing. It's obvious to everyone, except Michael's widow, that he intentionally overdosed on those pills."

"So, there's no chance—"

Peter cut Anne off. "Trust me."

Anne blinked, immediately wary. The bankers and traders employed by the firm were in the business of exploiting opportunities and capitalizing on ignorance. They were the last people anyone should trust.

"I have the inside scoop on this one."

Did he? She studied his worn, sagging face. Or was he just playing her.

"As Nick said before, that's the least of our worries." Peter leaned back heavily in his chair and peered over his glasses at her. "Of far greater importance is the fact that we've been in touch with someone well-placed at the SEC."

She felt her heart skip a beat. The Securities Exchange Commission oversaw the financial industry with the goal of protecting investors. And preventing fraud.

"They've started an investigation into these deals," Nick announced, glowering in the corner.

"And this source is reliable?" Alex asked.

"Very."

"That complicates matters," Alex said, furrowing his brows. "Within the next week or two, I expect the rest of the clowns who were a part of this charade will also find out about the investigation. They'll either be subpoenaed directly or hear about the investigation from one of their friends who was."

"What a shitstorm," Nick muttered under his breath.

"Any idea why the SEC has decided—"

"Evidently, somebody tipped them off," Nick said angrily, fixing his beady eyes first on Anne and then Alex, as if he was trying to see whether one of them was responsible.

"We don't know who," Peter replied, unaware or perhaps ignoring Nick. "But once they start digging, there's no telling what'll happen."

"Actually, I think we all have a pretty good idea of exactly what will happen," Alex said matter-of-factly, giving a slight nod toward the head trader. "I agree that we should dump everything we own. Quickly. Before word of this gets out."

It was as if the air had suddenly been released from a balloon. Nick stopped his pacing and unclenched his fists, looking at them like they were actually human.

"In small batches," Alex continued. "To avoid drawing attention."

"And we should probably sell them to larger players who can afford to take a hit," Nick added, taking a seat for the first time during the meeting.

"Good point," Peter replied. "If things go south, the smaller outfits might try to renege on the trades."

"Is that legal?" Anne scanned their faces.

"Perfectly," Alex said, his expression betraying nothing. "Caveat emptor."

Anne had never studied Latin, but was familiar with the expression nonetheless: *buyer beware*.

"They're big boys," Nick responded with a cavalier wave of his hand. "That's the nature of the business."

Peter nodded. "After we've sold everything we own, we can focus on getting our most important, institutional clients out of the bonds. With any luck, we can help them avoid large losses before the SEC gets too far along in its investigation."

"That would be good," Nick said, looking much calmer than when they had first begun.

"After that—" Peter said, looking at no one in particular. "Well—if we can—we should try to get the rest of our clients out of these bonds, including the mom-and-pop investors." He paused. "Hopefully, the price won't have dropped precipitously before that happens."

Yeah, right, Anne thought to herself. *Kind of like a snowball's chance in hell.*

Peter's eyes rested on Alex and Anne. "An SEC investigation is concerning."

Anne agreed completely. She wondered what kinds of shenanigans the firm would contemplate in order to avoid being held responsible.

"I want the two of you to go through Michael's files immediately and look for anything that might be—" he paused, searching for the right word, "—well, problematic. Anything that might raise the ire of the SEC."

Peter's secretary tapped on the door and peeked her head in. "Jason is on line one."

He nodded, and she disappeared. "I have to take this call."

Anne and Alex stood up to go.

"I hope you both realize," Peter spoke slowly, enunciating each word. "This has huge implications for our firm."

Anne felt a tinge of annoyance. Of course they realized the significance of an SEC investigation. What did he think they had just spent the last twenty minutes discussing?

"I want to review anything you find, in case something needs to be... handled."

She and Alex nodded in unison like well-trained monkeys and then slinked out of the dark office into the hustle and bustle of the trading floor.

"So, was it murder or suicide?" Anne asked as she and Alex made their way past barking traders, phones ringing on every side, and beleaguered assistants ferrying papers and other necessities around the room.

"I think Peter's got a pretty good handle on things," Alex replied, showing no hint of concern. "It's probably a suicide, just as he said."

"I hope so," Anne replied, still feeling uneasy. "But what if he's wrong?

"Let's hope he's not," Alex called over his shoulder. "I'll meet you back here in ten."

As she rounded the corner, she found the trader who had been arguing with her the previous day, hanging around one of the secretary's desks, debating the prospects for the New York Yankees. It soon became obvious he had been waiting for her in order to resume their conversation about the bonds she had told him to avoid.

Her smile promptly disappeared. "What do you mean you bought them? I told you they were, for lack of a better description, a piece of shit."

"They were incredibly cheap." He brought his straight fingers into a tight bunch and held his hand about a foot from her face in a gesture she recognized as an Italian finger purse. "I know a bargain when I see one. You don't even have current financial information. It could be the hospital's in great shape right now."

"And it could be that it's just filed for Chapter 11 bankruptcy protection," she retorted, thinking that she did not have time for him right now.

"Well, we won't know until you do the research. Will we." He glared at her.

She sighed. "I'll see what the newest financials show. But don't forget, last year, they had a $5 million loss on revenues of only $20 million. That's pretty bad." In point of fact, it was dismal.

"Maybe things have improved."

"I doubt it. That hospital is one of three hospitals in Bat Cave, North Dakota. It's a small town in the middle of nowhere." Anne crossed her arms and looked him straight in the eye. "In my opinion, Bat Cave can support, at most, one hospital. What this means is that you, as a trader, should only be considering purchasing the bonds of the one hospital that has a chance of surviving." She leaned closer to him and raised her voice slightly. "It's not clear to me that your bonds fit that description."

He rolled his eyes, looking unimpressed.

Anne took a step back again and continued in a more subdued tone of voice. "The annual reports show that the majority of the hospital's clientele rely upon Medicaid to pay their medical bills or worse, have no sort of ability to pay them at all." She ran her fingers through her hair in an effort to push it off of her face. "Need I remind you that Medicaid is the worst type of reimbursement a hospital can have?"

"Hospitals survive in Harlem, so they should be able to survive out in the boondocks as well," the trader shot back quickly.

"Inner-city hospitals are frequently subsidized by the State in one way or another. This hospital doesn't have any sort of guarantee like that." She shook her head. "You're comparing apples to oranges. The reality is that your hospital will likely default before year's end."

The trader remained undaunted. "Elise has a friend who's an investment banker at Stoddard Securities. He told her the bonds would be refunded. Maybe you should look into that angle."

"That's inside information. If you want it, ask Elise for it. I'm providing you with a financial analysis that says these bonds are garbage. Even if the people at Stoddard Securities were to lose their collective minds and attempt to bring a new bond issue to market in order to pay off the old one, no investors would be willing to buy the new bonds. The new deal would fall flat on its face. Don't hold your breath waiting for a refinancing to rescue you from this mess."

"You could be wrong, you know." He shot her a defiant look.

"It's possible," she said and then added silently to herself, *but not likely.*

The trader motioned toward the elevators. "I think he's waiting for you."

Anne turned to see Alex trying to stop the doors from closing. She had not made it back to her desk, and it was already time to start wading through the files in Michael's office.

"We can talk about this when I get back," Anne called out as she darted over to join him before the elevators began beeping angrily.

"Didn't mean to interrupt," Alex said, his face impenetrable.

"We were just finishing up." Anne said with a sigh. "Hopefully, the bonds he just bought won't turn into yet another project for you and me to tackle…."

* * *

When they arrived at Michael's office, they found his secretary, Betty, mumbling to herself as she angrily yanked a piece of paper out of the typewriter. Anne explained, in the gentlest tone she could muster, their purpose in being there and then asked where they could find information related to the deals that Michael had been involved with.

"Everything was kept in his office—" Betty's voice quivered when she spoke. "—in the file cabinets." She fished around her desk drawers and pulled out a set of keys.

When it looked like she was about to hand them over, Alex said, "It might be better if you let us in and showed us where things are situated."

She stood up and walked stiffly over to the door, as if she had just finished running a marathon and every muscle in her body was straining to make it possible for her to take a single step more.

Alex looked over at Anne and raised his eyebrows as if to suggest that it had been a mistake to ask for her help.

Probably, but it was too late now. Anne gave a little shrug in return.

Betty led them to a stack of antique wooden file drawers and pointed. "They should be unlocked," she said with a sigh and gave a slight tug on one of the brass handles to confirm her suspicions.

"Where else would any information pertaining to his deals be kept?" Anne watched Betty stand up slowly. "For example," Anne gestured to her right, "did he maintain any records on his personal computer here?"

Betty flinched when she looked over in the direction of his desk. "He might have. Any diskettes should be in the lower left drawer." She took a tentative step toward the door.

"Who else has a key to his office besides you?" Anne inquired, trying to sound casual.

Betty crumpled slightly and sighed. It looked like she wanted more than anything to get out of there. "All of the associates and analysts who worked closely with him," she replied, her voice dull and lifeless. "Kelsey, Bob, Dave, everyone. But he never locked it—though, somebody did, on Tuesday night after—" her voice began to break "—after everything that happened."

"How about the analysts and associates that worked with him on the deals?" Alex asked gently. "Did they maintain separate files anywhere else?"

"It's possible they kept copies of documents, but Michael would have kept anything pertinent himself. He was meticulous about stuff like that."

Anne felt they had put her through enough. "Thank you so much for helping us get oriented. I'm sorry we had to drag you back in here."

"Yes, thank you," Alex said, opening the office door and stepping aside.

"We can carry on from this point."

Betty smiled weakly and slowly scanned the room. "This is the first time I've been back in his office. I still can't believe he's gone." She motioned toward the desk and took a deep breath. "When I first found Michael, I kept looking back and forth at him and the half-eaten raspberry scone sitting on his desk, trying to understand why he hadn't finished it. He always ate his breakfast by 9 am and then got a mid-morning snack around ten. I could set my clock by it." She bit her lip.

Beyond Betty's periphery, Alex frowned and tipped his head toward the door. Anne nodded back ever so slightly, understanding that he wanted the conversation to end so they could get to work.

"It took a few seconds before the full impact of what I was seeing actually sank in."

Anne glanced over at Alex, who gave a resigned shrug of the shoulders. They were going to hear Betty's story, whether they were interested or not.

"I tried to yell for help, and my voice caught in my throat. It was as if the world was moving in slow motion."

Anne tensed, unsure what to say, as she watched Betty's face take on a mottled appearance. It looked as if she was about to cry.

Betty sighed heavily and took a step toward the door. "It wasn't until I stumbled out of the office that I finally was able to scream."

Anne gave an involuntary shudder as she imagined the realization slowly taking hold in Betty's mind. Her love. Her future. Everything she had expected to share with Michael now gone.

"It was just—" She stopped, her voice cracking.

Alex reached out and gently squeezed her shoulder. "You were in shock and are going to need some time to come to terms with everything that's happened."

Probably a lot of time, Anne surmised. The poor woman looked absolutely devastated.

"I remember hearing a rush of feet," Betty continued, a glazed look in her eyes, "and muffled voices and exclamations of surprise." She shook her head. "Somebody—I don't know who—called for an ambulance." She heaved another sigh. "The rest is just a blur."

They thanked her again and watched her slowly recede from the room.

"I can't believe she was sleeping with him," Alex shuddered as soon as Betty was out of earshot.

"He was obviously the love of her life," Anne said, choosing not to add, *despite the fact that he was already married and an inveterate womanizer.*

"Right." Alex nodded emphatically. "That's what I just don't get."

He was also damn good-looking and, for all they knew, a wonder in bed. "I expect he could be quite charming when he wanted," she replied with a casual toss of her hair.

"Evidently," Alex said drily.

Her eyes scanned the open drawers. "Strange. I thought Michael was exceptionally well-organized, but—" she pointed at the files, jam-packed together with no semblance of order, "—this is total chaos!" She smiled thinly and kicked off her shoes. "Let's get down to it."

Several hours later, they had separated out all of the files that looked similar to the Pandora deals. "I count seventeen," Anne said, "a few more than we had originally anticipated."

"I'm knackered," he replied. "Let's grab a bite to eat. We can work out what to do next after we return."

They stood up to see Kelsey open the door and enter the office. She was taller than Anne remembered and bigger-boned but not fat. Her body reflected the look of strength and stamina that comes only from hours of consistent, grueling exercise. As she took two more steps into the room, Anne saw that even Kelsey's iron constitution was susceptible to the ravages of emotional turmoil. Her eyes were ringed with dark circles, and her face looked pasty and dull.

"Betty mentioned you were digging around in here," she said with a sad smile. "Anything I can do to help?"

Anne felt a mixture of concern and pity. Standing in Michael's old office had to be as difficult for Kelsey as it had been for Betty. She hesitated, not wanting to be heartless, but was cognizant that she had been given a clear directive by her manager to get to the bottom of these deals. Anne pointed at the file drawers she and Alex had just finished perusing and asked whether there was additional information stored anywhere else.

"No." Kelsey shook her head. "Everything pertaining to the Pandora deals should be right there, where you've been looking. Or, on his computer," she added, jerking a thumb toward his desk. "Are those your shoes?" she asked suddenly, looking at the floor in front of the credenza.

Anne smiled sheepishly and explained that she took them off every chance she got.

"I do the same thing," Kelsey blinked at her in surprise, apparently not expecting that, "when I'm alone in my office. How funny."

She definitely seemed different today, less rushed and less harried. Anne wondered if Michael's death had caused her to re-evaluate her priorities.

"This whole thing has been something else, hasn't it?" Kelsey said, "And the newspaper article this morning—"

"Peter Eckert told us to ignore it," Anne said, curious to hear Kelsey's perspective. "—that there is no actual investigation."

"That's what my manager said as well," Kelsey replied, pulling out a cigarette. "And it isn't like there's police tape here, blocking his office off either. It's just his widow kicking up a bit of a fuss. She's high maintenance—if you know what I mean—this is par for the course with her." She lit the cigarette and carefully blew the smoke to one side.

"I've actually met Mrs. Kingston—" Alex chimed in, "—at some charity events. She was quite pleasant to chat with. Not the sharpest knife in the drawer, but—"

"That's putting it mildly," Kelsey said, curling her lip. "She's about as dumb as they come. But she also has a big trust fund. It's her main attraction."

Alex appeared at a loss for words. "Well," he said, eventually regaining his composure, "One thing's for sure, she certainly knows how to run a charity event. The gala she organized a few months ago was executed flawlessly. They raised a lot of money that evening for homeless dogs."

"Sounds like something right up her alley," Kelsey replied flatly. "All part of being a socialite."

Anne detected a hint of denigration in her tone.

"Yes," Alex continued, apparently unaware. "There's no doubt she enjoys the glitterati, but she's also very polished. An expert at working the room. She's a great person to have on these sorts of committees."

"It sounds like you find her attractive," Kelsey said, her emerald green eyes both dazzling and discerning at the same time.

"No. Well—yes. I mean—I guess so." Alex sounded flustered. "That wasn't my point." He furrowed his brow.

"Interesting," Kelsey said with a tinge of disdain. "My understanding is that she's had a ton of plastic surgery—" She took a long drag on her cigarette and expelled the smoke slowly, "—a complete overhaul, actually."

Anne cringed inwardly. She regarded plastic surgery as one of the sadder comments on society.

"Not that it really helped," Kelsey added with a light tap of her cigarette against the ashtray. "There's only so much they can do."

Anne's eyes were drawn to the family photo sitting on Michael's desk. His handsome face smiled back with one arm draped loosely around a woman wearing an elegant pantsuit, a diamond pendant, and matching earrings. The three children artfully arranged around them wore cute dresses in complementary colors and looked like mini-versions of their mother, who had an unusually small mouth and pointy chin. No doubt it had been an uneven match in the looks department. If Peter Eckert was right, Michael's wife may have been little more than a meal ticket.

"That's kind of sad," Anne said quietly.

"Poor little rich girl, you mean? I suppose that's one way of looking at it." Kelsey sounded almost philosophical. "The thing that surprised me was how tacky she is." She leaned toward Anne and wrinkled her nose. "I'm not sure how she manages it, coming from hoity-toity Short Hills, but every time I see her, she has the worst bleach job. Ever."

There was clearly no love lost here.

Kelsey took another drag on her cigarette and then turned to face Alex. "It's interesting that you've crossed paths with her socially. Do you live there as well?"

"No," Alex said quickly. "I have a flat in the city—on the upper west side."

He looked at Anne. "It's getting late. We should probably grab that lunch we were talking about."

Anne nodded and then asked Kelsey whether she would like to join them, but she declined, opting instead to lift weights in the gym. Anne thought she saw a wave of relief wash over Alex's face.

"That was strange," he announced as they stepped outside of the building and into the cold, fresh air. "Kelsey had a real bee in her bonnet about Michael's wife. I wasn't quite sure what to make of it."

Anne hesitated. Should she tell him that Kelsey had also had some sort of dalliance with Michael Kingston? It might explain why she had been so scathing in her remarks.

Alex blew on his hands to warm them and then pulled a pair of gloves out of his coat pocket. "It was surprisingly personal."

With that, Anne decided to spill the beans.

"Seriously?" Alex's eyes widened.

She nodded, uneasy about having divulged information that could come back to bite her.

"Blimey!"

She mentally pushed her fears to the side, the rational side of her brain arguing that he was a lawyer, often made privy to corporate secrets, and someone she knew to be trustworthy.

Alex gave a small shrug. "That would certainly account for her animosity."

Anne stressed that he was to keep this tidbit under his hat. She had no idea whether anyone in Kelsey's department was aware there had been a relationship.

"Would anyone even care?" he asked as they waited for the light to turn green. "I tend to think these investment banker types are willing to do just about anything to get ahead, whatever the cost, with no regard for the consequences."

"Some," Anne said.

"They're all cut from the same cloth."

"That's painting with a rather broad brush," Anne said, hitting the walk button firmly with her palm. "My best friend is an investment banker at

Holbein."

Alex laughed. "Don't get all cheesed off. I didn't mean to offend you. I'm sure your friend is perfectly nice." He stole a quick glance sidewise at Anne. "Besides, my comments are being colored by the negative vibes emanating from Michael's office."

"Oh, so that's your excuse?"

"Let me translate my comments into plain old English for you, Ms. Hardnose. His office gives me the creeps." He paused for a moment. "Maybe it's because you can't open the windows to get fresh air." They stepped off the curb and crossed the street.

"You can't open the windows in your office either," Anne retorted. "I'll bet they're designed that way to prevent people from throwing themselves onto the street below." She looked quickly to her left and right. "Which way to the pizzeria?"

He pointed down a street to her right, and they turned. "That way, the suicidal types end up taking digoxin instead," he said and made a face.

"Yes." A chill ran down Anne's spine. "But there's less of a mess that way." They both laughed nervously. "This subject is too morbid for my taste," she said with a shiver. "What shall we do next?"

"Eat!" Alex said and picked up the pace.

9

The Note

After lunch, Anne decided to swing by the trading floor to wrap up the conversation about the Bat Cave bonds.

"Let's make them the *High Yield Bond of the Week*," the hotshot trader said with a smirk. "I'll be able to sell them all within a week."

She immediately had a feeling of déjà vu. Wasn't this the same conversation she had had with the other trader just before her previous boss was fired?

"Give me a break," she said. "You and I both know this isn't an appropriate investment for retail investors. They're just regular people who have no business buying risky stuff like this. There's no way in hell I'm going to write a report recommending they buy this crap."

"You have to. You said the bonds were okay."

What?! She had told him to steer clear of the bonds. He knew it, and the junior traders sitting on either side of him did too. Anne glanced over at them, but they both looked away, clearly trying to avoid getting drawn into the fray. "That's not my recollection," she said firmly, drawing herself up tall.

"Well, that's how I remember it." He crossed his arms defiantly, as if daring her to challenge him. "And now I own them."

She debated how to respond. Investment banking was already breathing down her neck. The last thing she needed was to get herself embroiled in a battle with a trader at the same time. "Tell me," she said slowly, "what was the bargain-basement price you got them for?"

"Around ninety cents on the dollar." He leaned his head once to each side as he spoke, stretching his neck.

"And the next highest bid?" Anne had a hunch it was nowhere in the neighborhood of what he had paid.

He squirmed in his seat. "On the order of seventy-five cents on the dollar."

Bingo. Everyone else on the street thought they were total crap as well. She looked at him more closely and saw beads of sweat on his forehead. Beneath that swaggering façade was a nervous jackrabbit who was trying to bluff his way into a win. "And you bought about $7 million. Right?"

"About," he said, looking everywhere but at her.

No wonder he was being such a jerk. He was looking at a million-dollar loss if he sold them today. His only way out was for someone to help inflate the story, but there was no way she was going to be that someone.

"Here's what I propose we do," she said, rubbing her hands together as she formulated her response. "I'll go talk to Elise about the…idea…to refinance the bonds. Maybe there's more to this than initially meets the eye."

The lines on his face began to relax.

"Then we'll talk about what might go into a report." Or if there would even be a report since she was certain these bonds were a pile of junk.

"Sounds good." He turned away from her and picked up his phone.

Crisis averted.

For the meantime, anyway. She let out a deep breath and headed over to the elevators, making a mental note to book an appointment for a Swedish massage, perhaps an extra-long one this time.

"Everything alright on the home front?" Alex asked when she marched into Michael's office. He was searching through the many drawers of what appeared to be an antique postal chest.

"Just the usual fun and games," she said noncommittally and took a seat at Michael's desk to tackle his PC. As she began to systematically list the contents of each directory, it quickly became clear that the computer files (she guessed there were hundreds of them) were even more poorly organized than the physical files in his cabinet had been. She frowned. This was going to take forever.

Anne kicked off her shoes and resumed studying the screen in front of her, looking for a more optimal way to chug through the many files. *Sort them by date rather than name?* Before her fingers could begin typing, she was startled by a loud gasp followed by a bang from one of the cabinet drawers being slammed shut. Anne glanced up just in time to see the look of surprise on Alex's face as he fumbled with a square box perched precipitously in his hand. It began a slow descent to the floor, where it bounced and rolled, landing near her feet. With a graceful sweep, he leaped over and picked it up, quickly stowing it safely back in the cabinet, but not before she had read the label describing its contents and seen the disconcerted look on his face.

Condoms. In the office. At the ready.

"At least Michael practiced safe sex." The words were out of her mouth before she knew it. Had she just crossed a professional line? She looked over at Alex, uncertain of what he might think.

He froze.

She caught her breath, regretting the flippant comment. It was the sort of thing she could have said to Jennifer or Donna, not a strait-laced lawyer who was investigating fraudulent bonds. And to top things off, he probably had a British sense of humor, whatever that might be. Stiff upper lip and all that kind of emotional rigidity. What had come over her?

She saw his mouth break into a smile, and then he burst out laughing. "My thoughts, exactly...although I have to say that I feel sorry for his wife."

With the tension broken, Alex moved on to a different drawer, and she resumed studying the directory printouts.

"Crikey," he called out a few minutes later. "Look at this."

Anne lifted her head grudgingly, concerned she would lose track of what she was doing.

"It's marked personal," he said, waving a floppy disk in his hand.

"Then it probably doesn't have anything to do with the bonds," she said, quickly looking back at the screen.

"You never know." Alex set it down on the desk right in front of her.

"Maybe this is where he kept track of the money he was making on the side. I think we should check it out."

"Okay," she sighed, slipping it into the slot, certain the disk would contain nothing of interest. "But after this, I think we should focus our attention on the files sitting on his computer."

"Is that the only thing on the—" he began.

"Oh, my God!" Her eyes widened in surprise. "I think this is his suicide note."

"Farewell?" He murmured. "It certainly sounds rather ominous."

"Maybe it's just a guest list for a farewell party rather than—"

"I doubt it," he cut her off. "But there's only one way to find out."

She dropped her voice to a whisper and turned to face him. "You think we should open it?"

Alex gave a small shrug. "Why not?"

They glanced around to make sure no one was watching and then brought it up on the screen.

After careful deliberation, I have decided to end it all here and now. I'm not sure how I reached this point of no return. When I began my career, I was optimistic and full of idealism. Somewhere along the line, the money and prestige took on a life of their own, becoming the sole focal point of my energies. Now that the truth about my involvement in the Pandora deals has come to light, my reputation and my career are finished.

I'm sorry for any pain I have caused, but I cannot endure the humiliation of a trial and being sent to prison.

Respectfully,

Michael Kingston III

Anne closed the file as soon as they were done reading and stared at the blank screen in mute dismay. A mass of thoughts jumbled in her mind. This note was his last communication with the world. His tentative effort to reach out had been captured and then stored as nothing more than a few magnetic spots on a floppy disk. Without thinking, she mechanically typed the command for a directory printout again.

```
A>dir

Farewell.txt 12435 bytes 1-13-89 10:30p 1 File(s) 347565 bytes
free
```

The file name, size, and date glowed on the dark screen. Eventually, the text began to blur, and she had to blink and look away.

At first, the importance of what she had seen didn't register. Suddenly her eyes widened, and she sat bolt upright in her seat. "Check this out! His suicide note was written four days prior to his death at 10:30 pm. Don't you think that's kind of weird?"

Alex shrugged. "Not necessarily. It just means he'd been planning it for a while."

"Maybe," Anne said distantly, "but something about this bothers me. Where's his calendar? I want to see where he was on the 13th."

Alex lifted a small pile of papers and unearthed the spiral-bound book. They both just stared.

"If he was on a sailboat in San Diego, he couldn't possibly have written that letter," Anne whispered.

They wandered over to Betty's desk, where she confirmed that he had indeed been in San Diego for a client meeting on the 12th and had then taken a sailing trip to Catalina Island beginning on the morning of the 13th. Coloring slightly, she admitted she had accompanied him on the business trip in order to take notes and assist with logistics.

"Who would write a suicide note while on a business trip and then return and bring it in to work?" Anne spat the words out the moment they returned to the privacy of his office. "That makes no sense at all!"

"Unless he didn't want his wife to see it," Alex replied, his voice no more than a murmur, "so he brought the floppy here for safekeeping. I agree with you, though. It's a little weird."

Anne looked at him, incredulous. "And how could he have written it?"

"What do you mean?"

She motioned. "His computer is here."

"Unless he borrowed someone else's." Alex studied the dancing green lights on the computer screen, his hands gripping the back of the chair behind it. "Or maybe used one at the hotel."

"He was on a sailboat," Anne countered, her uneasiness growing. "It would have had a radio on board. But a computer? I don't think so."

"Maybe he had some sort of portable device…."

Anne shook her head. "They weigh a ton and cost a fortune. Nobody at Spencer Brothers has one that I know of."

Alex slowly looked away from the monitor and faced her directly. "I think you're probably right, but we should check with Betty to be sure. The other thing to remember is that the guy was rich. Maybe he owned a personal one."

Anne's eyes narrowed. "Not only were these deals illegal, unethical, and a bad idea from the start, but they appear to be dangerous. It looks like Michael got murdered over them, and I'm not sure I'm interested in finding out why."

"Hang on. Even if Michael's death wasn't a suicide—and that's a big if—then he probably did something specific to piss off the killer."

"And now we're poking our noses into his sketchy little enterprise. Seems like the perfect way to get his killer to take aim at us."

"We don't even know that these deals had anything to do with his death," Alex protested.

Anne couldn't believe Alex failed to see the risks they faced. "What do you think he was murdered over, his surgically reconstructed wife?"

"I'm just saying that it doesn't necessarily follow that we will become the next targets."

"I never said it would follow," Anne quipped, "—just that it was a possibility." Realizing that she was tired and starting to feel irritable, she stood up and pushed the chair under the desk. "Let's get out of here. I think we've accomplished more than enough for one day."

*   *   *

She was stopped on the way back to her cubicle by William, who greeted her in his usual stony manner and then asked her to come into his office.

What now? She looked at him, her heart beating furiously.

"I hear you recommended some Bat Cave, North Dakota hospital bonds, but are refusing to write them up."

Recommended? She clenched her hands in frustration. The trader was clearly getting desperate. Even so, she had half a mind to march out to the trading floor and let the little twerp know what a slimy piece of garbage he was. Instead, she took a deep breath and explained the situation to her manager. When she was through, he shook his head.

"I suspected as much. This isn't the first time he's pulled a stunt like this." She raised her eyebrows.

"You didn't hear it from me." William cracked a smile. "Relax. I'll get the matter resolved. Meanwhile, you should probably see what Elise has to say. Just to close the loop on this thing."

Ugh. The Ice Princess. Anne stood up and braced herself for another battle.

After walking all of ten feet to circle around the cluster of cubicles containing the research analysts, she reached her intended destination.

"Hi there," Anne addressed the unfriendly scowl staring at her from inside the cubicle, "I've got a quick question about the Bat Cave bonds."

Elise was wearing the same pea-green sweater she had been wearing the day before, except today, her skirt matched the sweater. Her legs were covered with dense, black tights that ended in black boots with large buckles, and she wore enough make-up to be performing in a Broadway Musical.

"Yeah." Elise shrugged, as if she could hardly be bothered to reply. "What about them?"

"Trading's under the impression they're going to be refunded."

Elise merely looked at her blankly. "So?"

"So—what's the story?"

Elise rolled her eyes and let out a long deep sigh. "I just told them what I heard from my friend upstairs."

"Upstairs?"

She froze. "I mean at Stoddard Securities."

Anne suddenly wondered where the Ice Princess was actually getting her information from. Could it be that someone in the investment banking group at Spencer Brothers was her true source? That would constitute insider trading. And be grounds for termination.

"And did this friend—"

"I haven't heard anything else since."

Anne paused, wondering how best to proceed. "It's just that I don't think the hospital has a hope in hell of selling new debt to refinance the old. It'll be lucky to avoid bankruptcy before year-end."

"Don't know what to tell you." Elise fiddled with the catch of a silver locket dangling loosely around her neck.

Anne felt like grabbing the necklace and jerking it off of her neck. "I was hoping you knew a little bit more about the basis for the proposed refinancing, because it doesn't make any sense based on the financials I've seen."

"Like I said before…." Elise yawned and began studying her nails.

"Right. Well, it sounds like—"

"Too bad you didn't warn Golden Boy *before* he bought the bonds." Elise's mouth took on an annoying smirk. "I hear he's pretty ticked off that you won't write them up."

Anne didn't need to be reminded that the trader who bought the bonds was good friends with Peter Eckert. They lived in the same town and often commuted to the office together. Because of that relationship, the other traders trod carefully around him.

Elise opened her eyes wide, all innocence, to deliver her final shot. "Especially with all the rumors about upcoming layoffs."

Anne's heart began beating more quickly. It was time to end the conversation with the Ice Princess before she said something she regretted. She stepped back to give herself more space. "Thanks for your help," she said as evenly as possible.

"Anytime," Elise said in a tone that could only be interpreted as mocking.

* * *

"What a bitch!" Jennifer said when Anne told her about the conversation a few minutes later.

"We need to come up with another name for her," Anne said, frowning. "Ice Princess doesn't sufficiently capture the essence of her horribleness."

"Maybe we should go with Loki," Jennifer said with a mischievous look. "The Nordic god of trickery."

"But he's male."

Jennifer waved her arms dismissively. "Loki changes his shape and sex at will, so sometimes *he's* a *she*. And Loki's blatantly malicious. Just like you-know-who."

Anne gave a small smile but did not feel much better. It seemed as if her world was held together with rubber bands and paper clips. One small misstep and everything would break apart. "I think I'm reaching the end of my rope."

"Cheer up!" Jennifer nudged her gently. "William said he'd take care of the issue with the Bat Cave Bonds, and who cares what Crazy Loki has to say."

True. That crisis had been averted, but what about Michael Kingston? Had he actually been murdered? Her mind flashed to his office, the stately wood desk, the plush leather chair where he had been sitting, and the antique cabinet to the side. It had a calm, dignified feeling. Restful even. And yet it had been the place of arguments, fury, and death.

And condoms...

"You won't believe what we found today while rummaging around Michael's—" Anne began before being interrupted by one of the secretaries who said she had an urgent personal call. She felt her heart skip a beat. Was there a problem with one of her parents? Or her sister?

Anne ran to pick up the phone and then felt a flash of irritation when she realized that it was just one of her neighbors complaining about another one's dog.

"She needs to be fined," he insisted.

"But if you didn't actually see Sparky do it—" Anne started to say.

"I saw it happen yesterday, and this looks exactly the same. If you want, I'll show you some samples."

Just what Anne needed. She closed her eyes and took a deep breath. "That's okay. I'll take your word for it."

"Look," he continued. "I'm not trying to be difficult, but I can't be stepping on doggy landmines every time I walk outside my door. This has got to stop."

She kept her annoyance in check. "I'll put it on the agenda for our next meeting. Thanks for bringing it to my attention."

Anne hung up and briefly wondered what had possessed her to accept the Condo Association Presidency. The guy in the first-floor unit was no longer speaking to her because of the yard maintenance fees, and now Sparky's owner would soon be angry, too. Four more months of this thankless job, and then her term would be finished. It couldn't come fast enough.

* * *

The following morning, Anne bounced out of bed and hurriedly dressed for work. She headed straight into William's office without removing her coat or changing out of her walking sneakers.

"I'm convinced that Michael was murdered," she greeted him without prelude.

"Good morning, Anne. Is there something you'd like to discuss?" He leaned back and assumed an air of quiet concentration.

"It wasn't suicide."

He looked at her blankly. "And what makes you say that?"

"Because when Alex and I were going through his computer files to look for information relating to the flaky deals, we found his suicide note."

He began swiveling back and forth in his chair.

"It was saved on a floppy disk."

He froze and gave her a cold, hard stare. "And did you indulge your morbid curiosity to sneak a peek at its contents?"

She squirmed. "There's no big secret about what the note said. Lots of people saw it the morning he was found."

"So that's a *yes*." His look was disapproving, as if she had disappointed him in the biggest way possible.

"The thing that's odd is the date."

"What do you mean?"

William bore an alertness about him that reminded Anne of a tiger surveying its prey before the kill. She blinked, unsure how this conversation was about to play out. "The suicide note was written four days before his *supposed* suicide."

The crevices on his forehead relaxed. "So, he wrote it in advance," he said, dismissing her concerns with a sweep of his hand.

"While he was in San Diego? Cavorting with his secretary? At 10:30 pm at night?"

He shrugged. "Maybe they had a fight."

"Or maybe he didn't actually write it."

"Anne—look at this logically." His tone was condescending, and she found it difficult to suppress her annoyance. "The man's life was caving in on him. You and Alex were hot on his heels, and he knew it. The only thing that floppy tells you is that Michael had been contemplating suicide for a while and just happened to have some time, while he was in San Diego, to put his thoughts on paper."

"But his computer was back here," Anne persisted, despite the small upward curve of William's lips that suggested he was now sneering at her.

"He could have used one at the hotel or at the local office." He shook his head. "You're searching for a mystery where there is none."

"I'm wondering if we should tell the police what we found."

"What?!" He jerked up in his chair, his hands flying to the desktop.

"Absolutely not! The next thing you know, we'll have the SEC breathing down our necks."

"But what if—"

"There is no *what if*," he snapped, as if he were a German shepherd guarding a private estate, and she had just walked too close to the fence.

She drew back in her chair, stung by both his tone and lack of support.

"Your job is to focus on the bonds and only the bonds!"

As he launched into a lecture about getting her priorities straight, she studied him abstractedly, like a painting at the Guggenheim. His white shirt did not have a single wrinkle, and his colorful silk tie was bold and trendy. Despite being a snappy dresser, the comb-over could not hide his ever-growing bald spot, and small white flakes of dandruff littered the shoulders of his hand-tailored, navy suit jacket.

"—understand these Pandora deals inside out."

As he continued talking at her, she noticed that he occasionally spit, when he said an 's', and a small red vein pulsed on his forehead where his hairline was receding.

"—spend less time listening to the scuttlebutt and more time wrapping up your inquiries."

The comment should have made her angry, but instead, she felt nothing. His words passed by like a rushing river while she stood to the side on the tree-lined bank, barely letting anything he said penetrate her consciousness. She was no longer letting him in.

Eventually, his mouth stopped moving.

"Is that everything?" she said evenly.

He nodded tersely.

Anne walked out feeling very dissatisfied with the outcome of her little chat with William.

10

The Party

Three Days After the Meeting

"Y ou're here?" the trader said. "I thought you hated these affairs."

"I do," Anne replied, looking around the semi-darkened bar and dance club where the department was holding its annual party. With striped umbrellas, colorful papier-mâché fish, and white lattice fencing on the walls, it was decorated in the style of a private beach club in the Hamptons.

"But?" He looked at her expectantly.

She gave a small shrug. "William specifically hunted me down and told me it was in my 'best interest' to make an appearance." She made air quotes around *best interest*. "I didn't feel I had much choice." A questionnaire had been passed out two weeks earlier, asking all departmental employees to indicate whether they would attend the function. *Response Required* was written in big letters across the top, like a note from the school principal sent to the parents of an unruly sixth grader.

He laughed. "I know what you mean. My girlfriend was upset she wasn't allowed to come, but I told her it was part of my job."

Typical for brokerage firm functions, spouses and significant others were specifically excluded. In addition, the functions were always held on Friday nights so that the heavy-duty partygoers would not miss work the following day.

He nodded toward the DJ, partially obscured by a partition in the corner. "This music sucks. I hope they bring out a live band later on."

"They will," Donna said, magically appearing by his side in a short mini-skirt with black fishnet tights. "They always do."

Tottering on six-inch stiletto heels, she looked like she might lose her balance at any moment. But the thing that caught Anne's attention was her eyes. They were rimmed with thick, black eyeliner and little wings on each corner, making her look like a leopard. The only thing missing were black spots.

The trader leaned toward Donna and pointed at his empty glass, "Ready for another?" She nodded, linked her arm around his, and the two disappeared toward the bar.

Anne spotted Jennifer halfway across the room, headed her way. "Brace yourself," Jennifer greeted her with a dramatic arm flourish. "Mr. Excitement is about to speak."

As if on cue, the lights came up, the music stopped, and the room went silent.

Everyone turned to look at the President standing on a small podium that had been erected near the front. He rolled up his sleeves, cleared his throat, and began to drone on and on. This time it was about the importance of teamwork, positive attitudes, and maintaining respect for one's fellow employees. From the stifled yawns and continual shifting of restless bodies in the seats, Anne read the general sentiment in the crowd as one of utter boredom. How could he not sense it, too? She looked over at Jennifer, who rolled her eyes as if to say, *See, I told you.*

When he was finally through, he was rewarded with a loud burst of applause. Anne assumed it was both out of politeness due to his high station in the company and also out of a sense of thrill and relief that the tedious part of the evening was finally over.

Everyone moved to the huge room reserved for dinner and partying, where Anne's suspicions were confirmed.

"Get real," one person said to her, "our firm is the most cutthroat in the business. I don't think most of our people even know the definition of teamwork."

Anne couldn't help but agree.

Another said to her, "If I don't stab someone else first, then I'll find myself bleeding all over the floor. A lot of good that would do my family."

An understandable concern, Anne conceded.

As she had expected, the room was dark, the band was pretty good, and the traders and salesmen, especially the married ones, were busy getting drunk and making passes at the young clerical help. Anne and Jennifer stood on the sidelines watching the antics unfold on the dance floor.

"Typical," Jennifer said as one of the traders removed his tie and started ripping his shirt.

"I think he did the same thing last year," Anne replied as he climbed up on a table and started chugging his beer. "But he looks a little more wobbly than I remember."

"The sad thing is I would actually enjoy dancing," Jennifer lamented. "But if we go out there, we'll just be relegated to the bimbo pond."

Anne nodded. "I know. That's why we're standing here like wallflowers." Two other guys started removing their ties, and a chorus of shouts could be heard egging them on to join the ripping frenzy. "Seems like a real waste of money. Those are probably expensive shirts."

"My wife would kill me if I did that," a voice boomed from the side. "She's already ticked off that she isn't allowed to come to the party in the first place." It was one of the traders Anne helped from time to time, who had been sitting by the bar drinking with his buddies. He was generally friendly and easy to deal with. "And they really ought to cut Renata off. She's barely able to walk."

Anne looked over to where he was pointing and saw one of the secretaries stumbling toward the ladies' room.

"She looks like she could use some help," Jennifer yelled, heading over toward the inebriated woman. The music was thumping loudly, making it hard to hear.

"We've almost finished dumping those bonds you worked on," the trader shouted over the din. "What a mess."

"You're telling me."

"Strange business, Michael Kingston killing himself last week. It's the last thing I would have expected him to do."

"You knew him?"

"Yeah. We went to high school together. Back when his name was Otis Reichenbach." He took a swig of his beer. "He was a real riot."

"You knew him in high school?" she shouted back, unsure whether she had heard him correctly. "But his name was different?"

"Yeah," he bellowed. The floor was now physically shaking, and she leaned closer to him, straining to hear his response. "His father worked the night shift at Hadley Machine Works. Like mine did. We both grew up in Paterson, New Jersey." He moved sideways as a gyrating body came dangerously close to knocking his beer, and she followed him. "Total dump. Back then, the only thing any of us wanted was to get outta there." He took another swig of his beer.

"And his name was different?" She asked again, in disbelief.

"Yeah. He changed it after he went to prison."

"Prison?" The music swelled up in a roaring frenzy, mimicking her furiously beating heart.

"He got caught stealing a car with another guy at school. Happened a few weeks before graduation. He was always pulling stunts like that. Conning people. Stealing things. He would make stuff up like it was nobody's business. And he got away with it a lot of the time too." The trader shrugged and then added, "He was a really sharp guy."

Anne was dumbfounded. Nothing that related to Michael Kingston was what it seemed. The lights began strobing as the music died down to a low rumble. She seized the opportunity to ask another question. "How long was he in prison?"

"Less than a year. Probably 9 months. When he got out—man, was he built! He must've lifted weights the entire time he was there. I ran into him a couple of times at Keene College." The music began another crescendo.

"I thought he went to Harvard," she screamed, trying to be heard over the deafening noise. "That's what the papers reported." She felt vaguely disoriented, unsure whether it was due to the contradictory information she was hearing or if she was simply suffering from sensory overload.

"That business about him going to Harvard and Stanford was all bullshit," the trader yelled back. "He went to Keene College for a few semesters and never even graduated. And the Rhode Island stuff? He must've just made it all up. He was a con artist through and through." He laughed as he spoke, as if he was impressed by how much the man had gotten away with, perhaps even envious.

"And you're sure that Michael Kingston was this Otis guy you knew in high school? Absolutely sure?" Anne's throat was starting to hurt from all the yelling.

"No question about it. I bumped into him on the elevator a few years ago. That's when I found out he worked at Spencer Brothers, just like me. It's a small world." He drained his beer.

"Did you tell anyone? Like his boss?"

He shook his head. "Why would I? He'd served his time. And he could've been a useful person to know if he hadn't gone and killed himself." He pointed at the empty bottle and said, "Time for a refill," and then headed back to the bar.

Anne tried to process what she had just heard, but the pounding music made it hard to think. Did it matter that Michael had changed his name? It certainly meant he had reinvented himself. But did that figure somehow into his murder? If he was indeed murdered. Maybe he had gotten tired of the charade and simply decided to throw in the towel. Or, maybe...

"How're you enjoying yourself?" It was one of the salesmen interrupting her train of thought. A nice guy she enjoyed helping on occasion, he took his fiduciary responsibilities seriously and would only sell risky bonds to sophisticated investors who understood the financial implications. Likewise, he appeared to imbibe responsibly, wandering around with a drink in hand but not completely plastered. They chatted amiably for a few minutes before he moved on and started talking with someone else. She looked over toward

113

the ladies' room and saw Jennifer emerging with Renata in tow.

"Does Vito have a girlfriend?" Renata asked with a loud slur after Jennifer had helped her over.

"I don't know," Anne replied.

"Let's find out," Renata said, rocking from side to side. "He's kind of cute." She turned around and saw him standing a few feet behind her. "Oh, God!" She gasped, followed by a loud burp. "Do you think he heard me?"

Anne had no idea but agreed to sleuth out his *availability status* when she got a chance. As the evening wore on, more salesmen and traders wandered by to say hello and chat for a few minutes, leaving no time for her to think about Michael Kingston. She was having a fairly pleasant time, all in all, until the band stopped playing, and a pair of secretaries wheeled out a cake for Peter Eckert. With some guidance from senior management, all three hundred members of the department sang happy birthday to him. Afterwards, someone yelled, "Make a wish!"

Peter smiled broadly as he looked around the room. "I probably shouldn't say this, but what I'd really like…" he raised his beer in the air, nodding in the direction of the secretaries, "is to take one of these pretty young girls home tonight."

Most of the crowd laughed.

Give me a break, Anne thought to herself and instantly decided the cake was her cue to leave. "I'm out of here," she told Jennifer. "I've made my obligatory appearance and seen enough for one night." She was anxious to get home and mull over what she had learned.

"Me too." Jennifer followed her to the coat check room, where they retrieved their jackets and headed out to the street to pick up one of the hired cars.

The firm had begun providing private car service after one of the traders had gotten behind the wheel of his fancy sports car following one of these parties, inebriated, killing an innocent bystander. Despite the sad history behind the benefit, Anne found it provided an easy and relaxed way to get home from these affairs. She settled into her seat and waited for Jennifer to climb in on the other side so they could be on their way.

"My seatbelt doesn't seem to connect—" Jennifer began, before being interrupted by a loud rapping on the window. It was one of the traders, looking to join them in their car.

"You guys live in Hoboken, right?" he asked after she had finally gotten the window down. "I'm going across the river too." His speech was slurred, and his movements uncoordinated. "To Morristown."

Indeed, their two stops were on the way to his house. The driver could easily drop them off first and then continue on. Jennifer shrugged and then slid into the middle, inviting him in.

As the car slowly snaked its way through Manhattan, Anne and Jennifer chatted quietly in the back. The trader eventually fell asleep, and Anne relayed what she had been told about Michael Kingston.

"From prison to Wall Street?" Jennifer said with obvious surprise. "I guess it kind of makes sense. In a twisted sort of way."

"I'm not sure it even matters." Anne looked out the side window. The car entered the Holland Tunnel and began to pick up speed, its yellow lights casting distorted shadows on the wall. "But for some reason, it's unnerved me."

"So what if he changed his name?" Jennifer replied. "People do that all the time. It sounds like he screwed up in high school and just wanted to leave it all behind."

"You're probably right," Anne said, but found herself unable to believe it.

They arrived at Jennifer's apartment first, and she got out, leaving Anne alone with the trader, who was still asleep. As the car pulled to a stop in front of her building a few minutes later, he jerked awake in surprise and then leaned forward, hurling the remains of his dinner all over the back seat. Anne sprang out of the vehicle, but not quickly enough. Her coat was going to need a trip to the cleaners.

The driver took one look and said, "I'm not taking him any further," and insisted the trader immediately exit the vehicle. He stumbled out and sat down on the stoop of her building.

"You can't leave him with me." Anne protested. "I hardly know him. He still needs to get home."

"Call a cab," the driver muttered and then sped off in a cloud of smoke.

Swearing under her breath, she brought him into the building so he could call his wife. As luck would have it, one of her neighbors walked by and caught a whiff of him just as she was unlocking her front door.

"A new boyfriend?" she asked, looking horrified.

"No!" Anne felt her face go red. "He's just someone I work with."

"Hmmm," her neighbor said in a judgmental sort of way.

"The driver refused to take him home," Anne said, thinking it might help to explain.

"I'm not surprised." Her neighbor gave a withering look.

Anne ushered him out of the hallway and shut the door from her neighbor's prying eyes. Her dog took one sniff and quickly moved away while Anne stood, mortified, replaying the interaction with her neighbor again in her mind.

He pointed at the couch. "How about if I just sleep here?"

She shook her head and handed him the phone. "While you call your wife, I'll make some coffee."

Red-faced and tight-lipped, a woman dripping with diamonds appeared about 30 minutes later, looking about as angry as Anne felt.

"Hi," the trader slurred as he stood up to greet her and began to sway. Anne hoped he was not about to throw up again.

His wife gave an exasperated sigh. "Let's get this show on the road."

Those were Anne's thoughts exactly as she watched him stagger toward the door.

His wife gave her a quick nod. "Nice to meet you."

"You too," Anne replied with a perfunctory smile, relieved when she was finally able to lock the door behind the two of them. She stepped out of her heels and peeled off her dress and hose, leaving a trail of clothes across the floor. The week had been exhausting, and she felt overrun with information. First suicide, then murder, then not really murder. And on top of that, Michael Kingston had fabricated huge parts of his life. As she dropped into bed, she wondered what she had gotten herself into.

11

The Clink

Monday, One Week After the Meeting

"And if you can believe it, we let him into the car," Anne said, rolling her eyes as she recounted her adventures the following Monday morning.

"You should make him pay for your dry cleaning," clucked Donna, whose bright purple eyeshadow and aqua eyeliner gave her the appearance of a tropical fish. "It's the least he can do."

"I don't know if he even remembers what happened. He hasn't said a word, and I've already been out near his desk twice this morning."

"Scumbag," Donna said, chomping on the ever-present wad of gum.

"Getting back to what I told you earlier—" Anne looked around to make sure no one was listening. "—about Michael Kingston. Do you think there's any chance…? I mean, we all know how the traders love to pull a fast one."

"No," Donna said firmly. "He wouldn't make up something like *that*. He might leave a wad of wet paper towels in your briefcase." She blew a big bubble. "Or arrange for the delivery of a dozen dead roses to liven up your cubicle…something more along those lines."

"But if Michael Kingston actually went to prison, he should never have been able to get his securities license or a job on Wall Street. It should have turned up on the background check."

Anne still remembered the lie detector test she had been required to take as a condition of employment. After being wired up with a metal sensor on her finger, a pressure cuff on her arm, and yet another pressure cuff wrapped around her stomach, the man operating the polygraph machine asked dozens of questions about whether she had a history of stealing or any motivation to do so (Had she ever shoplifted? Tried marijuana or snorted coke? Did she gamble? Did she live with people who did any of these things? The same questions asked multiple times, in different ways.) Presumably, Michael had had to pass a similar test as well.

"If he was a juvenile at the time he stole the car, his record was probably sealed, and then the whole thing expunged a few years later."

And armed with a new name, he'd have a squeaky-clean slate.

"Michael Kingston wouldn't be the only one around here to make things disappear," Donna chuckled. "One of the guys in the derivatives group was arrested last year for drunk driving after he totaled his car. A few weeks later, the case file magically vanished from the court docket." As she spoke, she smacked the gum in her mouth against her cheeks. "And Vito had a rap sheet a mile long. You just have to know who to pay off."

"Vito?" Anne lowered her voice to a whisper. "Renata was asking about him. She thinks he's kind of cute, but if he…"

"It was petty juvenile stuff. Nothing serious." Donna spat her gum into a nearby trash can. "But I'm pretty sure he has a girlfriend anyway." Her eyes darted over toward the figure slithering toward her office. "With William on vacation, I wasn't sure Elise was going to make it in today. You know that he's in the Bahamas this week, right?"

Of course Anne did. It meant they would be shorthanded. Hopefully, the Ice Princess would actually help take up some of the slack in his absence.

As she walked away, Donna called over her shoulder, "Make that cheapskate pay for your dry cleaning."

Anne started to walk back to her cubicle and then made a U-turn and headed for the corporate library on the 17th floor. When she arrived, she asked the librarian to help her search the local Paterson, New Jersey newspapers from 1976-1978. The woman looked pleased to have something to do and immediately set to work, pulling out microfiche boxes and scanning the indexes. After a few minutes, she handed Anne six rolls of film. Anne kicked off her pumps and began scrolling through the pages.

The trader who said he knew Michael Kingston from high school appeared in articles about the football team, credited with contributing to several big wins. In one, there was a photograph of the team with their names listed at the bottom. She zoomed in on the small grainy image of Otis Reichenbach. A handsome athlete, who could be a younger version of Michael Kingston, stared unsmiling at the camera. She studied the picture, looking for something she could definitely point to that would say without any doubt she was looking at Michael Kingston, but ultimately couldn't find that telltale clue.

She gave up on the photograph and continued scrolling until she reached the crime reports. Her eyes remained glued to the screen while her hand slowly turned the crank of the microfilm machine, stopping only after she had found the following:

Paterson Man Arrested after Joy Riding
May 28, 1978

Police arrested 17-year-old Otis Reichenbach after he stole a car and led authorities on a dangerous high-speed pursuit that began in Paterson and ended on the Garden State Parkway in Newark. He has been charged with grand larceny and is being held in the Paterson County Jail.

Anne nodded silently to herself. The story checked out.

After thanking the librarian for her help, she walked slowly to the elevator and headed back to the trading floor to grab her lunch. Jennifer flew out and grabbed her arm as she passed by the research cubicles, pulling her toward the table where the lunches were waiting.

"He didn't offer to pay for the dry cleaning?" She rolled her eyes. "Seriously?"

"Last time I'm sharing a car with him," Anne replied as she scanned the labels, looking for her name.

"Hey—that's mine!" Jennifer grabbed a bag from one of the salesmen's hands.

Anne finally spotted hers and pulled it out of the pile. "Quick standing lunch?"

Jennifer nodded, and they headed back to the long row of file cabinets.

"It's been a zoo around here this morning," Jennifer announced as she unwrapped her sandwich. "After I returned from having coffee with Kelsey, the secretaries were nowhere to be found. Plus, Donna and the Ice Princess were holed up in the conference room, leaving me alone to man the fort. Where were you?"

"In the library. And I'm heading up to Michael's office after I finish eating. Did you let Donna know that you need some help?"

"Yes. A few minutes ago. She said this afternoon they'd work in her office instead." Jennifer gave a surreptitious glance around and then jerked a thumb in the direction of Elise's cubicle. "And she also told me the engagement is off again."

"I didn't realize it was back on. It's sort of hard to keep track."

"He says he can't afford to buy a ring because he's decided to get a new car." Jennifer rolled her eyes.

Anne shrugged. "He's obviously got cold feet."

"Or perhaps he's simply biding his time to make sure nothing better comes along."

"You wouldn't think that would be very hard, judging by what she has to offer." Anne clapped a hand over her mouth in a mock gesture of horror at what she had just said.

Jennifer smiled contemptuously. "You haven't seen him."

Out of the corner of her eye, Anne saw something move. "Wait! Here she comes."

"Thanks for helping me understand those unusual bond provisions," Jennifer said loudly, followed by a wink.

Anne wolfed down her lunch and headed up to Michael Kingston's office to meet Alex. Their plan was to continue combing through his files to see if they had missed anything pertinent to the sleazy bond deals, but she began by telling him about her morning sleuthing in the library.

"He was an ex-con?" Alex raised an eyebrow. "I'm having a hard time imagining Mr. Dapper in the clink." He cocked his head to the side. "And this trader knew him in high school before he changed his name?"

She nodded.

"I'm not sure what to make of that."

"I flat out don't believe it," a voice said from behind her.

Anne turned to see Kelsey standing in the doorway, impeccably arrayed as always. She wore pearls and a navy sheath dress that skirted her body without clinging, hinting at the perfect figure beneath. With flawless make-up and neatly blown-dry hair, she stood in stark contrast to Anne, who threw herself together each morning in fifteen minutes flat. *How does she do it?* Anne wondered. It was as if she had an army of secret elves that helped her get ready every day.

Kelsey stepped forward. "I overheard you guys talking and thought I'd pop in."

"I'm glad you're here," Anne greeted her. "I've been doing some digging."

"That's what I gather. Are you actually buying this business about his name and education all being fake? This morning I tried to explain to Jennifer that it made no sense."

"Well, actually—" Anne began.

"He belonged to the Harvard Club," Kelsey scoffed.

"Even so—"

"He endowed a chair at Stanford," Kelsey said emphatically, shaking her head in disbelief. "I think I would've known if he'd made that up!"

"Except—"

"Except what?" Kelsey's eyes bored through her. "Some drunk trader is taking you for a ride. He probably stood at the bar laughing with his buddies about how gullible you are."

"You haven't even heard what she has to say," Alex snapped, causing Anne to look at him in surprise. He motioned toward the newspaper articles.

"Show her."

Anne set the pages on the table and then stepped back to give Kelsey room to study them.

She snatched the one with the photograph of the football team and brought it close to her face, scrutinizing it intently. When Kelsey finally raised her head, she looked like a cat on the prowl, her muscles tight and her eyes narrowed to tiny slits. "Is the trader in this photo as well?"

Anne nodded and pointed him out.

Kelsey bit her lip and slowly sank into one of Michael's guest chairs. "Maybe I didn't know him as well as I thought I did. He's turning out to be a man of many secrets."

Anne exchanged glances with Alex and then forged ahead. "There's something else I think you should be aware of."

"There's more?" Kelsey sighed heavily and began slowly massaging her temples.

"We've uncovered something on Michael's PC that makes his death look suspicious."

Kelsey's hands froze midair, and she looked up, confused. "What are you talking about? He killed himself."

Anne shook her head. "His suicide note was written four days prior to his death."

Kelsey's eyes widened. "What? No. What makes you think that?"

"We found a floppy disk in his office with the note on it," Anne said without skipping a beat. "Which reminds me...does it strike you as odd that he would have typed it?"

"No," Kelsey stammered. "That was totally his style. He either dictated memos onto a small recorder for his secretary to transcribe or typed them up himself on the computer. He never wrote anything in long-hand. But...but what were you saying about it being written earlier?"

"The file shows the date of last revisions, which was four days before he died...while he was away on a business trip in San Diego."

Kelsey looked at her, speechless.

"One of the Pandora partners must have murdered him and then slipped the diskette in with the others," Alex said, laying out their theory. "The question is, which one?"

Anne immediately set to work, considering the possibilities. "Walter Hughes was seething with anger toward Michael that day. Remember how he stomped out of the meeting? He had murderous rage written all over him." She could still see his perfectly combed silver hair bouncing with each step.

"It could've been Marvin Goldberg," Alex countered. "That bloke wasn't batting on a full wicket. While I went through the bond structure, he had this smug look on his face, as if he was the only smart person in the room."

Anne thought they had all seemed arrogant and self-absorbed. The thing that had struck her most about Marvin was the way his eyes had roved over her, like she was a piece of meat.

"And he kept blowing those damned smoke rings!" Alex continued, still obviously bothered by it. "Underneath that casual façade might've been a cold, calculating murderer biding his time until he could safely slip the drugs into Michael's coffee."

Kelsey nodded, the color slowly returning to her face.

"How about David Singer, the bond lawyer?" Anne considered the next obvious culprit. "He was as nervous as a jackrabbit. Maybe part of his jumpiness was a result of his plan to eliminate Michael."

"They all had motives," Alex said, throwing his hands up in despair.

"And they all had opportunity," Kelsey said quietly. She pulled a cigarette from her blazer pocket, carefully lit it, and drew a long, deep breath.

"Yet, senior management is convinced he committed suicide." Anne frowned. "So, we're stuck dealing with these people until the Pandora deals are straightened out."

"Thanks for filling me in," Kelsey said, her attitude considerably softer than when they had first begun the conversation. "I'm going to be very careful about any interactions I have with these guys going forward."

Anne was surprised by the earnest, almost grateful look in Kelsey's eyes as she spoke.

"This just shows that we really need to be working together," Kelsey continued. "The three of us. Even though we're in different parts of the company."

Alex shot Anne a sidelong glance that she was unable to decipher.

"I'm sorry." Kelsey hesitated, as if struggling to find the right words, "I think I was a bit short with you before."

Anne waved her off. "Don't worry about it."

Kelsey sighed. "I don't think...I just haven't been myself these last few days. And I have to admit, I'm rather floored by what you've found. His background and now this business with the suicide note."

"I know," Anne commiserated. "It's a lot to take in."

"I can't help wondering if there's a simpler explanation." Kelsey fiddled nervously with her earring. "Something obvious we should see that we're just missing. I don't know. Everything's jumbled in my mind right now."

Alex eyed the door. "Time for a break?"

Anne nodded. "I should probably get back to the trading floor. William's on vacation this week, so the rest of us are picking up the work he would normally handle."

"How about if we reconvene tomorrow morning after we've all had a chance to think a bit," Kelsey suggested. "Say 9 am? Unless something urgent comes up."

"Sure," Anne said immediately and then saw Alex shaking his head no in the background. But it was too late. She had already agreed.

"Now we're stuck meeting with her again," he whispered as they waited for the elevator to arrive. "She's just going to slow us down."

"We can use the opportunity to ask her more questions about the bonds."

He frowned. "I don't think she'll tell us anything useful."

Anne shrugged, wondering why he was making such a big deal about it. "Then we'll keep it short."

"Even so," he said as they stepped inside the elevator. "There's something about her attitude that bothers me. I can't quite put my finger on it—"

The elevator lurched, and Anne felt his arm brush against her shoulder.

"Sorry," he said, looking chagrined, and then moved further away. "I hate when the lift starts acting up. It makes me wonder if it's about to go into freefall."

She smiled. "I know what you mean. Sometimes I—Oh No!"

The elevator lurched again, and everything went dark.

"Bloody hell. This day just gets better and better."

"Maybe if we just give it a second, it'll—"

"Isn't there an emergency button on this contraption?"

"I think it's near the bottom of the panel," Anne said, putting her hand out, feeling along the wall. "But I'm not sure how well it works. The other day a couple of salesmen on my floor were trapped for a good thirty minutes before being rescued. I guess it rings, but no one can hear it unless they're fairly close by." Her hand suddenly bumped his, and she felt a little shock as they connected. "Oh, sorry!"

She had no idea he had been so close.

Reaching her other hand out toward the adjacent wall, she inched backwards, away from the elevator buttons. And from him.

"I think I found it," he said, followed by a pause. "No. That's not it. Maybe this one—"

There was a low rumble, and the lights came back on. Almost immediately, the elevator began moving.

"Yes!" they both said and then burst out laughing.

Anne waited a moment to make sure there were no more glitches and then picked up where they had left off. "Kelsey's not exactly a team player. Maybe that's what's bothering you."

"It's not that," he said slowly.

"And she can be kind of negative."

Alex shook his head. "I get the distinct impression she's playing with us. Kind of like a cat toying with a mouse."

Anne found herself feeling uneasy. Katie had warned her that Kelsey only thought about number one and had even gone so far as to nickname her the Wicked Witch, although she had retracted that appellation soon after. Now Alex was expressing reservations.

"Maybe I'm not being entirely fair," Alex allowed. "She has been through a lot recently."

"Big time," Anne said. "She and Michael were very close, and now she's learning that he kept huge aspects of his past hidden from her. Not only that, he might have been murdered by people she herself worked with. That would be enough to freak anyone out. But here's the thing, we can always back off from dealing with her if she doesn't have anything useful to add."

"I suppose," he said, noncommittally, as the elevator came to a smooth stop. "I'll bring doughnuts to help sweeten the atmosphere."

Anne gave him a thumbs up and exited the elevator, but continued mulling the discussion over in her mind as she made her way across the trading floor. What was it with those two? Alex was polite in his interactions with Kelsey, but also reserved, keeping a distance so large it would take light years to span. And it seemed like Kelsey could barely tolerate Alex's presence. Anne wished the three of them could just work together. Peacefully.

* * *

It wasn't until she was almost upon them that she became aware of Carter and Elise, huddled in what appeared to be a serious conversation in the corner near the salesmen. The Ice Princess looked like a vulture, dressed entirely in black, her long sleeves waving as she gestured in multiple directions. They stopped talking as she neared them, but not before Anne heard the words "get that bitch fired." She took a sharp left and walked over to Jennifer's cubicle to find out who they were talking about.

"Me," Jennifer said flatly.

"You? Why?"

"She's all bent out of shape because her boyfriend called while the secretaries were playing hooky this morning."

Anne shot her a look of disbelief. "You didn't take a message?"

"No." Jennifer sounded exasperated. "I transferred the call into the conference room where she and Donna were working."

"What's wrong with that?" Anne waited to hear more.

"They didn't bother to answer the phone." Jennifer blinked with feigned innocence. "I guess it just rang and rang and rang...."

Anne suppressed a chuckle. "That's not your fault."

"There's more." Jennifer sighed. "When her boyfriend finally reached her, he was totally pissed off. Next thing I know, she's yelling at me. Says I should've walked over to the conference room and found her when he called."

"Give me a break," Anne said, flashing annoyance. A mediocre analyst at best, Elise was frequently out of the office with random crises and always found a way to make things difficult for everyone else. And yet this drama queen had somehow survived the most recent restructuring. The only thing Anne could figure was that she had dirt on someone high up. "That's ridiculous."

"Exactly!" Jennifer crossed her arms. "It's way on the other side. I told her I'm not her personal secretary and walked away."

"Good for you."

"That's what I thought," Jennifer said, looking dismal, "but then she followed me over to the secretaries' desks and started wagging her finger in my face, calling me a low-life."

As if that wasn't the pot calling the kettle black. "You need to just ignore her."

"I wish I had."

Anne looked at Jennifer, unsure what she meant.

"I thought she was going to poke my eyes out, so I pushed her claw a safe distance away…And then I told her where to stick it."

Anne laughed. "Too bad I missed it. When did this happen?"

"Just after you went up to Michael's office. But that's not the worst of it. Now she's telling everybody that she's going to report me to Personnel for hitting her."

"Seriously?" Anne started to laugh.

"Seriously." Jennifer bit her fingernail nervously.

"She's such a spaz. I can't believe we have to put up with her ridiculousness."

"Fortunately, several people happened to witness the whole thing, so she doesn't have a leg to stand on. But still, can you believe it?!"

Anne didn't think anybody who mattered would believe that Jennifer had done anything wrong. Moreover, she was a good analyst, and the traders knew it. They were generally willing to overlook quite a bit at Spencer Brothers in the interest of making a profit.

"Elise won't get anywhere with a formal complaint about this little spat," Anne said firmly. "It's such small potatoes compared to everything else going on around here."

"Anne!" one of the secretaries called from the far side of the cubicles. "You've got a call on line one and two others holding."

"I better get back to the grindstone," she said dismally. "Try not to worry about this. Really. She's not worth it."

12

Midday Call

Tuesday, One Week After the Meeting

"I think we should reconstruct the sequence of events," Anne said after reconvening with Kelsey and Alex in Michael's office the following morning. "When people arrived…who he spent time alone with." She took a bite of her doughnut and nodded at Alex. "These are great."

"Glad you approve." He looked at Kelsey and pointed at the lone one remaining. "Aren't you going to have it?"

"Too many calories," Kelsey said dismissively and pulled out a cigarette instead.

Anne glanced down at hers, thinking about those five pounds she kept meaning to lose, then shrugged and took another bite.

Alex motioned toward the door. "You actually have a pretty good view of Michael's office from yours."

"I did," Kelsey corrected him.

"Right," Alex said evenly, his face inscrutable. "Why don't you begin by telling us what you saw that morning, and we'll fill in where we can." He leaned back and took a sip of his coffee.

"There's not much to tell. I hardly—" She stopped at the sound of the door opening behind her.

"Sorry to intrude." It was Betty with a man in overalls trailing behind. "We'll just be a minute."

"Take your time." Kelsey leaned back and took a drag on her cigarette.

Betty pointed to the wall where the antique file cabinet stood. "The marble table should go here and…" She looked at the floor-to-ceiling windows. "He wants the blinds replaced with the same type that Daniel has. Exact same style and color."

The man began scribbling furiously.

"And don't forget the carpet. Russell is adamant about it."

He pulled out a measuring tape and began confirming dimensions.

Russell? Anne mouthed to Kelsey.

Kelsey shrugged while mouthing back *He won the coin toss.*

When they had finally finished, Kelsey's eyes strayed to the row of windows overlooking the Hudson River. "This office has a breathtaking view. There was an all-out war over who would get it next."

"And it sounds like Russell won," Alex said drily as he glanced down at his watch. "So, on the morning that Michael died…"

Kelsey nodded absently. "It was clear and sunny. However, I don't think the sun had even risen when Michael got in. He was already here before I arrived at 7 am. And he seemed agitated. Definitely not his normal self." She looked at Anne. "That's what makes me think it really was suicide."

"But the date on the floppy—"

"I don't know how to explain that." Kelsey tapped her lighter on the desk, "—but I'm guessing there's a simple explanation." She lit her cigarette before continuing. "Walter showed up first, around 7:45, and the two of them were alone in here for a good fifteen minutes. When Marvin appeared, they all headed over to the conference room. Michael returned and—" She looked at Alex. "You came by. Around 8:10?"

"That sounds right," Alex said, caught in the middle of a doughnut bite.

"What?" Anne looked over at him, surprised. "I didn't realize the two of you met beforehand."

He shrugged nonchalantly. "It had nothing to do with the bonds. I had a quick question related to a charity we both support." He glanced at Kelsey.

"Supported."

She took a long drag on her cigarette and then made a series of smoke rings that drifted toward him. "David arrived a few minutes after that."

"Right." Alex leaned away from the incoming smoke. "I left him with Michael. The two of them joined the rest of us in the conference room about five minutes later."

"I know I showed up at 8:30 on the dot," Anne said. "After the commute from hell."

"How could we forget that?" Alex laughed. "I was beginning to wonder whether you were ever going to make it."

"Me too!" She saw a momentary look of confusion on Kelsey's face and then explained, "First, the ferry broke down, and then I got stuck in the elevator."

"Glad I live in the city," Kelsey said with what almost looked like a sneer. "There's a reason they call New Jersey the armpit of New York. Remember that trash barge that was floating around the Hudson last year?" She took another drag of her cigarette.

Anne felt a flash of anger at Kelsey's haughty attitude. Her Hoboken condo was enormous by New York City standards and very nicely equipped, although she did sometimes wonder whether the additional space she got by living across the river was worth the hassle of her daily commute.

"That trash came from New York City, as I recall," Alex's voice pierced her thoughts. "And didn't a bunch of hospital waste just wash up on Staten Island? It seems to me—"

Kelsey put up her hand. "Forget it. I shouldn't have said anything." She looked at Anne and softened her tone. "I'm sure your place is nice. Michael lived in New Jersey as well, and his house was gorgeous."

Anne wondered how she knew. Was it because she had met him there for a tryst while his wife was away? Or had it been something innocent, like a party, where everyone in the office had been invited? Regardless, she was not about to ask.

"I'm biased," Kelsey continued, "because I love living in the city. It's vibrant and alive. Sometimes it seems like it never sleeps. And you never have to worry about being late for work."

Anne gave a conciliatory smile, hoping Kelsey would move on.

"The bottom line is that Anne arrived, and we began our meeting," Alex said with a weary sigh. "Michael made introductions, and I reviewed the structure of the bonds. At some point, Walter got his knickers in a twist—"

Kelsey cocked her head to the side. "That had to have been around 9:00 because I remember seeing Walter stomp down the hall with Michael immediately after my teleconference ended. Does that sound about right?"

Anne and Alex looked at each other and nodded.

Kelsey laughed harshly. "His blood pressure must have risen about a hundred points, and I have to say even Michael looked a little ruffled—and he was generally impervious to everything. When they got in here, Walter exploded."

Anne looked around, imagining the scene. Walter furious. Michael doing what? Yelling back? Or perhaps sinking into resignation, getting ready to ingest the pills? Unless he had already taken them. "Where were Marvin and David?"

"Hovering around the door like starving rats, waiting to be let in."

"Could you hear what they were arguing about?" Alex asked.

"No," she stared straight back at him, a dour expression on her face, "These glass walls block sound surprisingly well." She took a quick puff and expelled the smoke in his direction.

Alex coughed and moved his chair back a foot.

"Walter was gesturing wildly, his face beet red. He looked like he was seconds away from a stroke. Then Michael called me on his speaker-phone." She sighed and looked at Anne. "He always did things like that whenever he had people in his office. To look impressive and powerful. You know what I mean?"

Anne gave a quick nod, hoping it would be sufficient to keep Kelsey from getting derailed onto a tangent about Michael's condescending tendencies. She wanted to stay focused on the events of the morning.

"Yeah," Kelsey nodded back. "I figured you'd understand. Anyway, he asked me to get a copy of some financials that had nothing to do with the

Pandora Deals." She clenched her fist. "It was so annoying. I have work to do as well." She sighed. "But he was my boss...."

Anne gave a sympathetic nod.

"When I returned a few minutes later, Marvin and the bond lawyer had joined them. Everyone was arguing. I dropped the spreadsheet off, and Michael asked me to let you guys know he would be delayed a few minutes."

"That gave you and me a chance to meet." Anne smiled.

"Yes," Kelsey paused. "In hindsight, that was the highlight of my day." She took another drag of her cigarette. "As soon as I left, somebody must have said something to set David off because the next thing I knew, he was storming down the hall."

Anne thought back to that moment and remembered him returning to the conference room, tight-lipped, obviously angry.

"I followed him in, and then while you and I were talking, Walter appeared, looking none too happy with Marvin right behind him."

"Right." Alex rolled his eyes. "Walter kept twiddling that damned gold pen of his. It drove me up the wall."

"What happened after you left us?" Anne asked.

"I don't know." The smoke from Kelsey's cigarette wafted in a thin line toward the ceiling. "Michael closed his office drapes, which was unusual. I'd never seen him do that. When I asked Betty about it, she said he didn't want to be disturbed while he made a phone call."

Alex looked at her quizzically. "And that was all? Until he was found?"

"As far as I know." Kelsey shrugged. "I went down the hall to meet with one of my colleagues on a deal we're planning to bring to market next week." She sighed. "We still have a ton of work on it remaining."

Anne shook her head. "You really ought to take a break..."

Kelsey gave a weak smile in return. "At some point, we started to hear a lot of commotion. By the time we figured out what was going on, somebody had already called for an ambulance. Betty handed me the suicide note and then just collapsed in a heap on the floor. She was a mess."

"That is so sad," Anne murmured.

"I know," Kelsey said with a strange look. "I keep thinking about what it must have been like to walk in there and find him. Especially since—well…" her voice trailed off as she snubbed out her cigarette.

"It had to have been devastating," Alex said brittlely.

"I'm sure," Kelsey replied, fixing her green eyes on him. "It was a shocking sight. When I looked past all the people, I could see Michael slumped in his chair. He looked gray with his hair plastered to his head, as if he'd just come out of the shower. It was obviously him, but at the same time, so unlike him. I mean, this was a man who was terribly concerned about appearances, and yet there he was, limp and pale, for all the world to see. Had he known, he would have been so upset…but of course, he didn't…"

Anne shifted in her seat and felt a small shiver go down her spine, glad she hadn't seen the body.

"For some reason, it suddenly dawned on me to go down to the conference room, so you wouldn't be left waiting there without an explanation." Kelsey shook her head. "Funny, the things that occur to you in the midst of a crisis."

Anne was struck by the dichotomy in the way Kelsey and Betty had handled the traumatic event: one collapsing in shock and the other rising up to take charge. Both had been very close to him, perhaps even in love. It said something about their very different personalities.

"So Marvin was the last one to meet with him," Alex began slowly, as if he was thinking out loud.

Kelsey shook her head. "I'm not convinced—"

"I'm just trying to summarize what we know at this point," Alex said sharply.

"Fine," Kelsey said dully, lifting both hands in surrender. "I just don't want us to get ahead of ourselves."

"Right." He gave her a cursory nod. "I don't think any of us wants that."

Anne looked back and forth at the two of them, once again wondering why they reacted so negatively to one another. Had they worked together in the past at some point, perhaps still carrying some residual baggage from that encounter?

"What we do know is that all three were alone with Michael at separate times." Alex ran his fingers through his sandy brown hair. "Really, any of them could have done it."

"I guess." Kelsey's face was oddly pinched, and her voice cracked slightly. "I find it hard to believe he was murdered. Maybe he just couldn't face being caught. Given his background and all."

"You've got to admit," Anne said. "If it was murder, it took nerve to pull off. I mean, the guilty party had to bring in a diskette with a suicide note already written, then dump the digoxin into—well—presumably his coffee, then boot up the PC, print out the suicide note, place it in an obvious place on his desk, turn off the PC, and then slip the floppy into his diskette holder." Anne shook her head in disbelief. "It seems like an extraordinary number of things to do while pulling off a murder that's staged to look like a suicide."

Alex nodded. "And incredibly risky."

Kelsey shook her head again. "It would be a miracle to pull something like that off successfully. It's much more likely that he was thinking about killing himself for a while and just happened to write the note a few days before he got around to doing it. The man was always planning his next move, months in advance. In fact, the more I think about it, four days is really nothing."

"Except," Alex chided her, "he was happily sailing off the coast of California when the note was written. So, the four days are, in fact, quite telling."

Kelsey's nostrils flared, and she crossed her arms firmly. "Maybe the date is somehow wrong."

"How?" Alex looked at her skeptically, despite the way she was obviously bristling at his tone. "How could it be wrong? When a person edits a file, the computer stores the date and time. It's legally admissible evidence for when a document was written, like a will, for example. Are you trying to suggest the courts are all wrong?"

"I don't know," she stammered, "I'm just saying..."

"The question is how the killer managed to do everything that morning."

"Unless—" Anne paused as she mentally scrolled through various alternatives, "—unless he didn't." She looked over at Alex, a small smile creeping onto her face, feeling the same sense of satisfaction that comes with suddenly discovering a puzzle piece that properly fits a difficult spot. "What if he'd already printed the note out earlier?"

"Earlier..." Alex said slowly, running his fingers through his hair. "Then all he'd have to do was place it on Michael's desk after administering the drug."

"Exactly," Anne said, feeling the pieces shift into place. "There'd be no nonsense of sitting at the desk, turning on the PC, and printing out the note. Activities that seem so likely to attract attention. And take time."

"And it would take just a second to drop the floppy into the holder to make it appear as if it were one of Michael's diskettes," Alex added.

Anne nodded.

"All he'd have to do is empty the pill bottle into the cup," Kelsey said with a tight expression on her face.

"That makes a lot more sense," Alex said, looking grim.

"The question is," Anne looked back and forth at the two of them, "which one of them hated him enough to do it."

* * *

"Has Carter been by yet?" Donna asked with a mischievous smile. She was wearing yellow eyeshadow, presumably to match her yellow jacket.

"No—but I just got back." Anne looked down at her watch and saw it was already eleven. The meeting with Alex and Kelsey had taken longer than expected.

"He's afraid William's been eavesdropping on our conversations," she cackled. "That he's installed some sort of listening devices in our phones."

"Seriously?" Anne looked warily at the mountain of messages that had accumulated and wondered how long this conversation was going to last.

Donna nodded, her smile so wide it squeezed her eyes shut. "He's absolutely convinced of it."

Anne sighed. As if any of their conversations were worth listening to.

"Not only that," Donna rasped with an accompanying laugh that sounded like she was almost choking, "he says he caught William snooping around our desks a few weeks ago. For what purpose, I can only imagine..."

Perhaps he needed a pen? Or a pad of paper?

"Now he's launching a petition to remove William from office."

Anne felt her jaw drop. "He's trying to get William fired?"

"No. Just demoted." Donna broke into a broad laugh. "Carter thinks numero uno should be in charge."

Anne drew a sharp breath. "Carter-the-Carper? Manager of the department?"

"It'll never happen. He's—"

A dark, gothic presence glided in next to Donna and asked, "Are you ready to go?" Just as quickly as she had appeared, Elise disappeared from Anne's view.

"I'll be right there," Donna called out.

"We can talk later," Anne said.

"That's actually what I came by to tell you. We're seeing the new hairstylist on Pearl Street during our lunch break." Donna studied her hand for a second. "I'm thinking about getting my nails done at the same time. We may be a while."

They hadn't been gone more than two minutes before a trader came by in search of a housing analyst. When the secretary informed him that they had both just left and would be gone for several hours, he became angry. Next thing Anne knew, he was squirming outside her cubicle, insisting she fill in. She wondered if this was how the rest of the week was going to play out while William was gone.

She pulled the files grudgingly, annoyed that the two women had skipped out of the office so cavalierly, and began to study the financial reports.

"Knock, Knock," The Carp's voice trumpeted out. He stood near the entrance to her cubicle, fidgeting awkwardly with his pink and green polka dot tie.

She groaned inwardly, wondering what he wanted.

"I'm concerned that morale is extremely low," he said, followed by a sneeze. "Allergies," he added, waving his hand dismissively. "I don't have a cold." His face took on a concerned expression. "The secretaries are on the verge of quitting."

"I wasn't aware," Anne said carefully, trying not to encourage him.

"Oh yeah. They've had it with William. He's rude and condescending." Carter paused and loudly blew his nose. "And the guy's sneaky. I'm worried he might've bugged our phones." He proceeded to pick up her handset and unscrew the ear and mouthpieces to check. "Yours look clear right now, but you should monitor them. I've spoken with Peter Eckert regarding this problem."

"About our phones?"

"No, that William isn't working out. We need a new manager." He paused and appeared to be studying her reaction. "Someone with more experience. Someone we actually respect. Don't you agree?"

There was an awkward pause as she considered how to answer him smoothly and deftly, without ruffling any feathers. "We definitely need a manager we respect," she said, unsure whether he recognized her response as non-committal. "I agree with you on that."

"I knew we could count on you," he said through his handkerchief and disappeared in the direction of his cubicle.

Count on her for what? She had no interest in throwing William under the bus. It was obvious he had the full support of management. And if that wasn't enough, the rumors of impending layoffs meant it was an especially bad time to make a fuss.

Almost immediately, her phone rang.

"Let it go," a muffled voice ordered in a low growl.

"That's got to be like the worst impersonation of William *ever*," she said, laughing.

"Let it go, or you'll be sorry," the voice repeated with a small cough and then hung up the phone.

She sprang over to Carter's cubicle. "Very funny. But I think you need more practice."

"What are you talking about?" he sniffed.

"Your imitation of William," she replied, wondering why he was being such a space cadet. "By the way, when you tap someone's phone, you sit there silently. You don't engage in conversation."

138

He looked at her with a quizzical expression.

She began to wonder. "That was you just now, calling me. Wasn't it?"

"No," he said, sneezing heavily into his hand.

As she stepped back to avoid the droplets, the realization washed over her. "It must have been one of the traders."

"They think it's funny that William is listening in on our conversations?" he asked incredulously.

Of course they did. The accusation was absurd. And politically dangerous. Even worse, he did not seem to realize how foolish he had been to assert it in the first place. "You know how they like to play practical jokes."

He looked crestfallen, like a student who had just learned that he had failed his final exam. "They wouldn't be laughing if they discovered their boss was eavesdropping on them."

"I don't think the secretaries are going to pick that up," Anne said, with a nod toward his ringing phone and headed back to the safety of her cubicle.

She finished her analysis and headed out to the trading floor to discuss her findings. Three hours and five inquiries later, Donna and Elise had still not returned. Anne was more than a little annoyed. With all of her energies being diverted to backing them up, in addition to answering the miscellaneous questions from salesmen and traders that she normally handled, she had no time left to study the Pandora deals. *When the cat's away, the mice will play,* she told herself, *but those little rodents may soon find themselves being eaten.*

Elise and Donna finally reappeared around 3:00 pm. With uneven bangs and layers that poofed the hair out in random places, they looked like they had gone to a blind barber. *Serves them right for taking so long,* she thought smugly to herself.

13

The Chinese Wall

Wednesday, One Week After the Meeting

"Y ou're wanted down there." The secretary pointed. "Now!"

Anne slipped her feet into her pumps and took a last sip of her morning tea before heading to Peter Eckert's office. As she walked across the trading floor, she straightened her blouse and attempted to get her hair in place, hoping she looked presentable.

"Before Alex arrives, I want to have a quick word with you," Peter said by way of greeting. "Several of your colleagues have expressed concern about William's management skills."

She carefully sat down, trying to maintain a neutral expression.

"I hear that everyone in the research group is on the verge of quitting."

She blinked, unsure how to respond. "That's a bit of an exaggeration." She glanced over at Nick Angelini standing quietly by the window, watching the salesmen and traders get started on their day.

Peter cleared his throat before continuing. "I was hoping you'd provide me with your candid appraisal of William's performance."

Nick turned and anchored his attention on her.

"Anything you say will stay within these four walls." Peter looked at her expectantly.

Anne was certain that neither this nor any other conversations with anyone else in her research group would remain confidential. The moment William returned from vacation, he'd be told exactly what sort of stunt The Carp had pulled in his absence.

"I haven't had any problems with him so far." She met his gaze.

"What about everyone else?"

She created a mental lineup of the research analysts in her group. Both Donna and Elise detested him, convinced he was self-serving and opportunistic. Carter thought him sneaky and had taken to calling him Wily Will behind his back, but he held an obvious grudge, having been passed over for the position. Jennifer held a more nuanced view. She maintained that William lacked empathy and was occasionally obnoxious, but was technically capable and certain to be an improvement over the previous guy. For the most part, Anne sat in Jennifer's camp.

"Some are happier with him than others," she said.

The room fell silent for a moment.

"Why do you think that is?" Peter asked, resting his chin on his hands but keeping his eyes focused intently on her.

She tried to choose her words carefully. "William's a very private individual, and his personal style is somewhat aloof. That may not resonate well with some people."

"So, they disliked him before he was put in the position?"

She nodded. "He wasn't everybody's first choice."

The normally stern and humorless trader cracked a smile.

"Hmmm," Peter said, giving no hint of how he might use this information. Anne heard the door open behind her.

"Alex!" Peter waved him in. "Perfect timing. We were just wrapping up."

He nodded and quickly slipped into the remaining chair, looking cheerful and relaxed. Was he sporting a new tie? Anne stole a quick sideways glance to confirm her suspicions. The blue and lavender colors were definitely brighter (and more stylish) than what she had seen him wear previously. Next to Mr. Chipper, she felt dowdy and boring, like something the cat had dragged in.

"How's work progressing on the Pandora bonds?" she heard Peter Eckert say, and snapped back to attention.

There was a pause as Anne and Alex looked at each other and tried to figure out which one of them would respond.

"We've spent the last week combing through everything in Michael's files," Anne finally replied. "A total of 17 appear to be problematic. Bottom line, the deals are structured exactly as expected."

"Anything else?"

She shifted in her seat. "We found his suicide note on a floppy disk."

"William mentioned that to me before he left."

"How long is he gone?" Nick's hawkish stare was focused on the trading floor again.

"Till the end of the week," Peter said, casting a quick glance in the same direction. "Is everything okay out there?"

Nick swiveled back to face them and gave a slight nod.

"Did he tell you it was written four days before Michael actually died?" When he did not reply, she continued, "I think that's a little strange."

Peter shrugged, his face impassive. "People do odd things when they decide to kill themselves."

"I've also learned that he was a juvenile delinquent who spent some time in prison for stealing a car. He changed his name when he got out and began fresh as Michael Kingston." She scrutinized Peter's face looking for a reaction.

"Hmmm." Peter didn't appear surprised, leading Anne to surmise that he had already heard about it from the same trader she had. "That would fit in with something else I wanted to discuss with you today."

She tensed.

"I think it would be a good idea to start working with our outside legal counsel. Make sure the firm is covered."

Anne raised her eyebrows, wondering what had prompted this sudden request. "Has something changed?"

Peter exchanged glances with Nick, who replied, "My friend at the SEC says Marvin Goldberg has turned State's witness."

Her eyes widened. A plea bargain.

Peter pursed his lips disapprovingly. "It's a pretty sure bet he'll try to incriminate everyone else."

Us. She looked at Alex, who sat stone-faced. Was he annoyed that they wanted him to consult with outside lawyers? It suggested they did not trust him to handle the situation.

"With our own key witness suddenly dead, we're not exactly in the best position to be defending ourselves."

Peter sounded more tired than usual, and his eyes had dark shadows beneath them. Anne wondered why he continued to work rather than step off the treadmill and enjoy what he had achieved. He had to be financially set for life, and it was obvious the stress of this job was taking a toll.

Alex leaned forward and cracked his knuckles. "So, you want us to marshal the outside troops and ready ourselves for battle?"

"The sooner, the better." Peter peered at him. "We need a clear strategy for extricating, or at least protecting, Spencer Brothers from this unfortunate situation."

Alex nodded. "I'll get on it."

"There might be a way to use Michael's criminal past to our advantage," Nick said, his mouth twisting into a smile.

"I'm certain of it," Peter replied, his eyes cold and hard. "The man was an operator. He probably kept the firm in the dark about many of his activities."

Had he? Or had management been blinded by the flashing dollar signs and ignored what they knew to be questionable business tactics? Anne tended to lean toward the latter.

Nick shrugged. "Given his background, no one will be surprised to learn that Spencer Brothers was taken in by some of his lies." There was something slightly malicious, almost diabolical, about his laugh that caused Anne to recoil inwardly.

Uncertain whether the meeting was over, she looked for a cue that it was time to get up and leave. Instead, Peter began drumming his fingers nervously on the table, looking first at Alex and then at her. "This probably goes without saying—"

She remained seated, waiting to hear whatever supposedly didn't need to be said.

"This information is strictly confidential." He clasped his hands together and rested them on his desk. "Absolutely no one is to be told about the SEC investigation, including our friends in the investment banking group. It's possible one or two of them might find themselves on the wrong side of the fence, if you catch my drift."

Anne caught her breath. He had to be referring to Kelsey. Was she more embroiled in these flaky bonds than appeared?

"Of course," Alex said with a quick nod and stood up to leave. Anne immediately followed suit.

Halfway to the door, she stopped and turned. "Michael Kingston's death. Do the police still believe it was a suicide?"

There was a long pause as he scrutinized her. Anne's heart began to thud. Had she just crossed some invisible boundary?

"One of the few things we know for sure is that Michael wasn't murdered." His voice was level, and the expression on his face flat, but his eyes were piercing. "Anne, I want you to remain fully focused on this investigation. The bonds. That's all you should be thinking about. Got it?"

"Just checking," she said quietly, feeling like a tiny ant in Peter's giant colony. Even if he knew more, would he have actually told her? *Probably not*, she thought. It had been foolish to even ask.

* * *

"We'll have to be mindful of what we say to Kelsey," Alex said as they walked back to her desk, the tiniest hint of a smile on his face.

Anne didn't share his glee at shutting Kelsey out, but understood the need to keep the SEC investigation confidential.

"Treat this like another example of the Chinese wall."

She nodded. In the securities business, they frequently had to be careful about passing information from one group to another that might lead to insider trading or some other conflict of interest. It was something that came with the job. Nonetheless, erecting an invisible barrier between them and Kelsey felt almost duplicitous. "We can still talk with her about the bond structure, though."

"Right. It's just the SEC stuff that's off-limits."

They slowed down as they reached the edge of the trading floor.

Alex turned to face her. "I'll buzz outside legal counsel as soon as I get back to my office. I daresay they'll be chuffed to get the business, although I think it's overkill myself...."

"You didn't look overly thrilled when he suggested it." Anne wondered if he would say more, but he just pursed his lips and shrugged.

"Anne?" Jennifer called out as she rounded the corner. "Oh. Sorry. I didn't mean to interrupt." She looked uncertain. "We can talk later."

"I was just leaving," Alex said, taking a step back. "Cheers."

"He's kind of cute," Jennifer observed as soon as he was gone. "And I love that British accent."

"You know I don't date people from the office." Anne stepped out of her shoes and kicked them under the desk.

"Maybe you should think about making an exception once in a while," Jennifer said, flinging her arms up in a gesture of exasperation. "Does he have a girlfriend?"

Anne smiled. "Did you have a real reason for finding me?"

"Yes," Jennifer sighed and then slumped back against the cubicle wall. "Unfortunately."

Anne looked at her, concerned.

"Donna just told me that the Ice Princess filed a formal complaint with Personnel yesterday afternoon, just before leaving work. All because she missed a phone call from that idiot she calls a boyfriend. Can you believe it?"

Anne wanted to laugh, it was so ridiculous, but seeing the distress in Jennifer's eyes, she thought better of it. "Nothing will come of her little ploy."

"I'm afraid she's going to get me fired."

"That's not going to happen." Anne's phone rang, but she ignored it, hoping one of the secretaries would pick up. "Don't expend energy worrying about this. She's making a mountain out of a molehill."

Jennifer looked morose. "But what if they don't believe me?"

"They will." And Anne couldn't believe anyone in trading would even care. If it didn't affect their bottom line, then it wouldn't make it into their periphery. She raised an eyebrow when her phone rang yet again. "Did you happen to notice if any of the secretaries were around?"

Jennifer shook her head. "It's like a morgue out there."

Anne sighed. Of course it was. And it was likely to remain that way for the rest of the day. They had been complaining about each other virtually nonstop, the insults growing daily. One had broken a fingernail (*She just sits there filing away while the phones ring off the hook. Who does she think she is? The Queen of Sheba?!*) and also tended to take long lunches (*I'm going to take an even longer one!*) Another had struggled to replace the paper in the microfiche reader, prompting comments about what an airhead she was. Both complained about the third, who had gotten in a fight with her new husband and spent hours on the phone with her sister asking for advice (*He always spends Saturday night drinking with his friends. She knew that before she married the loser!*) The tight row of desks where the secretaries sat had become a war zone. Anne took a deep breath as the phone rang yet again.

"And the Ice Princess called in sick," Jennifer added brightly.

She felt a flash of irritation. With William on vacation, they were already short-staffed as it was. And on top of the turmoil with the secretaries…Anne shook her head. "So typical."

Her phone rang a fourth time.

Jennifer shrugged. "Better see who it is."

Anne gritted her teeth and picked up the receiver.

"Ms. Scott? I work for the *Wall Street Chronicle*."

The reporter they had been warned about. She felt a jolt of adrenaline and caught her breath. How had he gotten her name? Or telephone number?

"I understand you were meeting with Michael Kingston on the day he died. Now that the SEC has begun an investigation—"

"I'm sorry. I have no comment."

Jennifer took a step into Anne's cubicle and pointed at the phone. *Reporter?* she mouthed, a wide-eyed expression on her face.

Anne nodded, gripping the receiver.

"Wait!" the reporter continued. "Can we talk off the record?"

"I don't think so."

"Anything you say will stay between you and me. I'm just trying to get a better understanding of what happened that morning."

Jennifer started waving her arms back and forth like a ground operations person guiding a plane into the jetway. Her meaning was clear. *Get off the phone! Get off the phone now!*

"If it wasn't actually suicide—" the reporter persisted.

"I'm sorry. I can't help you."

"But—"

"Good luck with your story." Anne hung up and felt her heart beating in her chest. "We need to find those damn secretaries!" She let out an exasperated sigh.

"Oh good," a deep male voice called out. "Jennifer's here as well."

Anne turned to see two traders standing at the entrance to her cubicle and groaned inwardly. When was she ever going to get caught up on everything she needed to do?

"We have a bid list that just came in."

The rest of her day was consumed with putting out one brush fire after another. When Anne finally made it home that evening, she was exhausted. Her nerves were frayed from the pressure of responding to dozens of trading inquiries, and all she could see was a mountain of work in front of her for the evening as well.

She kicked off her shoes and wandered into the kitchen to start making dinner. After opening a new can of food for Muffin and pouring herself a glass of wine, she began listening to the messages on her answering machine.

The first one began cheerily enough. "Hi. This is Bob. I want to add another item to the agenda for our condo board meeting."

She began rummaging through the refrigerator to find something edible while the recording played on, pulling out some leftover lasagna just as it ended with a small beep.

"Hi. This is Louise." the next one began. "I need to talk to you about the guy in unit four."

Anne groaned. She began reheating the pasta in the microwave while Louise complained about her neighbor leaving the lid off of the garbage can, inviting raccoons to paw through the contents and leave a giant mess. The message finished at the same time her dinner was done nuking. Beep!

The last message was delivered in a hoarse whisper. "Back off! I'm warning you! Just back off!"

The glass of wine Anne was holding slipped and shattered on her kitchen floor, startling Muffin, who jumped back in surprise. "Damn!" she exclaimed and then checked the caller ID box.

"Unavailable," it read.

"Of course," she said aloud to herself.

As she retrieved a broom and dustpan from the pantry close, she noticed her hands shaking and was surprised at how unnerved she felt. *Back off from what?* She poured a new glass of wine and debated the significance of what she had just heard.

Was the caller somehow related to the Pandora deals and Michael's death? If so, she should probably notify Peter Eckert immediately and contact the police as well. But what if it was just her neighbor on the first floor who was annoyed about the flower garden fees. He had stood up at the last meeting and complained bitterly that they were exorbitant, specifically calling her out as *The Worst President of the Condominium Association Ever*, with a strong emphasis on *Ever*. Screaming that his rights were being trampled and demanding that the association remove the lien on his condo, he had been quite menacing at the time. *Back off now*, the message had said. Perhaps this was simply Mr. Irate giving her more of the same.

She frowned and took a sip of her wine. The last thing Anne wanted to do was make a big deal about something at work that had nothing to do with work. She would look overwrought, as if she didn't belong in a professional position with serious responsibilities. Recognizing that she wasn't giving senior management much credit, she also knew they didn't deserve it. She had seen too many examples of women at Spencer Brothers being held to a different standard.

As the debate played back and forth in her mind, Anne started to lean toward the option of ignoring the call for the time being. She made a mental note to ask around to determine if other board members had received similar calls and tried to get her mind to focus on something else, anything else, except the strange message.

She wandered into the living room and flipped on the television. Nothing good was playing. She turned it off and picked up a book. Unable to concentrate, she set it down again after a few minutes. *Back off*, he had said. What was he going to do if she ignored him? Appear at her front door? And why the weird whispering? Mr. Irate had shown no fear in confronting her in person at the meeting.

Suddenly the phone rang. Her heart leapt to her throat, the shrill tone cutting across the stillness of her apartment. She hesitated before picking it up and then cautiously put the receiver to her ear. When the voice on the other end began talking without identifying himself, it took her a moment to recognize the caller as her friend, Jim.

"Are you okay?" He asked after a few seconds.

"Yes. Why?"

"You sound a little distracted."

"Oh," she paused, uncertain whether to say anymore. "I'm fine. It's been a long week."

"Are you still planning to go skiing this weekend?"

"Absolutely!"

"It's a bummer that Katie won't be able to make it."

"I know, but it means I'll win the big race for sure," Anne said with a laugh.

"I wouldn't get too cocky if I were you. Kevin quit his job in December and has been hitting the slopes nonstop ever since. He could present some formidable competition...."

As they talked, she found that the accumulated tension began to dissipate, and by the time they hung up, she had put the strange message out of her mind entirely.

14

The Weekend Beckons

A Week and a Half After the Meeting

Anne woke up Friday morning feeling relieved. With William's weeklong absence from the office almost over, the chaos would finally be coming to an end. More importantly, the weekend stretched open, inviting, and completely before her.

She struggled to get her baggage down the flight of stairs and out the doors and then faced the prospect of carrying everything a good seven blocks to the PATH tubes. Ordinarily a brisk ten-minute walk, it took over twenty minutes. As the subway car rumbled beneath the river separating New Jersey from Manhattan, people stared at her as if they had never seen a pair of skis before. She ignored them and focused her thoughts on the upcoming weekend. Friends. Fresh mountain air. No angry condo people. And no Pandora bonds. Anne took a deep breath and let it out slowly. This group ski trip had become an annual tradition, and she was very much looking forward to it.

At the office, the security people furrowed their brows and debated whether to inspect her ski bag for dangerous weapons. She smiled coquettishly, and they eventually waved her through.

"Going on holiday?"

She turned to see Alex sprinting toward the elevator. To keep the doors from closing, she waved her foot back and forth in front of them. "Skiing. In Vermont this weekend, with some old college friends."

"That should be fun." He pushed the button for his floor. "Although I prefer Colorado, where the conditions are always perfect. New England can be a little dicey."

She smiled. Compared with the powder out in the Rockies, there was no question that the typical ice and refrozen snow in the northeast could be a challenge. "I'm just glad to get away," she replied. "It's been awful with William out of town."

He smiled. "Office truants wreaking havoc down in research?"

She nodded. "Donna and Elise keep sneaking off for long lunches, and the secretaries have gone totally AWOL. Yesterday, the phones were left unmanned for hours, and it was a nightmare trying to keep up with the calls." She debated whether to mention the strange message left on her answering machine.

"William will restore order on Monday."

Anne nodded. She was actually looking forward to his return. With all of the distractions this week, she had not been able to make enough progress on the Pandora bonds. "Hey, I was wondering—"

The elevator beeped, indicating they had reached her floor.

"Have you gotten any weird phone calls?"

He laughed. "What do you mean?"

She stepped off of the elevator, banging her skis against the door. "Oh—" She suddenly felt foolish for having brought it up. "It's probably nothing." He looked at her quizzically, so she tried to quickly explain. "Someone left a message in a creepy, guttural whisper, saying to 'back off' or something along those lines."

He pushed the button to hold the door. "At home?"

"Yes," she sighed. "So, it wouldn't make sense for it to be work-related."

"Not really."

He studied her for a moment, and she found herself feeling self-conscious. *Had she overdone it on the blush?* She liked to add just a hint of color so she didn't look like death warmed over, but still keeping the overall look natural.

"Were you thinking it had something to do with the Pandora deals?"

"It crossed my mind," she admitted, brushing a strand of hair off of her face. "But I'm also President of the Condo Association and—"

"President? Seriously?"

She shuddered theatrically. "Don't ever make that mistake. It's the worst non-paying job in the world. We're in the midst of fending off a lawsuit from a guy on the first floor who doesn't think he should have to pay for the flower beds out front." She shrugged. "The call was probably from him."

"What a wanker." Alex made a face. "Avoid him at all cost."

The elevator started beeping.

"That's what I'm thinking too." She waved. "See you later."

When she got to her cubicle, she saw that again, none of the secretaries were anywhere to be found, and the phones were already ringing nonstop.

"This is ridiculous," Jennifer greeted her with a wave at the empty desks. "And Donna just told me that the Ice Princess will be late."

Anne shook her head. Thank god it was Friday.

"Is that your phone?"

Anne groaned and went to answer it. After the fifth call in a row was yet another broker inquiring about the status of a particular defaulted hospital in Philadelphia, she became exasperated. "I wrote the story up last week precisely so I could avoid these very calls," she addressed one of her cubicle walls. "If you would read what I've written, then I could work on other things."

The phone rang for the sixth time. She glared at it and debated letting it go, her hand hovering just above the receiver as she flirted with the idea. And then she relented and picked it up.

"Do you realize what Marvin has done?"

Walter's anguished voice emanated loudly through the line, along with an annoying clicking sound. More like a tapping. *His gold pen?*

"Do you have any idea at all?"

The rate of tapping increased, becoming more like a drum roll. Anne held her breath and waited for him to continue.

"He's gone to the SEC behind our backs and shot off his mouth. He plans to save his own ship by sinking ours."

There was a loud thud, and the tapping came to an abrupt halt. She guessed that Walter had thrown the pen down. Hard. Clearly, this wasn't a good day for him.

"Interesting," Anne said, trying to give a neutral response. She wondered how he had found out so quickly.

"Interesting?" he roared back. "Problematic is more like it! Can you imagine what he must be saying?"

She most certainly could, and none of it bode well for Spencer Brothers. "Well—I certainly appreciate the heads up," she said gingerly, wondering what he actually wanted.

"I should think so," he sniffed.

"And you're calling because—" she left the rest of the sentence dangling.

"—Because we have to work together on this. Get our stories straight. My firm isn't about to take the rap on this one, and I assume yours isn't either."

"Which stories?"

"The entire story! What's with you people?"

Presumably, he was referring to the bonds and the substantial fees they had all collected, but what if there was more that was yet to be uncovered, such as bribes or illegal payoffs. "To be honest," she said, "we're still trying to understand the extent of our involvement in these deals."

"Honest, my foot," Walter's voice screamed out. "You know damn well that Michael was up to his eyeballs in these things. Your firm underwrote the bonds and, for all intents and purposes, is responsible for bringing them to market. Now that Marvin is singing to the SEC, it's only a matter of time before we're all contacted. I thought perhaps we could work together to ensure the SEC doesn't find out any more than it has to. Obviously, you fail to see the importance of this matter!" He hung up without saying goodbye.

"You have a nice day, too," she said to the dead telephone line.

"I wonder how he found out," Alex said when she reported the conversation a few minutes later.

"Most likely the same big mouth who tipped Nick off," Anne said derisively.

"So much for quiet investigations. This business is incredible."

"Quite. I'll give our outside legal counsel a ring and see what they advise."

As she put the phone down, she heard a light sneeze. She whirled around in her chair to see Carter leaning against her cubicle wall with that false-friendly look she had come to recognize. *Will this day never end?* She took a deep breath and braced herself.

"What have you been up to lately?" he squeaked. "You've been virtually incommunicado for weeks." He blew his nose again, more loudly.

She shrugged. "Trading inquiries and everything else we do. You know how it is."

"What about those bonds you were working on? The ones that Michael Kingston—"

"I'm still working on them." She glanced at her watch, wondering how long it would take for him to get to the point.

"Elise was asking."

Anne furrowed her brow. *Why would the Ice Princess care?* The good thing was it meant she was actually in the office.

"She seems to think that you're spending an awful lot of time on them. That it's unfair to the rest of us."

And why ask Carter, of all people? Wouldn't the Puff Queen make more sense?

"And William just made things worse when he told her the Pandora Bonds were none of her business. She was furious after that. He has the worst interpersonal skills."

Anne looked at him, flabbergasted. "When did she—"

"Just before he left on vacation. Which reminds me. He gets back on Monday. Elise is hoping they'll fire him on the spot. But I doubt that will happen."

Anne agreed with him there.

"He's a perfectly good bond analyst, so my recommendation is to keep him." His eyes darted back and forth. "I mean, that's what I would say if I were asked."

As if Carter would ever have any say in the matter.

"Just between you and me," he leaned toward her and lowered his voice, "I think there will be some big changes coming to our group. Very soon."

"Wow," she said, keeping her voice and demeanor even.

"He's just not right for the manager job." Carter put on a sad face. "It'll be hard for him at first, but I think he'll eventually appreciate the advantages of letting someone else take the reins. Once he sees someone with real talent in charge."

Anne was not sure she could stand to listen to the self-aggrandizing twerp list the particular strengths and skills he had that would so obviously make him better suited for the position. "Thanks for the update." She turned to look at the papers on her desk, hoping he would get the message that it was time to leave.

"If you ever have any ideas about how things should be run around here, I'm all ears."

Perhaps a little less backbiting? She glanced briefly at him. "Okay."

"You know." He rearranged his features into a small smile and began acting like a politician addressing a crowd. "I try not to make a big deal about this, but Peter Eckert maintains an open door with me. He trusts my judgment...because of my experience...So really, if you have any concerns..."

This time she kept her eyes aimed down at her desk. "Thanks."

At 4:30 pm, she practically ran out of the office. With just two hours standing between her and her flight, she wasn't about to risk a horrible traffic jam in the tunnel or some other random natural disaster. She spotted one of her friends at the Eastern Airlines departure gate and waved, firmly resolving to put everything about her job out of her mind until after the weekend.

"Hey," he greeted her. "Did you know that investment banker who killed himself?"

She looked at him and sighed.

15

Let's Make a Deal

Sunday, Two Weeks After the Meeting

After an action-packed weekend of skiing in the blustery cold, Anne returned home on Sunday evening. She immediately headed over to her neighbor's place to pick up Muffin.

"She missed you," he said as the dog ran over to greet her, jumping up excitedly with a big sloppy kiss.

"Thanks so much for watching her," Anne replied, stroking Muffin's soft, warm fur. "Any word from our friend in unit one?"

"Yes. As a matter of fact, I bumped into him on Saturday. He seems to have cooled down."

"That's good to hear." She leaned down to attach the leash.

"He even apologized for yelling at our last meeting. Said his girlfriend had just dumped him...."

Anne stood back up, ready to go. "What about the lawsuit?"

"I got the impression he doesn't plan to go forward with it."

"Well, that's a relief." Her mind jumped to the weird message. Had the guy in unit one left it on her answering machine while he was still angry? Or did this mean the call had come from someone else? "By the way," she tried to sound casual, "have you gotten any odd phone calls recently?"

"No." Anne's neighbor looked at her, puzzled. "Why?"

"Just wondering," she shrugged. "Probably a wrong number. Thanks again for taking care of Muffin."

The following morning, Anne bumped into two more of her neighbors who had supported the condo plant fees, and they gave her the same response—none had received strange phone calls either. As she stood on the upper deck of the ferry, watching the Manhattan skyscrapers come into view, she began to consider the strong possibility that her irate neighbor had no connection to the strange message. She disembarked and headed toward her building feeling vaguely disconcerted. If the call was related to the Pandora bonds, why hadn't Alex received one as well?

"How was your weekend?" A cheerful voice sang out. She turned to see Jennifer on the escalator nearby.

"The conditions were great, and I got to catch up with some of my classmates from college. I can't believe it's been almost ten years since we graduated. How about yours?"

"I got engaged!" She thrust her hand toward Anne. "Isn't it beautiful?"

Her diamond looked like a headlamp, ready to illuminate everything in sight.

"Wow!" Anne said as they stepped off and began walking toward the elevators. "Is that your grandmother's ring?"

"No," Jennifer laughed. "Mel worked with a jeweler and had it custom-made."

"It's lovely."

The elevator doors opened, and the throng of people waiting to enter began to flow in and fill the space.

"Have you set a date?" Anne whispered once they were settled inside.

"Not yet, but we're thinking about doing it in the fall at a vineyard in California."

There was a loud buzz as the doors tried to close, and someone's briefcase or jacket stuck out too far, tripping the sensor. The crowd shifted toward the back to make room and waited for the doors to close again.

"That will be great."

"I was hoping you'd be one of my bridesmaids."

"I'd love that," Anne said, secretly wondering how to ensure that the dress would be more flattering than the one she had worn for the last wedding she was in.

The elevator continued its slow rise until it finally reached their floor with a bump and flash of lights. Breathing a sigh of relief, she tightened the grip on her bag and prepared to exit. The doors opened, and she saw that the base of the carriage was at least a foot above the floor.

"Wait a second, and the elevator will move down," someone said authoritatively, and indeed, it slowly drifted into place.

"Remind me to take the stairs next time," Jennifer said after they were safely off.

"You and me both," Anne said, shaking her head.

They made their way to the research cubicles and found William looking relaxed and tan after his vacation in the Bahamas.

"Good morning," he smiled. "I trust things went well last week?"

"It was interesting," Anne replied, thinking it best to give him some time to settle back in before venting her frustration about the chaos that had ensued in his absence.

"That's one way of putting it," Jennifer said poker-faced.

He looked at them quizzically. "Should I—"

"William?" one of the secretaries called out.

Within minutes of his arrival, he was being summoned to the corner office. Anne exchanged glances with Jennifer and then headed to her cubicle and began untying her sneakers.

"What do you think is happening?"

She paused and looked up. Donna was walking into her cubicle with a prankish smile. Purple glitter was splattered all over her eyelids, and her eyes were heavily rimmed in aqua.

"The Carp's strutting around the trading floor like he owns the place."

Anne shook her head. The poor guy actually believed he was in the running for the manager position. "He doesn't have a clue."

"The traders are taking bets right now. Nobody's willing to put a dime on

Carter."

Donna's maniacal cackle could probably be heard halfway across the floor. It was going to be a free-for-all.

"And not only that—" Donna snickered.

"Have you seen my ring?" Jennifer's outstretched arm popped into view.

The engagement. The battle for control of the research group. General trading floor chaos. Anne could tell it was going to be one of those days. She would be lucky if she managed to make any progress at all on the Pandora bonds.

"Two carats?"

As the secretaries came over to admire Jennifer's rock, Anne kicked off her sneakers and pulled her pumps out of the drawer. Her phone rang, and she turned to answer it.

"I recommend you sell it immediately," she said after learning which bond the broker was asking about. "It could default any time."

"But my client will take a twenty percent loss."

"His losses will be larger if he waits."

"Are you absolutely certain?"

"I spoke with the financial officer just last week because someone else was asking about this very same bond. There's no question the place is on the verge of collapse. If it were my money, I'd bail now."

She hung up and gathered the files that were sitting on her desk. Faced with the prospect of having one of the secretaries slowly and grudgingly file them away, Anne decided to head over to the cabinets and do the job quickly herself. She stood up after putting the last set of financials in place and spotted William crossing the trading floor, his mouth drawn and his muscles tight.

"What a thing to return to," Jennifer said quietly, drawing up by her side. "It's got to be kind of depressing to discover that one of your people has been plotting for your demotion, or worse, during your vacation."

He headed straight for Carter, who was joking with one of the traders, and tapped him on the shoulder. Carter turned, looking surprised, and followed William into his office.

"Doesn't look good," Jennifer said. "I bet Peter Eckert told him everything. Even that stupid eavesdropping stuff."

"I'm sure," Anne replied, suddenly reminded of Carter's paranoia and the odd phone call she had received after he went through his ridiculous song and dance about their phones being bugged. At the time, she had assumed the person on the line was Carter or one of the traders pulling a prank, pretending to be William listening in on their conversations. *Let it go*, the mystery caller had said, which suddenly seemed eerily similar to the *Back off* message left on her answering machine at home.

"Anne?" a trader called out, interrupting her train of thought. "Could you take a quick look at this bond for me? I have twenty minutes to make a decision."

She ran over to the coffee bar, grabbed a cup of tea, and then set to work gathering the necessary information.

When Carter finally emerged from William's office, he looked like he had been put through the wringer. His tie was loosened, his hair was oddly disheveled, and his face was a ghastly shade of white. There was no question in Anne's mind as to whose side management had thrown their weight. She looked down and started scribbling some notes in order to avoid making eye contact as he shuffled past her cubicle. She did not want to get drawn into a conversation about what had transpired and how unfair it all was.

She paused in her writing and noticed that his feet had stopped moving. A sense of dread began to envelop her.

"Anne?"

Just then, the phone on her desk rang, and she felt a flood of relief. There was no way Carter could corner her if she was tied up in a telephone conversation.

"Sorry. I've got to take this," she said and picked up the receiver. "Hello?"

She heard David Singer's voice on the line and was momentarily taken aback. First Walter and now David. These guys were scurrying around like rats trying to flee a sinking ship. What were they so scared of?

"I'm concerned about Marvin's disclosures to the SEC," he began. "My firm provided the legal opinion, and I'm afraid my job could be on the line."

He sounded distraught, and she found herself feeling sorry for him. "I'm not sure how I can help."

"Well, I think you should be aware that Michael was involved in other deals for which we provided legal opinions as well. They're structured very differently from the Pandora bonds, but are also chock full of problems. Perhaps, if we were to work together, I could help your firm save some major headaches down the road."

"And in return?" Anne asked, feeling like a contestant trying to win cash and prizes on a game show.

"I would expect you to let me know what you plan to say to the SEC and what you've heard Marvin has told them."

"Can you hold for a second?"

When she returned to the phone, she told him she was heading up to Alex's office and that they would call him back in a couple of minutes. She slipped her feet into her pumps and ran to the elevator.

"Before we even consider striking any sort of agreement, we need to know a bit more about these *other* deals," Alex said firmly once they had put David Singer on speakerphone, resuming the conversation.

"Fair enough," David replied. "I'm talking about a set of bond issues, put together in Arkansas, in which a group of individuals created various separate financial institutions that were identified as banks on the official statements. These so-called banks are on the brink of financial ruin, and the projects that were financed with these bonds are on rocky ground as well."

"So, we're talking sham banks and *what* kinds of projects?" Anne asked.

"Hotels." He laughed harshly. "In the middle of cornfields."

"Underwritten by—"

"Your firm."

"Bloody hell." Alex rolled his eyes. "You're telling us that the projects will likely fail and that the banks providing the guarantee on the bonds will be unable to protect the bondholders."

"You got it." David Singer's voice crackled as the speakerphone cut in and out throughout his discourse. "And just to top things off, these bonds were sold by *your* firm to retail investors…little old ladies living on fixed incomes…hardworking people trying to save for retirement…ordinary people like your parents and mine."

His tone was disparaging, accusatory even, suggesting their firm was somehow more to blame than he was.

"If I were to become sufficiently morally outraged, I could take this information to the press, which your firm might find rather embarrassing. But I could be persuaded from doing so if I felt you were going to be friendly toward me in these *other* proceedings." He paused briefly. "What do you say?"

Extortion is a crime? Anne thought to herself.

"Interesting proposal," Alex replied.

She gave him a quizzical look. Why would they consider getting into bed with him, of all people? The guy was a total sleazebag.

Alex put his hand up as if to say, *don't worry, I'm not getting sucked into this any more than you are.* "We'll have to talk to our senior management and get back to you with a response."

"When can I expect an answer?"

"We'll try to have something by the end of the week. Just so you understand our position—we're still in the midst of an internal investigation. Michael's death has obviously made matters somewhat more difficult for us."

"Of course. His death is what allows me to make this proposal at all."

A chill ran down Anne's spine. "What do you think about the suggestion that he was murdered?"

"I wouldn't be surprised if someone became fed up with Michael's game-playing and power trips and finally decided to bump him off. He could be extremely difficult to work with."

"I take it you didn't really care for the man," Alex addressed the gray box with a wry smile.

"That's the understatement of the year. But nobody really liked him. Anybody who says otherwise is probably lying."

Anne exchanged glances with Alex across the table.

"If he was murdered," she asked slowly, "who do you think did it?"

"Walter. And his damn pen."

She drew a sharp breath in. "Why?"

"He had the most to lose. From what I could tell, he and Michael were entangled in a whole lot of stuff—way more than just these bonds."

"You don't think there's any chance it could have been Marvin?"

"Why would he bother murdering Michael if he was willing to cooperate with the authorities? It doesn't make sense."

Anne tended to agree.

"Which leaves me and Walter," he continued, "and I know it wasn't me."

"Or Michael," Alex said quietly. "For all we know, this was his way of pulling a final, cruel joke on the people involved in the Pandora deals. He had to know his death would stir up a ruckus."

Anne was surprised he thought there was any chance it had been a suicide, given everything they knew at this point.

"That ruckus, as you call it, has presented us with a golden opportunity—" David paused and cleared his throat "—to rearrange matters more to our own liking. We might as well take advantage of the situation and find a solution that is favorable to the rest of us who have been left behind."

"Right. By the way," Alex winked at Anne. "Have you received any strange phone calls recently?"

"Sure, I get them all the time from my ex-wife. Can you be a little more specific?"

"Communications from an unnamed individual regarding these deals."

"No phone calls." David coughed. "But someone left a dead rat on my office stoop the other day."

Alex shot a sidelong glance at Anne, who raised her eyebrows.

"Probably just a disgruntled client." He chuckled. "In my line of business, I don't tend to make a lot of friends. But...are you saying you got an anonymous phone call related to these deals?"

"A weird message telling me to *Back off!*" she clarified. "It was left on my answering machine and delivered in a low, creepy whisper."

David gave a loud, full-throated laugh. "Sounds like a line from a B-rated horror movie. Next thing, ax-carrying ghosts will materialize and begin swooping around your place."

She might have found it funnier if she knew who had actually left the message and why. "At first, I thought it might've been one of my neighbors, although now I'm not so sure."

"Nice neighbors," David said wryly.

Alex nodded. "That's what I thought."

"Well, if it was related to these deals, I'd put my money on Walter." David's light tone became harsh and his manner abrasive. "The guy has the imagination of a slug. Only he would think that a message like that communicated anything useful."

"Hmmmm," she said quietly. "Why do you think Walter would have felt the need to do it."

"Who knows what's going through that pea-sized brain of his, but he knows that Marvin has an agreement with the SEC. Perhaps he's afraid you'll do the same...as if a lame message like that would stop you. I hope—" He paused, and they heard some murmuring in the background. "I'm sorry. There's a call I need to take."

"We'll be in touch on the other matter," Alex said.

"Wow," Anne said as soon as he had clicked off.

"These guys are something else," Alex said with obvious disdain. "How did you like the fact that he, too, had heard about Marvin Goldberg's secret change of face."

"What else is new?" She gave a small shrug.

* * *

When Anne returned to her cubicle, she saw a stack of messages, piles of unopened mail, unread articles, and pending inquiries. And now, thanks to David Singer's recent disclosures, she had a whole new set of questionable deals to investigate. She kicked off her pumps and thought about where to begin. *With a chocolate bar*, she decided and headed over to the candy machine.

Just as she put her first quarter into the slot, one of the secretaries appeared and began complaining about the Carter fiasco. "Do you realize that everyone was called into Peter's office to talk about William except us?"

Anne knew that comments from the administrative staff would not have changed the outcome one iota, but saw the obvious message that they were invisible to management. "No."

"This place sucks. They treat us like we're such peons."

Anne finished inserting the rest of her coins and waited for the candy bar to drop.

The secretary lowered her voice a notch and jerked her thumb in Carter's direction. "He would have changed everything if he'd been put in charge of the department."

"Really?" Anne peeled away the foil wrapper and took a small bite. "How?"

"For starters, he wasn't going to make us answer everybody's phones anymore."

Seriously? Anne thought to herself. *Then who would answer them instead?*

"And, he was going to make each of the analysts do their own filing."

Leaving the admins to do what exactly?

Gwen continued relaying the litany of ridiculous changes that would occur with Mr. Power-trip in charge: larger desks, mythical raises, reduced workload. Meanwhile, Anne found her mind wandering. Why was David Singer trying to work with them? Was there a chance he had also made a deal with the SEC? And how come there was so much animosity between him and Walter?

"Especially Renata," the angry woman prattled on. "She's always making personal phone calls and running errands. And I get stuck picking up the slack. Just yesterday—"

Anne's mind continued whirring. What if one of the Pandora partners felt exploited like Gwen? Or better yet, Cheated? *Did one of them decide to kill Michael because he felt used?* Gwen was still going on about Renata. *I tried to explain how unfair it is, but Renata just laughed. So, then I told her—*

Generally, Anne found Gwen likable. And occasionally helpful. But with all of the work she had to do, she resented being trapped in the hallway, her limited time getting soaked up by this endless complaining.

The corners of Gwen's lips pulled down in a sulky pout. "I can't believe they chose William over Carter."

Anne would have been shocked if Carter's coup d'état had succeeded. Despite his longevity with the firm, he carried far less influence than William. *Had it been the same with the Pandora partners?* Maybe Michael had had an outsized amount of power and control relative to the others. Or perhaps he had taken a larger distribution of their ill-gotten gains. Money often brought up all sorts of buried emotions.

"My job will continue to be the pits," Gwen said with a loud sigh.

Anne cast around for a way to escape the conversation. If she walked back to her cubicle, Gwen would undoubtedly follow. *Head for the elevators and duck into the ladies' room?* She suddenly realized that Gwen had gone silent and was looking at her with a dejected expression.

"I think you should wait and see what actually happens," Anne said, trying to sound upbeat. "After William gets the lay of the land, he may start to make some changes that will improve things." She glanced down at her watch. "Oh no! I'm late for a meeting on another floor."

As she stood in the bathroom stall hiding, she wondered if this was how the killer had felt, hemmed in with no way of breaking free, except by getting rid of Michael.

16

The Check

Tuesday, Two Weeks After the Meeting

"It was 2 am!"

Anne cradled the receiver against her shoulder while she spread cream cheese on her bagel, unwilling to let this latest condo crisis interrupt her breakfast.

"Not all of us are independently wealthy," her neighbor continued his tirade. "Some of us actually have to work for a living."

"I agree," she said, turning to see who had just tapped her on the arm. She raised a finger, motioning for the secretary to wait a moment, and then set the plastic knife down. "We can remind everyone about the noise rules at our next meeting and send a note to *him*, in particular, so that he's aware there was a problem with his party."

Anne covered the receiver with her hand and leaned toward the secretary, who whispered, "Alex Hunter from legal is on your other line." She nodded and put the phone back to her ear.

"—empty beer bottles near my front door the next morning. I'm assuming it was one of his drunk friends."

"While we're at it, we'll review the guest policy," Anne said, taking a small bite.

"I think he should be fined."

The secretary tapped Anne again and whispered, "He said it was urgent."

Anne nodded. "I'll bring it up with the board. Look, I've got to go. There's—"

"Is our esteemed condo leadership actually going to do anything about it? When I complained about the lights last time, they just laughed."

It was true that his suggestion for reducing light pollution by limiting the number of glowing Christmas decorations had met with some resistance due to its anti-festive nature. For a while afterwards, he had been dubbed The Grinch by several board members. But this was obviously different. There was no question that 2:00 in the morning was pretty late. She repeated her promise to address the issue at their next board meeting and then pushed the button for her second line. "Alex?"

"I've got Walter on the phone. I think he wants to strike a deal."

"I'll be right there."

She wrapped the bagel in a napkin, slipped her pumps back on, and walked to the elevator. A morose-looking Jennifer paced back and forth, already waiting for it to arrive.

"What's up?" Anne asked, pushing the elevator button by force of habit, even though it was already lit.

Jennifer's face darkened. "I just got a call from Personnel about the *alleged incident of abuse* with Elise." She made quotation marks with her fingers as she spoke. "Can you believe it? We're talking about a missed phone call, and they used the word *abuse*!"

"Seriously?" Anne pushed the button again, even though the rational part of her brain knew it would not make the elevator arrive any sooner.

"I almost asked if I should bring my attorney, as a joke, and then thought better of it." Jennifer spied the bagel in Anne's hand. "Is that your breakfast?"

Anne nodded. "Probably not the best idea. I'd be very careful in these proceedings if I were you. We all know she's a nutcase, but Personnel may not have any idea what they are dealing with."

The elevator dinged, signaling its arrival.

"I don't understand how she manages to keep her job. She calls in sick half the time and is always—" Jennifer froze as the elevator doors opened to reveal Elise facing them squarely from within. The two locked eyes on one another with obvious hostility.

"Are you going to let me out?" Elise growled.

Anne glanced at the wide space already available and took a step to the side.

"Thank you," Elise said with a cold sneer and then proceeded to look Jennifer up and down, obviously waiting for her to do the same. Jennifer crossed her arms and stared straight back, refusing to budge. As the seconds ticked by, Anne began to wonder how to break the impasse.

And then the elevator doors began to close.

Anne waved her foot just inside the door, and they reversed their direction. Without lowering her gaze, Elise slowly walked out, making a point of continuing to eyeball Jennifer until she was well past and the doors had closed again.

"Well, that was awkward," Anne said, unable to suppress a laugh.

"Wish me luck this afternoon," Jennifer replied with a sigh. "I'm going to need it."

The elevator glided to a stop, and Anne gave Jennifer a quick thumbs-up before hopping off and running to Alex's office.

"My wife and I always get a couple of spots in the center of the action and throw a big party," she heard Walter's voice as she entered the room. "Our caterer makes the best hors d'oeuvres. You should drop by and say hello."

"We were just talking about *The Hunt*," Alex explained. "Have you ever been?"

"No," she said, surprised. She had no idea he enjoyed killing animals. "Does the party happen before or after you go shooting?"

Alex smiled. "Neither. It's a steeplechase event where horses race around a track and jump over small fences."

Feeling like an idiot, Anne gave a sheepish grin.

"You should check it out sometime," Walter said, reminding her that he was on the speakerphone and that they were supposed to be discussing the Pandora bonds.

"And we should probably get back to business," Alex said congenially. "So, you said you had a proposal?"

"Indeed. I think it's in your best interest as well as mine."

"We're listening." Alex looked at Anne as he spoke to the gray box sitting innocuously on the desk.

"With Michael's sudden death, matters have changed enormously," Walter began.

Anne glanced down at her bagel and wondered if she dared eat it. She did not want to get caught mid-way through chewing and then need to say something with her mouth full.

"He's unable to testify as to what exactly occurred in these various transactions, and you don't really know for sure."

Anne brought the bagel to her lips and took a small bite.

"Together, we could work to make events satisfactory for both of us," Walter finished pleasantly.

"By which, you mean *damage control* with the SEC?" Alex said, cocking his head to one side.

She swallowed and debated whether she had time for another nibble.

"Indeed. Things will be a lot easier for all of us if our stories are in sync and we aren't contradicting one another. There's no reason that we can't both emerge from this unfortunate set of circumstances…unscathed."

Clearly, whatever alliance had existed amongst the Pandora partners had developed a major fracture. More like a chasm. This was essentially the same idea that David had floated the day before, and it appeared neither was aware of the other's efforts. Next, Anne expected him to suggest that David Singer was the murderer.

"What about David?" she asked to confirm her suspicions, glad she had decided to set the bagel aside. "Are you interested in working with him as well?"

Walter paused before responding, "I'm not sure that's a good idea. Given the stories in the paper, it's possible Michael was murdered the morning we met. And—well, I'm starting to think that David had pretty good reason to want Michael out of the picture."

"Reason enough to kill him?" Alex rested his chin on his hand.

"Perhaps. Michael had all of the Pandora documents in his possession. In the wrong hands, they had the potential to be very problematic."

Anne took a sharp breath. What was he referring to? *Something incriminating?* Did that mean there was more yet to be found?

"David often intimated that Michael couldn't be trusted to keep everything secure."

Doubt and suspicion. The death knell for a conspiracy. Anne wondered what had divided these two men. Presumably, they had been friends at one point, or at least held a modicum of respect for one another. Why else would they have chosen to collude on the Pandora Bonds?

"And did you agree with him?"

"Of course not," Walter replied tersely. "It made no sense for Michael to do anything foolish with the information, especially since it was just as damaging to him as it was to the rest of us."

"Why would David think any differently?"

"He wasn't part of our social circle, and I think he felt somewhat alienated. He probably thought that Michael and I would conspire to hang this whole thing on him."

Excluded. The word played in Anne's mind. Had David felt like a second-class citizen to their coterie? Or downright rejected by the clique? Taken to an extreme, these sorts of feelings could be a motive for murder. On the other hand, Walter might be intentionally painting this negative picture of David, misleading them in an effort to direct attention away from himself.

"I assume you knew nothing about Michael's past?"

"God no," he gasped. "And I always thought Michael and I were very close. We belonged to the same country club and played golf every weekend. I would never have guessed that he was a convicted felon."

Anne could imagine Walter's silver hair shivering in horror at the mere thought of it.

"And I'm not the only one," Walter sniffed. "At the club, we pride ourselves on having a very elite and well-respected body of membership. This business with Michael has been a terrible shock to *everyone*. A close friend of mine is on the board, and he is beside himself…as I'm sure you can imagine."

"I'm sure," Anne said, tapping her fingers lightly on the desk. "These documents that David was so concerned about…what damaging things could Michael have done with them?"

"Gone to the authorities. Or the press. Gotten David disbarred. I don't know. It would have hurt everybody involved, so it doesn't really make sense."

"I agree," Alex said. "By the way, have you received any odd communications lately?" His eyes narrowed as he waited for the response.

"Funny you should ask. I got the strangest phone call the other day. You too?"

Anne locked eyes with Alex.

"Not me, but Anne did," Alex answered. "We weren't quite sure what to make of it."

"Did he tell you to 'back off' in a hoarse whisper?" Walter chuckled.

"Yes," Anne replied, stunned. Word for word, it was exactly the same.

"I told him to *not* give up his day job and hung up."

Anne sat back in her chair, relieved. She wasn't the only one.

Walter sighed. "It had to be David. That's one of the many reasons I don't think we should try to work with him on this matter with the SEC."

Except David had been the recipient of a dead rat. Or so he had said.

Alex cracked his knuckles and then asked, "So what do you propose?"

"I think we should cooperate with the investigation, up to a point. A carefully calculated point."

"Meaning what exactly?"

"That we should selectively share information. Just enough to make it clear that Michael was responsible for this mess. And that David helped him. We can argue that the rest of us were duped."

Blame Michael and David. Simple enough. "What about Marvin?" Anne asked. "He's already cooperating and may have painted a very different picture."

"He hasn't got the proof. Michael and I held onto everything. If we coordinate what we share, we can take control of this investigation."

Anne saw Alex's eyes widen. As a lawyer, this conversation had to be rather alarming.

"Which documents, in particular, are you suggesting we hold back?" Anne asked.

"Which ones have you found?"

Alex frowned. "Come on, Walter. We're not going to blurt out a laundry list of potentially problematic items. You know that."

"I'm starting to get the distinct impression you have no idea what I'm talking about," Walter said crisply. "But maybe that's a good thing if it means David has them instead. Presumably, he'll make sure they never see the light of day."

"On the other hand," Anne said quietly, "it might be helpful if we knew which documents you think are problematic so that we can talk about why."

"I suggest you two start by giving me an answer to my proposal. Until then…"

"We'll need to talk to our senior management first to get their buy-in," Alex said firmly.

"Wonderful. I'll be waiting."

"Bloody hell," Alex said as soon as the telephone line had been disconnected. "This slippery prat wants to throw Dodgy Dave under the bus! And if that weren't enough, he wants to collude with us to deceive the SEC! As if we could trust him!" He shook his head in disbelief. "Michael really knew how to pick 'em…."

"There's obviously something important that we haven't uncovered. And whatever it is—" Anne bit her lip, "—it must implicate them."

"Unless there's nothing for us to find because the murderer took the evidence away with him." Alex leaned back, resting his head in his hands.

"Except that would mean that neither Walter nor David is the murderer since both are still trying to get their hands on these all-important documents. And if Marvin had them, there'd be no reason to bother cooperating with the authorities. My guess is that *none* of them have whatever it is."

They just had to figure out what *it* was and where it was hidden.

* * *

After returning to her desk, Anne quickly finished the bagel and began racking her brain. She'd been through all seventeen of the offering statements for the bonds and found nothing hair-raising there. They looked like they had been stamped out by the same cookie cutter. She'd reviewed the agreements with Oko Sychaito Bank, which Walter undoubtedly had copies of as well, and seen nothing particularly incriminating there either. *Could it have something to do with the unusual fees they failed to disclose to potential purchasers?* That was certainly unethical at best, but Anne had already brought that up in the grand showdown before Michael's death. There was no obvious reason for Walter and David to suddenly be worried about that. She twisted her hair into a small bun and put a pencil through the center to secure it in place.

There had to be something else they had overlooked. *But what?* She decided to go back to Michael's office and take a second gander at his files.

When she got within view of his office, she saw a thirty-something man with sandy blond hair sitting behind a modern-looking, glass-topped desk, a phone glued to his ear. Evidently, Russell had already moved in.

"What happened to Michael's stuff?" Anne asked Betty as she greeted her.

"It was moved down the hall to an empty storage room," Betty said with a hint of sadness. "Just a sec. I'll show you where it is."

Anne followed her past hushed offices guarded by industrious-looking secretaries, glass-walled conference rooms, and a collection of photocopiers and printers spitting out reams of paper until they finally reached an interior room hidden off a small corridor near the restrooms. Betty unlocked the door, flipped on the lights, and moved to the side. Anne stepped into the small, dimly lit storage area and surveyed the situation.

The room looked neat and orderly, offering no hint as to where she should begin. Her eyes roved over the desk and a stack of boxes before settling on the bottom two drawers of the credenza. Since Betty had said they contained personnel information, she hadn't looked at them previously.

"Ordinarily, I was never supposed to open these cabinets for anyone,"

Betty sighed as she jiggled the key in the slot. "But now..." her voice trailed off.

Anne watched her struggle with the lock, unsure whether to help, but Betty's jaw was set with a determined expression on her face. A few seconds later, there was an audible click.

"I'll be at my desk if you need anything else," Betty said, straightening up and floating quietly out of the room.

Anne was unprepared for what she found.

One drawer was empty, and the other had five skinny folders in it, each marked with the name of one of the people who had reported to Michael. Otherwise, they were completely bare. *Another dead end. I thought for sure there'd be something here.* She looked around to make sure no one was looking and then peeked into Kelsey's file. A six-figure salary. *Not bad for someone without an MBA.* Anne quickly put the file away and admonished herself for giving in to her curiosity.

She continued looking around the room and next spied his desk drawers. But they, too, proved to be a disappointment. She sat down in his comfortable, executive-style chair and rocked back and forth. *What else was left?* Her eyes came to rest on the file cabinet. Anne had looked through it previously and pulled everything that described how the bond issues worked. She hesitated and then opened the topmost drawer. A quick perusal confirmed her memory. The only other thing in there that she hadn't reviewed carefully was a thick file with signed copies of the various agreements marked "closing documents."

She sighed and pulled it out. As expected, the same people's signatures appeared again and again, and the documents were standard boilerplate. Anne shook her head. *Nothing of interest here.* She closed the file and tried to reinsert it in the same place it had come from, but found the space too small. As she struggled to wiggle it into the overpacked drawer, her finger caught on the edge, and she pulled back sharply, dropping the file on the floor.

"Damn!" she swore and then began gathering the papers scattered around her.

As she slipped them back into order, something fluttered to the ground. She bent down and picked up what appeared to be a check. Ripped in the corner, it had obviously worked itself free from the packet of papers. Anne drew a sharp breath. It was made out in the amount of $27 million dollars, and after turning it over, she saw it had never been cashed.

She looked at the front again and furrowed her brow. It was drawn upon The Caribbean Trust, a bank she had never heard of, with an address in the Virgin Islands. Re-examining the other sets of closing documents, Anne found that all of them had checks drawn on that same bank attached in the same manner. None of them had been cashed. They were all written for huge sums of money that were equivalent to the size of each bond issue. Now that, she decided, was very odd.

Anne gathered her things together and headed down to Alex's office.

"Do you have a way to look up the names of the corporate officers of this Caribbean Trust bank?" she asked after explaining what she had found.

"I'll do some digging and see what I find," he said. "I'm willing to bet it won't be pretty."

Anne was fairly certain it would be downright ugly, but there was a good chance it would bring them closer to understanding what the Pandora partners were trying to hide.

And why.

17

The Three Musketeers

Wednesday, Two Weeks After the Meeting

"My cousin's wedding was a disaster," Katie said. "And to think I could have been skiing instead."

Anne shifted the receiver onto her shoulder and unwrapped her candy bar. "Besides the bright purple dress—"

"It cost me $200 and looked like a tent!"

"All bridesmaids' dresses look awful. That's part of the fun of being in a wedding. But what else went wrong?" Anne popped a piece of chocolate into her mouth.

"Where do I even begin?" Katie sighed. "My cousin had a total meltdown because the person who was supposed to do her hair and make-up came down with the flu and the replacement was clueless. I actually thought her hair looked fine myself. It just wasn't quite what she was expecting."

The background noise from the trading floor was louder than usual, so Anne pushed the receiver more forcefully against her ear.

"The best man showed up looking like he'd had a few too many, and then just before the ceremony was supposed to begin, there was this torrential downpour—"

Anne heard loud laughter and turned to see Donna passing quickly by.

"—we all got drenched making our way from the parking lot to the tent. Then as my cousin was walking down the aisle, the best man tripped over her veil. It was twenty feet long, but still, I don't think that would've happened if he'd been sober. Did I mention that he also managed to lose the rings?"

"No way." Anne became aware that something was different. The trading floor did not have its usual hum. There was thumping. Or was it clapping?"

"Yes, way! And when he fell—"

Anne stretched the cord of her phone as far as it would reach, trying to figure out what was causing the commotion she was hearing, but couldn't get beyond the confines of her cubicle.

"—heard this loud ripping sound that reverberated across the beach, and then he tumbled, face forward, onto an elegantly dressed woman. I bet you'll never guess who it was."

"Who?"

"Michael Kingston's widow."

"What?!"

"Turns out she knows my cousin's new husband. They're all members of the same snooty country club. And she was telling everybody that Michael didn't commit suicide. She's convinced he was murdered by his secretary."

"Betty?"

"The one he was having a fling with. Evidently, she knew all about it."

Anne sat bolt upright. "She knew? Wow! And yet she stayed with him. Why?"

"That's what I was wondering."

"Unless...maybe they were talking about getting divorced."

"My cousin's husband said he didn't think so. I thought it strange that she was there at all. It's been just two weeks since he died, although I guess she has to move on with her life at some point...." Katie paused.

Anne heard a dull roar followed by yelling and screaming and then saw Carter and Elise race past her cubicle.

"I'm hearing weird stuff in the background," Katie said.

"I think something is happening on the trading floor. I should probably check it out."

Anne sprang out of her chair and narrowly avoided a collision with William running past. When she reached the trading floor, she scanned the room and finally found the object of interest.

Seriously?

A woman, partially clothed, was in the process of removing the rest of her outfit slowly, piece by piece. She twirled each article of clothing high above her head and then flung it into the expectant crowd while a nearby boombox provided accompanying music. As the next item made its acrobatic journey, some salesmen started making their way closer to her, waving dollar bills. Meanwhile, the rest of the pack was hooting and hollering, including Nick Angelini and Peter Eckert, clearly enjoying the show.

Anne spied Jennifer in the multitude who mouthed *Benny's Birthday* and *Stripper.*

She sighed and returned to her desk. With everyone distracted by the exotic dancer, maybe she could actually get some work done. Anne sat down, and her mind immediately went to the conversation she had just finished with Katie.

Betty? A murderer? It would mean Michael's death had nothing to do with these shady deals. Anne frowned. It didn't make sense. Betty didn't have it in her to do something so calculated. And vengeful. *Or did she?* And what about his globetrotting wife? Could she have been fed up with his philandering and exacted her own revenge? It would be masterful to have Michael's young lover find his body and ultimately get blamed for his death. Anne kicked off her shoes and leaned back in her chair.

A plan like that would take cunning and a lot of nerve, but it did not fit with the woman's behavior. The police had been ready to call it a suicide, and the widow was the one trumpeting the idea that he had been murdered. Not exactly the smartest thing to do if she had actually killed him. *And what about the bonds?* The problem deals stared up at her from her cluttered desk, a stark reminder that she had work to do.

Lots of it.

Anne made a mental note to think about Michael's murder later. Right now, she had to focus on the Pandora bonds. Trying to ignore the clapping and whistling in the background, she began to chart the chain of events leading up to their issuance.

Everything she had or knew about them was spread out before her. She picked up the offering statement of one at random and examined it closely. It had a closing date of August 2, 1986. The check stapled to the back of it had the same date and was made in the proper amount to pay for the bond certificates–$27 million. And yet, the check had never been cashed. *Why not?* Instead, it had been tucked away in the recesses of Michael's file drawers. She popped the top of her Coke and took a long sip to quench her thirst.

She thumbed through the various legal pages and then froze on the last page of the investment contract with the Oko Sychaito Bank. The date next to the signatures on that page was different from everything else in the entire file.

It was approximately six months later.

And could mean only one thing.

The bonds did not actually sell in 1986. Instead, they sat around, inactive for six months, and actually sold in 1987, despite what the certificates and various paperwork all stated. *Why hide the true date of the bond sale?*

She clasped her hands and stretched her arms back as far as they could reach. Startled to see a shadow in the periphery of her vision, she jerked up and swung her chair around to find Kelsey standing at the entrance of her cubicle. She wore a high-waisted green skirt that flared beautifully, drawing the eye toward her thin, elegant frame. And as usual, her hair and make-up looked perfect. Anne looked down at her own stocking feet and was relieved to see that at least her hose had not developed a run.

"Is this typical?" Kelsey asked, nodding her head toward the trading floor.

"It happens occasionally." Strippers. Crude jokes. Profanity-laced tirades. It was all part of the rough and tumble adventure called *working on the trading floor*.

"Hmmm." Kelsey shifted back and forth, fidgeting with her pearls.

Anne rolled her eyes and shrugged. "I do my best to ignore it."

"Yeah…Do you have a few minutes?"

"Certainly," Anne said, looking around the small confines of her cubicle. "Would you like to move to one of the conference rooms?"

Kelsey shook her head, a worried expression on her face. "I only have a few minutes before I need to get back upstairs."

Anne looked at her, curious what was on her mind.

"There's something I neglected to tell you earlier."

"Oh?" Anne's ears perked up.

There was a pause, and then Kelsey blurted the words quickly and clumsily. "After Michael's death, I got a call from Marvin Goldberg." Kelsey gulped. "I'm not sure what came over me."

Anne felt a prickle of dread. What had Kelsey done?

"The day had obviously been very disturbing," she continued, tugging harder on the pearls. "So I wasn't thinking clearly."

Anne raised her eyebrows and waited for the train to come roaring in.

"They wanted to meet. That evening."

Anne felt her stomach drop as she searched Kelsey's face. "You met with the Pandora partners the day Michael died?"

Kelsey nodded mutely, her expression dull, her green eyes flat.

"Where?"

"In the same conference room where you guys had your summit in the morning."

Anne tried to keep her face impassive. Why had Kelsey met with them that day, of all days? And why was she telling her about it now?

"They said they wanted to discuss something of *mutual importance*." Kelsey ran her fingers through her perfectly blown-dry hair. "My curiosity was piqued, so I agreed."

A deal. With Kelsey. Which means she had something of value that they wanted. Anne took a deep breath and shifted in her chair. Finally! Some answers. She could feel the anticipation building within her.

"When Marvin arrived, he explained that they were interested in certain papers Michael had retained from the deals. He offered me $10,000 in exchange for them."

"Cash?"

"I guess so. We didn't get far enough in the discussion for me to find out how the transaction would actually work." She looked at Anne quizzically and then quickly added, "I said no immediately. There was no way I was going to jeopardize the firm."

Yeah, right, Anne thought. *The money he offered was obviously not worth the risk of being found out.*

"David tried to intimidate me with the threat of lawsuits and my future job prospects if I refused to hand the papers over." Kelsey sniffed. "Typical lawyerly crap."

Anne gave a thin smile.

"And Walter was just plain condescending." Kelsey pursed her lips. "All I wanted to do was wipe that smug smile right off his face."

Anne tried to sound casual. "Which documents were they so hot to trot for?"

"The closing documents."

Bingo! The pieces were finally starting to come together. She could hardly wait to tell Alex.

"I'm not sure what they were so worried about. Perhaps they meant to alter them. Hide their tracks. I don't know." Kelsey shrugged. "But there's no question they were desperate to get their grubby little hands on them. When everyone was grabbing their coats and getting ready to leave, Walter said he was going to hit the men's room first. A few minutes later, I caught him red-handed, snooping in Michael's office."

"You're kidding!"

"No. I ran in and asked him what he thought he was doing, and he just looked at me, speechless."

"That's pretty nervy." Anne shook her head.

"I told him to leave, and he became angry. He insisted I show him where the papers were kept. He didn't give up until I threatened to call security." She paused and looked down at her feet. "If he'd had more time, I'm sure he would've found what he was looking for. I just thought you should know in case one of them happened to mention the meeting."

Why would it matter if they did? Anne still didn't understand what had driven Kelsey to suddenly spill her guts about this debacle. "Except for the incident with Walter, were you with the others the entire time?"

She hesitated and then said, "No…When they first arrived, David said he had to make a private phone call. I told him to go ahead and use my office…at the time, I thought nothing of it."

Anne was surprised that Kelsey had allowed any of them to roam around the floor unsupervised. It had been both foolish and dangerous.

She cringed. "I can't believe I was so stupid."

"You couldn't have known," Anne said, trying to be supportive. "And it had been an incredibly stressful day."

Kelsey's face clouded, and then her eyes flashed with anger. "I can't get over how brazen they were. Michael's body was hardly cold, and the only thought in their minds was raiding his files so they could cover their little derrières." Her lip curled. "Men. All they think about is themselves."

"You know," Anne said, a disturbing thought beginning to creep into her mind, "it's possible one of them wanted more than the files."

"That's what's worrying me." Kelsey fixed her green eyes on Anne. "It was the perfect opportunity to hide something in his office, such as the diskette you found with Michael's suicide note written on it…."

Anne's thoughts exactly.

"We could never prove—" Kelsey stopped abruptly as Alex stepped into view.

"Is this typical?" He nodded his head toward the trading floor.

Anne gave an exasperated sigh.

"I was asking the same thing," Kelsey said.

There was an awkward silence.

"What brings you down here?" Alex finally asked.

Kelsey locked eyes with Anne.

He looked back and forth at the two of them, obviously confused. "Should I come back later?"

"No," Anne said quickly. "We were just talking…" She stopped, unsure of how much to say, hoping that Kelsey would tell Alex what she had already told her.

"The Three Musketeers," Kelsey blurted out. "I met with them the night Michael was murdered."

"What?" Alex looked at her with an incredulous expression. "Why?"

Kelsey shook her head and looked away. "I don't know what I was thinking."

"I think they wanted the uncashed checks from the Pandora deals," Anne explained. "They were filed away with the closing documents."

"Oh my God," Kelsey said slowly. "That hadn't even occurred to me...I knew something was off when Marvin called this morning."

Anne drew in a sharp breath. Kelsey had no idea he was cooperating with the SEC. He had probably telephoned at the behest of the investigators and recorded the conversation.

"Marvin?" Anne and Alex both said at the same time.

"Yes. Out of the blue. Asking about the closing documents."

That explained why Kelsey had come down. She was worried that one of the Pandora partners might tell someone about their meeting the night of the murder and that it would reflect poorly on her.

"What did you tell him?" Alex studied her carefully, his jaw tight.

"I told him to contact our legal department if he wanted anything related to those deals." She crossed her arms, a smug look on her face. "The last thing I was going to do was help that little weasel. Does he actually think I don't read the newspaper? He's obviously worried about the SEC launching an investigation into their fishy deals. As far as I'm concerned, those slimeballs are on their own. I was just following orders."

Anne breathed a sigh of relief. If the conversation was being recorded, it did not sound like she had said anything incriminating. "What was the purpose of those checks that he's so worried about?"

"Drawn on a bank that has no assets to speak of?" Alex's face looked hard and unyielding. "That's what I came down to tell you."

Kelsey sighed. "It was a way for Michael to buy time."

Anne and Alex exchanged puzzled glances.

"Time?" Alex echoed back.

"You know what?" Kelsey looked at Anne. "I've changed my mind. Let's move into that conference room after all. I need a cigarette."

18

The Club

"By the time Michael had come up with the Pandora scheme," Kelsey paused. "Hmmm…I don't see my lighter."

While she rummaged through her purse, Anne fought the urge to grab it and dump the contents of the bag out on the table. She was anxious to move on and talk about the bonds.

"Got it!" Kelsey finally said with a triumphant flick and proceeded to light her cigarette. "It was near the end of 1986, and the tax law was about to change." Her eyes darted around the room. "Is there an ashtray around here?"

Alex glanced at the wall clock, his mouth tight, and then stood up and retrieved one from the side table.

Kelsey slowly inhaled and carefully blew the smoke out to her side. "As you both know, the Tax Reform Act imposed all sorts of restrictions on municipal bonds issued after that year. So, Michael devised a scheme to *artificially* close the deals prior to that happening." She gave a sly smile. "On paper, the bonds would supposedly be sold, except that *no money would actually change hands*."

Anne looked at her dumbfounded. She had just admitted to fraud by saying that the Pandora bond documents contained false information. Intentionally! Moreover, the purpose had been to mislead investors into believing that the bonds were not subject to the harsh post-1986 tax provisions. When in fact, they were! But Anne still did not see how the uncashed checks fit in.

"Walk us through how it worked," Alex said, his voice expressionless.

"Michael would hand Marvin a check drawn for the necessary amount on their bogus Caribbean bank." Kelsey took a quick puff. "Marvin held the check as a supposed proof that the bonds had been issued prior to the tax reform act, and Michael tucked the bonds away in a file drawer. They sat there, inactive for six months or so, and then eventually were resold to the general public when the timing seemed right."

"Bloody hell," Alex said, shaking his head. "Why go through this whole charade with the checks when you could have just sold the bonds in the first place?"

"We couldn't exactly flood the market with $300 million of securities on December 31st," Kelsey said with a snort, as if it should have been obvious to a first grader. "That would have aroused too much suspicion, and there wouldn't have been sufficient demand. By holding off for a few months, the bond sales could be spread out. Don't forget. When we marketed them to the general public, real money changed hands. We had to actually sell the damn things."

Of course they did. Those sales were what generated those big fat fees they collected. Anne tilted her head to one side. "How did Michael end up with the uncashed checks?"

"I'm not sure how he finagled that one, but it was a constant source of friction between him and the other Pandora partners, David especially."

"It's interesting," Anne said quietly. "On the one hand, the checks provided the illusion of a bond closing in 1986, but at the same time, they also provided tangible evidence that the bonds had been illegally issued in 1987."

"I know," Kelsey replied. "He really should have destroyed them after the bonds had been truly brought to market. I told him that several times." She shook her head. "He could be so stubborn."

Anne exchanged glances with Alex. If Kelsey were to speak this frankly with investigators from the SEC, she might find herself in pretty hot water. Not to mention that those checks might very well have been the motive for his murder.

"Why do you think he chose to hold onto them?" Alex's sharp eyes studied her.

"It provided him with a sense of power and control." Kelsey's face flushed red, and she took another drag on her cigarette. "Michael had a mean streak. Most people never saw that side of him. But I did. And the Pandora partners did as well." She looked down and fumbled with the latch on her purse. "In retrospect, I'm not all that surprised one of them decided to do him in. He did and said a number of things to make many people very angry with him." She set her bag to the side and looked up, pensive.

"You mentioned that he and David wrangled over those checks," Anne said. "And it's pretty clear that David and Walter don't get along well. How did they end up as business partners?"

"It wasn't always like that. Initially, the three of them were friends. But over time...things gradually deteriorated."

Like the slow dissolution of a marriage, except the build-up of tension and distrust had ended in murder instead of divorce.

"At one point, David and Walter weren't even on speaking terms. I had to relay things from one to the other and back again." Kelsey rolled her eyes. "It was ridiculous."

Not to mention unprofessional and inefficient, Anne felt like adding. "Do you have any idea what caused the big fallout?"

Kelsey gave a thin-lipped smile. "The three of them all lived in the same moneyed community, but on a social basis, David didn't cut the mustard. Walter made the mistake of trying to explain this to him."

"That he was too tacky?"

"He's Jewish."

Anne did a double take.

Kelsey nodded slowly. "The Harbor Ridge Country Club is about as Waspy as they come. Membership is by invitation only, and you have to have a certain income or the right pedigree to be considered. It's only recently that they even started allowing Catholics."

Anne was finally starting to understand. It had to have been galling to learn he was no more than a second-class citizen to someone he had regarded as a friend.

A smile briefly crossed Kelsey's lips. "Let's just say the conversation didn't go very well." She took a quick puff of her cigarette and blew the smoke carefully to one side.

"Harbor Ridge…" Anne toyed with the name in her mind. "For some reason, it sounds familiar."

"The US Open holds its golf tournament there sometimes," Alex said, his face tight.

Despite the club's exclusionary practices, Anne thought, *which the golf organizers had to be well aware of.*

"Even women aren't true members of this club." Kelsey gestured with air quotes when she said *true members*. "They're tag-along spouses, given membership on a special associate type basis." The term *special associate* got air quotes plus an exaggerated eye roll.

"You mean their membership is tied to their husband's?" Anne had no idea organizations like that still existed in the modern era. It was legal?

"You got it. In the event of divorce, the wife's membership is automatically revoked, regardless of whether her family connections are what got the two of them admitted in the first place. The man, however, remains a full member of the club."

Alex just shook his head.

"Not only that, the club has a male-only grill room. A few years ago, Michael arranged a Christmas party there for the company's senior investment bankers and *forgot* that the one female managing director we have wouldn't be allowed entry into that space."

"Seriously?"

"I couldn't make this stuff up if I tried," Kelsey snorted. "When she showed up and was turned away at the door…well…I guess all hell broke loose. I heard they gave her a special gift of company stock to compensate…."

This was the club that David wanted to join? And that Walter and Michael actually belonged to? Anne's mind was still reeling that an institution like this even existed and that the US Golf Open used it for its tournaments.

Kelsey shrugged. "The list goes on and on. They designate certain tee-off times, like virtually all-day Saturday when only men are allowed to golf. And on the days when the women are allowed to play, they aren't allowed to wear shorts on the course, even though the men are."

"I wonder why the wives put up with it," Anne said.

"It's the most prestigious social organization in the area," Kelsey replied coolly. "Pretty medieval, in my view."

Anne agreed. Downright depressing, to be honest. But focusing on the club wasn't bringing them any closer to understanding who might have murdered Michael and why. "So, David wanted to be part of this throw-back to the dark ages. What about Walter?" she asked in an effort to bring them back to the subject at hand. "How close were he and Michael?"

"Fair-weather friends," Kelsey replied. "Sometimes on and sometimes off. They maintained a semblance of allegiance because of their membership at the club and also because it was convenient at times for business, but I don't think they respected each other. They both wanted to be in charge, to be the top dog calling the shots."

While Kelsey took a long drag on her cigarette, Anne thought about the similarities between the two men. Both were hyper-focused on money, prestige, and social standing, willing to do anything to stay in the lead. Had Walter lost one battle too many and lashed out to regain his footing?

"What about Marvin? How did Michael get along with him?"

"Surprisingly well." Kelsey bit her lip again. "Despite the fact that Marvin was a bit of an oddball. He came to meetings looking like he had just climbed out of a dumpster and would say whatever was on the top of his head. Yet Michael dealt easily with him. Their relationship appeared cordial and relaxed, even friendly to me. I think Marvin is fundamentally secure in his sense of self, so he didn't strive to defeat Michael or act in ways to establish superiority. That's probably why they didn't have any issues."

Anne did not totally buy it. Marvin may not have been outwardly competitive, but he had certainly taken a pre-emptive, self-preserving strike against the others by cooperating with the SEC early on in the investigation, virtually guaranteeing leniency for himself, meanwhile leaving his partners to twist in the wind. His ability to get along with Michael probably indicated that he was the smoothest operator of the Pandora partners. Perhaps even the most dangerous.

"The battle for control is interesting." Anne saw Alex's head bobbing up and down in agreement. "It can't have set up a good dynamic within the group."

"You're right," Kelsey said. "It created unnecessary tension and squabbling. Michael wanted to succeed in every major way to prove something to himself, no matter what the cost. Now that his past has come to light, I suspect he was trying to leave his low-class background as far behind as possible. That had to have been the root of his low self-esteem."

Did he lack self-confidence, as Kelsey was suggesting, or was he seeking recognition, approval, and respect? Anne wondered if this desire to achieve also explained his philandering, but was not about to broach that subject with his former mistress. Instead, she said, "Yet he had everything; a beautiful house in an elite neighborhood, a well-connected wife, and a great job."

"He certainly had a lavish lifestyle, the job of many people's dreams, and what might have appeared to be a storybook life." Kelsey's voice had begun to crack, and she paused for a moment. "But it was never enough for him. He always had to have more."

"I guess money can be addicting," Alex said with a shrug.

Kelsey dismissed his comment with a wave of her hand. "It wasn't just the money. It was more than that." She fixed her green eyes on Anne. "He wanted to be king."

The most important chess piece in the game of life. Anne nodded silently to herself. *That fit.*

Kelsey's eyes narrowed. "The power was exhilarating to him. He loved bilking the system and getting away with it." She leaned back and crossed her arms over her chest. "It's amazing what you learn about a person in the years you work together. In some ways, a co-worker can know more about you than your spouse."

Anne tended to think she was right in that observation.

"There never was any expectation of building the projects then, was there?" Alex said more as a statement of fact than a question.

"No," Kelsey replied quietly. "All of the deals were brought to market solely to generate fees, fees, and more fees." She shook her head and looked away.

"Are you familiar with a group of bonds that were issued to build hotels in Arkansas?" Anne asked.

Kelsey grimaced. "The Corn Dog deals. It's only a matter of time before they ultimately fail, leaving investors holding the bag. Those deals weren't structured as elegantly as the Pandora ones. At least with the Pandora bonds, no one gets hurt financially."

"That's not true if the IRS finds out about them," Alex said with a frown.

"Of course." Kelsey lifted her hands up as if to surrender. "My point was simply that the Corn Dog deals were doomed to failure from the start. The firm was downright irresponsible for bringing projects with such crappy potential to market. I don't think, however, that there was anything illegal about them."

"What type of investors were they sold to?" Anne asked, dreading the answer.

Kelsey averted her eyes. "Retail customers."

Just as David Something-or-Other had said.

"They specifically targeted the uninformed mom-and-pop buyers knowing that sophisticated institutional investors wouldn't touch these things with a ten-foot pole." Kelsey gave a rueful laugh. "Doesn't make a pretty picture, does it?"

It most certainly did not. Anne could not understand how any of this had made it past the firm's internal review committee unless Michael himself chaired it.

"Just so you know, I didn't work as closely on those deals. Another associate was the primary on the first ten or so of them. Michael brought me in near the end when she left the firm."

Alex gave her a quizzical look.

"For personal reasons. Nothing to do with the bonds."

Anne couldn't help but wonder if Michael had made unwelcome advances that contributed to the woman's departure. She glanced at her watch. "It's getting late."

Kelsey nodded and stood up. "I should get back upstairs before they send out a search party for me. We're bringing a deal to market tomorrow, and I still need to finish one of the key charts."

"Bloody Hell," Alex said the moment Kelsey was out of earshot. "She just confirmed what David said about these dodgy Arkansas bonds being targeted at people who had no business buying them. I guess she missed the question on the securities exam that had to do with the basic requirement of *know your customer.*"

"How about the part where you agree to *follow the law*?" Anne threw her arms in the air. "Or does the tax revenue code suddenly not count?"

He shook his head while she ticked the offenses off, one by one, on her fingers. "After those bonds were *illegally* issued, the Pandora partners *collected* their generous fees and then probably *skimmed* some of the interest income from the investment contract as well. They were in fat-city until we came along."

"No wonder their sudden desire to collaborate with us."

She nodded. "And no wonder Marvin Goldberg has become friendly with the SEC."

Alex's steel blue eyes looked straight at her. "Kelsey didn't have a good explanation for how Michael ended up with the uncashed checks."

"She sure didn't." Anne returned his gaze. "But I wonder if that's the reason somebody made the executive decision to eliminate him."

"I'm gobsmacked that she let those guys run around the floor the day he was found dead." Alex put his hands on his head as if he was about to pull his hair out. "What was she thinking?"

"It means any one of them could have planted that diskette in his office." Anne shook her head. "The closing documents weren't exactly hidden in an armored truck either. We're lucky none of them managed to actually find them, and I suspect she's lucky she wasn't murdered in the process."

Alex stood up. "I've had enough of this dreary business for one day. Let's get out of here and reconvene in the morning."

* * *

Anne was met at the door by a happily wagging tail when she got home that evening. As Muffin wolfed down her dinner, Anne perused her mail. Another letter from mother. She raised her eyebrows and opened that envelope first. She was rewarded with a yellow stick-it note on top of a long test. *This will help you figure out your personality type*, it said, *so you can select a marital partner who is a good fit*. Anne groaned and set it aside for when she had more time and energy.

She changed for aerobics and headed out. After returning and fixing supper, she showered and settled down to read. At 10:30 pm, the phone rang. When she answered, a hoarse voice whispered, "Back off now! I'm warning you! Just back off!" Anne yelled into the receiver, "I've got caller ID. I'm tracing your call right now." He laughed and repeated the message.

She hung up the phone feeling weak and shaky. Who was making these calls? And why? Suddenly she felt a bolt of panic flash through her system. Perhaps the mysterious caller had been calling from New York and knew, as she did, that such calls couldn't be traced through the caller ID system in New Jersey. If so, it would have been obvious she had been bluffing. Besides, if a number had really been traced, it would have appeared on the screen of the special unit before she had even answered the call.

You idiot, she berated herself, *what a stupid thing to blurt out. Now the caller knows he's made you nervous.* She marched directly upstairs to her bedroom and pulled out a can of mace from the bureau. She resolved to carry it everywhere she went. Just in case.

19

The Widow

Thursday, Two Weeks After the Meeting

Alex was on the phone when she arrived, his desk covered in papers and his jacket thrown casually on the chair.

"I'll be off in a minute," he whispered and then continued jotting some notes.

"I've been on pins and needles ever since I got your message," she said as soon as he finished. "Why all the intrigue?"

"I wanted to be sure no one would overhear us."

She tensed in anticipation.

He chuckled. "Someone left a 'back off' message on my answering machine yesterday. Just like what you and Walter described."

Was that it? She had rushed up there thinking he had something earth-shattering to report.

"So now the mysterious caller has been in touch with all of us."

Anne shrugged. "I don't know what this person hopes to achieve."

"Me neither." His grey eyes studied her for a moment, and his face took on a serious expression. "But the reason I wanted to meet privately is that I ran into a buddy of mine last night."

Alex leaned toward her.

"He told me that he saw Peter Eckert having dinner with Michael Kingston's wife last week."

"What?!"

"That's what I thought, but then I realized it isn't so surprising. They belong to the same country club—"

"Peter belongs too?"

"Yes. I thought you knew."

How would she have? It wasn't like she had access to the club's member registry. "No…This is the first I'm hearing it."

"Oh. Sorry. I think they all golf together occasionally, and since he knows I work at Spencer Brothers too…"

She tried to come to terms with what he had just told her. The Senior VP of municipals at Spencer Brothers—her boss's boss—someone she met with on a routine basis and who determined her bonus each year—belonged to a country club that treated women like second-class citizens.

Lovely.

Anne cocked her head. "So that means Peter is friends with Michael's widow? Or is there more between them?"

"It's unclear. My friend thought they looked pretty chummy, but it could be that Peter was just trying to be supportive given everything she's been through. It does suggest he might have been closer to Michael than I realized."

"You don't think Peter could've had anything to do with Michael's murder, do you?" she asked slowly.

"He wasn't at our meeting. I don't see how."

A heavy weight settled on Anne's chest. "Unless the two of them met early that morning before anyone else got in."

"That's why I thought we should discuss this in my office. If we're going to start looking in Peter's direction, we sure as hell don't want him to get wind of it."

The political fallout would be huge. They might as well sign their own death warrants and hire a band to play the funeral march. She looked at him appreciatively. He had done the right thing to make sure they had total privacy for this discussion. "We could ask Kelsey."

Alex sighed deeply.

"She was in that morning and saw who was around."

"But then we have to trust her to keep this quiet," Alex said with a frown.

"Do you have a better idea?"

* * *

After a quick phone call to make sure she was available, they were knocking on Kelsey's office door.

"We're still trying to get this deal finished up, so I don't have a lot of time," she greeted them, wearing a double-breasted navy pinstripe suit and her hair up in an elegant knot.

"We were wondering about the morning of Michael's death again," Anne began, all the while resisting the urge to fuss with her own tousled hair.

Kelsey stiffened.

"Did anyone else meet with him really early that day?" Anne gave up and ran her fingers from front to back, pulling the loose strands off of her face and tucking them behind each ear.

"I don't know..." Kelsey said slowly, a puzzled expression on her face. "It's possible."

"Is there some way you could find out?"

"Possibly..." She fixed her eyes on Anne. "Is there someone, in particular, you have in mind?"

"Peter Eckert," Anne replied.

"Whoa."

"He may be close with Michael Kingston's widow."

"I'll do a little digging around. Maybe you could do the same on your end with Peter's activities."

"That's my plan. But we've got to keep this just amongst the three of us."

* * *

Anne stopped on the way back to her desk to grab a candy bar and then considered ways to get a look at Peter's calendar. With no immediate ideas coming to mind, she decided to set that problem to the side and focus instead on the Arkansas hotel deals.

After some back and forth with one of the secretaries, she got copies of the offering statements for the deals. She studied them and quickly found they were virtually identical to one another, except each one was guaranteed by a different bank. Typically, a bank promising to pay off the bonds in the event of default would make them a safer investment, but these bonds were unrated by any of the national services, a red flag that they were inherently risky, maybe even junk bonds.

She pulled out a publication that gave financial information on all banks in the country and scanned the listing for the twenty-five used in these deals. Only one of them appeared, Skyward Savings, and its financial condition was rated as deplorable.

She picked up the phone and began dialing. When she asked the finance officer about one of the other banks involved in the deals, he paused and put her through to the president, who answered, "Why yes. They are a subsidiary of ours. But you should be familiar with that already since your firm underwrote the bond issues."

Anne asked about the remaining no-name banks involved in the deals. Each and every one of them was a subsidiary of Skyward Savings. Of course, this detail had not been disclosed in the offering statement. In addition, he claimed that the hotel projects were all in very good shape. After asking for a copy of their most recent financial statements, she hung up the phone and called Alex to let him know about the inter-relationships amongst the banks on this set of bonds. He sounded about as pleased as a dead bird.

She stood up to stretch and found the entrance to her cubicle blocked by Carter. He immediately pounced upon her, flashing an insincere smile. "How're you doing?"

She eyed him warily, immediately on guard. He wanted something. The question was, what. "Fine," she replied, trying to keep her tone light.

There were bags under his eyes, and he looked shaky, as if his small frame were crumbling under the constant weight of too much pressure. She assumed he was worried about his future at Spencer Brothers, given the spectacular failure of his recent coup attempt.

"Are you mad at me for anything?"

"No," Anne said slowly, wondering where this was leading.

"It seems like you've been avoiding me ever since William returned from vacation."

She shrugged. "I've been busy."

"Still working on those Pandora Bonds?" He pulled a Kleenex out of his pocket and prepared to sneeze. "That project seems to be taking forever."

"Yes," she paused, suddenly seeing an opening. "I was just about to grab a Coke. Do you want anything?" She took a step forward, but he did not move.

He shook his head and then gave a loud sneeze. "How come you're working on it rather than Donna? Housing bonds fall within her area of expertise, after all?"

They also fell within Anne's. She debated whether to point that out and thought better of it. "She was too busy when the initial request came in."

"Oh," he said smugly as if he knew better.

Her curiosity was immediately piqued. She sensed an underlying current of animosity and wanted to know what was behind it. And then she thought of Kelsey, being asked to meet with Marvin, Walter, and David the night of Michael's death? With everything that had happened that day, she must have been intrigued. Was it really that strange that she had agreed to see them? Suddenly she noticed Carter staring intently at her. "I'm sorry," she said, "would you repeat that?"

"Has William mentioned anything to you about what happened while he was gone?"

Finally. The real reason he was standing in her cubicle, chattering away. "No," she said curtly and then immediately regretted her tone. Even though The Carp was annoying, there was no need to antagonize him. "Why would he?"

"Well, Elise said the two of you talked for a long time on Monday afternoon."

A tight smile crossed her lips. *Leave it to the Ice Princess to try to stir things up.* "I don't recall."

He stuffed the wet Kleenex back into his pocket. "I just thought he might have confided in you about it."

"Why?" She stole a quick glance at her watch.

"You know." He cocked his head toward William's office and then toward Anne's cubicle. "Because of your special friendship."

Anne stared at him, trying to understand what the waving head was supposed to communicate.

"Nobody else can stand the guy," he chortled. "Yet you two are virtually best friends." He finished with a suggestive wink.

She looked at him, wondering what planet he was on, and then it slowly dawned on her. *He thinks I'm having an affair with William. Is everybody sleeping with their boss except for me?* Anne was beyond annoyed. She was downright offended. "Oh, you mean our *special* relationship," she said coyly and raised her eyebrows.

He nodded.

She trained her eyes on him and then fired. "I hate to break it to you, but if I were going to attempt to sleep my way to the top, I wouldn't bother with a low-life like William. I'd go after someone much higher up. The kind of person who owns a gulf coast island with beautiful white beaches and horses…and a private jet." She brushed past Carter, feeling annoyed that she had allowed him to waste her time.

"I understand your position," he twittered after her. "Elise said you were trying to keep it a secret."

Anne stopped abruptly and wordlessly turned back to face him.

"But don't worry," he warbled, "I won't tell anyone."

That evening when she told Katie about the conversation, enough time had elapsed that she was able to see some humor in the situation. "I'm thinking that aliens must have landed on Earth and experimented with his brain."

"I'm seriously starting to wonder about the people you work with," Katie said. "I don't know how you stand it."

"Me neither," she replied.

20

One Hundred Pennies

Monday, Three Weeks After the Meeting

Jennifer gave a surreptitious glance around and then lowered her voice. "First of all, the Ice Princess shows up wearing this tacky, leopard-like catsuit and pounds of makeup smeared onto her face."

"I know exactly the outfit you're talking about," Anne whispered back. "It's a hideous shade of orange and green."

"Exactly," Jennifer said with a disapproving sniff. "She doesn't have the figure to wear it. Plus, it's totally unprofessional."

"I wonder what the woman in Personnel thought."

"It can't have been good." Jennifer laughed. "But get ready for this. She hobbles into her chair and puts on this pathetic act about being a victim."

Anne shook her head. "Elise? Injured because she missed a phone call from her boyfriend? Spare me."

"Yeah." Jennifer rolled her eyes. "Fortunately, she barely managed to say more than three sentences before she'd already contradicted herself. I had the shock of my life when the HR woman actually noticed the inconsistencies and asked Elise to clarify her statements. Of course, all she could manage was to trip all over herself again. Eventually, Pauline—that's the HR woman—told her to just stop. Case dismissed."

"That's great! You must be so relieved!"

"Totally. And it was hilarious to see the Ice Princess storm out of there in a huff. But that's not all...."

Anne looked at her, puzzled.

"After she left, Pauline told me that this wasn't the first time she'd had this sort of ridiculousness with Elise."

"Figures," Anne muttered. "And yet no one has bothered to rein in the self-righteous little queen, despite everything."

Jennifer's mouth widened into a broad smile. "That's what's so interesting. Pauline went on to say that Elise wouldn't get away with this anymore, because—" she paused to make air quotes, *"Michael Kingston is no longer around to protect her."*

"What?!"

"That's what I thought. But it totally makes sense. How else do you explain her longevity around here?"

Indeed. It was the perfect explanation. And then Anne was struck by another, more sobering thought. She had spotted Elise on the investment banking floor the morning Michael was killed. *Could Elise have had something to do with his murder?*

Jennifer's smile became smug. "I'm guessing she had dirt on him."

"I'm sure," Anne answered absently, her mind focused on Elise's behavior that day. She had left early, with a migraine, after reporting Michael's death to the trading floor. Perhaps she needed to get away from it all. Regroup and collect herself.

"I was so happy to wash my hands of the mess. Yet, I have to admit, it was kind of funny at the same time."

"You've got a better attitude about it than I would," Anne said. "What she put you through was terrible."

"Well, a summary of the situation is going to be put in her file." Jennifer gave a conspiratorial smile. "And from the look of things, I would guess it won't be positive." She finished off in a sing-song voice, "Not the best thing to have happen around bonus time...."

Anne shrugged. "It's her own doing." She slipped into her pumps and grabbed a pen and pad of paper. "I'm going to have to run. I've got a meeting with Alex."

"Hey," Jennifer said as she exited the cubicle. "Maybe you should ask him to join us for drinks one night after work." When Anne did not reply, she continued, "Just a suggestion."

"No comment," Anne called out over her shoulder.

* * *

The sun streamed through the windows of Alex's office as Anne, and he listened to advice from the firm's outside legal counsel.

"At this point, we think the best course of action is to negotiate a settlement with the SEC," a disembodied voice boomed out of the speakerphone. "We'll indicate that Spencer Brothers had absolutely no knowledge of the activities of Mr. Kingston and that he exceeded his power immensely."

Anne locked eyes with Alex, a tight smile plastered on her face. This was very close to what she had proposed three weeks earlier when they had been talking with the dark-haired Oko Sychaito lawyer, trying to figure out how best to proceed.

"We might want to consider an even stronger message than that," another deeper voice added. "We could say the firm would have fired Mr. Kingston for these transgressions, had he not chosen to take his own life."

"That's an option as well," the first voice agreed. "In addition, we'll indicate that new policies have been introduced to prevent such wrongdoing in the future."

"We might want to avoid using the word *wrongdoing*," the deeper voice piped up again. "Maybe say *activities* instead."

"All good suggestions," Alex said amiably. "Our management is keen to avoid the SEC levying heavy fines. I expect they'll concur with the proposed strategy."

There was a scraping of chairs in the background and some murmuring that Anne could not make out, and then one of the lawyers began talking again.

"We'll need to finish reviewing the documents you've unearthed before deciding which ones to allow the SEC to be privy to...uh...it's possible that some may fall under attorney-client-privilege, in which case we wouldn't forward them...."

"Right. We'll send you copies of everything as soon as we can."

"It's a good thing the firm hired these hotshot attorneys at the cost of an arm and a leg," Anne said as soon as the conference call was finished. "Where would we be without their innovative solutions to these daunting problems?" She began gathering her papers.

"We'd sink down the toilet faster than anyone we know." Alex raised one eyebrow pointedly. "Wait until I hand this stuff to my secretary to copy. She's going to freak."

"At least you won't get three hours of argument over the matter—" Anne replied, heading toward the door, "—and a discussion about how the other secretaries do so much less, etc. etc. etc."

* * *

When she got back to her cubicle, there was a lone, small envelope sitting dead center on her chair. It was addressed to simply Anne. She picked it up and felt her nerves go taut, her mind wildly speculating about its contents. *A pink slip?* Had Peter somehow caught wind of their suspicions about him and decided to cut her loose? Or perhaps the investment banking group had grown tired of her poking her nose into their shady deals and thrown their weight around in the C-suite? Fingers shaking, she ripped the envelope open and found a short, handwritten note tucked neatly inside.

> *Anne,*
> *As a token of our appreciation for your efforts, we enclose the following bonus. Keep up the good work.*
> *Peter Eckert*
> *VP of Municipal Bonds, Spencer Brothers*

Included were a handful of pennies.

She gave a small start as she realized she wasn't being fired and then began to laugh as she absorbed the humor of the joke.

Jennifer poked her head in sideways. "Thought you'd enjoy that."

It was hilarious, except that it had almost given her a heart attack when she had initially assumed the worst.

"How about if we haul this pile of metal to the cafeteria and buy ourselves an apple muffin or two?" Anne said, grateful for fun friends.

Jennifer gave a thumbs up. "Great idea. I'll grab my purse in case we're a tad short."

After they returned, Anne began calling the developers of the various Arkansas hotel projects, one by one, to determine their financial condition. Either they all happened, coincidentally, to be very difficult individuals, or they had been told by somebody not to cooperate. Whatever the case, Anne knew she was going to have to find a different way of sleuthing out what she wanted. She turned the matter over in her mind for a moment and then called Kelsey.

Five minutes later, she was sitting in a plush investment banking office, tea in hand. "Thanks for meeting with me on such short notice."

"No problem," Kelsey said, flashing a big smile. No longer appearing to carry the weight of the world on her shoulders, she looked relaxed and at ease.

"I'm having a hard time getting status updates for any of the Corn Dog projects—" Anne began.

"They're on the brink of failure," Kelsey said, sounding grave.

Anne nodded. This was exactly what she had expected.

"I chatted with one of the other investment bankers on our floor after you asked about them a few days ago and even managed to get copies of their most recent financial statements. I'll have my secretary make copies for you."

Anne asked about the banks.

"A total disaster—" Kelsey delivered the news with a dismissive sweep of her hand "—all related to one another somewhat incestuously. I'm fairly certain there's been double counting of the assets on some of the balance sheets, so the financial picture could be even grimmer than it appears at first glance."

"Why aren't I surprised?" Anne sighed.

"As you've probably guessed, the banks received *unusually* generous fees for providing guarantees on the bonds. Unfortunately, they're not adequately capitalized to honor their promises. All hell will break loose when those projects begin to fall apart."

Anne sank deeper in her chair. The bonds would likely be in default in less than a year.

"Sorry to be the bearer of bad news." The corners of Kelsey's mouth turned down in a gesture of commiseration.

"It's not your fault, and I want you to know that I appreciate your candor." Anne stood up to leave. "At least now I know what I'm up against."

"Unlike poor Jennifer who was broadsided by that shrew Elise."

Elise. Perhaps Kelsey could shed some light on what the HR woman had intimated about Michael being her protector. Anne tried to sound casual as she asked, "How well did Michael know her?"

Kelsey's mouth twisted sideways, and she gave a small laugh. "I guess you haven't heard."

Anne felt her stomach knot.

"He's the one who got her hired...but he made sure she wasn't in *his* department."

Of course not. Instead, Elise had been dumped ten floors below for others to cope with. *But why?*

"She's a distant niece or cousin. I forget which." Kelsey's voice hardened. "Nothing like having the right connections."

Indeed. For years, the link with Michael seemed to have made her invincible.

"Although, in some respects, they probably helped each other. He occasionally fed her tidbits about upcoming deals so that she could tip off the traders. In return, I assume she kept his working-class background a secret." Kelsey winked. "I wonder how long the little tyrant will last without him around to provide a safety net."

Not very, if the HR woman's comments were any indication. Which also meant that Elise had no obvious reason for wanting Michael dead. In fact, his death was probably a major hiccup for her.

"Have you heard anything more about the SEC investigation?" Kelsey's luminous green eyes searched her face.

Anne shook her head slowly, all the while trying to convince herself that she wasn't really lying. She hadn't heard anything she was allowed to tell.

"Me neither," Kelsey said, looking slightly puzzled. "By the way—"

Anne's ears perked up.

"—Our department has tickets to *Madame Butterfly* at the Met for Thursday. Would you like to join me?" Kelsey looked at her expectantly.

"I've never been," Anne replied, slightly taken aback. Opera? She'd always assumed it would be kind of boring, but it was a nice gesture for Kelsey to extend the invitation. "I'd love to see what it's all about."

"Great," Kelsey said, a smile filling her face. "I'll make sure to snag them."

Anne left feeling conflicted about the conversation. She had asked Kelsey for information but had not reciprocated by sharing what she knew. The word *traitor* kept popping into her mind, and she began to second-guess her decision to keep the SEC information under wraps. Kelsey obviously trusted her and was reaching out, wanting to be friends. Moreover, she was turning out to be a big help in unraveling the details of these bonds.

"You *couldn't* tell her about Marvin turning state's witness," Alex said tersely when she reported the exchange. "Peter Eckert was crystal clear on that point."

"I know," she demurred. "But still, I felt bad."

"Well, don't. We still don't know for sure how big a role she played in all of this."

"That's true, but if she was just doing what she was told—"

"—then she'll come out of this mess just fine."

And if Kelsey eventually learned that Anne had kept her in the dark, she might rescind her friendship, convinced that Anne was a two-faced snake in the grass.

"Instead of trying to bring Kelsey into a loop that she has been specifically *excluded* from," Alex eyed her sternly, "you should be keeping the guy in the corner office fully informed...and his Man Friday."

She sighed. Alex was right. "He's going to blow a gasket when he hears about this second set of problem deals."

Alex nodded. "Now would be a good time for us to come up with a strategy."

Just as they finished laying out the key points to be addressed, Alex's phone rang. "Yes." He looked at Anne, his mouth widening into a smile. "She's here."

Dismayed that her hideout had been discovered, she groaned.

"Sorry," he whispered sympathetically.

Evidently, there had been a flurry of trading inquiries, and one of the secretaries had been told to track her down. She headed toward her desk to face the onslaught. No rest for the weary. It was back to the grind.

* * *

By the time they convened with Peter Eckert and Nick Angelini that afternoon, the meeting with Kelsey had disappeared into the far recesses of Anne's mind.

"The use of an offshore bank was an interesting twist to the whole affair," Peter said when they told him about the uncashed checks.

"But it also makes it obvious that they were trying to skirt the IRS laws and regulations. If they hadn't done that..." Nick's voice trailed off as he shook his head.

"They might very well have gotten away with it," Peter murmured.

Perhaps, Anne thought to herself, but she wasn't entirely convinced. She had discovered the Pandora bonds without knowing anything about the banks or the uncashed checks. While they certainly provided proof of a fraudulent structure, the strange structure of the deals themselves was enough to raise eyebrows and start an investigation.

"You said that the incriminating evidence is stapled to the back of the closing documents?" Nick said, his eyes darting back and forth between Anne and Alex.

They both nodded.

"Collect anything and everything that refers to these Caribbean banks and bring it down to my secretary." Peter's voice sounded dry and dusty. He tilted his head and cleared his throat. "Also, if you've made any photocopies—destroy them."

Anne's eyes widened. They appeared to be moving into slash-and-burn mode.

He brushed a piece of lint off of his sleeve. "Now tell me about this second set of deals, the ones from Arkansas."

As Anne explained the risky nature of the Corn Dog bonds, how they were on the verge of collapse, and that they had been sold exclusively to retail investors, Nick began anxiously pacing around the room. He waited for her to finish and then stood very still. "My men need a full list ASAP."

Peter nodded. "Dump anything that looks problematic and avoid picking up anything new." He turned to buzz his secretary. "Get Little Rock trading desk on the phone immediately!"

"We got approval from the research department to bring these deals to market." Anne cringed inwardly as the head of the Arkansas desk began to defend himself on the speakerphone. "We *explicitly* asked whether we could sell them to retail customers."

"Who?" Nick barked. "Who gave the okay?"

"Peggy."

Peggy? Anne tried to keep her face emotionless as the discussion zeroed in on a junior analyst who had been let go in the most recent corporate restructuring.

"What possessed you to listen to that dimwit?"

"She was in the research group. Why wouldn't we?"

Peter rolled his eyes at the speakerphone. "Because that was just a temporary assignment until we could get rid of her."

"How the hell would we have known that?"

Peggy's brief tenure as a junior analyst in Research had followed a two-year stint as Peter's secretary. Local gossip held that in that role, she had abused her power by limiting who could get in to see him and which telephone messages he received. He had solved the problem by transferring her to the research group, which the poor woman had erroneously thought was a promotion. Friendly, but not particularly hard-working, Peggy spent a great deal of time making a point of letting everybody know how much power she supposedly pulled in the corner office.

"Great," Peter muttered and abruptly terminated the call. He buzzed his current secretary again. "Get William in here."

"Peggy didn't have authority to okay deals for sale to retail investors," William said once he had been briefed on the matter at hand. "If Little Rock had a question about the suitability of these bonds for their retail customers, they should have contacted one of the senior analysts." He paused and looked directly at Peter. "They know that."

Peter's lips twitched as he absorbed the information.

"Furthermore," William added drily, "she was assigned to work on straightforward, investment-grade bonds that didn't require any expertise. The type a monkey could handle."

Anne bristled at the condescending description of Peggy's responsibilities. She had been a trainee, learning the basics of the job, who had ultimately failed. Despite her many shortcomings, she had genuinely tried to get up to speed. There was no need to rip her apart so callously.

"Who was responsible for overseeing her work?" Nick asked sharply.

William's mouth curled up very slightly. "My predecessor, Tom."

Anne remembered their recently fired manager, strutting around the cubicles, talking loudly to Peggy, making sure everyone within earshot could hear him instructing her on the basics of bonds. It was as if he thought she could influence the senior executives and wanted everyone to see that he was tightly linked with her.

Nick gave Peter a quizzical look. "Another pay-off?"

Anne blinked. *Pay-off? Tom was in the business of writing glowing reports on crappy bonds for personal gain?*

"Wouldn't surprise me," Peter said with an edge to his voice. "Whose dumb-ass idea was it to make that idiot a manager anyway?"

Yours, as Anne recalled. She looked over at Nick, who was standing unusually still, his steely gaze focused on Peter.

"Tom frequently evaluated complex, risky deals such as these," William said with a small shrug. "He probably gave the okay, and Peggy simply delivered the message."

Because Michael had made it worth his while to do so? The room was silent except for the ticking of a large, round clock on the wall to her right.

Peter looked sternly at Anne and Alex. "None of what you two have just heard is to be repeated."

"Of course not," Alex said firmly.

Peter gave a perfunctory nod toward the door. "William, Nick, and I have a few more things to discuss. Privately."

Anne and Alex stood up simultaneously and made a beeline for the exit. Outside the office, Alex took off his jacket and stretched. "Things were definitely getting a little hot in there. Interesting tidbit about your ex-manager's little side business."

"I always assumed he was incompetent," Anne said, still feeling dumbfounded. "And that was the reason he was fired. It never occurred to me that he might have been pushing crappy bonds on purpose because he was profiting personally."

Alex shook his head. "This business corrupts people."

Or perhaps, Anne thought, corruptible people were drawn to this business.

He cocked his head and squinted at her. "What do you think they'll do about our retail customers? The ones who bought the Arkansas bonds."

"My guess is that they'll wait until the projects default and then deal with the lawsuits individually," Anne replied. "Let's face it. There's too much money on the line for them to buy the bonds back at par today."

"This business never ceases to amaze me," Alex said as he turned toward the elevators.

* * *

212

Anne wandered back to the research enclave and popped her head into Jennifer's cubicle.

"Guess what? Kelsey has invited me to join her at the opera."

"That's nice." Jennifer leaned back in her chair and stretched. "She's really into it. Personally, I've found it's not my cup of tea."

"I'm not sure it's mine either, but I feel kind of sorry for her," Anne said. "She seems kind of alone up there, and I don't get the impression she has many friends outside of work either."

"Ever since graduating from college—" Jennifer gave a small shrug "—her job has been her total life."

"That's what I gather," Anne said. "It seems like her entire identity is wrapped up in it."

Jennifer's face took on a pitying smile. "I don't think she's had a date in years."

Anne decided against mentioning the affair Kelsey had had with Michael. Instead, she said, "Maybe these recent events have caused her to re-evaluate her priorities."

"Could be."

"I'm kind of surprised she hasn't been promoted to VP by now."

"I know. It's strange," Jennifer replied. "I've wondered about that myself. But she's always seemed happy with her job. Perhaps she makes so much money that the title doesn't matter to her."

Anne didn't buy that for one second. Kelsey was way too competitive to ignore the prestige associated with a promotion. She would want it all.

"Which reminds me," Jennifer continued, "I hear that bonus numbers will probably be released next week. Rumor has it that the bonus pool is only 60% of the size it was last year."

"But I thought we had a good year. I know the trading desk made a lot of money."

"Equities lost a lot, so we're getting screwed. The Ice Princess and Donna have been talking nonstop about it all day."

"How do they ever manage to accomplish anything?"

"They don't," Jennifer made a face and then motioned toward her ringing phone. "I better take this."

* * *

It was dark when Anne stepped out of the terminal and headed briskly toward her apartment. It had been a long day, and she was looking forward to relaxing with Muffin. As her footsteps echoed on the pavement, she became aware of a second set of steps behind her, slowly gaining ground. She rounded the corner and heard whoever was behind her do the same. She glanced back and saw a man completely bundled up, his face not visible. Looking forward, she saw that one of the streetlamps was out and that she was about to pass a dark alley. She picked up her pace and heard him do the same. Her heart began racing. Was he following her? If so, why? Her fingers found the can of mace in her pocket and held it tight.

She crossed the street, slowing down to let him get in front, and saw two eyes peer at her from across the way. He turned at the corner and gave one last look before disappearing from view. With a sigh of relief, Anne ducked into a small neighborhood store where the presence of people and bright lights made her feel instantly safer. Only then did she slowly let go of the mace.

After spending a few minutes browsing the aisles, she exited the market. The street was silent, the full moon clearly visible in the sky. Suddenly she heard quick footsteps approaching from behind. She gripped the mace again and whirled.

"Hi," Anne's neighbor from unit three greeted her. "I'm glad I happened to see you. I've been having an issue with the gate to our garage. It keeps jamming partway down. By the way, are you planning to continue on as President when your term expires?"

21

The Opera

Three and a Half Weeks After the Meeting

O n Thursday morning, Anne pulled her scarf tight and hunched against the wind as she stepped out from the warmth of her building and began walking toward the ferry. The clouds had already begun to gather in anticipation of a major snowstorm that was forecast to hit the region overnight.

"Anne," she heard a voice calling faintly from somewhere behind. She turned and eventually spotted a dark figure in the throng waiting to board.

"Alex, what are you doing here?"

"Same thing as you." He wove his way up to her. "Trying to cross the Hudson for another fun-filled day at work."

"I thought you lived in the city."

"I do." He smiled. "I stayed in the 'burbs last night with some friends."

They stepped onto the ferry and looked for a place to stand.

"Get ready for this." Alex leaned toward her conspiratorially, and she felt her heart quicken. "Walter's been sacked."

"Our Walter? From the Pandora bonds?"

He nodded. "Word is that management at the Oko Sychaito was very unhappy about the *embarrassment* he caused the firm with these deals. Now that he's been cut loose, it will be interesting to see what his next step is. He's no longer in any position to make a deal with us."

"Do you think he'll try to turn state's witness?"

"Wouldn't surprise me. The question is whether he has anything more to offer beyond what Marvin has already told them."

The ferry jolted as it left the dock, and Alex lost his balance, falling against someone standing nearby.

"Hold on to the bar," the person muttered angrily.

"Sorry," Alex said, looking chagrined.

"We better tell Peter Eckert and Nick Angelini as soon as we get in."

* * *

That evening, she met Kelsey in the lobby at 5:30. They hailed a cab and headed uptown to a French restaurant that had recently opened to rave reviews.

"I can't believe you've never been to the opera," Kelsey said while they sipped their wine. "It's such a wonderful way to escape into another world."

"My parents took me to the Symphony when I was a child, and it bored me stiff. I've always assumed opera would be even worse."

Kelsey laughed, her perfect white teeth visible despite the dim light of the restaurant. "At least your parents tried. I'm sure it never occurred to mine. As far as they were concerned, the local football game was a major cultural event."

Anne looked at the smartly dressed woman sitting beside her, not a hair out of place, who looked like she had lived in New York City her entire life. Except she obviously hadn't. "Where are you from originally?"

"A small town in Pennsylvania that I'm sure you've never heard of. It had nothing going on except the factory. Everyone I knew worked there. My mother. My father. The people I went to school with."

"But not you."

"Not me." Kelsey's lips came together in a straight line. "Every month, there was always an argument about which bills to pay. Sometimes my father even worked double shifts to make extra money. But it was never enough. After living through years of that, I was determined to have a better life." She leaned back in her chair and took a sip of wine. "How about you? I'm guessing you're from the northeast."

"A suburb of Boston," Anne said carefully, not wanting to reveal her upper-middle-class upbringing to someone who had obviously come from a family struggling to pay the rent.

"Such a fun city! I would have loved to go to school there." Kelsey bit her lip. "But, I had to pay my own way through."

Anne nodded, thinking how fortunate she was to be the child of a physician. It meant she could attend the college of her choice and graduate with no student debt. "Jennifer and you both attended—"

"The same state university." Kelsey finished the sentence for her. "But we didn't travel in the same circles. I was there on a full-ride scholarship, working ten hours a week in the cafeteria, while she hobnobbed around with the sorority girls that wouldn't take a second look at someone like me." Kelsey leaned back and took a sip of wine.

"The whole Greek system—" Anne began, but Kelsey waved her off.

"It all worked out fine in the end. Once I had that accounting degree, I knew I'd never starve. Someone always needs help keeping the books."

The woman was a fighter. Like Michael. Self-made and self-reliant. Anne lifted her glass in a toast. "And now you have a high-powered career, live in the Big Apple, and get free tickets to the opera."

"They were meant for some clients, but something came up, and they couldn't use them." Kelsey adjusted the emerald ring on her finger so that the stone-faced directly up. A deep shade of green, it caught the light from the candle and perfectly matched her eyes. "It happens a lot, actually. One of the perks of the job."

"All we get is a free lunch."

"At least you don't have to work weekends or routinely pull all-nighters." Kelsey sighed. "I can't remember the last time I slept in or had a vacation, for that matter. I really ought to take some time off."

They were interrupted by the waitress bringing their entrees to the table.

"I've been toying with the idea of going to Vail for a week." Kelsey began to carefully cut her steak into small, square pieces. "Michael brought a group of us out to his condo there one time. That place was just amazing. It had a hot tub that overlooked the slopes. And you could ski in and out of it." She took a bite. "This is excellent, by the way. How's yours?"

"Cooked to perfection," Anne replied.

"He took two weeks off every winter to go skiing. Said he found it relaxing…." Her voice trailed off. "I guess his wife will get the place now. Or maybe it was hers all along, anyway."

"How are you faring these days with him gone?" Anne asked gingerly.

"As well as can be expected. Things are pretty hectic in the office, and the shift in responsibilities has been less than clear. You know how that goes."

"I meant personally." Anne hesitated, debating whether she dared probe any deeper. "I understand you were very close to him. I imagine his death has hit you quite hard."

Kelsey stiffened visibly, and Anne instantly regretted asking. "I'm sorry—" she stuttered, "I probably shouldn't have—"

Kelsey raised a hand to interrupt her. "I guess you've heard through the grapevine that Michael and I were more than friends for a while?" She gave a nervous laugh and looked away.

"Um-hum." Anne nodded.

"I didn't think anyone knew about it." Kelsey took a sip of her wine. "Very naïve on my part."

"He had something of a reputation," Anne replied quietly.

Kelsey sighed. "Wish I'd known that before I got involved with him. It was so *stupid* to sleep with my boss, of all people."

Anne agreed, but instead gave a small shrug, trying to suggest it was no big deal.

"I feel so embarrassed when I look back on it." Her face took on a pained expression, as if she were being physically stabbed.

"Don't." Anne waved her hand dismissively. "We all do things we later regret. Besides—" she smiled, "—he *was* very handsome."

Kelsey nodded. "*Very.*"

Anne was relieved that she had successfully confirmed the affair without alienating Kelsey in the process. She took a bite of her steak and began to chew, thinking about possible things to say next.

"Even so—" she heard Kelsey say, "I didn't exactly have a choice."

Anne tried to swallow quickly and felt the food catch in her throat. "You felt pressured?"

Kelsey nodded. "If I'd said no, he would've stopped mentoring me, and my bonus would've been hit big time."

"He said that?"

"Essentially." She picked up the cigarette she had been smoking a few minutes earlier and ground it into the ashtray until there was nothing left but the filter.

Anne bit her lip, unsure of what to say.

"He claimed that he was *drawn* to me and felt trapped in his marriage. That we had a unique bond, and he couldn't help himself," Kelsey sneered. "And at first, I believed him." She laughed harshly. "I thought he recognized that I was talented and hard-working. I thought he actually saw me as someone special."

"He probably did."

"No." Her face looked hard. "He was just using me. But it took a long time before I realized that. Before I really understood."

It had never even occurred to Anne that the affair might have been coerced. She had simply assumed Kelsey was a conniving vixen, trying to sleep her way to the top. Seeing the pain on Kelsey's face as they sat in the restaurant talking, she realized how wrong she had been.

"He put you in a very difficult position," Anne said firmly. "He should *never* have done that."

"No." Kelsey agreed, her vivid green eyes fixed on Anne. "It makes me sick to my stomach when I think about it now."

"Did you ever consider requesting a transfer or going to HR and filing a complaint?"

"I thought about it. But it would have been my word against his." She gave a weak smile. "We both know how that generally turns out...."

219

Anne saw the impossible position in which Kelsey had found herself and wondered what she would have done in the same place.

"The hardest part was the humiliation." Kelsey's face froze in a mask of contempt. "Being kicked to the curb like a piece of trash."

"What do you mean?"

"I discovered he was having a fling with Jane, our floor receptionist." Her eyes became tiny slits. "And then he started sleeping with Betty."

Anne looked down at her dinner getting cold. He had also propositioned Katie during that same time period. Anne thought it likely there had been a number of women, many of whom Kelsey had no idea about.

"Of all the people he could have chosen," Kelsey continued. "He chose her! Someone I had to work with every day. It shouldn't have shocked me, but for some reason, it did."

Anne felt her stomach tighten. "I don't know how you maintained a cordial working relationship with him after all of this."

"There was *no way* I was going to give up everything I had worked so hard to build." Kelsey looked resolute and unwavering with her arms crossed firmly in front of her. "I focused every ounce of my mental energy on two things: my bonus and getting myself promoted. Whenever I interacted with him, that's all I thought about. Everything else was just noise."

Anne picked up her knife and fork. "Do you think his wife has any idea this was going on?"

"I doubt it. She's about as dumb as they come. Spending money on cars, furs, and jewelry without a clue as to where it comes from or what it takes to generate that kind of cash. I was amazed she even conceived of the idea of his death being a murder. The process required her to conceptualize two separate, concrete thoughts." Kelsey laughed bitterly. "Maybe one of her country club friends suggested the idea. She couldn't have come up with it on her own."

"What's amazing is that it looks like she was right, after all," Anne replied, relieved that they had moved on to a less distressing topic.

Kelsey nodded but didn't appear to be listening. Anne wondered whether that meant she was still thinking about their prior conversation or perhaps disagreed about Michael's death being a murder.

"I've been wondering—" Kelsey cocked her head. "How did Alex hear about Walter being fired?"

"He was at a charity event last night for one of the dog rescues and bumped into a mutual friend."

"Hmmm." Kelsey looked quizzical. "Kind of a strange coincidence. Wouldn't you say? It suggests they travel in the same social circles."

Anne was momentarily stunned. She had assumed that whoever he talked with was just a casual acquaintance. "He certainly didn't sound like the country club type when we talked about it with him before."

"No," Kelsey said slowly. "He certainly did not." She picked up her wine glass, gently swirling it, before finally bringing it carefully to her lips.

"I'm wondering how this might change the investigation. I wouldn't be surprised if Walter approached the SEC and tried to turn state's witness." Anne paused to let her words sink in. In her mind, she had given Kelsey a warning of what might happen without telling her what she actually knew.

"I expect he will," Kelsey replied. "He'll do anything to save his skin."

"And maybe the phone calls I've been getting will finally stop," Anne said without thinking. "If he's behind them, that is."

Kelsey's eyes widened in surprise. "What kind of phone calls?"

Anne instantly regretted her comment. This was not territory she had intended to traverse.

"Oh." She tried to sound nonchalant. "Someone has been calling up in no more than a whisper, insisting that I drop my investigation into the deals. It always sends a chill down my spine."

"You're kidding!"

"No, Alex has been receiving them as well."

Kelsey looked incredulous. "Welcome to the club."

Anne stared at her for a long moment. "It never occurred to me—"

"Me neither." Kelsey rolled her eyes. "I thought I was the only one."

Anne felt her shoulders relax as she let out the breath she had been holding in. Kelsey was in the same boat she and Alex were in. There was no harm in telling her. "Walter got one, and someone left a dead rat on David's doorstep."

Kelsey smirked. "He always has to be the outlier, doesn't he."

"They each blame the other."

"That's par for the course when it comes to the two of them. What about Marvin?"

"I don't know." Anne bit her lip, her mind on instant alert again. Peter Eckert would have her head if she revealed that Marvin was cooperating with the SEC. "We haven't heard from him in a while."

"I wish we'd talked sooner," Kelsey said with a sigh. "These calls have been giving me the creeps, but I figured I shouldn't make a big fuss about them. I didn't want to look weak and powerless to my new boss."

Anne's sentiments exactly. She was surprised how much the two of them had in common.

Kelsey rolled her eyes. "It's not like anybody at Spencer Brothers would give a crap anyway."

Wasn't that the truth. Anne often felt like she was lost in a vast corporate enterprise, just a single grain of sand that could be washed out to sea with a misspoken word. "I should've realized you'd be a target as well. You worked closely on the deals. You know how they work and who took what part in their design and marketing."

"True here as well, I'm sure." Kelsey caught the waitress's attention and asked for the check.

"I'd reached the point of actually considering a phone tap," Anne confided.

"That's an interesting idea. Plus, you might want to increase the basic security around your condo. If Walter's behind them, I don't really think either of us has anything to fear, because my sense is that he's all bark and no bite. But you might feel better if you do something proactive."

"I have a guard dog that would never let anybody come near me," Anne said with false bravado. (In point of fact, Muffin would probably greet an intruder with a big hello and happily lead them to her jewelry.) "But for additional protection, I could look into some sort of alarm system, I suppose."

"Why not?" Kelsey said.

They paid their bill and started walking over to the Lincoln Center to enjoy their evening entertainment. Snow was just starting to fall and a foggy mist had settled over the city.

"Personally, I'm toying with the idea of getting a gun."

Anne paused for a moment, taken aback. "Guns make me nervous," she replied. "Plus, it seems like there are a lot of hassles in getting the permits and all."

Kelsey shrugged. "I have to look into it and see what's involved."

They picked up the pace in an effort to get out of the blustery cold.

"Living in the city," she continued, "I sometimes feel like I'm taking my life in my hands. Regardless of whether the calls stop or not, I still might like the security of one for my day-to-day living."

* * *

When Anne woke in the morning, the world was blanketed in snow. She snuggled under her comforter until the alarm broke the stillness, angrily insisting she get up. She reluctantly dressed and headed out into the cold crisp morning, wondering what the day would have in store.

"Late night?" Alex greeted her when she arrived at her cubicle an hour later.

She stifled a yawn and then told him about her evening at the opera.

"With Kelsey?" Alex sounded surprised. "I'd have been afraid there'd be a lot of awkward silences during dinner. What did you talk about?"

Anne debated whether to tell him about Kelsey being sexually harassed by Michael. "I learned that she's also received threatening phone calls."

"That's interesting," Alex said, in a tone that suggested it was anything but.

"Kelsey's a lot more relaxed in private than she is at work." Unsure why Alex seemed to dislike her so much, Anne felt a need to defend her. "We had a wonderful time."

"That's great," he said, not sounding overly enthusiastic.

She decided to change the subject. "Have you heard anything more about Walter?"

"Not really." He chuckled. "Poor chap is trying to come to terms with being summarily dismissed like that. He never saw it coming, if you can believe it."

"I thought you didn't know him personally." Anne looked at him, surprised. "That it was a friend who gave you the news."

"I don't really," Alex uttered with uncharacteristic nervousness. "That's just what I heard."

Anne nodded, wondering what to make of his reaction.

"I've been meaning to ask you something…" he began.

She mentally braced herself.

"But it's rather…."

She felt her pulse quicken. What was he struggling to say?

"Would you like to have dinner and see *Les Misérables*?"

A date. With Alex. She felt a surge of excitement.

"The reviews say it's brilliant, and I happen to know someone who can get tickets for the performance next Saturday night." He paused and looked at her nervously.

She took a deep breath. Alex was charming but also a co-worker. She should probably say no.

"I can't promise, but we might also have an opportunity to meet the cast after the show."

Ignoring the warnings blaring from the rational side of her brain, she thought about the unacknowledged sexual tension that permeated their relationship. It made the air crackle between them, and her mouth go dry. "That would be great," she replied, immediately wondering what to wear.

"I love British accents!" Katie bubbled on the phone a few minutes later. "If you marry him, you could have the wedding in a castle up in Scotland. Or, perhaps further south, closer to…what part of Britain is he from?"

"I don't know," she replied. "I'll have to ask. The thing is, we work together. Do you think it was a mistake to accept?"

Katie sighed. "He works on a different floor in a separate part of the company. And you're obviously interested. Don't overthink it!"

How could she help but consider the ramifications? If things went south, she would still have to see him occasionally. Deal with him. Perhaps even work with him. Like Kelsey and Michael. She drew a sharp breath. But, of course, that was completely different.

"The message you left on my phone this morning said you'd gone to the Opera. I'm having a hard time picturing it after the piccolo escapade in college."

The gentle, round face of Anne's freshman roommate flashed into her mind. She had been a music major and invited them to attend her spring recital.

"As I recall, you couldn't get out of there fast enough," Katie chided.

The sound had been so shrill it hurt Anne's ears, and then there had been the business with her date. "Remember Mr. Universe?" He had probably been the best-looking boyfriend Anne had ever had. Tall. Ruggedly handsome with a perfect smile. Model material.

"How could I forget. All brawn and no brains."

"Exactly." Anne laughed. "That was the night we broke up."

"Everything about that evening was a disaster! I thought his bumper was going to fall off after he backed into the tree."

Anne sighed as the memories flooded back. "It was my roommate I was worried about. She looked devastated when I told her we couldn't make her other performance. I said we had to study for our final exams, but still...."

"So, who managed to talk you into the opera?"

Anne gulped. She knew Katie would not approve. "Kelsey. Investment banking had extra tickets."

"What?" Katie gasped. "You went with the Wicked Witch? Why?"

"It's been a tough couple of weeks for her. I get the impression she doesn't get out much."

"There's a reason for that..." Katie said disparagingly.

"She's really not that bad when you get to know her. During dinner, she opened up to me about her relationship with Michael Kingston."

"Really?"

"He put her in a very tough position. She didn't feel like she could say no when he propositioned her. She was terrified he would destroy her career."

"Hmmmm."

"And then he dumped her to sleep with the secretary *they both shared*. It had to have been mortifying."

"I can definitely believe he initiated things—" Katie began.

"—which was totally inappropriate. He was her boss."

"I agree," Katie said firmly. "Total abuse of power by Michael. No question the guy's a class A jerk."

Anne knew before she said it that there was a *but* lingering in there.

"But…I have a hard time seeing Kelsey as anyone's victim. She really struck me as a user. Whatever you do, make sure you don't fall under her spell…Enough about her, though. Let's talk about what you're going to wear on this date of yours."

22

An Untimely Death

One Month After the Meeting

Monday morning, Anne set her tea down and opened the paper. She never got beyond the top story.

The Wall Street Chronicle
Monday, February 13, 1989

Brokers Falling Faster than Interest Rates

In yet another bizarre twist to the Michael Kingston affair, police have confirmed reports that a close business partner, Walter Hughes of the Oko Sychaito Bank, was found dead of an apparent suicide after falling ten stories from his apartment window.

His death comes just weeks after the death of prominent investment banker Michael Kingston III, who died of an apparent overdose of digoxin in the Spencer Brothers Offices where he worked. Mr. Kingston's death is currently classified as suspicious

227

and under investigation.

This second mysterious death, on the heels of the first, raises additional questions about the nature of the financial transactions the two were involved in and whether investigators have done enough to solve these cases.

"Isn't that one of the guys you were meeting with a few weeks ago?" Anne heard Donna cackle as she pointed at the paper. "The day Michael kicked the bucket?"

Anne's heart was thumping, yet she felt like the world was moving in slow motion. "Yes," she heard herself reply.

"Those Pandora deals have been nothing but trouble." Donna's aqua and iridescent green eyeshadow made her look like a peacock today. "I'm glad I have nothing to do with them."

"Yes," Anne heard herself say again.

"Unbelievable," Alex chimed in, appearing magically at the entrance to her cubicle just as Donna disappeared. "I just got off the phone with a friend of mine. He said Walter didn't leave a note or give any indication that he was about to take a nosedive off the balcony. His wife is absolutely devastated."

"She had no idea?"

"None." He looked grim. "He told her he needed to wrap some things up in the city. She expected him to be home in time for dinner, and then they were going to attend a big birthday bash for one of their friends."

As Alex spoke, Anne could see Kelsey in the background, walking up quietly behind him. "Wow!" she interjected, causing him to start. "I just saw the paper. So tragic."

Alex stiffened. "We were just saying."

"Do you think he did it out of remorse for killing Michael?" Anne looked at both of them.

Kelsey shrugged.

"We might never know," Alex said grimly. "It certainly would tie things up nicely and neatly for us, but it's also just as likely that he couldn't deal with being fired from the bank."

"I don't like the high mortality rate of people involved with the Pandora deals," Anne said, unable to shake her feelings of unease. "Statistically speaking, the numbers are—"

"Striking," Alex said, looking pensive.

"Is something wrong?" Kelsey asked.

"Not at all." He waved her away. "I'm just thinking about how his death might change things."

Anne was about to reel off some comments about the SEC investigation and then caught herself. Kelsey still didn't know about Marvin Goldberg cooperating with the regulators. The last thing she needed to do was inadvertently give that away.

"Well—I didn't get any weird phone calls this weekend," Kelsey replied cheerfully.

"Me neither," Anne said, watching Alex fuss with his tie. He looked hot and uncomfortable, almost nervous. She hoped their upcoming theater date would not make it awkward to interact at work.

"I think we're into a whole new era," Kelsey said confidently.

"Maybe," he said. "The whole thing is just so weird. First Michael and now Walter. I wouldn't have pegged either of them as murderers or as suicidal."

"It just shows how little we ever know someone," Kelsey replied.

Anne nodded, thinking about everything they had learned in the last few weeks about Michael, things they would never have known if they hadn't stumbled across the Pandora deals.

Out of the corner of her eye, she saw Jennifer coming towards them.

"You'll never believe what happened," she said breathlessly.

"We already know," Kelsey replied, leaving Jennifer looking deflated.

"I've got to get back upstairs," Alex said with a quick nod toward Anne. "I'll catch you later."

"How did you hear?" Jennifer asked.

"It was in the paper," Anne said. "He was fired last week. I guess he couldn't take it."

"He? Fired?"

"Walter." Kelsey thrust the paper at her.

"From the Pandora Deals," Anne added.

Jennifer glanced down. "Another one of those people killed themselves?" She shook her head. "It's becoming an epidemic."

"What were you talking about?" Anne and Kelsey asked simultaneously and then laughed, recognizing they were both on the same wavelength.

"Elise." Jennifer looked like the cat who had swallowed the canary. "She walked in on her boyfriend while he was having sex with the bimbo who lives in the apartment above. So, she won't be coming in to work today."

Yet again, the Ice Princess would be out. Although, for once, Anne could actually understand why.

"And Donna says the engagement is now definitely off."

They were interrupted by a trader looking to buy a block of bonds.

"It's been fun," Kelsey announced, looking at her watch, "but I've got to get back upstairs."

After some back and forth with the trader, Anne and Jennifer decided to work together, figuring it would ultimately save time. They headed over to the bank of file cabinets and began searching for relevant files.

"Kelsey seems so much happier these days." Jennifer tossed some financial statements onto the cabinet top. "It's nice to see. She used to sound like an indentured servant. It's like she's finally been emancipated."

Anne nodded, thinking that Jennifer was more on target than she realized. With Michael Kingston dead, Kelsey was free from seeing him prance around with Betty on a daily basis. And she no longer needed to worry about him interfering with her bonus or standing in the way of her getting a much-deserved promotion. Kelsey might not realize it now, but his death was probably a good thing for her. Anne added some papers to the growing pile.

"And I'm sensing something different about you, too," Jennifer gave her a coy look. "There's definite chemistry between you and Alex."

"You know my cardinal rule," Anne stammered.

"Cardinal. Schmardinal. He's cute. You need to lighten up."

Anne did not want to lie, but she also did not want anyone in the research group to know about her budding relationship. It was too early. Things might not work out. "If there's anything to tell, you'll be the first to know." She looked at Jennifer, confident she had managed to walk the thin line between deception and truth.

"Maybe you can bring him to my wedding." Jennifer flashed her ring.

"We'll see." Anne bent down to the lower drawer and pulled out one more document. "I think that's everything."

"What are you doing down here again?" Jennifer said in a playful tone.

Anne looked up to see Alex.

He looked at Anne. "Can we have a quick chat? In private?"

Jennifer smiled knowingly, and Anne felt her face go red. What was he doing? If he wasn't careful, everyone would start to realize there was something between them. This was exactly what she had been afraid of.

"Sure," she said, trying to sound nonchalant. "The conference room is probably empty."

"Go," Jennifer ordered and then pointed at the papers they had gathered. "I can take care of this."

Anne and Alex walked over in silence, the trading floor buzzing around them. With each step, Anne found herself becoming more annoyed. He shut the door with a click, and she turned, fuming. He was going to have to learn that her private life needed to stay that way. Private.

"I just got a call from the detective investigating Michael's death."

Anne blinked in surprise, feeling like an idiot.

"He wanted to know why Spencer Brothers hadn't turned the diskette containing the suicide note over to them. Since I'm the in-house legal counsel...well...you can imagine how ridiculous I sounded."

Ridiculous? He had no idea how close she had come to taking off his head. That would have been the epitome of ridiculous. She swallowed hard and tried to focus on what he was telling her.

"The official word all along has been that Michael's death was a suicide. I reminded him of that little fact, but I think he was trying to push my buttons to see if I knew anything more."

"But that suggests they *are* conducting a murder investigation."

"Exactly." His steel blue eyes studied her. "Just like the papers have said."

"How did he even hear about the diskette in the first place?"

"That's the interesting part." He crossed his arms. "Evidently, Michael's widow told them about it. I assume she heard from Peter Eckert…."

Anne felt her world turn sideways. Nothing was as it had seemed. "He's the one who told us there was no murder investigation."

Alex nodded.

"And now he's gone and told her about the suicide note?"

They locked eyes, in perfect understanding. Peter Eckert was not to be trusted.

Anne walked back to her desk, determined to get a look at Peter's calendar. She needed to know if he had met with Michael on the morning he died. If it turned out he had…she was unable to complete the thought. Instead, she headed out to the trading floor and slowly surveyed the room.

Peter's office was in the corner, on the periphery, with a clear view of the trading operation. His secretary, Jane, sat right outside. A quick glance through the windows showed it to be empty. *Where was he?* Anne scanned the floor once more. He was definitely gone. Somewhere.

She set to work manufacturing a diversion.

"Next week is Secretary Appreciation Day," she said to one of the traders. "I want to do something special to thank them for all their help, but I need to check Peter Eckert's calendar to make sure the timing is okay, and I don't want to spoil the surprise for Jane. Can you distract her while I take a peek? Maybe ask her to go for coffee?" Thanks to the rumor mill, she knew the two of them had begun dating recently, so it would be easy for him to pull off. And she figured he might actually like the excuse to spend time with her.

After the two lovebirds had retreated around the corner, she opened Peter's calendar and began flipping the pages. He was an extremely busy person. Flip. Flip. Always in meetings. Flip. And then she found the week.

"Anne?"

She froze at the sound of Peter Eckert's voice before slowly raising her head to find him towering over her.

"What are you doing?"

She rattled off the same story she had given the trader and then held her breath, unsure whether he would fall for it.

"Nice idea," he said and disappeared into his office.

After letting out a sigh of relief, she resumed looking at the calendar entries. The day in question was blocked out completely with one notation.

Golfing—Palm Beach, Florida.

He had been nowhere near Michael Kingston's office the morning he died.

23

The Evidence

The Wall Street Chronicle
Wednesday, February 15, 1989

Suicide Note Reveals All

Before jumping out the window of his tenth-story Park Avenue apartment on Saturday night, Walter Hughes confessed to the murder of Michael Kingston III in a letter sent to Kingston's widow. Kingston was found dead in his office on January 17 of an apparent overdose of digoxin, and a note found next to his body indicated he had committed suicide. However, his widow has steadfastly maintained that her husband was murdered and convinced police to open an investigation.

In Hughes's long and rambling note, he expressed remorse for killing Kingston. In addition, he described business transactions involving falsified records with offshore Caribbean banks that he feared were on the brink of discovery by investigative authorities. He railed against one of his partners, David Singer, a corporate bond lawyer, complaining bitterly that he expected Singer to cooperate with the authorities and testify against both him and Marvin Goldberg, another co-conspirator. Police have announced that the Kingston murder case is now officially closed.

Anne whirled around in her chair in preparation for heading up to Alex's office and then saw him rushing breathlessly toward her cubicle.

"Have you seen—" he began, and then in response to her nod, continued, "It's a load of rubbish."

"I know!" she replied. "Whoever wrote this letter to Michael Kingston's widow doesn't know that Marvin has already spilled his guts to the SEC. There's *no way* Walter wrote it."

Alex furrowed his brows. "We've hit our second fake suicide note this month."

"It can mean only one thing." She looked straight at him. "He was murdered. Just like Michael was."

Alex nodded, his face terse. "And neither Marvin nor David Singer is the killer."

"Right." Anne leaned back in her chair. "Whoever wrote this note must be someone more on the periphery, or better yet, a non-participant in the deals."

"Which leaves just about anybody, since we both know the guy was detested by virtually all." Alex rested his hand on his chin.

"Except," Anne continued her line of analysis, "whoever's been harassing us with the threatening calls and letters knows who each of the participants is, despite the fact that we've not been publicly identified in the papers. That means the person must have an intimate knowledge of who Michael was meeting and working with. Someone like...his secretary, for example."

Alex looked taken aback. "Betty seemed genuinely disturbed about his death. And every time we've seen her, she's reminded me of a little bird with a broken wing, not some cold-blooded murderer."

"It could be a ploy," Anne countered. "Are you aware that Michael's widow has been running around telling people that Betty killed him?"

"What?" Alex's voice sounded almost strangled. "Where did you hear that?"

"My best friend bumped into her at a wedding a few weeks ago. In Hawaii, of all places."

"Hawaii?" He shook his head. "That was fast."

Anne shrugged, thinking it best to defer a conversation on that topic until later. "You've got to hand it to her. She's the one who initially insisted that he'd been murdered when everyone else thought it was just suicide. What if she's right about Betty as well?"

"Hang on," Alex paused. "Betty was with Michael in San Diego when the note was written. When would she possibly have had time—or opportunity—to access a computer?"

"Are we sure she was with him for the entire trip?" Anne mentally tried to reconstruct the conversation they had had with her.

"I thought that's what she said."

"I remember her saying she accompanied him to *take notes and assist*," Anne made air quotes.

"Right." He nodded in agreement.

"But I can't recall whether we then *assumed* that meant she was with him the whole time. Did she explicitly say that?"

Alex furrowed his brows. "I don't know. I think we were so floored about the *assist*—" he coughed dramatically, "i.e., *the affair*, that we might not have prodded any deeper."

"What if she flew separately? Joined him partway through?"

"That would mean she flew out for a tryst *after* writing the suicide note," he said, looking skeptical.

"Or returned early and wrote it then." Anne bit her lip. Given what she'd seen of Betty, it was hard to believe either of those scenarios. It would mean she was a cold-blooded killer, pretending to be in love while secretly looking for an opportunity to take Michael out.

"If so, what was her motive?"

"Maybe he'd begun an affair with yet someone else?"

"She certainly had opportunity. Remember?" He cocked his head. "Michael left his coffee behind in the office. Betty brought it in for him just as we were starting."

Anne had forgotten that detail.

"No doubt she had access to whatever he ate or drank and before the meeting as well." Alex shook his head. "Even so, I still don't buy it."

"Me neither," Anne paused, "but I think we need to find a way to confirm where she actually was on the day the suicide note was written. To rule her out for sure."

Anne began to picture the conference room that morning with the Pandora Partners seated around the table and Walter angrily flicking his gold pen. Was there anyone else to consider besides Betty? She froze as another memory came to mind.

The Ice Princess.

Elise was the one who told everyone down on the trading floor that Michael had been murdered. Not only that, Anne had seen her wafting around the floor shortly before he died. Anne's heart began beating faster as she laid the information out for Alex.

"She's been passing confidential information about upcoming bond sales between the investment banking floor and trading?" He looked grim. "That needs to be reported up the chain immediately. Separate and apart from that, we need to figure out if she could possibly have anything to do with Michael's murder."

"Maybe we—" Anne began.

They were interrupted by one of the secretaries saying they were wanted down in Peter Eckert's office immediately. They looked at each other and headed toward the trading floor.

"Damn that Walter!" As usual, Nick Angelini paced back and forth while he spoke. "Why did he have to mention the un-cashed checks in his suicide letter? Now everybody knows about the offshore bank. I had hoped we could make that entire business quietly disappear from the picture."

Anne and Alex exchanged glances. No doubt, he had planned to destroy the checks. And if they had been asked about it later by the SEC? He probably would have instructed them to lie. She took a deep breath and let it out slowly.

"Okay," Peter Eckert said gruffly. "Send them along to our outside legal counsel. We'll let them deal with them." He scrutinized Anne. "Looks like his widow was right about Michael being murdered. And that you were right to be concerned."

"Unfortunately," Anne replied, wondering what exactly his relationship with the widow was.

"And now she gets to collect the insurance." Nick raised his eyebrows pointedly. "Regardless of whether she actually *needs* the money or not. From what I hear, it's an *unusually* large policy."

Anne briefly considered telling them there was no doubt that Walter had also been killed as well. Would they believe her? Probably not. She looked over at Alex fidgeting in his seat. Was he thinking the same thing?

"Everyone is dismissed."

She hesitated for just a second and then stood up, emerging from the meeting drained.

"I didn't think it was the right time to bring up the inconsistencies in Walter's suicide note," Alex said sheepishly, as if reading her mind. "I didn't see what it would buy us."

"Me neither." For all they knew, Peter could be the murderer. Or Elise. Or Betty. They needed to narrow the field before they started leveling accusations.

She returned to her desk and found two messages from Kelsey imploring her to call back as soon as possible. The second was marked urgent.

"Have you seen the papers?" Kelsey sounded virtually hysterical. "It was Walter all along."

"We need to talk," Anne replied and then said she would be up immediately.

The elevator took an eternity to arrive. While she waited, she grew uneasy. How was she going to explain everything?

"Walter always seemed like such a nice guy," Kelsey said the moment Anne stepped foot through the door. "A bit pompous for my taste—" she stopped suddenly, seeing the expression on Anne's face. "What?"

Anne tried to figure out how to begin. "Well—"

"I know." Kelsey flashed an impish grin. "It's bad to speak ill of the dead." She sighed. "I'm just thrilled that it's finally over."

"The thing is—"

"No more anxiously looking behind our backs, hesitantly answering our phones, wondering what the next weird phone call or letter will bring." Kelsey broke into a broad smile. "It's such a relief that the pieces have finally come together."

Anne hated to burst her bubble, but Kelsey needed to know she was still in danger. "Not as tightly as you think."

Kelsey froze. "What do you mean?"

"Whoever wrote that letter to Michael's widow doesn't realize that Marvin has already turned state's evidence. He's been cooperating with the SEC for weeks." There, she had done it, told Kelsey exactly what she had been forbidden to tell.

Kelsey's jaw dropped in mute surprise.

"I'm sorry. Peter Eckert was explicit that nobody was to be told, not even you."

"But we both work for Spencer Brothers." Kelsey's voice was barely audible. "I thought we were on the same team...."

"We are," Anne replied, knowing her words rang hollow. "But Peter's only concern is the trading floor. And he insisted...." Anne felt terrible watching the animation drain from Kelsey's face, as if a plug had been pulled.

"You're sure Walter knew?"

Anne nodded. "He tried to make a deal with us."

Kelsey sat down, obviously trying to absorb the information. "Who else knows?" she asked slowly.

"Alex, a few of our very senior traders, David Singer, and our outside legal counsel...." Anne paused, trying to determine whether she had forgotten anybody. "That's it."

"Everybody but me," Kelsey said flatly.

Anne sighed, unsure what else to say. "I'm really sorry I couldn't tell you."

Kelsey appeared to recede, as if she was tightening from within.

"But I'm telling you now, despite Peter Eckert, because you need to know that Michael's killer is still on the loose. You and I could still be potential targets."

Kelsey looked at her blankly.

Anne summed up the implications for her shell-shocked friend. "What this means is that the murderer isn't one of the people intimately involved with the deals. That leaves someone more on the periphery. One possibility is that it's Betty."

"Betty?"

Kelsey sounded distant. Anne wondered how well she was registering the conversation.

"She was his most recent paramour. Maybe he screwed her over too. No question she had opportunity on the day of the murder. I know she seems sort of timid, but…." Anne felt like she was babbling.

"I suppose it's possible."

"We're also wondering if it could be Elise."

"But Michael always protected the little shrew," Kelsey said slowly. "And I don't see how she could have slipped the suicide note into his office or planted the drugs in his coffee…whereas Betty…."

They all kept coming back to Betty. She made the most sense. And at the same time, she didn't.

Kelsey's eyes took on an intensity that made it clear she was fully focused on the conversation. "A few months ago, Michael bought a condo in Manhattan for her. None of us would have even known about it except that Michael's wife has recently discovered the purchase and is threatening to sue for it."

"But why would Betty murder him for giving her a condo?"

Kelsey raised her eyebrows. "Evidently, there was a loan on the place for $500,000 that was forgiven as a result of Michael's death."

"So, she killed him for the money? To own it free and clear?"

"Why not? She doesn't make all that much as a secretary. It's a penthouse suite in a very nice neighborhood."

Anne tried to make sense of what she was hearing.

"However, Betty may end up being thwarted in the end." Kelsey gave a tight smile. "Michael's wife is trying to circumvent his will and call the loan in."

240

"Wow," Anne replied. "If she murdered him to get the condo and then doesn't even get to keep it in the end, that would be a bummer."

"You think? Betty's in a major twit over the situation. She's been running around asking everyone what she should do."

"Interesting. I still think the key here is the suicide note. We know she was in San Diego with Michael for at least part of his business trip, but was it the entire time? Maybe we've overlooked some opportunity she had to write it. How about if you ask around and see if anything weird turns up?"

"I'll get on it right away," Kelsey paused, an odd expression on her face. "Have you told anybody else about this?"

"Oh God, no. Without proof, we can't go arbitrarily accusing people. Plus, we don't want her to know she's under suspicion."

"Exactly. She might do something brash, like disappear." Kelsey's voice sounded tense and edgy.

"And since you work on the same floor, you should, obviously, be very careful in your dealings with her. She's a potentially dangerous individual."

Kelsey gave a terse nod, her jaw set in a tight line.

"I know." Anne stood up to leave. "Hopefully, this will all be over soon."

When she returned to her desk, she felt a wave of relief. It had been stressful keeping Kelsey in the dark. Now that she had finally shared what she knew, they could work together and determine whether Betty had indeed murdered Michael. But if Betty didn't do it, who did?

She was interrupted in her thoughts by the arrival of Carter, who stopped by to say the traders had already been told their bonuses.

"Have you heard anything about when we might be told ours?"

"No," she said, realizing she had not had time to even think about how big it might be or when they would be dispensed.

Carter squinted his eyes at her as if he thought she was lying.

"Maybe William can give you some idea of the timing," she suggested. He was their manager, after all.

"I already asked." Carter turned sideways and gave a big sneeze. "All I got was an icy stare."

"Oh." She took a small step back to avoid the cloud of droplets and then began searching her mind for another way to get rid of him. "You could try asking Donna."

"She said it would happen at the end of the week."

"Well then, why are you asking me?" she asked, exasperated and not really caring if he knew it.

"I thought you might know something more specific," he said as he trundled away.

Anne swore a silent epithet to herself and then wandered over to the row of secretaries' desks. Gwen was alone, single-handedly answering all of the incoming calls, having been abandoned by the two other admins.

"He's on the other line. Can you please hold?" Gwen set the phone down, and the hold light blinked. "What's up?"

"Do you fill out time cards?" Anne asked.

"You bet," was the sharp reply. "Anything to make us feel inferior and less professional than we already do."

The phone rang, and while Gwen took a message, Anne saw Elise slink into Donna's office.

"That's the third time Elise's boyfriend has called. He sounded kind of annoyed."

"I just saw her—" Anne said.

"If she wants her messages, she can come get them," Gwen replied tartly. "Why were you asking about the timesheets?"

"Well—if I wanted to find out whether a particular secretary was out of the office one day, how would I go about doing it?"

"You could call up Susan in Personnel and ask her to pull the card for that individual for that week."

"What about a secretary up in the public finance area?"

"Same thing. Susan handles all of them. But you know, there's an easier way."

Anne's ears perked up. "Really?"

"Sure, just ask the other secretaries who work up there. Find out who covered for her. I can do it easily enough. Who is it?"

"Betty Manchester."

Gwen looked intrigued. "She's the one who worked for Michael Kingston, right?"

Anne nodded. "I'm specifically interested in Friday, January 13th, which was the week before his death. I want to know where she was that day."

"I'll ask around and let you know what I find." The phone rang, and she cupped her hand over the receiver. "If I come up with something, you'd better let me know why."

"It's a deal," Anne said.

24

Betty

One Month After the Meeting

Thursday turned out to be bonus day. One by one, they were each tapped on the shoulder and invited into the quiet chambers of William's office, their faces scrutinized by the others for any sign of emotion when they emerged. Making sure to hide the ecstatic thrill she felt upon hearing her unbelievable bonus amount, Anne put on a poker face and walked calmly and carefully back to her desk.

"Are you going to buy a fur this year?" Gwen's voice shattered her internal reverie.

Try a Mercedes Benz or something on that order, Anne thought obnoxiously to herself. "Definitely not," she said, maintaining her cool façade despite the excitement churning within her. "I feel sorry for the animals."

"There's no way my bonus will be big enough to buy me anything major." Gwen crossed her arms indignantly. "And my credit cards are all maxed out. I can barely make my monthly payments. Sometimes I think I should just file for bankruptcy so it can all be wiped away."

Anne groaned inwardly. Clearly, Gwen was getting warmed up for another whining session.

"It's so maddening." She gestured back toward the other two secretaries chatting away in the distance. "I do so much more than they do. And yet I'll probably still get the same piddly amount."

Anne nodded while thinking about possible ways to invest her money.

"And not only that, William said it might be two or three weeks before we even hear."

"Really?" The words tumbled out absently, her mind continuing to wander.

"Yeah," Gwen continued to huff. "It's unbelievable. We're treated like scum."

With effort, Anne redirected her attention to Gwen's moving mouth.

"I really ought to look for another job. That's what Carter says."

Ugh. Anne had completely forgotten about him. He would probably come by next and start badgering her about her number. Maybe she should go up to Alex's floor and hide for a little while. Or she could give Kelsey a call and suggest they meet for coffee.

"But that's not the reason I came over. I got some information about Betty."

Anne snapped back to attention.

"She was definitely out of town on those days you asked about, on a business trip, with Michael Kingston."

"The whole time? You're sure?" Anne kept her face expressionless.

"My friend in accounts payable pulled her expense report. She and Michael took the same flights and ate at the same restaurants. The firm paid for *everything*. Talk about unfair," Gwen practically spat. "We never get to travel down here."

"I don't think secretaries up there commonly travel with their bosses either. There were probably extenuating circumstances." Anne saw no need to spread more gossip about the affair.

"The fact that she was boinking the boss didn't hurt." Gwen winked.

"Everyone up there knows?" Anne asked sheepishly.

"Is the pope Catholic?"

Anne kicked herself for being so naïve. Of course they did. Kelsey announced it on the day of Michael's murder to everybody sitting in the conference room. She had undoubtedly told her co-workers as well. And in later conversations, even Anne's manager, William, claimed to have heard the rumors. What had she been thinking?

Gwen gave her a shrewd look. "She was flashing a *huge* sapphire ring around when she returned. And he gave her a luxurious fox fur a few months before that. It sure would be nice if someone rescued *me* from this dungeon and threw in a fur for good measure." She turned on her heel and strode away.

Anne considered this newest information. *Perhaps Betty found her way to a computer while in San Diego, managed to write the suicide note, and then worked on her tan.* She frowned. *After frolicking in the sun and lazing in bed with Michael, Betty gazed at her beautiful new ring and decided she was fed up with being his mistress and—no!* She frowned again. *It was highly unlikely Betty had anything to do with the fake suicide note. But if not Betty, then who?* Out of the corner of her eye, she saw Carter ambling toward her cubicle. She leapt out of her chair to avoid being trapped in yet another useless conversation.

"I'm late!" she called out, edging past him toward the elevators, breathing a sigh when the doors closed.

Alex looked exhausted when she appeared in his office. "Quarterly filings." He waved at some papers on his desk. "I'm ready for a break."

She explained her need for a quick escape and then told him what she had learned about Betty. "Do you think Michael was actually planning to marry her?"

"Hard to say." Alex shrugged. "A mistress that everyone knows about? Not the best way to begin divorce proceedings. I'm surprised they weren't more discreet."

Anne thought of Kelsey and cringed. It had to have been galling for her to see him lavish one expensive gift after another on Betty.

"Kelsey was just one of many women he slept with," Alex said dismissively. "I feel sorry for his wife, who may not have had any idea this was going on."

"Or perhaps she knew exactly what was going on. That would be pretty sad as well." Anne imagined his pampered wife, mortified by her husband's philandering, afraid to get divorced for fear she would be affected financially, and hoping that no one in the country club would discover her dreadful secret. "On the other hand, that could also be a motive for murder."

Alex looked dubious. "His wife?"

"She stands to inherit." Anne shrugged. "And she knew about the affairs. She may even have picked up a lover herself."

"Peter, you mean."

Anne nodded. "What if they're in it together? And we're feeding him everything we know...."

Alex grimaced. "A sobering thought."

"His wife could have easily written the suicide note while he was playing with Betty in San Diego. The only question is how she put the digoxin in his coffee."

"Unless it wasn't in his coffee...."

Anne felt her heart skip a beat. "Oh, my god. Maybe it was in something else he ate instead...."

"Something he brought from home?

"Exactly. Perhaps Betty would know." Anne paused. "Except we need to be absolutely certain she didn't murder him before we start asking questions about his eating habits that morning."

"Right. Maybe Kelsey instead." He checked his watch. "Bloody hell. I need to finish these reviews. Let's sleep on it and decide in the morning."

* * *

"Pretty early showing for an investment banker," Anne said half-jokingly when Kelsey appeared at the entrance of her cubicle at 8 am.

"I wanted to catch you before you got into your day."

"As long as it isn't about bonuses." Anne popped the rest of the bagel and cream cheese hastily into her mouth. "Everyone here is obsessed."

Kelsey gave a tepid laugh and began to fidget with her earring, leading Anne to wonder if she was uncomfortable with the topic.

"I'm glad you stopped by," Anne said, attempting to reset the conversation. "Alex and I came up with a new idea yesterday, but first, I want to fill you in on what we've learned about Betty."

She became aware of Kelsey's clear green eyes studying her intently.

"I've discovered, through my own sleazy means—" Anne paused to wash the food down with some orange juice before continuing, "—that she was in San Diego all four days, including the day the suicide note was written. Now that doesn't entirely rule her out, but—"

"I'm way ahead of you," Kelsey broke in quickly with a wary edge to her voice. "Not only did Betty accompany Michael on his trip to California, but the two of them were sailing with our clients in a lovely yacht at the time the note was written." She shook her head. "There's absolutely no way Betty could have done it, even if there were a computer at her disposal."

"That really puts the nail in the coffin." Anne carefully wiped the corners of her mouth. She always felt self-conscious eating at her desk.

"Exactly." Kelsey tapped her foot nervously. "And your new idea?"

"The wife."

Kelsey raised an eyebrow.

"What if something other than the coffee was laced with digoxin? Something he brought from home? Like the half-eaten breakfast pastry that was found at his side?"

"It's possible," Kelsey said evenly. "But—"

Anne was puzzled by her reaction. "You don't think so?"

Kelsey hesitated. "I've identified someone else."

Anne started in surprise. "Elise?"

Kelsey took a half step backwards and looked away. "I think we should wait until Alex can join us."

She tensed. Kelsey seemed different this morning, remote and distracted. It was disconcerting. "Okay. Let's see if he's available." She turned to pick up her phone.

"Not now."

Anne stopped, disappointed and slightly annoyed. She was impatient to hear why Kelsey had changed her mind about Elise. "But—"

"I've got a *million* things on my plate," Kelsey interrupted and glanced down at her watch. "I really shouldn't have even come down here in the first place."

Kelsey's smile felt disingenuous, but Anne shrugged her shoulders in what she hoped was a casual, acquiescing manner. "When would you like to do it instead?"

"Soon. I'll check my calendar and get back to you."

Anne nodded and watched Kelsey retreat silently from her cubicle. After she was certain Kelsey was out of earshot, she turned to dial Alex's number.

"Why is she leaving us so completely in the dark? Frankly, I found her manner a little bizarre."

"Don't forget she and Michael were very close." Alex sounded unconcerned. "She's always a bit high-strung. Perhaps the hunt for Michael's killer has set her into an emotional tailspin."

"Maybe," Anne said, unconvinced. "But she was really dismissive of the idea that it might be his wife. She acted as if she had found something really damning that was going to shock us out of our socks. And we're the ones who suggested it might be Elise in the first place!"

"Leave it to Kelsey to insist upon creating all this tension and hype." His disapproval echoed down the line. "A normal person would have simply told you what they knew. Instead, she acts like you're out to lunch, makes this big dramatic production, and holds you in suspense until it is convenient for her to unveil her mastery. Doesn't that strike you as just a little unnecessary?"

It did, but Anne didn't want to compound his already jaundiced view of Kelsey. "She did sound really busy—"

"Give me a break," Alex retorted. "It would've taken her all of five seconds to tell you her theory. You need to stop defending her and call a spade a spade."

Anne drew a sharp breath. Was she making excuses for Kelsey, or was he being overly negative? The animosity between the two of them seemed to have grown stronger in the last few weeks. Neither of them seemed able to tolerate the other for more than a few minutes at a time.

"I'll hear what she has to say," he continued, sounding resigned, "but I'm not holding my breath. Until then, I'm going to finish my summary of those quarterly filings. Accomplish something useful."

"And I'll start writing up what I've learned about those junky Corn Dog bonds so that everyone knows to stay clear of them."

She hung up the phone feeling rattled. Like Alex, she was annoyed by Kelsey's latest stunt, but she also was put off by his negative attitude toward her friend. It seemed unnecessarily hostile, and she did not like being caught between the two of them. Going forward, Anne resolved to step out of any conflict that might arise and let them manage it themselves. She turned to face her computer and began to compose her report.

"Knock. Knock."

She looked up from her typing a few hours later.

Jennifer was rubbing her hands together fiendishly, like a cartoon villain. "Brace yourself."

Anne tensed with anticipation. Was she about to announce that she had received a gigantic bonus? Or perhaps the opposite, and was quitting her job?

"Elise was just fired."

"No!"

"Yes!" Jennifer did a little victory dance. "Finally! The gods have spoken!"

"That's great," Anne said, shocked to realize how much she relished the downfall of a fellow employee. But Elise wasn't just any co-worker. She was the most difficult person Anne had ever worked with. And possibly a murderer. "Do you know why?"

"She told one of the traders that some crappy nursing home bond was a sure bet, so he bought a ton of them. Anyone could see the place was on the verge of bankruptcy and, sure enough, it defaulted the next day. The trading desk took a *huge* loss." Jennifer motioned toward the head trader's office. "When Mr. Intense found out, he blew his stack."

"I never thought we'd see the day."

"You're telling me." Jennifer beamed. "I'm so excited I can hardly stand it, but I can't stay and gloat. I have twenty minutes to dig up some information for Vito. You know how he is. If I show up empty-handed, he'll have a cow."

Anne watched Jennifer float happily away and then placed her hands on the keyboard and resumed typing. A few minutes later, the phone rang.

"I've found what I need," Kelsey said. "Let's meet in Alex's office at 5:30 pm."

25

Alex

One Month After the Meeting

"I thought we might get thirsty," Kelsey announced when she arrived and started popping open the cans of cold soda she had brought along. Anne was surprised, but also impressed, by Kelsey's thoughtfulness. She hoped it boded well for the meeting.

"I can tell you don't work on the trading floor." Anne motioned toward the cups. "Downstairs, we drink our soda directly out of the can."

"It tastes better this way." Kelsey's eyes sparkled with amusement. "Would anyone care for some chips?"

"My favorite!" Alex grabbed a bag and immediately started munching.

"Excellent idea." Anne leaned over to steal one from him.

"Hey!"

"I just want a couple."

"We've been on pins and needles all day." Alex relented and handed her the bag. "We're dying to know what *sordid* information you've amassed."

Kelsey passed one of the cups to Anne and then looked at Alex. "I assume you've heard that Betty's not our *man.*"

He nodded. "Or *woman,* for that matter. Even though she's always blushed guiltily at the very mention of Michael's name."

The quizzical expression on Kelsey's face was at odds with his light attempt at humor.

"And she had *ample* opportunity to drug his coffee," he hastened to add. "That's the real reason we considered her."

"She was embarrassed." Kelsey finished pouring soda into the other two cups. "For some reason, she didn't think anyone knew about her little dalliance."

"And yet she returned from San Diego flashing that big rock." Alex chuckled. "Not exactly the best way to keep things under wraps. It certainly—"

"I've checked her story out thoroughly," Kelsey cut him off.

Alex stiffened.

"There's no way she could have done it." Kelsey seemed oblivious to his discomfort. "Once she realizes you're accusing her of Michael's murder, she'll—"

"Wait a minute. I'm not—"

"It's common knowledge in our department that the two of them were together all weekend. You can't hang it on her."

Anne became uneasy. They had been meeting for all of five minutes, and the two of them were already crosswise. She debated whether to intervene and say something to try to help defuse the tension.

"I'm not hanging it on anybody," he responded testily. "I was just trying to explain why we suspected her at all." He raised his eyebrows and gave Anne a sideways glance. "Betty's clearly no longer in the running. Anne and I have been wondering whether it could be Michael's wife. I mean widow."

Kelsey peered at him. "An interesting idea, but I'm skeptical."

"So tell us why you think it's Elise," he said with a wry smile. "Enlighten us."

"Once I lay everything out, I wonder if you'll still feel that way."

A faint chill ran down Anne's spine. "What do you mean?"

Kelsey leaned back and took a long sip. "I mean that I've been doing a little research and have discovered some rather startling information." She gave Alex a withering look. "Some might even call it *damning*."

Anne felt a growing sense of alarm spread through her chest.

"Alex," Kelsey continued, "where do your parents live?"

He surveyed her coldly before answering. "New Jersey."

"In Short Hills, New Jersey, is what you mean."

Anne started in surprise. Alex came from the same town as Michael Kingston?

"Yes," he replied icily. "Not that it's any business of yours."

"I believe your family belongs to the same golf club that Michael and Walter did—" Kelsey's voice was syrupy sweet, "—that is, prior to their premature exits from life as we know it."

Anne stared at him in disbelief. He had been socially friendly with them outside of work?

He shrugged his shoulders. "Where," he asked calmly, "might I be so bold as to ask, is all this leading?"

Kelsey ignored the question and plodded on. "The same club you acted so disgusted and revolted by. Please correct me if I'm wrong."

Anne found herself struggling to make sense of what she was hearing. The Alex she knew was a down-to-earth guy who acted like he respected women. Not some racist jerk who hobnobbed around with the country club set. And yet, it explained why he and Michael had been meeting to discuss a charity event the morning of his death, why Walter was chatting up the steeplechase fundraiser with him before their teleconference a few weeks earlier, and how he had "heard" about Walter being fired so quickly. They were all part of the same tight little social circle.

Alex gave her a level look. "I don't belong to any of those clubs."

"That may be true today, but that wasn't the case some years ago."

He looked uncomfortable and annoyed at the same time.

"As a teenager, you belonged to those very clubs through your parents' membership. Didn't you?" She sounded like a prosecutor, relentlessly grilling a recalcitrant witness. "Consequently, your horrified reaction was something of a put-on."

"Not at all. I detest their practices."

Alex's face looked strangely different. The crooked smile, that had previously seemed so cute, now had a slightly malicious, almost sinister quality.

"In fact, you've been holding quite a bit back from us."

The two locked eyes, each looking like they would eat the other for dinner.

"Like what?" he said in a baiting tone, daring her to continue.

"Like the fact that Michael Kingston and your parents were fairly chummy up until his death."

Alex snorted.

She turned and spoke directly to Anne, as if he were no longer in the room. "They served on a board together for some local cancer charity, and yet—"

"Yet what?" Alex shot back.

She turned to face him again. "You never mentioned that tiny little detail to us."

"It wasn't relevant."

Anne could practically see the frost forming on each and every one of his words.

"Oh really?" Kelsey scoffed. "I've got it on good authority that you were in Michael's office the day he died. After everyone had left. Is that irrelevant as well?"

"That's not true," he sputtered, his face starting to turn red.

"What were you looking for? Were you hiding evidence of something related to the crime, something like the digoxin you'd crushed into his sugar?"

"I wasn't looking for anything! I wasn't there!" Alex exclaimed, looking back and forth at Anne and Kelsey like a confused squirrel, desperately trying to decide whether to turn back or continue crossing the road as a car barreled straight toward it.

She looked smug. "You've always had it out for Michael. Probably jealous of his success and secretly pining for that mannequin of a wife he married. And then, finally, you saw your chance."

Alex became eerily still.

"You were there that fateful morning. Alone with him. You put the digoxin in his drink and killed him."

255

Anne sank back heavily in her chair and absorbed the weight of Kelsey's words.

"No!" Alex looked frantically at Anne. "You don't believe any of this, do you?"

She sat in stunned silence, not knowing what to believe anymore.

"The reason I never mentioned my Short Hills background," he began in a rush of words, "is because it would be obvious that I come from a wealthy family. I never mention it to anyone if I can help it. I don't want to alert gold diggers that there's a treasure trove in their midst. And I want to succeed as a lawyer on my own merit, without the benefit or crutch of my family name."

Anne mentally registered the explanation. It was plausible, but was it true?

"I had no idea my parents served on some board with Michael," he continued in the same frenzied tone. "They're involved with a number of charities. So am I for that matter, but I don't tell them every single person I interact with. The fact is, I detest the country clubs and their racist practices and resigned my membership after law school."

Anne turned to look at Kelsey, curious to see her reaction to his explanation, and found her studying Alex, as if he were some newly discovered creature she had never seen before.

"I should have known that you had a load of tosh like this cooked up and ready to serve." In addition to being angry, he sounded hurt. "Who's to say you're not the killer trying to pin it on me!"

"You're forgetting one thing, Alex," Kelsey paused before continuing triumphantly. "Our ominous phone caller was a man, not a woman. Therefore, a man, not a woman, is responsible for this murder. That man was you!" she finished, sounding like a venomous snake.

"That's rubbish! You're suggesting I fabricated the phone calls, and yet I've got them on tape. Rubbish!"

"Anne, you received the calls." Kelsey looked at her expectantly. "It must have been obvious to you they were made by a man."

Anne suddenly realized she had no idea what sex the mysterious caller actually was. All she had ever heard was a threatening, guttural whisper that she had assumed was a man, but in point of fact, could just as easily have been a woman. A flood of thoughts immediately began racing around her mind, clamoring for attention that she couldn't even begin to process, like why she had assumed one gender over the other and whether that characterized her as sexist. She kept trying to reconcile what she was hearing from Kelsey with what she thought she knew about Alex. Was it possible she had completely misjudged him?

"I couldn't really tell," she replied.

"My caller," Kelsey said decisively, "was a man."

"This is ludicrous!" Alex shot back angrily. "You're out of your mind to accuse me of such a thing. I don't know what your problem is and whether you actually believe this rubbish, but I've heard enough. This conversation is over. Get out of my office." His finger shook as he pointed at the door. "Now!"

Anne had never seen him this angry. His lips had narrowed, there was a wrinkle between his brows, and his face was colored a bright, splotchy red.

Kelsey stood up and took a few steps. "Come on, Anne. You shouldn't stay here alone."

She started to rise and then sank back into her chair again.

Alex lifted both hands in a show of despair. "She's off her trolley. You can't possibly believe her."

Anne saw the pleading in his eyes and looked down, unable to meet his gaze. Was he capable of murder?

"We've worked together for years. You know that's not who I am."

It's certainly not who she had thought he was. She had been looking forward to her date with the handsome, but slightly shy, lawyer with the fun British accent that she knew from work. *Thought* she knew. But did she? It could be that he was a psychopath who had been planning to murder her at the end of the evening.

Anne became aware of her hands, clasped tightly in her lap, turning white from the pressure. "I can't believe—" she began.

Alex went perfectly still, watching Anne struggle with her thoughts.

"Come on," Kelsey repeated, taking another step toward the door. "Let's go."

Anne felt trapped in a tug of war, paralyzed by uncertainty. Whatever decision she made at this point would infuriate one of them.

"Alex—" Kelsey said after a long moment, "You should turn yourself in."

He jumped up, his nostrils flaring, and put both hands on the polished wooden desk. "I've done nothing wrong!"

"If you don't—" she finished quietly but firmly, "—we will."

Breathing heavily, he glared at Kelsey, then slowly and deliberately picked up his drink and took a sip. "Anne, I'd like to be alone right now if you don't mind."

She felt a sharp pang in her chest. He obviously felt betrayed by her lack of trust in him. She stood up reluctantly and joined Kelsey.

"It's just—" she groped for the right words as they walked toward the elevator, "—so unexpected...so out of the blue...so opposite of his general character to have done something like this." It didn't seem possible.

"I know how much of a shock this must have been." Kelsey touched Anne's elbow lightly. "I'm sorry you had to be there and see that. To be honest—I was afraid to confront him alone."

Anne shook her head. "There must be some other explanation."

"There is no other explanation." Kelsey spoke slowly and firmly, her face impassive. "You have to look at the facts here. He's not who you think he is."

Anne scrutinized her face, but could not read what was behind the mask. "Are you really going to go to the police?"

"Not yet. I think Alex will probably come forward on his own."

Anne was dubious. "He seemed pretty firm in his denials."

They stepped onto the elevator and began to ride down to Anne's floor.

"How about if we go out for a drink and try to forget about this mess?"

A drink was the last thing Anne wanted right now, especially with Kelsey, who was so closely wrapped up in all of this. She felt overwhelmed and needed some distance to process everything she had just learned. "I think I'd rather just go home."

"Okay." Kelsey gave a small shrug. "Another time."

Anne nodded mutely, thinking about Alex alone in his office, stewing. What would he do now? Escape to Europe and hide out in the family castle? More likely, a man of his means would hire the best criminal defense lawyer in the country and mount a strong defense. But was he actually guilty?

"Let's at least walk out together."

Whatever, Anne felt saying. She really didn't care. She just wanted to get away from this place, from everyone in it, and sort things out in her mind.

"We could both use the company—" Kelsey began.

Suddenly Anne knew that she needed to talk to someone about everything that had happened. But who? Her mind jumped to her best friend, Katie. She would call her the instant she got to her desk and see if she was free for dinner. If not, they could just as easily talk on the phone. The two of them would lay everything out, calmly, and figure out what she should do. Or not do.

The elevator jolted and came to a stop.

"Damn!" Kelsey put her hand in front of the door to keep it from closing as Anne stepped out. "I just realized I need to grab something from my office. I'll pop up and meet you back here in a couple of minutes."

"That's okay. I can—"

"No," Kelsey interrupted. "I won't be long. Just wait—"

The doors closed, cutting her last words off. With everyone gone for the day, the floor felt dark and empty. There were no voices to drown out the hum of the ventilation system, which now seemed obtrusive, almost suffocating. Anne made her way quickly to her desk, picked up her calendar, and flipped it to the back page, where she kept Katie's work number. Her hands shook as she punched the numbers into the phone and put the receiver next to her ear. She heard it ring and ring and ring.

No answer.

Katie wasn't there.

She sat down, kicked off her pumps, and pulled her sneakers out of the drawer. And then she remembered that Katie was in Omaha, Nebraska, finalizing a deal. If everything went according to plan, she would be returning later that evening. Anne picked up the phone again and began dialing. She would leave a message on Katie's answering machine at home.

"You've reached Daisy and me," a voice sang out cheerfully.

Anne always smiled when she heard this recording. Daisy was Katie's little Yorkie, a dog she had adopted from the pound. Anyone who did not know that was probably someone who did not actually know Katie either. She used it as a way to screen unsolicited sales pitches and the occasional crank call.

"We're not available right now," the rest of it played out, "but if you leave a message, we'll get back to you as soon as possible."

"It's me," Anne said breathlessly, trying to compose her note on the fly. "I've just come from a meeting with Alex, and I'm concerned. I've learned some strange things."

She paused and then corrected herself.

"Actually, I don't know if they're strange, but they're things I didn't know. That I should have known. That he should have told me. And Kelsey—"

She paused again. Katie had no respect for the woman. It was probably better to avoid mentioning her right now.

"Forget Kelsey. The thing is—I'm not sure, but he may have more to hide. Please call me as soon as you get this message. I'll be home all evening."

She sat still for a moment and thought about what she had just recorded. It sounded jumbled and confused, verging on hysterical. She took a deep breath and picked up the phone once more.

"Hi. It's me again." She could tell she sounded calmer this time. "I'm not sure my other message was very clear. It turns out that Alex is from a very wealthy family. The thing is, they belong to the same country club that Michael Kingston's family belongs to, and Kelsey thinks he murdered Michael. He's obviously furious, and I'm not sure what to think. The whole thing's been a shock. I've known him for years, so I'm finding this very hard to take in. I really need to talk. Please give me a call as soon as you get this."

She hung up and looked around her cubicle, uneasy. Something was wrong, but she couldn't put her finger on it. She felt as if she were being manipulated, like a marionette. But by who? Kelsey? No. She was just laying out the facts.

Anne bent over to tie her shoelaces.

Was it something Alex had said? She tried to reconstruct the conversation in her mind. He seemed genuinely shocked by Kelsey's accusations, and his explanations had seemed reasonable, but clearly, there were whole aspects of his life that she had no clue about. Could that include murder?

Finished, she stood up.

But why? What could have driven him to murder Michael? She gathered her coat and bag and then paused in the middle of tightening her belt.

"Anne," she groaned inwardly as she heard a voice call out. "Are you ready to go?" Kelsey came into view a few seconds later. "Let's get out of here. I'm beat."

As they walked to the elevator, Anne continued turning things over in her mind.

"If Alex did it…." She gave Kelsey a quizzical look, "…then why did he send a suicide note to Michael's widow that was obviously a fake?"

"To cast suspicion on Betty," Kelsey replied matter-of-factly. "And the scary thing is that it almost worked."

Anne shifted her weight from one leg to the other, unable to stand still, as they waited for the elevator to arrive.

"I think it's supposed to snow again this weekend," Kelsey said amiably.

"Yes," Anne replied absently, focused on the nagging feeling that she had missed something crucial.

"I was hoping the storm would come a little later so we might have a snow day from work."

"Wouldn't that be nice." Anne managed a small smile.

Kelsey's face lit up. "Sometimes I imagine my phone ringing some morning while I'm still in bed, and it's one of the secretaries calling to say *Work's canceled! Stay home! Catch up on your rest!*"

Anne gave a dismissive wave. "There'd have to be a nuclear war knocking out the entire stock exchange for something like that to happen." Her mind flashed to the image of Kelsey groggily rolling over to pick up the phone. And then she tensed as she suddenly realized what was bothering her. "And, they'd have to know your home number," she finished dully.

Kelsey nodded. "You're right. We'd be lucky if the firm even bothered to make an announcement on the radio." She hesitated. "Is everything alright?"

Anne turned and pushed the *up* button for the elevator. "You go ahead without me. I just realized I need to ask Alex something."

Kelsey looked concerned. "I think that's a big mistake. Now that the truth is out, he needs time *alone* to think." She shook her head. "Besides, it's too dangerous."

"Alex would never hurt me. I'm certain of that."

Kelsey bit her lip. "You can never be certain of anything. He's already killed two people."

"What if you're wrong? And it was Michael Kingston's wife?"

"I'm not wrong." Kelsey looked at her earnestly. "And I'm worried about you. It's not safe to be alone with him."

Anne's mind was made up. She was determined to talk to Alex.

"Listen to me!" Kelsey threw her arms up in exasperation. "It's not his wife!" A frantic look crossed her face, and then her tone changed subtly. "Don't even think about doing this."

Anne sensed a hard fury underlying Kelsey's words and felt her heart begin to race. She put her thumb on the trigger of the mace in her coat pocket and wrapped her fingers around the body of the canister. When the elevator bell rang out, they both turned to see which way it was headed.

Down.

The doors opened. For a long second, they both just stared at each other in stony silence. Anne tried to hide her thoughts and keep her face unflinching. Kelsey seemed to be doing the same.

All at once, Kelsey's face distorted.

The elevator doors began to close, and Kelsey looked toward them and then back at Anne. And then Kelsey lunged. Anne stepped back, pulled the mace out of her pocket, and sprayed. It hit Kelsey in the face. She reeled backwards and fell against the wall. Tears coursed down her cheeks, and she coughed uncontrollably before finally collapsing in a heap.

Anne stepped toward the elevator and pushed the *up* button over and over, terrified the pepper spray would begin to lose its effectiveness while she stood there waiting for it to arrive. When the doors finally opened, she quickly stepped around Kelsey, still coughing and crying on the ground, then punched the button for Alex's floor and waited anxiously for the car to ascend.

The instant the doors opened, she sprang off the elevator and began to sprint. She burst into Alex's office and stopped short. He was slumped in his chair, motionless. Her eyes moved to his desk, where she saw a single piece of paper. Feeling panic rise within, Anne stepped closer and found a neatly typed note explaining his remorse for killing Michael Kingston. She picked up his soda and saw that most of it was gone.

"No!" she screamed and then picked up the phone to call for an ambulance. She couldn't bring herself to touch him and see if he was even breathing. She just kept hoping she hadn't been too late.

26

A Failure to Pin

One Month After the Meeting

The Wall Street Chronicle
Monday, February 20, 1989

A Crime of Passion

The Manhattan District Attorney's office has charged longtime Spencer Brothers employee Kelsey O'Brien with the murder of her former boss, Michael Kingston III, and attempted murder of Alex Hunter, a lawyer who also works at the firm.

Kingston was found dead of an apparent overdose of digoxin on January 16, 1989, some months after breaking off an affair with O'Brien. His death was initially ruled a suicide, but police reopened the investigation at the behest of his widow.

Fearing she would be found out, O'Brien poisoned Hunter in an effort to make it appear that he had murdered Kingston and then committed suicide. Hunter was rushed to the hospital after being found unconscious in his office by a co-worker and is expected to make a full recovery.

"I always thought she was a piece of work," Donna said with what looked like a spit toward the floor. "Although I never pegged her as a murderer. My money was always on the wife."

They were standing around the file cabinets before the morning rush, with the newspaper strewn casually beside them.

"Things have worked out well for her," Jennifer said, cradling her coffee. "Now she gets to collect the insurance."

"She's already filthy rich," Carter peeped before Anne could point out that collecting on a life insurance policy was probably the least of the woman's concerns, given that she was independently wealthy.

"The mansion in Short Hills. Probably millions, stashed away in bank accounts. What more does she need?" He picked up his doughnut and took a large bite.

Donna's nose scrunched up, creating a series of radiating lines through the orange and yellow eyeshadow that caked her face. "All those affairs? The woman *deserves* to be compensated for putting up with that dick."

As if a pile of money could make up for the string of women Michael had kept on the side. He had lied to his wife for years. Hopefully, she hadn't contracted any sexually transmitted diseases along the way.

"In fact, Kelsey ought to get a medal for taking out that piece of trash." Donna blew a big bubble as if to emphasize her point.

Anne smiled in agreement, but at the same time, thought Donna was starting to get carried away.

"Is Kelsey the really athletic one who always runs around looking like the building's on fire?" Carter trilled.

"You got that right." Donna's bright green blouse waved back and forth as she gestured toward the trading floor. "She could probably wrestle any of the guys out there down to the ground. Even Vito. The woman's a powerhouse."

Anne imagined Kelsey locked up in a jail cell, unable to work out. She had to be climbing the walls.

"It's a good thing you went back up to check on Alex Hunter," William joined the conversation.

"That was you?" Carter said.

Anne and Jennifer stepped aside to avoid the small pieces of food that flew out of his mouth.

"Yes." Anne sighed. "We'd all been meeting shortly before it happened."

"Do you know how he's doing?" William asked, carefully stirring his latte.

Anne smiled. "He got out of the hospital yesterday and expects to return to work on Wednesday." Although their Saturday night plans to see *Les Misérables* had been scuttled by the poisoning, he had already suggested they reschedule for the following weekend. She was looking forward to having a real date with him.

"What are you glowing about?" Donna gave her an odd look.

"Nothing!" Anne answered and then kicked herself, thinking she had been over-emphatic in her response. "It's fortunate that he's recovering. That's all."

Jennifer gave Anne a quizzical look. "You've spoken with him since he got home?"

Anne groaned inwardly. She had not meant to reveal anything about her budding relationship with Alex. Although technically, she reasoned to herself; they had not yet gone on a date, so they were still friends. "I wanted to make sure he was doing okay after everything that happened."

Jennifer pointed at the newspaper sitting on the cabinets beside them, a pained expression on her face. "I still can't get over the fact that Kelsey did all this."

Anne knew it must be particularly hard for Jennifer to accept. The two had known each other for years.

"Even the most polished investment banker can have a dark side," William said with a wry smile.

"We should have been on to her much sooner, but we were so focused on the Pandora deals that we totally overlooked the most basic motive of all."

William brushed the paper aside. "*Crime of Passion* doesn't really capture the essence of what happened. It seems to me that *Jilted Lover turns out to be Nutcase* would've been a more apt headline."

Anne thought that a bit harsh.

"How about *Inveterate Womanizer Finally Meets His Match*?" Donna suggested with a cackle.

At least that idea presented Michael as part of the problem.

"I vote for *Spurned Girlfriend Takes Revenge*," Jennifer said quietly.

Anne thought that pretty much summed things up.

"The thing is," Jennifer continued, looking perplexed, "Michael must have dumped dozens of women over the years, and yet none of them resorted to murder."

What had set Kelsey apart from the others? The question lingered in Anne's mind for just a moment. "I think she actually thought he was going to leave his wife for her."

"Really?" Donna rolled her eyes. "Men never do that. They just string their clueless mistresses along with a bunch of empty promises."

"Wait a minute," Carter chirped. "Not all men do that. Some might genuinely be interested, just unable to limit themselves to—"

"Spare me." Donna cut him off.

"But that doesn't mean—" Carter began to protest.

"I would have thought Kelsey was savvy enough to see through that BS," Donna continued, completely ignoring Carter, her eyes narrowing. "She was smart. And shrewd."

Anne waved her comments away. "Even if she was, it had to have been mortifying when he began his fling with Betty. Every day, right outside her office, the two of them were interacting within plain view. And I don't get the impression they were particularly discreet."

"No one wants to be used and then discarded without a second thought." Jennifer cast a disparaging glance at Carter. "It had to have been totally demoralizing."

"How about his wife?" William said, raising an eyebrow. "If you're going to feel sorry for anybody, it probably ought to be her."

"She's also a victim here," Jennifer allowed a grim expression on her face. "The jerk in this story is Michael."

"So, getting thrown over by that loser was enough to push her over the edge?" Donna looked dubious. "Murder is rather extreme."

"You're right," Anne said, setting her half-eaten bagel back down. "To add insult to injury, Michael had promised her a rather substantial bonus and then had the nerve to screw her over on the money after ending the affair. Kelsey told me about it the night we went to the opera."

Donna's eyes lit up. "Now, that sounds like something that would cut Kelsey to the core. No wonder she lost it."

"I think there's a good chance she would have gotten away with Michael's murder if she hadn't screwed up the date on the suicide note," William said matter of factly.

"I agree," Anne said, remembering how William had obnoxiously dismissed the discrepancy when she had initially told him about it. Perhaps this was his way of apologizing? "Kelsey should have re-saved the document the morning she killed him so it would appear that he wrote it just before ingesting the pills."

William readjusted his tie. "It's fortunate Kelsey didn't think to do that."

"I'll never forget the look on her face when we initially pointed it out."

"You told her?" Donna smacked her ubiquitous wad of gum.

Anne nodded. "She turned white as a sheet. At the time, I thought Kelsey was shocked that he might have been killed by one of the Pandora Partners. I think that's when she panicked and came up with Plan B—*pin it on somebody else*."

"Which wasn't such a bad idea, in principle, given the mess she was in." Seeing the look on the faces around him, William quickly added, "Not that I'm advocating murder...."

"So, she decided to frame Alex?" Carter twittered, little flakes of doughnut glaze now scattered on his shirt.

"She went after Walter first. When he took that dive to his death, she thought she'd found the perfect patsy. Too bad she screwed that note up too."

"How did you know it was a fake?" Jennifer twirled her finger around the top of her coffee mug.

"Because whoever had written it was unaware the SEC had already struck a deal with Marvin in exchange for immunity—something Walter was fully aware of."

"That scamming punk got an immunity deal?" Donna looked incredulous.

Anne suddenly realized she had let another piece of information slip that she probably shouldn't have.

"Everybody needs to keep that under their hat," William said gruffly.

"Of course we will," Donna said, looking annoyed.

"Does he get to keep the profits as well?" Carter squeaked.

"Who knows," Anne said dismissively. "We aren't privy to the terms."

"Did the other Pandora Partners know that he'd made a deal with the SEC?" Jennifer set her coffee down and picked up a muffin.

"Within hours," Anne said, rolling her eyes. "They all knew. Everyone except for Kelsey." She felt a wave of guilt wash over her. Kelsey had looked genuinely hurt when she learned Anne had not shared that information with her. But if Anne had...Anne did not want to even contemplate that possibility.

"So then they all must have known that Walter's suicide note was a fake," Jennifer said.

William's eyes narrowed. "I don't recall you sharing that little tidbit with me."

"Alex and I were trying to get more information before approaching you," Anne said quickly. "Once we realized the note had been fabricated, we began to focus on Betty."

"Betty?" William and Donna said at the same time.

"That reminds me," Carter said with a sneeze. "I've been meaning to swing by and say hello. Now that she's available again..."

Anne saw Jennifer clench her hands and look down at the floor, obviously trying to refrain from taking Carter's head off.

"She brought his coffee into the meeting that morning," Anne explained. "It was a prime opportunity."

As Donna and William stared at her in disbelief, she saw no need to mention the part where she and Alex had wondered about Peter Eckert and the widow.

"I think Kelsey was hoping she could pin it on Betty as well," Anne continued, thinking how different things looked in hindsight, "but after doing a little of her own digging, she discovered there was no way that was going to fly, so instead she focused on Alex."

"Is he really British?" Carter asked, wadding his wet napkin into a ball. "His accent sounds put on to me. Maybe it grated on Kelsey's nerves as well."

Anne thought back to all the times she had felt caught between the two of them, wondering why they kept sniping at one another. She had even criticized Alex for being overly negative about Kelsey. In retrospect, he had been a better judge of character than she had. "I think it's fair to say the two of them didn't really get along, although I don't think it had anything to do with his accent."

"She almost succeeded in pulling it off. If you hadn't returned..." William gave Anne a quizzical look. "How did you know?"

Anne flashed to the fateful evening when she was sitting in her chair, putting on her socks and sneakers, and the nagging feeling at the back of her mind that something was wrong. "I kept going back to the logic of it all. If Alex wanted to point the finger at Walter, why would he send a letter to Michael's widow, riddled with errors about the SEC investigation? It didn't make sense. As I sat there fussing about it in my mind, Kelsey came by so we could walk out together, and then she said something off the cuff about snow days."

"Snow days?" William gave her an incredulous look. "How could that possibly relate to Michael's murder?"

"It was the idea of being called at home to take the day off. She was saying how wonderful that would be."

"She's right," Donna said, pausing in her gum chomping. "I don't think we've ever had one, and I've been working here for 20 years. But why in hell's name does it matter?"

"When we went to the opera, she made a point of telling me she had an unlisted number that she refused to give to anyone, even the secretaries up in investment banking, and yet she supposedly received threatening phone calls like I did. How would Alex have possibly gotten her number? And then it suddenly snapped into my mind that she had a motive. She certainly had opportunity, and she was unfamiliar with the details of the

SEC investigation. Suddenly, it all made sense."

Carter stepped toward the cabinets to grab another napkin, and everyone backed away. "How did she get the digoxin?"

"Guess what her brother does for a living?" Anne queried, a smile playing on her lips.

"Doctor?" He sneezed again.

"Close," she replied. "Pharmacist. Here in New York City."

"And Walter's suicide?" Donna piped up.

"He really killed himself," Anne answered somberly. "He was depressed about being fired."

Out of the corner of her eye, Anne saw Gwen storming over toward them.

"While you guys have been standing around shooting the breeze, the phones have been ringing off the hook." She slammed a small pile of messages on the file cabinets and turned on her heel. "I need to get back to my desk since I'm the only one actually working around here!"

Donna rolled her eyes and began sorting through the heap before stopping suddenly to turn and look at Anne. "There's one here from Alex."

Anne took a sharp breath and tried to look nonchalant. "Thanks."

Donna raised an eyebrow. "He must have called you from home...."

Anne shrugged. "Maybe he needs to file something with Personnel. About what happened with Kelsey."

Donna handed out the remaining messages, and everyone began to scatter.

"Anne!" Donna called out.

She turned, hoping Donna was not about to start grilling her about Alex.

Donna winked and slipped something into her hand. "There's a second one from him too."

27

Epilogue

A year later, Anne sat on her sofa sipping a cup of tea. Muffin lay nestled quietly beside her, a paw draped over Alex's knee.

"Here!" she pointed toward the bottom section of the page.

"Might as well save it for posterity." Alex pulled a pair of silver scissors out of the drawer. "Or," he winked, "target practice."

She nodded and began clipping:

The Wall Street Chronicle

February 12, 1990

Spencer Brothers Fined $10.7 million

Spencer Brothers was ordered to pay a record fine of $10.7 million to the Securities Exchange Commission for unethical sales and underwriting practices.

In a report compiled by the commission, the firm's senior management was accused of ignoring and, in some cases, encouraging employees to bring unethical bond deals to market in order to generate fees for the firm. In addition, firm salesmen were accused of recommending securities to individual customers for whom they were far too risky, in violation of their fiduciary duty. These practices reportedly led to hundreds of customer complaints and millions of dollars in legal settlements.

Two divisional managers, one trader, and three investment banking professionals were suspended for up to two weeks and ordered to pay fines totaling $50,000. The report charges that investment banking personnel created and then subsequently marketed certain municipal bond issues in flagrant violation of the Tax Reform Act of 1986. When the IRS ruled that interest on the bonds was taxable, the firm was deluged with investor lawsuits. A spokesman was unwilling to estimate the amount paid out to settle those matters. They are believed, however, to have spent upwards of $15 million.

The report also charges that another series of deals were created and marketed in the West Coast offices. These bond issues were characteristically high-risk securities in which every project defaulted, and the banks guaranteeing the loans were found to be non-existent. In response to these findings, the SEC has announced plans to review the underwriting practices of the entire industry in order to provide more stringent guidelines and penalties for firms that knowingly violate the rules.

In the settlement, the firm neither admitted nor denied any wrongdoing.

Glossary of Terms

bond. A debt security issued by a company or government to raise money to cover spending needs (a loan). The borrower promises to pay the loan back, with interest, over a certain period of time.

bond counsel. A lawyer who reviews the bonds when they are first being offered for sale to ensure that they have been validly issued.

bond proceeds. The money that is received from the sale of the bonds.

bondholder. A person who owns a bond.

C-suite. The highest-ranking executives in an organization (e.g., Chief Financial Officer, General Counsel, CEO, etc.)

Chapter 11 bankruptcy. A form of bankruptcy that allows a struggling business to restructure its finances so that it can continue to operate (rather than being forced to sell off its assets to pay debts).

Chinese wall. A business policy that blocks the sharing of information among departments. In financial firms it is intended to prevent the misuse of inside information in securities trading.

cover bid. The second-highest bid in an auction or competitive sale.

default. Failure to repay a loan or debt.

equities. Shares (stock) in a company. Stockholders often receive dividends based on the company's profits. Equities trading is the buying and selling of stock shares.

municipal bonds. Debt securities issued by states, cities, counties, and other local governmental entities to finance projects such as parks, libraries, highways, and other community infrastructure. The interest paid to bondholders is generally exempt from federal taxes and most state and local taxes (for residents) making them especially attractive to people in higher income tax brackets.

guaranteed investment contract (GIC). An investment agreement with an insurance company in which the insurance company pays a fixed rate of interest for an agreed-upon time. It is similar to a certificate of deposit (CD) except only insurance companies or non-bank financial institutions sell them.

offering statement (or official statement or prospectus). A document that gives detailed financial information about the investment.

outside legal counsel. A lawyer or law firm that has been hired to provide legal advice. They generally have many clients and bill their time hourly. They differ from in house legal counsel who are employed by a company (as regular corporate employees) to handle legal matters for the business.

oversight fees. Payments to a person or entity who is monitoring the progress of a project and ensuring that activities comply with laws and regulations. (It is intended to make sure that money is properly spent.)

par. The face value of a bond or other security (which may not match its market value).

prospectus. (see offering statement)

receiver. A court-appointed person who oversees the assets of a company that is deeply in debt (insolvent) in order to preserve the best value for creditors.

receivership. A situation in which control of a company is handed over to a receiver.

redemption provisions. The rules governing when bonds can be paid back early.

tax exempt status. Interest paid to bondholders on municipal bonds is typically exempt from federal income tax; however, if the bonds lack a public purpose they may not qualify for this status. A lawyer specializing in bond law provides a legal opinion as to whether the bonds qualify.

the project. What the money from the bonds is supposed to build or be used for.

the Street. A colloquial term for Wall Street which is both a physical street located in New York City and an umbrella term used to describe the financial markets (e.g., the New York Stock Exchange).

trustee. A bond trustee is a financial institution that enforces the terms of a bond issue (e.g., makes sure that interest is paid on time and that the borrower is fulfilling all obligations). A trustee is supposed to ensure that the interests of the bondholders are represented.

Acknowledgements

My warmest thanks to Philip Tracadas for his never-ending encouragement and Ginger Driver for her insight, help, and patience in reading the manuscript multiple times. The novel was greatly improved by comments from Ollie Stevenson, Elaine Krieg, Rhonda Boehm, Jean Nunnally, Brett Schultz, and Sharon Raymond of the Houston Writers Guild Critique Group, Becky Browder, Carol Chenault, Richard Cunningham, Sue Dauser, Kirsten Dodge, Christine Doyle, Stephanie Jaye Evans, Eve Grubb, Lydia Luz, Joy Oden, Maneesha Patil, Helen Robinson, Sarah Saltzer, and Renee Spangler. I also wish to thank Harriette Sackler and the entire team at Level Best Books for their help in getting this book published and my mother for being such a strong supporter of my various endeavors.

About the Author

Rebecca Saltzer worked as a bond analyst on the trading floor at Lehman Brothers in New York City in the financial heyday of the eighties. Like the protagonist in her novel, she sometimes encountered fraud and other questionable business practices, except in real life, none of it led to murder. In 2021, Rebecca received the William F. Deeck-Malice Domestic Grant for unpublished writers. When she's not writing, she enjoys hiking with her two rescue dogs and exploring the great outdoors.

SOCIAL MEDIA HANDLES:
  Twitter: @RebeccaSaltzer – www.twitter.com/RebeccaSaltzer
  Facebook: Rebecca Saltzer – www.facebook.com/rebecca.saltzer.14
  LinkedIn: Rebecca Saltzer – www.linkedin.com/in/rebecca-saltzer-86822b9

AUTHOR WEBSITE:
  www.saltzerbooks.com